T0146909

WOMEN RISING

A Novel By
Lark Edlim

WOMEN RISING
A NOVEL

iUniverse books may be ordered through booksellers or by contacting:

iUniverse
1663 Liberty Drive
Bloomington, IN 47403
www.iuniverse.com
1-800-Authors (1-800-288-4677)

ISBN: 978-1-5320-2635-5 (sc)
ISBN: 978-1-5320-2637-9 (hc)
ISBN: 978-1-5320-2636-2 (e)

Library of Congress Control Number: 2017911164

Print information available on the last page.

iUniverse rev. date: 07/19/2017

Acknowledgements

For the beautiful book cover, I wish to thank Marguerite Chadwick-Juner, a graphic designer and illustrator of extraordinary ability and creativity. She imagined and drew our protagonist, Courtney, and made her real.

Marguerite can be found in an idyllic little
village on the coast of North Carolina:

Marguerite Chadwick-Juner
4015 Schooner Circle, Oriental, NC 28571
Phone/Fax: 252-249-2996

I wish to acknowledge and thank Vincent Dacquino, founder and leader of the "Mahopac Writers Group" in Mahopac, New York, for his invaluable assistance in reading and editing the manuscript of this novel. As the story unfolded, chapter-by- chapter, during the seven months that it was written, Vin provided an invaluable reality check of both plot and character and on many occasions kept this imaginary train from slipping off the rails.

I also wish to thank my friend Steve Griffee for lending his knowledge and expertise on the inner workings of hedge funds, the stated purpose of which is to extract profits from the financial markets, thereby allowing wealthy individuals to continually draw cash out of the retirement funds of hard-working Americans.

And finally, I would like to express my sincerest gratitude to my editor, Pamela Johnson – pamtheeditor@yahoo.com - for her brilliant work in spotting logical errors, changes in POV, weak passages and just plain typos, and for her many, many suggestions for making the story stronger and dynamic.

"The desire for sex...always creates some trouble."
The Dalai Lama, on the morning of his 80th Birthday, July 6, 2015

Chapter 1

Courtney Stillwell had the sexes figured out.

Men were the problem.

What bothered her wasn't that men were such homely creatures. Men were, more often than not, self-centered and demanding. No man would admit it, but deep down they thought themselves superior and their actions reflected this attitude.

It just wasn't right.

Men also committed the majority of crimes – burglary, fraud and larceny – and the *vast* majority of violent crimes – murder, rape and robbery.

Life was a daily struggle between the sexes and with her young magazine, *Women Rising,* she was committed to making women aware. Like her, they should be *pissed off* at men and *fight back.*

She sat alone in her office on 44th Street, a few doors west of Fifth Avenue. It was an old building filled with literary history. The small suite – only a small reception area, her personal office and a conference room – took part of the space formerly occupied by *The New Yorker* magazine before it moved to nicer digs in the city.

Courtney focused on her work, editing one of those stories of a philandering husband that made a woman's blood boil. Illustrated by the striking image of an aggrieved wife gripping a smoking gun with two hands, it was to be the cover story for her magazine's October issue.

She became aware of her desk phone ringing and answered just in time before it went to voicemail, hiding her annoyance at being distracted.

"I'm so glad I reached you." The voice sounded breathless.

She recognized one of her writers, Veronica, and immediately experienced a wave of mixed feelings. Veronica, whom she called "Ronnie" was young and inexperienced.

"Great to hear from you," she said, injecting an upbeat tone she hoped would elicit whatever potential story Ronnie might have.

"Have I got a *story* for you. A *great* story. Breaking news." The intensity of the voice was palpable. Courtney was not in the business of breaking news, but the prospect sounded promising and Courtney always gave her novice writers a chance. It was a tough world out there for writers, as well she knew. "Okay, I'm listening."

"It's about my boyfriend…"

Right off the bat Courtney saw the story evaporating. She had met the guy once and the image of a bald-headed, tattooed redneck came to mind. One of a band of bikers.

"Billy's, like, *changed* Courtney. He doesn't come on to me any more. He's lost all interest. He didn't call for the longest time so I thought he had another girl. He didn't. I asked around."

This problem didn't sound life threatening or even interesting. "So? What's the problem?"

"I wasn't getting any, so I called *him*. Casual like. To find out what's going on."

"Let me guess: He was in a fight with another guy?"

"No, no, nothing like that. As I said, he's *lost interest*." Ronnie emphasized the last two words as if it were impossible for a guy to lose interest in having sex with her. Ronnie had the looks men went for. Curly blonde locks. A cute face. Hourglass figure. Slender legs. Young. A virtual man magnet.

"So, that's your story? He dumped you? Newsflash: it happens to women every day."

"The story isn't *that* he lost interest but *why* he lost interest. He's part of an *experiment* by the U.S. Army."

An experiment? Was she hearing right?

"He and his gang. They're getting paid to try this drug. They're testing some new stuff they just put in the water and it turns men off. They don't want to fight any more."

"Wait, you lost me. I thought you were talking about losing interest in sex."

"That's just part of it. They don't want sex and they don't want to fight. If this thing works, they're going to stick it to the enemy – you know, like the bad guys in the Middle East? Turn them all into yooks."

"Excuse me?"

"Yooks. Those guys that guard the harems."

"Eunuchs?"

"That's it. Yooks. The sheiks trust them not to – you know, *fuck*."

"You've made this up, right?"

"No, *really*. That's the idea of it. He didn't say *yook*, but—"

"What did he say, exactly?"

"He said some military guy – his name was Roger something – approached them and they made this deal: He'd pay each guy ten thousand bucks a month to try the stuff and report on the effects."

Courtney finally realized this may not be a joke. An *experiment*, like the Army's use of mustard gas on our soldiers at Edgewood Arsenal? "How did you find this out?"

"Billy told me. He wasn't supposed to, but he did when I pressed him. He said it was *top secret* and he's signed some kind of confidentiality agreement. But I didn't sign anything and I want to write about it. You'll print the story, right?"

Courtney said nothing for a moment. She could scarcely believe what she was hearing.

After a beat she replied, "Okay, sure. Tell me everything you can find out about this, and we'll talk about what we do. First, though, let me send you a contract giving *Women Rising* an exclusive."

"*Great*. And here's the best part," Ronnie added. "The part that really got to me—"

She waited.

"They call the stuff '*Ballzoff*'."

Chapter 2

By the time he'd reached twenty-eight years of age, Roger was already one of the "go to" guys in the United States for answers about the potential side effects of new drugs. His abilities as a scientist did not go unnoticed by the government, and the U.S. Army recruited him.

Since age thirty, Roger led an Army research laboratory at Aberdeen Proving Ground, Maryland. It was a coveted position that nobody knew about, at a lab that nobody knew about either. If you were to ask anyone in government about a "biochem skunkworks" at APG they would answer, "Lab? What lab?" Even DARPA, the defense agency research arm that funded the lab's research, was kept in the dark about the project he undertook.

But that suited Roger just fine. He didn't care about fame or fortune. He loved only his work, which he found intensely interesting. He had neither a wife nor girlfriend, nor even a dog or other distractions like that.

When Roger was initially contacted to lead the lab, he learned at the first meeting what the Army wanted to do. He was intrigued by the project they outlined - to find a way to change men temporarily into pacifists who did not want to fight – and thought it was doable. This seemed a worthy objective at the time, and he still considered the concept a game changer. Having now achieved some measure of success, as proven by his Stage Three trials to prove efficacy, he had become more and more concerned that information about the program might leak out. He was torn between being elated by the success of the program and anxiety due to this very same success.

Every month, Roger held a meeting with a particularly cantakerous gang of bikers to monitor their behavior. He had chosen these men for human trials because they were the meanest, fiercest, fight-prone group he could find within a fifty-mile radius of his laboratory. If his biochemical compound could pacify these angry individuals, it could do the same for the enemy. And thus far, things were going well. Very well, in fact. Far beyond his expectations. Nearly finished now, Stage Three was providing remarkable proof that his compound, which was really a "biochemical weapon," actually *worked*.

As the biker group filed into the meeting room and took their seats, he stood in front and observed their demeanor. It had changed markedly from that first day, nearly a year ago, when he had welcomed them and explained the program. At that time they were all ego and bluster, each in his own way, and they displayed an attitude with their every movement. Today they were different: Calm to the point of being almost docile and even polite. "Mind if I sit here?" asked one of them to another. "Please do," the bald and bearded biker replied.

When all had assembled and quieted down, looking up at him expectantly, Roger began: "How's everyone feeling?" A few of bikers tentatively raised their hands, but Roger continued. "I'll be more specific. Does anyone feel particularly depressed?" All the raised hands came back down. None went up.

Roger looked around the room making eye contact with many of the men. "All right then. Have you had any fights since you were here last month? Fights with other gangs? Fights among yourselves? " No hands went up.

"Are you feeling alright?" No hands went up. "Are you guys still *alive*?"

The bikers looked at each other for a moment, then glared at him for the insult. One of them demanded, "What kind of a question is *that*, you son-of-a—." The man checked himself.

Roger was actually relieved to hear the backtalk. The compound would not meet its specifications if it emasculated the men completely. "I don't mean to antagonize. I was wondering why you're just sitting there, not responding. That's not like you."

"Just answerin' your dumb questions, man." A titter of stifled laughter filled the room.

"Okay, thank you. Well now, you know the drill. When you fill out this form," he held up a packet of questionnaires, "you'll receive your monthly check. Oh, and we're going to do it differently this time. We're not giving you any more of the special water to drink. When you come back next month, I'll want to see if the effects of the compound have worn off."

One of the bikers raised his hand. Roger looked his way. "Question, Joe?"

"Yeah. Suppose we want to continue? Can we get more water?"

"Sorry, no. We'll need to monitor you when you stop taking it. It's kind of a drug, you know. We want to be sure you continue to feel all right."

"The stuff calms us down. Now you want to take it away? I don't think so, man."

Roger was taken aback at this remark, but found it interesting and pursued the issue. "Calms you down? In what way?"

"We don't fight so much. We kind of like each other now." The biker looked around the room for approval and found several others nodding their heads. "This water makes us feel…*better*. We're not so pissed off all the time."

"I'm glad to hear that. Now you know it's possible to have some harmony in your lives, maybe you'll stay that way."

"Not with these bastards, we won't." Joe stood up, holding his hands out, palms up. He smirked, indicating he meant the quip to be funny, but no one in the room laughed.

"One final thing…" Roger continued. "You kept the program absolutely confidential, right? Spoken to no one about it, like it says in the contract you signed?"

The bikers looked at each other and nodded. All but one.

"No leaks?"

Billy's hand went up.

"Yes, Billy?"

"Can I speak to you, privately?"

"Sure, come with me right now, while everyone is filling out the form."

Billy rose from his seat and sheepishly went forward while the others stared at him. "Start filling out your forms, everyone," instructed Roger. "We'll be right back."

Roger walked out with the biker through a side door and quietly closed it behind them.

"What's on your mind, Billy?"

"I did tell someone, and I wish I didn't."

"Oh? Who?"

"My broad, Ronnie. She said I'd changed. She wanted to know why."

"She said you changed? Changed how?" Roger was interested to learn this.

"We don't get together so much. You know, *sex*." Billy nearly blushed.

"That's not a problem for you, is it?"

"She's gonna blab."

"Blab?"

"You know. Tell."

"Uh-oh. We have to nip this in the bud. Why don't you bring her in here. We'll have her sign a non-disclosure form."

"I'm afraid it's too late for that."

"Why?"

"She's writing an article about it, and it's going to be published in a fuckin' magazine."

Chapter 3

Courtney skimmed through the article, frowning. She would have to completely rewrite it, she realized, because it was totally trashy and not really appropriate for her magazine.

"MY BIKER BOYFRIEND STOPPED WANTING SEX"
by Veronica Miller

On my first date with Joe (not his real name) I could feel the heat. He picked me up from my apartment with his blue and chrome Harley and, while my roommates watched with envy, we roared off to meet his biker friends at a local watering hole. He couldn't take his eyes off me all evening and treated me like an exotic princess, even with the other members of his gang vying for his attention. In the parking lot, when it was time to go, he pressed himself against me, and my temperature shot through the roof. One of his soul kisses was all I needed. The sex we had on the grass under the stars was the best I'd ever had.

I was hooked from that day on. I lived for the times we could be together. Riding behind Joe astride that Harley could be a bone chilling experience when the outside temperature dropped into the forties, and it could be searing and sweaty when it rose above ninety, but I was having the time of my life. Joe may not have been much to look at with his tattooed, bald head and his scraggly beard, and he talked a lot more than he listened to what I had to say, but I loved the attention and, most of all, the hot sex.

I was biding my time as a typist temp while I struggled to get my writing career off the ground. Fame and fortune as a writer were an impossible dream, it seemed, but I kept at it, waiting for the big break.

My "real life" was not anything to write home to Mom about either. The two gals with whom I shared the apartment kept odd hours so we couldn't connect very often. They were my friends, to be sure, but there was a limit on how much I could stand hearing their complaints about their miserable lives. I desperately wanted to move out to my own apartment but that was financially out of the question. My life was miserable too, but at least I had my dream to be the next J.K. Rowling.

And I could look forward to my times with Joe. That was then. Before he began to change.

My experience with men had been rather limited when we started dating, but I knew one thing: You could count on a guy to try to get into your underpants.

Joe was a typical guy in that regard and he wasn't at all shy about it. He didn't pretend to hold back as some guys do – the ones you might call "gentlemen" if they weren't too nerdy or gay. He went straight for it and, as far as I was concerned, he could have all he wanted. It was what I lived for.

That's the way it was until he and his gang were recruited to enter some secret government program. Then slowly, so slowly that I didn't understand it at first, Joe lost his interest in sex. The first thing I noticed was a change in his kisses: They weren't as fiery as they used to be. When I finally realized this, I thought about it and noticed he had also stopped pressing his body against mine. We continued to have sex, just like before, but it wasn't the same. It was not like he had to have me. And then eventually he stopped coming on to me and, because I was too shy to come on to him, the sex just stopped. It's hard to imagine, but it's true.

I was sure the government program had something to do with my "problem" so I began to ask questions about it. Although Joe's a talker not a listener, he wouldn't tell me much. He said he was sworn to secrecy, and anyway it was none of my business. At first he pretended not to know what I was talking about. He said he still wanted to have sex but his heart just wasn't in it. He began to enjoy the company of his biker friends more than spending time with me.

As time went on I became more and more frustrated and, yes, even obsessed about sex. It's what you can't have that makes you crazy. When I was getting enough – too much sometimes, in fact – I never thought about sex. But now the sex has dried up I think about it all the time. I think about those deep soul kisses and can feel the juices flowing "down there" where my little Sindy needs to be penetrated and satisfied.

What is a girl to do in this situation? I'm not ready to give up sex and I'm not going to beg for it. If my biker boyfriend can't deliver, I'll have to give the bum the boot and start looking for someone who can.

This article would be perfect for *Cosmopolitan* magazine, Courtney thought, but not *Women Rising*. *Cosmo* was all about women reveling in their role as men's sex objects. Conversely, *Women Rising* was about women reveling in their role as men's equal partners.

But the secret government program, now *that* was interesting. If this program were a success, as it appeared to be, the problems of male violence and male domination might be made to disappear. Men, she reasoned, would become more like *women*. This was almost too good to be true.

Sensing a sensational story in this government program, she set about the task of learning the *what, why, where and when* of the secret sauce that could turn bikers into candidates for membership in a Rotary Club.

Chapter 4

Before founding *Women Rising* Courtney had majored in journalism and, upon graduation from Barnard College, worked as a researcher for *Vogue* Magazine, fact checking stories before their publication. After serving two years at this editorial desk and learning the basics, she jumped ship and became a free-lancer on a mission to uncover skullduggery. Digging deeply to unearth the secrets of corrupt politicians, the fraudulent schemes of lawyers and businessmen and, though less often, the sexual proclivities of media celebrities, she wrote stories that got real results: Powerful men were cut down to size and some even spent time in "Club Fed."

In short, Courtney Stillwell became a Master – or in this case, a *Mistress* – at finding out whatever she wanted to know.

She started her digging by calling Veronica's mobile. The wannabe-writer picked up on the first ring.

"You liked my story? It was great, wasn't it?"

"I was pleasantly surprised, Ronnie. It was really good." Courtney bit her tongue.

"I could hug you, Courtney, right through the phone. So you'll print it?"

"It needs work, but if you're willing to make changes, I will."

"Needs work? How?" Ronnie's tone turned slightly icy.

"It's too little about Ballzoff, too much about you."

"Well, thanks for nothing."

Ronnie was easily offended, Courtney knew, and she needed to get her young writer back on track to get the information she needed. "I'm sorry," she said. "But my magazine is about what men do to women, not the other way around. I'd like to publish your story if we can just agree on changing the emphasis."

"You would?"

"Yes, I would and I will."

"Okay then. Tell me. What do you want changed?"

Having gotten the hard part out of the way, Courtney moved to the real reason for her call. "I'm sorry about what happened to you and your boyfriend. What's his name by the way?"

"Billy. You met him once."

"Oh, yes. Billy. What did you say his last name was?"

"Oh, no you don't. I know your tricks."

"What?"

"You want to interview him."

"So?"

"No can do. He's mine."

"Oh, come *on*. You introduced us. And I need to interview him to vet your story."

"And you forgot his name. Shows how much you cared who my boyfriend was."

"I'm sorry."

"You keep saying that."

"Saying what?"

"'I'm sorry.' You're a phony, you know that?"

"I'm sorry you think that..." Courtney realized she'd done it again. This conversation was not going as planned. She decided to take the direct route. "But I confess, I do want to meet Billy. I *need* to meet him to flesh out details for your article."

"Fat chance, Courtney. It's *my* story or *no* story." Veronica disconnected.

Courtney sat there, stunned and stumped. Without this smallest sliver of information – Billy's full name – she had no way of confirming the secret government program.

She speed-dialed her friend Emily, the editor of *Cosmo*.

"Helloo." Emily's familiar voice came over the wire.

"Emily, It's Courtney." She affected cheerfulness she didn't feel. "At *Women Rising*."

"I know. CallerID, remember?"

"I need a favor."

"Well, now, the Mountain seems to have come to Mohammad."

"Actually, I'm going to do *you* a favor but I want one in return."

"Now what can that be I wonder? Giving *Cosmo* a plug in your highbrow magazine? Sorry, Courtney, but we don't really need your help. We're one hundred times your circulation."

"Your sexist rag will emulate us someday. Women will turn to my magazine in droves when they finally realize what men do behind our backs. And believe me, it's not pretty."

"You're forgetting one thing, my foxy female friend. Sex *sells*. Helen Gurley Brown proved that with *Sex and the Single Girl*, thank you very much, and *Cosmo* women have been on a quest for the big 'O' ever since."

"Shameless pandering, but I'm sure you know that. Whatever. Let me get to the point. One of my writers came up with an article that's so hot it *bangs*. It could be your next cover story. But before I send it over, I want you to promise me something."

"We'll see—"

"When you fact-check this story, let me know the real name of the guy."

"That's easy enough to do. Why's that so important?"

"I want to know the story behind the story. Get me the name and I'll do some digging."

"Okay, done. If we run with the story, you'll get your man."

"You're going to love it." Courtney pressed *send*. "I don't have the rights to this but I'm sure this author won't mind if you grab it. She's looking for a break."

"Aren't they all? I'll take a look and get back to you." Emily disconnected.

Courtney sat motionless for a moment, smiling to herself. The man's name would enable her to get to the bottom of Ronnie's story.

Her desk phone rang, interrupting her thoughts. She looked at the caller ID but didn't recognize the name. She had a vague recollection of hearing the name "Roger" recently, but she couldn't place the context. She lifted the receiver.

"Hello," came the voice. "My name is Roger Thornwood. I need to speak to the editor of your magazine."

"I'm the editor and publisher, Courtney Stillwell."

"Do you have a writer named Veronica Miller?" There was something in the caller's voice that Courtney liked. The tone was confident and self-assured, yet friendly. Damn *men*, she thought to herself. They're attractive to women in spite of themselves.

"Yes," she replied coolly. "She's freelance. Not employed here."

"Has she discussed writing an article about something called 'Nemow'?"

"*Nemow*?"

"Nemow. The word 'Women' spelled backwards."

"I'm sorry. What did you say your name was?"

"How about '*Ballzoff*'? It's called that too."

Courtney blinked. She realized instantly who this was. She couldn't believe her luck. "Yes, I know all about it," she lied.

"You do? Then it's imperative we talk. Can I see you?"

"Yes, of course. What date would be convenient?"

"Right now."

"Now?"

"I happen to be right here."

"Where?"

"I'm right outside your door."

Chapter 5

Courtney got up from behind her desk and walked out to the front door of the office suite. Opening it, she stared for a moment at the face of a man, about her own age, staring back at her with intense blue eyes.

"Hello, I'm Roger." He held out his hand. Courtney took it and held it firmly while studying his face for a moment. He was pleasant enough to look at, she thought. Then she remembered her manners, greeted him warmly and invited him in.

"You call it 'Nemow'?" She said, making conversation while leading him to her private office. "That's a nice name. Better than 'Ballzoff,' don't you think?"

"'Nemo' for short," Roger replied, glancing briefly around her modest office. "But it's a serious matter that has to be kept strictly confidential."

"I'm afraid it's too late for that, isn't it, Mr. er, what did you say your name was?"

"Thornwood. Roger Thornwood."

"Do you have a business card?"

Roger handed her a card and Courtney glanced at it while motioning for him to take one of the two seats in front of her desk. Under his name, which listed him as a PhD, she saw "**Director, Bioweapons Research. United States Army.**" The address was Aberdeen Proving Ground, Maryland.

Courtney took her seat behind the desk. "Now then, Dr. Thornwood…"

"Roger. Please call me Roger."

"Roger that," Courtney winked. She was doing her best to connect with this man but was getting few signals coming back. "You're the one in charge of the Ballzoff program, aren't you?" She held up the card as if she were holding the man himself.

"Yes, I am. But it's *Nemo*, not Balzoff. And I'm here to warn you: It's a top-secret government project. Even the names 'Nemow' or 'Nemo' are confidential, but I assumed you knew them. Whatever you do know you cannot reveal publicly. That would jeopardize the entire program."

"It's breaking news, and my magazine is about to tell the world," Courtney said matter-of-factly. She certainly didn't have enough information about the program for a news story, nor even a confirmation for that matter. It was time to bluff. "We have a good source."

"I've heard."

"You've already confirmed the program exists."

"I thought you knew."

"Then I assume you know our source too."

"I do. It's a man named Billy." Roger made a disgusted face.

"Which Billy?"

"Billy Donner."

"That's true." She smiled while giving herself a silent pat on the back. "He told Veronica everything, and she told me."

"Then you know what this is about, and you know the program's a State Secret."

"I know you've developed a secret potion, something that can turn men into *women*. That's a 'good thing'."

"I won't confirm anything. I can only say that if used improperly, it could cause havoc."

"It could end war as we know it, reduce the crime rate, eliminate *rape*." Courtney's eyes opened wider as she thought of the possible benefits.

"It's not meant to ever be used. Under treaty it is forbidden."

"We need it right here at home, right now. It's the perfect solution to the difficulty with—" Courtney hesitated to say "*men*." She knew not everyone agreed with her that such a difficulty existed.

"You have no idea, do you?"

"Idea about what?"

"How important this is to our national security. You can't breathe a word of it. It's a potential A-bomb."

"You tried it on bikers. If it were so dangerous, would you have done that?"

"That was a very low dose, at least initially. We had to learn its effectiveness and how long it would last. Also the side effects."

"Were there any?"

"That's need-to-know. I'm not at liberty to say."

"You know Veronica has already written an article that's about to be published?"

"That can't happen. You and Veronica can't reveal anything to anyone."

"I'm afraid it's too late for that. I haven't signed a non-disclosure agreement and neither has Veronica. I'm going ahead with my story, and I sent Veronica's article over to the editor *Cosmopolitan* magazine. She said it would come out in their very next issue," Courtney lied. "And their worldwide circulation is *huge*."

Chapter 6

Emily Platt sat in her windowed corner office and twice reread Veronica's article. It had the essential three ingredients for a *Cosmo* cover – sex, sex and more sex - but more than that it piqued her curiosity: What were these bikers up to, she wondered. Why would they act this way? *What was this secret government program?*

She lifted the phone and called Veronica. It rang four times and went to voicemail. Emily immediately hung up and called Courtney. She was sure Veronica would get back to *her* just as soon as she saw who called. Things worked that way in the women's magazine business.

Courtney answered on the first ring. "Well, hello Emily. How'd you like Ronnie's story?"

"The writing is crap, but the topic is spot on what we like here at *Cosmo*. I might just pull the cover we set for the November issue. With some edits, make it the lead article."

"I knew you'd go for it. You owe me, *big time.*"

"Yeah, well, not so fast. We've got a lot of "t's" to cross before it goes out. We need to contact this Joe the Biker. We have to fact check and get his clearance."

"When you do, remember to let me know. That was the deal. I want to interview him."

"You're doing a story too? On what? The badness of bikers?"

"None of your business."

"I don't want you encroaching."

"Don't worry. Sex is your beat, Emily. Not mine."

"I'll send over the info when I get it."

"Maybe you should Google him. LOL"

"Yeah, or we could check LinkedIn."

"I know his real name at least. It's Billy Donner."

"I'll get his contact info. I have a call in to Veronica."

"She won't tell you. I tried."

"We'll see. When I dangle the publication of her story, she'll come around."

"You may get a call from someone else."

"Yeah?"

"A guy named Roger Thornwood. When he rings up, take the call."

"Oh? Who's this Roger?"

"He's the U.S. Military. He'll want you to kill Ronnie's story."

"Fat chance."

"Just saying—."

"Bye."

As soon as Emily hung up, her intercom buzzed and she pressed a button. "Yes?"

"A call on line two, Says he's from the Army. Name's Roger Thornwood."

"Put him through, Chester."

"You're taking calls from the Army now? What gives, Emily?"

"Something new, Chester. I'll explain later."

"Okay, Here you go—." Emily's desk phone buzzed and she picked up. "Emily Platt," she said. "Courtney Stillwell told me you'd be calling."

"Did she say why?" the male voice asked.

"She told me to take your call. So talk to me, but please make it quick. I just have a minute, starting now."

"Did she send you a magazine article by a Veronica Miller?"

"Yes, she did. What about it?"

"Did you show it to anyone?"

"That's none of your business."

"It contains information that's classified Top Secret. We need to talk."

"I'm not following. You're going to tell me what I can and cannot do?" Emily's voice turned cold.

"I'm head of bio-weapons research for the U.S. Army. I believe that article reveals some classified information."

Emily paused for a moment to take that in, then replied, "All right. I agree to meet."

"I can come over right now."

"I'm very busy. How about at five."

"I'll come to your office"

"No. There's a private room at 'The Lambs Club' we can use."

"The Lambs Club?"

"Google it. It's on Forthy-Fourth Street, right near Times Square. It's where Broadway actors used to stay overnight, back in the day."

"Wouldn't your office be more convenient?"

"Yes, but there's a problem with that. This office has ears. Besides, my magazine runs on estrogen with loads of drop-dead gorgeous women. Much too distracting for a man."

"I see," Roger replied. "I'll be at the Lambs Club at five. Please bring your copy of the article."

Emily hung up and sat quietly in her chair for a moment, thinking to herself while staring at the printout of the article in her hand. If whatever it was that they gave those bikers were added to New York City water, *it could ruin everything.*

Chapter 7

Roger walked into The Lambs Club on the stroke of five and gave his name to the uniformed man at the door. Roger noticed he wore white gloves. The man nodded in recognition and smiled warmly. "Ms. Platt is waiting for you in a private room. I'll show you the way." Roger took a quick look around as he followed the man up a majestic wooden staircase to a room on the second floor. The place had the feel of a nineteenth century men's club in London, with cherry wood walls and ornate ceilings. Entering the room, he saw Emily sitting comfortably in a lounge chair before a glowing fireplace. "Thank you for coming, Roger," she said, rising to greet him. "I thought this was a more appropriate place to have a heart-to-heart talk."

The doorman retreated without a word and quietly closed the door to the room as he left.

"What *is* this place? Like I'm in a time warp." Roger's eyes scanned the room. He felt transported to another world in another era.

"This building opened in 1905 as home to the 'Lambs'," Emily explained. "It was America's first professional theatrical club that took the name from a theater group in London in the 1880's. Over the years there were maybe 6,000 Lambs, Some of the famous ones were Irving Berlin, Charlie Chaplin, John Wayne, Richard Rodgers, Oscar Hammerstein, Spencer Tracy," She ticked off the names while counting on her fingers. "Oh and *Fred Astaire*. When he was made a Lamb he said he felt like he'd been knighted."

Roger shook his head in wonder. "Are you a member of the Club?"

"Oh, no. The Lambs are history here on The Great White Way. Anyone can have drinks or a dinner. I like the old fashioned elegance so I come here now and again. Speaking of drinks, can I offer you anything?"

"A cup of coffee would be nice. I have to get back to Maryland this evening."

"Well let's get to it then, shall we?" Emily lifted the phone on the small table next to her chair and ordered coffee and pastry for two. "Here's Ms. Miller's article, by the way." She handed a copy to Roger who quickly scanned through it while she placed the order.

"It's not too bad, really. It's easily fixable. You could just delete mention of the 'government program' and say these bikers were growing weed or something. Maybe a new kind of weed that made them temporarily sterile."

"No problem. I can do that for you."

"You will?" Roger had come prepared to use the full weight and might of the U.S. government to bear on containing information about the program.

"We won't allow one single word of your program to leak out." Emily added. "Our national security comes first and foremost." Roger silently exhaled a sigh of relief. "However, you are going to have a real problem with Courtney. She's a very determined young woman and I'm afraid she's latched onto this. I know she won't let go."

"Do you know her well?"

"We're polar opposites, but that makes us special friends. She's like the daughter I never had. I'm single, you know, but not by choice. Men are unfortunately intimidated by me and never ask. With her it's by choice. We're both in the same business so we're joined at the hip that way. But there's more. Much more. She confides in me and tells me things she wouldn't tell even her therapist. I do the same for her."

Roger smiled. "All I know is that she publishes a magazine, *Women Rising*, with a rather feminist agenda. Is she getting any traction with her point of view?"

"Not much, I'm afraid. She keeps her list of subscribers confidential from everyone, including me, but her circulation figures are public. They have to be to attract advertising. Her circulation is small, but it's growing. I'd say a quarter million, tops."

"It's all just a matter of business then? Bashing men is a good way to make money?" Roger furled his brow. He had to understand what he had to deal with here.

"Not so. With her it's very real. She's on a crusade to raise women's consciousness. Make them aware. She wants women to rise up and push back at their oppressors. For her it's some kind of a quest, I'm afraid."

Roger stared at Emily not knowing what to say in reply. Just at this moment a waiter gave three knocks on the door, then opened it and entered the room with a elaborate wooden tray with the coffee service and a plate of delicious looking Danish.

"Pastry?" the waiter asked, to neither one in particular.

Emily demurred and looked at Roger expectantly. "I'd like one very much," Roger replied. "I could use a pick-me-up." Roger watched as the waiter carefully manipulated a pair of tongs to place two delecate patries on a small plate and offered it to him. Roger took the plate and thanked him.

"That will be all, Walter. I'll pick one out myself, perhaps. Thank you."

Walter smiled at her and quietly left the room.

"Now then, where were we? Oh, yes: your Top Secret program. It's going to be difficult to stop Courtney once she gets the bit in her teeth. From what I gather, she thinks your program is the answer to a feminist prayer: making men more like women. She's not going to be easily deterred."

"The government has ways to stop people from disclosing government secrets, but it won't be pretty. Can you help me with this? Convince her that national security is paramount?"

"She won't listen to me. As I said, she's like a daughter and that works both ways. I'm like a mother to her and daughters tend to rebel against the advice of their mothers."

"What do you recommend then?"

"You need to treat this matter with utmost sensitivity. I'm on your side, but I can only help you behind the scenes."

"I'm deadly serious about stopping a leak. I'll have to do whatever it takes, including going to court. I want to avoid that route, though, because it could generate publicity."

"All right then. For you to understand what you are up against, I need to tell you something confidential. Somethng I'd like you to keep under your hat but I think it's important for you to know if you are going to deal seriously with Courtney."

Roger took a sip of his coffee and leaned forward to Emily. "I need all the help I can get. "But if I can't tell anyone, how can it help?"

"You'll understand that when I tell you."

"All right then. What you say will not leave this room."

"Your lips are sealed."

"Yes," Roger agreed. "It is just between us."

"Courtney has had an unfortunate history. She was raped – and I mean brutally raped – when she was in college by several members of the Columbia Lions basketball team. She reported the rape to the school officials but Columbia did nothing. They took the attitude that 'boys will be boys'."

Chapter 8

Veronica was not happy. Try as she might, she could not get her boyfriend to turn up the heat. Billy loved having her around and having her ride on the back of his bike, but he treated her like a sister. She wanted *more*, and she was determined to get it.

Whenever she asked what was wrong, he'd say "Nothing's wrong. What's your problem?" or "What the fuck do you want from me anyway?"

She felt it wasn't right for a girl to say she wanted to *fuck*. No woman should have to lower herself like that, but as his strange behavior continued she began to feel sorry for herself. She didn't deserve this. No woman did, but least of all a *real* woman like her. She had needs and those needs required a man: a *real* man.

The issue came to a head one evening while the entire gang was carousing at Cunningham's, their favorite watering hole. Veronica felt like an outsider as the men chatted away amongst themselves like a bunch of old women instead of hitting on her.

Then it came to her, like a stroke out of the blue. *Genesis 9:30.* She shot a lusty smirk at Billy. If Lot's two daughters could do the dirty, she could too. She signaled the bartender, took two twenties out of her purse and slapped them down on the bar. "Give me two shot glasses and a fresh bottle of tequila." She then turned to the bikers crowding around and announced loudly, "Billy, you and I are going to get shitfaced."

"We are?" Billy asked, surprised by her action. "What's the occasion?"

"You deserve a night to howl. My treat."

"Go for it, Billy!" shouted one of the bikers.

"Go, Billy. Go, Billy. Go…" the others looked on curiously and then began to chime in.

"How do you expect me to ride my bike?"

"Remember that first night, Billy?" Veronica asked with wistful toss of her hair. "We can sleep outside under the stars like we did then."

"We didn't sleep…"

"Oh, really? You remember?"

"Geez, Ronnie. Those were the old days."

"And this is now." Veronica held out one of the two glasses that the bartender had filled. "Take this, and let's go at it." With her other hand she grabbed the other glass from the bar and held it up. "To us."

The gang of bikers cheered. "Drink, Billy. Drink, Billy. Drink...."

Billy took the bait. He grabbed the glass and downed the tequila in one gulp. Veronica did the same then poured another shot, for Billy, and pretended to pour one for herself. In fact she poured a short shot but no one paid attention. She handed the refill to Billy and he downed that too.

Between shots, Billy refreshed his mouth with long draughts of beer.

It took only half an hour for Veronica to get the results she was aiming for. Billy could scarcely remain standing. When his friends saw him teetering, they steadied him and, with one man on each side, they walked him out through a back door of the building to a grassy area beyond the parking lot. Veronica followed, telling the men where to take him. She said she would stay with Billy all night if necessary to make sure he survived the ordeal. They lowered him carefully onto the grass, laughing loudly at his inebriated condition, where he lay flat on his back.

"Lights out, Billy," called one of the men and the gang departed. Rather than reentering the bar the men walked around to the front where their motorcycles were waiting. Veronica heard their engines start up with a roar, then idle briefly as gears were engaged and the cycles headed out, one by one, onto the highway.

Veronica looked down at Billy, spread-eagled with his eyes closed. She knelt down beside him, unbuckled his belt and, moving down to his feet, untied and yanked off his boots. She then tugged at his pant legs, pulling his jeans down, and tossed them aside. Moving back to his waist, she grabbed hold of his underpants and slid them down over his legs, exposing a flaccid penis. The feeling she had on that first date, when they made love under the stars, came rushing back and warmed her body as she admired his organ. A strong, unquenchable urge possessed her. "I've got you now, you big burly bastard." she uttered,

She grabbed hold of the penis in her right hand and massaged it gently, until she felt it awaken and become stiffer. Within a minute it stood upright, like a disciplined soldier waiting for a command. Veronica rubbed it up and down, slowly at first and then faster as she felt the rod swell in her hand. As she did so she watched Billy's face, which was blank at first but then, as if he were dreaming, began to show expression. She pumped his penis harder and harder until it virtually exploded in her hand. Looking over, she saw a wide grin on Billy's sleeping face.

* * * *

In the parking lot on the side of the bar, Courtney sat in the darkness at the driver's seat of her car, watching Veronica's actions with a special fascination. When Veronica finally finished, Courtney got out of the car and walked up to her. "I assume you realize," she said calmly, "you just raped a man."

Chapter 9

Veronica looked up at Courtney, aghast and embarrassed at first, but then suddenly angry. "Where *in Hell* did you come from?"

"I followed you. I need to talk to Billy, and this was the only way I knew to find him."

"Well you can see that he's *indisposed* right now." She climbed off Billy's half naked body and stood up, smoothing her skirt.

"I'll wait." Courtney replied, "If it takes all night."

"Yeah, you do that. He'll tell you *nothing*, as long as I'm with him."

"You'll keep him from talking to me after all I've done for you? You *owe* me, Veronica."

"I don't owe you shit. You wouldn't even publish my article."

"You mean you haven't received a call about that?"

"Call? What call?"

"I sent your article to Emily Platt, editor of *Cosmo*. She's going to publish it."

Veronica reached into her shirt pocket and plucked out her cell phone. She glanced at the missed calls and saw Emily's name.

"Probably the cover story in November," Courtney added.

"Egads." Veronica screamed. She opened her arms wide and embraced Courtney, hugging her tightly. "That's my big break." she cried. "I'm going to be a *famous writer.*"

"The article wasn't that good. Don't let it go to your head."

"I've been trying for *years* to get published," Veronica said. "Nobody even answers my calls."

"I did."

"That doesn't count."

"I published one of your articles in *Women Rising,.*" Courtney protested, feigning hurt. It was her practice, in fact, to help novice authors, especially young women who were trying their best to enter the field.

"Well, yes but, pardon my saying so, it's a crappy magazine. No one reads it."

"You ungrateful…. I won't say it."

"Yeah, because Bitch is *your* name. You're an embarrassment to the fucking female gender with your holy attitude. You hate men and men hate you. Women would too if they knew what's good for them."

"Watch what you say, Veronica. You piss me off and I'll never published you again. Ever."

"Once I'm published in *Cosmo* there's no stopping me. But okay." Veronica held up her hands in a posture of surrender. "Truce."

"You'll let me talk to Billy?"

"Yeah, you can talk to the bum."

"And you'll persuade him to talk about that government program?"

"You don't ask for much, do you?"

"Just that," Courtney said.

"Okay, yeah."

"Alright then. It's a deal." Veronica accepted Courtney's proffered hand and shook it firmly. "Now, what about it? When is this biker going to wake up?"

"How about *now*?" Veronica gave Billy a kick in the side and stared down at his ashen face. "Wake up, you son-of-a-bitch."

"Uh, what? Wha…where am I?" Billy rubbed his eyes and opened them wide.

"You're on the lawn behind the bar. You just came, big time."

"I did? It wasn't a dream?"

"Yeah it was. A big fuckin' wet dream. I hope you liked it because that's the last time I'm doing it to you."

"I… What are you talking about?"

"Never mind. Get up." Veronica kicked him again. "This lady wants to talk to you. *Now*."

Billy climbed to his feet and stood as tall as he could in front of the two women. "What the fuck is this? A female posse?"

"No," Veronica replied. "We're your next nightmare, unless you talk to her." She nodded to Courtney. "Courtney, this is Billy. Billy, this is Courtney, publisher of a bitchy women's magazine called *Women Rising*. About women with a penis that *rises*, unlike yours recently I must tell you."

"This may not be a good time," Courtney spoke up. "Could we make an appointment to speak, either in person or on the phone?"

"About what?"

"I understand you and your biker friends took part in a government program."

"Can't talk to you about that."

"Why not?"

"S'posed to keep it secret."

"Would a thousand dollars help you to talk?"

"Fuck no. They paid us a lot more."

"How much more."

"Ten thou apiece."

"Wow, that's a lot of money. I can't match that."

"A hundred thou would do it," Billy said, forcing a huge grin.

"That's crazy. Hmmm. How about fifty?"

"Seventy-five."

"If I pay you seventy five thousand will you tell me everything you know?"

"I'm not saying I know anything."

"You'd be surprised how much you know. Give me your address and cell number and I'll have my lawyer draw up the papers."

"When do I get the money?"

"Hopefully soon. First I've got to find someone who'll make an investment."

"You mean you don't even have it?"

"No, not many people have that kind of money sitting in the bank. But I have a good idea who does, so you might even stand a chance of getting paid."

Chapter 10

George Cleary didn't *think* he was a Master of the Universe. He *was* a Master of the Universe.

His hedge fund had bested the S&P every year for the last five years and he knew why. He had developed a mathematical algorithm that continuously sucked dollars out of the stock market, like a vacuum cleaner sucking dust out of a rug.

Except for its general rise and fall, the financial markets were a zero sum game: there is only so much money to go around at any given time. For every winner, there was a loser, and George had no intention of losing. George's computer traded stocks at microsecond speeds and, being located right next to the New York Stock Exchange server in Newark, New Jersey, it executed trades a full femtosecond ahead of most everyone else. What George took from the trough, other investors, including professional stock fund managers, had to supply.

Notwithstanding the unfairness of George's system, no politician ever complained. To the contrary, he was rewarded with special provisions in the Internal Revenue Code that reduced his income taxes to a fraction of the percentages levied upon ordinary citizens.

And for all these benefits he, and other hedge fund managers like him, did not contribute one iota to the U.S. economy. They did not make products or offer services to anyone. They had no factories or stores that made or sold anything, no companies or organizations that provided jobs. They invented nothing and created nothing. They just sucked money, tons of money, out of the market, year in and year out.

George had long since put behind him his miserable college days when, as a geek, he was viewed with disdain by the popular athletes on campus. He had tried to emulate their boisterous and self-confident banter, but this pretending had never worked for him. He would hang out with members of the basketball team in hopes that their affable attitude would rub off, but that had not worked either. If anything, it made things worse because he often became the butt of their sarcastic humor. The more he looked up to these boys, the more they looked down at him, so he eventually stopped trying to be this person he wanted to be, but wasn't.

That was ancient history, now faded, but still a part of who he was. He had learned to compensate well but, now and again when he found himself outside his element, that old feeling would materialize, like fog creeping in on a cool fall evening, and would cause him to scurry back inside his comfort zone. He hated that feeling, but there was nothing he knew to do to keep it away.

He was all right now. He knew where the zone boundary was. He had only one regret: that night when the feeling kept him from stepping up and stopping the guys from raping that girl. Try as he might to suppress the memory, he couldn't help thinking about what that girl had suffered, and it haunted him still. He sincerely wished he could make amends but he knew that would never happen. Maybe if he could replay the memory with all its detail he could process the guilt and lay it to rest.

Thoughts of this brain-searing moment were the farthest from his mind, however, when an email from _courtney@womenrising.com_ popped up in his inbox. Subject: *You Owe Me.*

George considered it for a moment, then clicked on the message.

Dear George:

You probably don't remember me, but I remember you. You were there at Columbia when I was attacked by those boys. I reached out to you, screaming, to save me but you didn't. You just stood there watching, frozen with your eyes wide open, big as saucers.

Now I need you, again. *Email, or better yet, phone me. I have a proposition for you.*
Cordially, Courtney Stillwell

Her complete contact information appeared below her name.

George was stunned. For a very long moment he sat looking at the screen, thinking about what he should do, and then dialed her number. She answered on the first ring.

Chapter 11

"Courtney speaking."

George liked her voice. He had always liked her voice and he had always liked *her*, although he could never let her know. "It's me, George Cleary. I got your email, just now," he said hesitantly. It was ten years since he'd last seen her.

"*That* was fast," she said brightly. "I sent it only a minute ago. Thanks for calling me."

"What...are you up to?" he managed to say. After leaving Columbia, George had tried his best to put thoughts of his college days behind him. He had not contacted anyone he knew back then, least of all her. Now that she had reached out to him, he found himself intensely curious. More than that, his feelings of sadness and empathy for her terrible ordeal came flooding back.

"I started a magazine...a women's magazine. It's called *Women Rising*. Ever heard of it?"

"Can't say as I have."

"It's for women, to raise their consciousness."

"Their what?"

"Consciousness. You know, about women's issues?"

George could well imagine that a woman who was gang raped might have "women's issues." "Oh," was all he could think to say. He then added, "Can you send me a copy of a back issue?"

"It's online too. Just go to womenrising.com."

George typed in the web address and a perky web site appeared on the computer screen in front of him. The home page showed a cartoon image of a girl with long hair Roger satand big breasts kicking a man in the rear. The headline read, "GIRLS, IT'S TIME TO KICK BUTT."

"That's funny."

"Yeah, I try to keep it light, sometimes."

"I like that. Funny is good."

"It's a serious topic though."

"I know," George acknowledged

"I've been watching your career," she said. "From afar. You've made quite a name for yourself. They say you were a billionaire at age thirty."

"Don't believe everything they say. I'm not even close to a billion, yet."

"How close are you?"

"Now that's kind of personal, though I don't really know myself. It's complicated."

"I do. I know exactly what's in my bank account. If I didn't, I'd be overdrawn in a heartbeat."

"Is your magazine doing well?"

"Yes, it's doing quite well, thank you. It's, how shall I say, *rising*. Women are catching on."

"I'm glad," George said.

"I'm on a kind of crusade, to lift women up."

"It's good to have a goal. Whatever it is."

"Frankly, I think men are the problem."

"You do?"

"Yes, but most women don't even know it. I aim to fix that."

"What's wrong with men?"

"Men cause most of the problems in the world, when you really think about it. And women accept it. Men take and take while women continue to give and give."

"You're saying it's tough to be a woman?"

"You have no idea."

"Try me."

"Just for starters, you can't deny that men have most of the money and most of the power."

"Now that you mention it…"

"And in the little things: Ever think of what it takes for a woman to get ready in the morning? Fixing her hair, doing her nails, the eye shadow, the layers of lipstick."

"No. I never—"

"Do you know why? At first women do it to look like their big sister, or like Barbie. That's all in fun. But then women do whatever they can to look hot and compete for men. Finally, sucking up to men becomes such a damned ingrained habit, they're stuck with it the rest of their lives."

"God, that does sound awful."

"And there's more—"

"Yeah?"

"After all these years women still insist on stumbling around in those unwearable high heels. And don't get me started about women's breasts. *Time Magazine* predicts that, within a few years, a quarter of the women you'll see out there will have breast implants. Sometimes I think women are their own worst enemies."

"That's *terrible*."

"And they do this for *men*, because they think men like it."

"Well, I have to admit—."

"It's all true, unfortunately."

"I'd like to meet you and talk some more."

"So ask me," Courtney said.

"Ask you what?"

"Take a chance, and ask me to meet."

"Well, of course."

"You dare?"

"Why not? Do you bite?"

"Sometimes I do. Yes," Courtney laughed.

"Okay, let's meet at Daniels."

"I've heard of it. But I can't afford that place. It's way over my budget."

"That's not a problem." George replied. "Just to be clear, I'm going to pay."

"This is *not* a date you understand, but since you're a man…"

"It's the old fashioned way, Courtney."

"Sometimes, now and again, that works for a woman," she said. "I can meet you there at eight."

Chapter 12

On the drive back to Maryland after meeting Emily, Roger was beside himself with worry. He had tried calling, emailing and even messaging, but Courtney didn't answer. He eventually pulled into a rest stop on the Jersey Turnpike. The more time went by without an answer the more anxious he became. Not knowing what else to do, he called information for the Army JAG Corps. He dialed the number, then decided against it and ended the call before someone picked up. He first had to speak with the base commander at APG.

He needed to go back to New York, Roger realized. He would stay the night and show up at Courtney's office first thing in the morning. He'd try reasoning with her before reporting the problem, if there was one, to his superior in the chain of command, Brigadier General Mason.

In less than two hours Roger had valet parked and was ensconced in a single room in the City. He slept poorly that night, despite the comfortable bed at the hotel. He'd found Courtney to be strangely elusive and that unnerved him. He had tried to connect with her but couldn't even though he felt comfortable in her presence.

The next morning he showered and dressed and went down to the lobby. It was time to have a heart-to-heart with Courtney and to explain the consequences if she wouldn't agree to keep Nemo a secret. From what Emily had told him about her background, he felt sorry for her and hoped that his usual sensitive manner would win her over. He tried calling her first to tell her he was coming, but she didn't pick up. He took a chance and went to her office anyway which was two long blocks from his hotel.

He arrived at eight thirty and knocked on the door. No one answered so he tried the handle. It was locked. He sat down on the floor next to the door with his back to the wall and waited. To keep busy he sent messages to his office for half an hour, but still no one came. He called Courtney's number for the umpteenth time but was diverted once more to voicemail. By nine thirty he was beginning to think she wasn't coming. He decided to stay until ten and then head back to APG. He was unnerved and started to pace back and forth on the hallway floor.

At five minutes to ten the doors of the elevator down the hall opened, and Courtney stepped out.

"You're late," Roger said, trying hard to keep his deep annoyance in check.

"It's not even ten o'clock," Courtney replied, clearly surprised to see him there. "This is New York City. Most people here don't start work until ten."

"I've been waiting for almost two hours."

"So?" Courtney calmly put her key in the lock and opened the office door. Roger followed her in.

"I'm here to get your agreement not to publish anything about Nemo," he said before she even put down her purse.

Courtney turned and faced him. "And if I don't agree?"

"The government will stop you."

"Ever heard of freedom of the press? It's in the Constitution in case you forgot."

"National security trumps the Constitution."

"I doubt that seriously. And anyway, it's too late. I know all about your 'Little Nemo' and I'm going forward with the article."

"I told you, you can't. Unless we keep the Nemo program a secret, we'll lose whatever advantage it can provide on the battlefield."

"I've already prepared a promo about our next issue. I sent it out to all our subscribers."

Roger glared at her. He hoped to God she was bluffing. She couldn't possibly have obtained further information from Billy Donner overnight, but if that were so, he didn't think she could have written an announcement in this short amount of time.

"Let me make myself clear. If you reveal so much as a hint about the program, you will go to jail. Have you ever heard of Daniel Ellsberg? Julian Assange? Edward Snowden?"

"You can't intimidate me," Courtney said firmly. "Charging me with a crime would be the best thing that could happen to *Women Rising*. All the women in the country would rise up against you. A nasty man bullies a poor defenseless woman. It would make national news."

Roger stood there, speechless. As a scientist he had never known controversy like this. Because he couldn't think of what else to say, he turned around and walked out of the office. He was not at all prepared to deal with a person as stubborn and determined as Courtney.

Chapter 13

Brigadier General Thomas ("Tommy-gun") Mason sat in his office and brooded. Yes, he had been appointed Commander of Aberdeen Proving Grounds but, unless he were able to impress the Joint Chiefs in some way, this would be the last post of his career and all he could expect to wear on his shoulder until he retired was a single lousy star.

It was five to three in the afternoon and at precisely three he expected Thornwood, his Director of Research, to appear and tell him some bad news. It was always bad news at APG. Some ordnance accidentally cooked off in the summer heat, blowing up an entire bunker of ammo; some private first class killed himself while firing an anti-tank weapon; some junior officer got himself into a fight at the Officer's Club bar and punched out a more senior officer.

This time that geeky snit, Thornwood, had called in to make an appointment, saying there was some kind of emergency that needed his urgent attention. The life of the Post Commander was all shit, and more shit.

When he heard the anticipated knock on the door, General Mason stood up. He would soldier on and hope to God lucky lightning would strike. He needed to get out of this routine job in this hellhole and make a name for himself.

His orderly, a young female who more than filled out her uniform, opened the door and announced, "Doctor Thornwood, Sir."

"Show him in, Eve."

The orderly stood aside allowing Roger to enter and then disappeared, closing the door behind her.

"Sit down, Thornwood." General Mason motioned to the wooden chair in front of his massive mahogany desk and waited until Roger complied. He remained standing himself, as was his habit, partly as a way to intimidate his subordinate and partly to buck himself up against whatever new crises had apparently occurred.

"I've heard you've been on a business trip," he said, almost reluctantly for he really didn't want to hear about Thornwood's problem.

"Yes, I went to New York," Roger began. "It's about our program—"

"Our program?"

"The Nemo Program."

"Oh yes, of course." General Mason had almost forgotten the secret skunk-works program that was going on at APG when he became post commander two years earlier. "I've heard you've been working night and day on this. How're you doing?"

"We're just about ready. We have completed our testing."

"Bioweapons research, right?" Not useful as far as the General was concerned. The deployment of bioweapons in the battlefield was forbidden by the Geneva Conventions.

"Yes. I believe we have a formula that works."

"What does the weapon do precisely?"

"It makes men less aggressive. Nicer. More like… well, *women* are. It could significantly aid our troops, Sir."

"I see," the General mused, but after a pause exclaimed, "*Wait*. If they behaved like a bunch of *women*? Are you *kidding*?"

"Oh, no. It would be used against the *enemy*. *They* would act like women. Maybe think like them too."

"Oh, I see." The General tried to imagine this. The idea had seemed bizarre at the time he was initially briefed about the program, and it seemed even more so now. "Go on," he said gruffly. "We would deploy this against who?"

"Against insurgents. Against ISIS."

"And how would we do that exactly?"

"We would add it to the public water supply. Like fluoridation."

"I see. And how do you propose we do that?" This scheme was becoming stranger by the second.

"Lots of ways. We only need to add trace amounts: about a milligram per liter. We can deliver it in powder form or as a liquid. We can use the same technology as fluoridation."

"Same equipment as fluoridation?"

"Yes and it comes in water-soluble white crystals, just like sodium fluoride. It's odorless and tasteless. We can even mix the crystals together. Nobody would know it's there."

"And it does what to the enemy, you say?"

"It's kind of hard to imagine. But suppose – just suppose – the enemy troops were all women. Our guys would have a field day."

"I'm sure they would." The General grinned widely at the thought.

"Well, yeah. I didn't mean it that way. I mean the enemy won't want to fight with deadly weapons. They might want to scream and talk us to death, but they'll pull their punches. Women are more like, uh...lovers than fighters."

The General furled his brow. "You don't know my wife."

It was Roger's turn to smile. He quickly added, "I didn't mean any disrespect, Sir."

"I know. I know. None taken."

"History shows they prefer not to use force."

"I guess that's true. They can sure get pissed off though, believe me. Whew." The General shook his head from side to side and shuddered.

"I wouldn't know about that, Sir."

"No, I guess you wouldn't. You're not married, are you?" It was a statement more than a question.

"No, Sir, I'm not. Never had the opportunity—"

"You didn't miss anything, believe me."

"We have a problem now, Sir."

"Oh? A problem?" The General winced. Here it comes, he thought, though he couldn't imagine what the problem could be. The program was totally illegal so it was going nowhere anyway. It would be locked up in the files of the DOD and forgotten like so many other hair-brained schemes of war.

"There's a woman up in New York City, Courtney Stillwell, who threatens to disclose the existence of the program."

"I see." General Mason winced again. "Now that would certainly be a problem, wouldn't it? You just tell her the government has classified this program as *Top Secret*. End of story."

"I did, Sir. She seems willing to go to jail if we try and stop her. She's had a serious issue with men in the past and she sees this as 'The Answer.' It's a personal thing."

"What kind of issue? With men I mean."

"I can't tell you, but you can imagine, Sir. It's the usual."

"She was *raped*? Damn."

"She's not going to change her mind," Roger said.

"You think? Well, what if she goes ahead and blabs? She tells the world about the program. What's the absolute worst that can happen? What's the downside?"

"That would forever ruin our chances of using Nemo against the enemy."

"It would? Suppose we were to slip it into their water. You know we can't do that anyway because it would contravene the Geneva Conventions, but just suppose. What is the enemy going to do, stop drinking water?"

"They would test for it. If they found it in the water supply they wouldn't let on so we wouldn't know it, but they'd secretly turn to drinking something else."

"What, booze? Come on, Thornwood. Get serious."

"Bottled water; water from another source."

The General couldn't believe what he was hearing. This was getting too ridiculous. "Oh yeah, *right*. I supposed they'll go to the supermarket and buy cases of Poland Spring."

Roger didn't answer. He looked upset.

"You know, Director. I have an idea. Why don't you call up this woman and tell her to go ahead. Disclose the program. Make it public. Tell the world."

"Tell the world?"

"She thinks men should act prissy, like women. Okay. Fair enough. Let's assume that this Nemo stuff's as good as you say, for the sake of argument. If she tells the world, no self-respecting guy would want to, or even dare to use it. *But*, on the other hand, if the stuff were kept secret and slipped into the water supply on the sly, men would drink it and would become prissy and sissy, just like she wants. So you see, if she's smart she won't tell anyone." General Mason's face broke into a broad smile and he leaned in toward Roger, conspiratorially. "We should give the stuff a try up there in New York City. Sneak it into their water system and see what happens."

Roger looked up at the man standing over him, his face aghast.

"Just *kidding*," the General said, grinning. "Thornwood, you should lighten up."

Chapter 14

Roger was stunned. This was not at all what he expected. He thought General Mason would immediately place a call to the Judge Advocate General of the U.S. Army, telling him to blast Courtney Stillwell to kingdom come with both barrels blazing. However, knowing Courtney and what she had endured, he was very glad the General had held his fire.

He didn't want to make trouble for her, but she was sure making things difficult for the Army and something had to be done.

Now it seems that he, Roger, was supposed to tell Courtney she was free to break the news about the new bioweapon called "Nemow." Didn't the General realize what a game-changer it would be if Nemo were deployed *secretly* against enemy troops? If *anyone*, not to mention *everyone*, knew about the weapon, this could never happen.

The news might even result in a media firestorm. Unless the bioweapon were first used successfully on the battlefield, as Roger had always assumed it would, its very existence might reflect badly on the DOD and it could even embarrass the POTUS.

He needed to turn General Mason around, and there was only one sure way to do it. He had to prove to him how well the weapon worked.

The officers' homes at APG were pretty much all alike, although the base commander's home was notably more prestigious. Because Roger lived in one of the APG homes himself, he knew the General's probably included a water filter in the basement. His home did, and all of these homes were built at pretty much the same time. Being the scientist that he was – some would derogatorily call him "anal" – he had changed the water filter regularly every six months, on the first day of the month, from a stock of new filters he kept in his kitchen cabinet.

After leaving the post commander's office Roger went home, grabbed one of his filters, and headed for the lab. Setting himself up in a separate room away from the prying eyes of his colleagues, he went to work. It took overnight to soak the cylinder-shaped membrane, but by morning it was impregnated with the Nemo formula. Now he was faced with the final step of the process: a task he'd rather avoid. He had to install it in the basement of the General's home.

Roger brought the doctored filter to his own home and changed his clothes. He donned a denim shirt and a pair of well-worn jeans and topped it with a baseball cap. Looking in the mirror he was reminded that he hadn't shaved for two days but he decided to leave the manly growth for the task he was about to perform. He grabbed the filter and a small toolkit, and walked out the door.

The General's house was less than a quarter mile down the road. It stood alone among the row of neatly trimmed brick homes that married officers were assigned when serving on base during their tour of duty. It was notably larger and recessed farther from the road and on a larger lot than the other homes, giving it an aloof appearance, just as the base commander was expected to be standoffish from his fellow officers. He was supposed to be friendly and approachable to a point, but not a friend. That seemed to suit General Mason just fine. In fact he was neither friendly nor a friend to his troops. He would remain in his office from eight in the morning until six at night, rarely going out to inspect his domain.

Roger knocked politely on the handsome wooden door and waited for Mrs. Mason to appear. The officers on base rarely saw her, except during infrequent social gatherings at the officer's club, celebrating an officer's birthday or engagement for example. No one saw her leave her house, even to buy groceries at the PX. Groceries and practically all other home necessities were delivered to her by orderlies, making her somewhat of an enigma at APG. Roger, who believed socializing was not a good use of his time, thought this was quite normal but for a general's wife, expected to lead the social life on base, it wasn't common at all. She was a recluse and that was that.

The door opened and Roger found himself looking at an unfamiliar, deadpan face. It was without a trace of make-up and topped with unruly twists of white hair, yet the woman was not unattractive. Although it was eight thirty in the morning when everyone on the base had long since started their day, she wore a bathrobe and slippers.

"Mrs. Mason?"

"Yeess?" The General's wife drew out the one syllable word as a question.

"I'm Phillip Morris," Roger said, unable to quickly think of a good alias when suddenly confronted. "I have been assigned to replace your water filter." Roger held up the white filter rod, partly as a "show and tell" and partly a show of his legitimacy.

"Oh," was all she said and stepped aside to let him in.

Roger stepped into the foyer and looked around. The layout was quite different from that of his own home, but he knew the filter unit was located in the basement where the main water pipe entered the house. "Your basement door?" he asked politely.

Mrs. Mason nodded perfunctorily and said, "Follow me." She turned and led Roger toward the back of the house, opened a basement door and flicked a light switch on the inside wall. This was going to be easier than I expected, Roger thought. He didn't like lying and he had never in his life pretended to be someone he wasn't. He wanted to install the filter so the General would try the KoolAid, and then get of there as fast as he could.

He walked carefully down the wooden steps to the basement and looked quickly around for the water facility. Spotting it, he walked over and went to work with his tools.

As he knelt and unscrewed the cap in the filter, he became aware that someone was right behind him, watching intently. He turned and saw Mrs. Mason, still in her bathrobe.

"Your old filter is horribly dirty," Roger said to make small talk and keep his nervousness from showing. "I'll replace it and you'll be good for another whole year."

"I don't think its been replaced since we got here, two years ago," she replied. "Thank you for doing this."

"No problem, Ma'am. It's my job." Roger inserted the new filter rod and screwed on the cap. Picking up the old one from the floor, he stood up and faced Mrs. Mason. She seemed somewhat forlorn to him, but he couldn't read her face. She stood there looking at him, apparently wanting something. "I'll be going now," he said.

"Can I offer you some tea? Coffee?" Her voice was nearly pleading.

Roger felt a tug of sympathy for the woman and acquiesced, although he would have preferred to leave right away and run straight home as fast as his legs could take him. "Coffee would be nice," he said.

Roger followed Mrs. Mason upstairs to her kitchen and took a seat at the kitchen table. The lady produced a cup of coffee in an instant, as if by magic, and placed it in front of him. "Cream and sugar?" she asked.

"Yes, please. I like both," Roger replied looking up at her face. It had a few wrinkles, showing character he thought, and a cupid's bow mouth without lipstick. In his opinion she was fairly attractive with that head of unruly white hair.

She sat down opposite him at the table and said, almost meekly, "I rarely have visitors."

"Do you work?"

"No. I really can't. Just as soon as I got settled somewhere, my husband would be transferred somewhere else and I'd have to quit."

"I'm sorry."

"Don't be. The life of an army general is not so bad, but it's lonely. *I'm* lonely. You may call me Beth, by the way." Mrs. Mason stared at Roger to emphasize what she meant. She was trying to tell him something, clearly, but as a general's wife she could not come out and say it, or even hint at any impropriety. Scientist that he was, though, Roger was totally inept at reading body language so any such hint would have gone unnoticed. "My husband rarely comes home."

"It's a tough job he has. A lot of responsibility."

"He could come home for supper, but he never does. I'm always asleep when he gets home and he leaves early in the morning."

"What do you do to keep busy?"

"Well, like I said, I'm lonely." Mrs. Mason shot Roger a knowing look. To change the subject he asked a question:

"Does your husband tell you what goes on here at APG?"

"We don't talk very much. Like I said he's never home. Our marriage is not doing so well." Mrs. Mason gazed at Roger again with that same forlorn look as before. "Can I tell you a secret?"

"A secret? Okay."

"My husband cheats. That's in his nature, I suppose. He's always had someone on the side."

For a moment Roger didn't know how to respond, but then he had an idea. "Can I tell *you* a secret?"

Mrs. Mason smiled seductively and leaned forward, her eyes glistening. "Tell me."

"I think the cheating's going to stop."

"Stop?"

"Yes. Don't ask me why, but you should see a change in his behavior very soon."

"I don't believe it."

"You'll see. Give it a few days. He'll start coming home in the evening, I'll bet."

"I'm not sure I'd like that." Mrs. Mason winked at Roger with a wry smile.

Roger took that as a cue that his visit was over. He stood up and backed away slightly from the table. "I'm sorry, but I have to go." He gave a light bow.

Mrs. Mason rose and, facing Roger, undid the cloth belt that kept her bathrobe tightly closed. The two sides of the garment parted, revealing a line of pearl-white skin from the nape of her neck down to the dark hair on her crotch. Roger couldn't help but stop for a moment to stare before he turned and made a hasty exit from the house and ran home in flat-out sprint.

.

Chapter 15

Courtney Stillwell could hardly wait to tell her colleagues at *Women Rising* the news. At ten o'clock they assembled.

The editorial board met on the second Wednesday of each month to discuss and decide upon the content of the next issue of the magazine. The board consisted of Courtney Stillwell, Editor in Chief, and three other women, all accomplished writers in their own right, who had their own individual agendas about the issues with men – so much so that the word "men" was almost a dirty word.

The ages of the three other board members ranged from twenty-six to forty-seven. Ashley, the youngest, had been invited to join the board after submitting a well-researched article about the Skull and Bones at Yale, an exclusive club that, according to its original bylaws, only men were eligible to join. Ashley was shocked when reading about its influential members, including the father and son Presidents, George H.W. Bush and George W. Bush, to name just two, and felt a angry rage well up within. When her article was published in *Women Rising,* it trended in the media and resulted in doubling the number of subscriptions for the magazine.

Bailey was African-American and thirty-two, close in age to Courtney and a close friend of hers since their days together at Barnard College. She was the only one on the board that knew about Courtney's ordeal with members of the basketball team because Courtney had asked her to keep it confidential. Courtney's personal life was not relevant subject for the magazine and she wanted to keep it that way.

Her claim to fame was a well-publicized class-action lawsuit she instituted against her then employer for sex discrimination. She won the suit by proving that men were paid more than women for doing the same job, that men were selectively promoted over women and that men held all the managerial positions in the high-tech company. It didn't hurt that the chief executive himself had texted misogynist messages to another CEO.

Delores, or "Deedee" for short, was the oldest and most seasoned member of the board. She had been Courtney's first recruit when the idea of starting the magazine was only a daydream. Deedee had been a writer and eventually an editor for 'Ms.', and knew the ups and downs of the magazine business. She became Courtney's mentor and a source of her strength and confidence when launching *Women Rising*.

All four women were handsome, each in her own way. Known as the "Alphabet Soup" because of its member's first names, the editorial board was a collegial and cohesive group of women who enjoyed each other's company as much as their mission of holding a mirror up to the machinations of the male gender. And for this work they had a never-ending surfeit of material to work with.

Before broaching her own subject, which she was eager to reveal, Courtney went around the table and asked each person in turn what material she had to offer. She always started with the letter "A," by asking the youngest editorial board member to speak first.

"So Ashley, what have you got?"

"A woman reporter for *USA Today* just did a study of all the mass killings for the last five years and found a startling statistic. Guess what that is?"

"Okay, before we guess," Courtney moderated, "you have to tell us: What's a 'mass killing'?"

"When someone kills more than four people in a single day," Ashley replied, then quickly added, "Besides *himself*, that is."

This kicked off the discussion and the comments came in rapid succession.

"The killer came from a broken home."

"No."

"A single parent home?"

"Isn't everyone these days?"

"The guns were stolen?"

"Actually only rarely."

"The murders took place inside."

"Inside what?"

"A building, dummy."

"I already gave you a hint, dummy yourself."

"Children were killed."

"What children?"

"The murderer killed his own children."

"Not usually."

"People were killed by someone they knew."

"Okay, okay, that's enough." Courtney interrupted. "We're wasting time. What's the answer, Ashley?"

"Ninety-four percent of the mass murderers were *men*."

"Well, *duh*." Courtney said. "That's not news, but it's a higher percentage than I thought. Woman reporter, huh. Have you spoken with her."

"No, but I will. Just give me the go-ahead and I'll build a story around her, what she found out and how she found it."

Courtney looked around the table and everyone nodded. "Okay great. We'll go with that. Bailey, your turn."

"I saw an article in the *Star* that said Jennifer Aniston cheated on Brad Pitt, her husband back in the day. How about researching that?"

"A woman cheating on a man?"

"That's trash. We're a serious magazine," Ashley pointed out. "I don't see the point."

"Alright, I'll spell it out," Bailey said. "Let's say seventy-five percent of the cheaters are men. Here's a woman who goes out there and cheats on her hot husband, *Brad Pitt* for God's sake. Don't you get it? If men can do it, women can too. What's good for the goose is good for the gander."

"You have it backwards," Deedee commented. "You should say, 'What's good for the gander, is good for the goose.' Gander's a male don't you know."

"Okay, let's vote," Courtney moderated. There were one in favor, two against. Courtney exercised her swing vote. "Let's save that. I've got something much better to tell you about in a minute."

"Tell us now."

"Not yet. Bailey, try again."

"Okay then. It's about that income divide out there. You all know that one percent of the population in the U.S. hold seventy percent of the wealth. I'd like to break that down between male and female. I'll bet if you do that you'll find ninety percent of the one percent are men."

"Any comment?" Courtney looked around.

"Probably worth the research," Ashley said. "But the answer won't surprise anyone. We all assume that to be the case."

Deedee interjected, "What might be interesting is just who those ten percent of women are? Did they make the money themselves or inherit it from their rich husbands?"

"Or get it through a divorce," Ashley added. "Like Ivana Trump got the Plaza Hotel."

"Go Ivana!" Bailey raised her hand in mock salute.

"We're curious, and I'm sure our readers are too," Courtney said. "See what you can find out, Bailey. Deedee, you're up."

"I've been thinking about an article on women inventors. Easy to research from the Patent Office website. What percentage of patentees are women? What kinds of things did they invent? The Patent Office classifies the patented technology, you know, so we could get percentages of women inventors based on these classes. Baby products, kitchen appliances, clothing fashions, that sort of thing."

"That's sexist. Women must have inventions in other fields too," Ashley said.

"It is what it is," Deedee responded. "Society says we should be homemakers, and we're supposed to invent high-tech stuff? I don't think so."

"Any objections?" Courtney scanned the faces. She was biased in her mentor's favor so she probably would have gone with the concept anyway. "Great idea, Deedee. Go with it."

Everyone now looked at Courtney with anticipation. "Okay, Courtney, your turn." Deedee spoke for the group. "What have you got?"

Courtney stood up dramatically and headed for the door. "I'll just be a moment. There's someone waiting in my office." In less than a minute she returned and stepped aside to let Billy enter "I'd like to introduce Veronica Miller's boyfriend. He's a member of a motorcycle gang with a great story to tell."

Chapter 16

The eyes of the three women were fixed on his face as the man entered the room looking his natural rugged self. Billy's shiny baldpate made his beard seem all the more scruffy. He wore faded blue jeans and a black T-shirt as most bikers do, and he looked around without speaking. He made eye contact with each woman in turn.

"His name is Billy Donner," Courtney said, as he stood there awkwardly. "His gang was contacted by the U.S. Army to test a new biological weapon. I have asked Billy to come here to explain the program which, I understand, is classified by the government as *Top Secret*. Billy signed a confidentiality agreement to keep it secret but he is willing to tell us everything. Isn't that true, Billy?"

"Yeah, I am."

"Why is that?"

"It ain't right. I think everyone should know."

"What isn't right?"

"The stuff really makes you feel relaxed, and they oughta make it available."

"You're also getting paid to speak to us. Are you not?" Courtney asked rhetorically.

"Uh, yeah. Seventy-five thousand bucks."

An audible gasp could be heard from the women at the conference table, one of them echoing, "Seventy-five—."

"We'll get into that," Courtney said, smiling pleasantly. "Have a seat, Billy." She motioned to her own seat at the head of the table. When Billy hesitated, she added, "Go right ahead. We're eager to hear what you have to say." As Billy settled into his seat she walked around to the opposite end of the table and took that chair.

Billy sat there a moment and glared at his audience, looking uncomfortable but not in the least bit intimidated. Then he took a breath and began. "Almost a year ago we were at this place in Cherry Hill, drinken' an' smokin' and having a grand ol' time when this guy walks in. Dressed real nice but lookin' real nerdy. Says his name is 'Roger' – like

Roy Rogers – and wants to speak to us. We start crowdin' around an' pullin' his leg, fun like, but you can see he don't go for that. So we ask what he's doin' there at this bar. Says he works for the Army and they need human guinea pigs to test this new drug they're workin' on. Doesn't call us guinea pigs, o'course; we woulda' took offense if he did, but we get the message. Right off the bat he tells us there's five thousand bucks in it for each of us if we do this thing. That gets our attention real quick. Know what I mean?"

The four women all nodded in unison without saying anything. Their eyes were focused on Billy as they hung on his every word.

"Frankie, he's the big Kahuna in the gang, says right away five thousand ain't enough. He asks this Roger to double it, and he does. Just like that. Like that was to be the pay for us anyway. We're to get ten thou apiece, he says, but it will be paid when we drink this stuff and meet once a month to answer his questions about it. He also hands us this paper. He says, take it home, talk to our lawyers if we want – our *lawyers*, ha! – an' to come back in a week if we want to do this thing. Frankie asks, why wait a week? We all want the money. But Roger, he says it's important to think about it some before we sign.

"All of us wondered what this drug was for. At first this Roger says it'll calm us down. Like we need calmin'. We ask why he chose us for doin' this thing and he says he's heard we're the baddest ass bikers in the State of New Jersey. We asked how he found us and he says it was easy. He asked the *po*leece. Pretty much every cop in the state knew where we were. So he started drivin' aroun' an' saw a bunch of our bikes parked at this bar."

"Did you read the paper he gave you? What did it say?" Courtney asked.

"Yeah, but not at first. We took the papers home to read. One thing though: This Roger told us not to tell anyone but our lawyers – like we had *lawyers* – because he didn't want anyone to know what we were doin' Before he gave us the paper he made us all sign another piece of paper sayin' we'd keep that first paper secret. We signed the second paper and he gave us a copy of that along with the first paper. Real business-like. We took the papers home and I showed them to Ronnie my girlfriend."

"But you weren't supposed to tell anyone," Deedee commented.

"Shit, what did I know? I had to find out if I should be doin' this thing. Ronnie said 'Go for it. You need the money.' So we met Roger a week later at that same place and I signed on. So did the other guys."

"You all did?" Courtney asked.

"Yeah. One of the guys gave Roger some trouble at first. He didn't want to sign, but we told him he had to or he was out of the gang. He signed on real quick. We each got a thousand bucks that very night. I'll never forget it. We roasted this guy Roger and got him real drunk. We had to carry him out to his car when the bar closed. He was *gone*, man. Slept it off in the back seat. I'll bet he remembers that night too – or maybe not."

"About that paper you signed," Deedee said, still staring and under the spell of the narrative. "What did it say?"

"I brought my copy. I thought you might want to see it," Billy replied, leaning over and fishing into his back pocket. He pulled out a folded sheet of paper and carefully opened it on the table. The women's eyes followed Billy's hands as he produced the wrinkled document.

"I'd like to make a copy," Courtney said. "Is that okay?"

"Sure," Billy replied. "No problem." He handed the sheet to Ashley who sat next to him on his left, and she handed it up the line to Courtney. Courtney stood and said, "I'll make copies for everyone. Be right back. Billy, don't tell any more of the story until I'm here, okay?"

"Yeah, sure." Billy looked around the table glaring hungrily. "I'll stay right here with these nice ladies." Two of the women moved uncomfortably in their seats, adjusting their positions. "You all look so pretty." Billy grinned showing his white teeth. "So, you ladies got any questions?"

Ashley, always unabashed, started the small talk. "Ronnie's your girlfriend?"

"Yeah. You know her?"

"She writes for the magazine sometimes. I met her once. She's really nice."

"She's gonna make it big someday. I'm always tellin' her to keep writin'."

"A girl needs encouragement. Good for you."

"Yeah, well that's the least I could do. She takes care of my needs. Ya' know what I mean? Now that the drug has worn off and all."

"Yes, I think so." Ashley glanced at the other women to make sure they understood, and they apparently did. "I've heard that one of her articles will be published in *Cosmo*."

"Yeah. She's real excited about that. Says it's her big break."

"*Cosmopolitan*? That's huge." Bailey chimed in.

"Yeah. We had a good fuck when she heard. I'm glad she's makin' it."

"We are too. Glad that is. She's one of us," Bailey said with some sisterly pride. Billy looked at her as if to ask, "Who the hell are *you* to say that?"

"What I want to know is, why aren't *we* publishing her article ourselves?" Ashley wondered aloud.

"Too trashy." Courtney appeared at the door to the room with copies in her hand. "But *we're* going to break *this* story," she added as she handed one copy to each of the three women. She gave the original back to Billy and returned to her seat. "Now Billy," she said, "please tell us what happened next."

Chapter 17

"You can see from that paper, this new drug we was takin' was some pretty mean shit. Paper says we accepted all the risks. Says we was told about the things that could happen if we took it and we was takin' the stuff of our own free will. Also says we agreed not to sue, but we knew damn well that wouldn't hold up if we got hurt bad. We'd sue anyway. Damn straight.

"It was scary, but we went ahead. The money was good. That's all we really cared about."

"Roger told you what the drug was for?" Courtney asked. She was anxious to get to the point of the meeting: the reason *Women Rising* should publish the story.

"Yeah, he did. First thing. He told us the military was developing this new weapon that would calm us down. Yep, that's just what he said. He said it could end all wars if it worked like it was supposed to. We didn't believe it at first – thought it was some kind of a joke – but he was serious and pretty convincing. Said he'd been inventing this stuff for 'bout four years and it worked pretty well on pigs. He asked if we were willing to try it, 'cause he needed to prove that it worked on humans."

Courtney's three board members stared at Billy, incredulous, unable to speak. Courtney summed it up for them. "Did Roger tell you at any time that you would be…*transgendered*? That you would turn into *women*?"

"No, no, nothing like that. But matter of fact, though, he said we might *act* like girls…" Billy paused, looked at his audience for a beat and then corrected himself. "I mean women. Never said we'd *become* women. And he promised the effects would wear off after we stopped takin' it."

"Did he say what it might be like to…huh, *act* like women do?"

"No. We asked him that. He said no one ever tried it before."

"Okay, then what happened?" Courtney pressed on.

"Like I said, we met at the bar a week later and signed the papers. He gave us each a thousand bucks and seven bottles of water. Told us to drink one every day for a week."

"When did you start?"

"Right there at the bar. We wanted to add it to beer, but Roger said no. So we all drank a bottle right there. Jimmy the bartender was real surprised and asked us what we were doin'. Thought we were nuts, drinkin' this water."

"So you drank your first bottle at the bar? What did it taste like?"

"That's the funny thing: there warn't any taste. It was like drinkin' regular water."

"Did you feel any different when you drank it?"

"Nope. Wasn't like drinkin' coffee, say. Roger told us it would take awhile to kick in. You know those steroid packs where you're supposed to take maybe eight or ten pills the first day and then one less pill every day? It was like that. Roger said the stuff builds up in your body. Once it does, you can take less to keep it goin'."

"When did it start to…uh, kick in?"

"A week maybe. After drinkin' a bottle every day."

"What did it feel like?" Courtney asked. She and her three colleagues collectively held their breath. This was what they really wanted to know.

"It was okay."

"That's *it*? *Okay*?"

"Well, yeah, at first anyway. Kind of crept up on you."

"How was it…later? Did you have any problem with it?"

"No, it was okay. I'm just sayin'. Some guys liked it even; some not so much. I didn't mind it really."

"Did it make you act like a woman?"

"I dunno. What's that like?"

"Did you feel any different?"

"Yeah, I did."

"Different how?"

"I stopped pickin' fights. I started complainin' a lot, just like women do. Every li'l fuckin' thing that bothered me, I bitched about it."

"Welcome to our world." Deedee interjected.

"I kept tellin' myself it wasn't so bad," Billy continued, "so long as it would wear off when I stopped drinkin' the stuff. The money was good."

"How long did you take it?"

"Nine months. Thousand dollars a month."

"When did you stop?"

"'Bout a month ago. Roger said the program was over."

"Did he say why?"

"Yeah, he said his program was a success. His words were, 'It was ready to use against the enemies of the United States.' Never forget that."

"Were you glad about that?"

"Yeah, I was glad. But he said something else—"

"Oh, what's that?"

"He said the President would never let the Army use it."

"Why not?"

"He said it was against some fuckin' Conventions to do that. Geneva Conventions."

"Do you have a problem with that?"

"Hell, yeah. They should fuckin' use it. Figuring the way the stuff worked on me, the enemy wouldn't want to fight. Shit, if the enemy also got ahold of it and used it on our guys, we wouldn't want to fight either. There'd be no wars any more."

One could hear an audible gasp from some women at the table. Courtney pressed on, "Did you want to continue taking the drug when Roger stopped the test?"

"Some of the guys did. I figured they wanted the money, but they said they liked the stuff too. I don't know. Anyway, I'd had enough."

"Did the effect 'wear off' like you said?"

"It took a week. I was actually getting worried. But Roger told us the stuff was like aspirin: When it builds up in your body it takes awhile to taper off."

"Do you feel normal now?"

"Yeah, I'm *back*." Billy looked at the four women at the table like he was about to eat them up. "I'm ready to go. Know what I mean?"

"I think we do, yes." Courtney replied, eyeing the other women. "So what did it feel like, uh, …before the effects wore off?"

"Let me tell you…" Billy paused for a moment and the four women leaned in to catch every word. "If they ever put this stuff in the water, it would make an unbelievable weapon. You don't feel like fightin', you don't feel like fuckin', you don't feel like foolin' around. The enemy's gonna let us roll right over them. End of story."

"Is that such a bad feeling?"

"It sure was a shitty way to experience the world. If that's what *you* people feel like, it really *sucks* to be a woman."

Chapter 18

Billy got up from the table after saying his peace and announced, "I guess I'm done here. You gonna pay me now?"

"That was the deal," Courtney said, also standing. "Ten thousand down and sixty-five now. I'll get the cash."

"Cash?" Deedee asked, visibly surprised and perturbed. She and the other women remained in their seats. "You should write a check. It's a business expense." Ashley and Bailey nodded in agreement.

"Billy insists on cash so it can't be traced," Courtney told them. "He's totally in breach of his agreement with the government."

"They'll find out anyway," Ashley argued.

"No they won't. He's a source. Under New York law we can protect our sources."

Ashley frowned. "You sure?"

"Sure, I'm sure. There are lots of cases on this. Remember 'Deep Throat'? No one found out who he was until the guy died. I still can't remember his name."

"That was in Washington. And it didn't matter, as long as the story was true. They just wanted to stick it to President Nixon."

"Same thing here. If we do it right, this story can be as big as Watergate. As long as it's true, no one's going to care where the leak came from."

"The government will," Deedee said. "And this Roger guy will. Big time. It's all on him."

"Don't worry about that. I can take care of Roger," Courtney said, stifling a smile. "Now excuse me while I get the cash. And I have a receipt for you to sign, Billy."

"Receipt?" Billy looked perplexed. "I thought this would be secret. No paper."

"You're getting your seventy-five thousand. I don't want you to come back and say you want more."

"I'm not gonna—" Billy thought a moment. "Oh, okay. S'long as the receipt don't say why you're payin' me."

"It won't. It doesn't." Courtney left the room leaving Billy standing there, looking somewhat smug while the other women looked on.

"So you think it sucks to be a woman?" Ashley asked, pointedly.

"Yeah, kinda. I suppose it takes some getting used to. I can't figure what you women do to have fun."

"We do just fine, thank you very much. Don't you worry about us." There was an edge to Ashley's voice.

"Never you mind, Ma'am," Billy said calmly. "I won't."

Courtney walked in with the cash and the receipt. Billy signed it, took the cash, and left the room and then the office. The women heard the office door slam.

Courtney sat down at the conference table where Billy had been seated and asked, "So, my dear friends, what do you think? Let's go around the table. Ashley?"

"Pure dynamite. This story will put this magazine on the map. I say go with it, ASAP."

"Bailey?"

"Who'll write the story? Can I? I'd like to run with this one."

"No, this story is mine," Courtney said firmly. "I found this guy and I found and paid the seventy-five thousand bucks."

"How about we all work on it?" Bailey replied. "It can be a collaborative effort. We do it right and we all get bragging rights."

"I like Bailey's idea," Deedee said. "You're too close to it, Courtney. You might miss something. Some new angle. There are a lot of ramifications to this Army project."

Courtney looked at Deedee with pleading eyes. "That's not fair. You guys haven't done anything to land this."

Deedee wasn't about to be hurried. She cocked her head reflectively and blinked her eyes twice before speaking. "I'm not sure we should go with this story at all," she said carefully. "It would bring the wrath of the federal government down upon our little magazine. We are still on tender feet and that would be something we cannot afford."

"Yes we can," Courtney replied. "Trust me on that."

"Alright then, explain. Transparency here." Deedee eyed Courtney earnestly.

"I have this friend…uh, George. He's very wealthy and he's funded us to the tune of a million dollars."

All three members of the board stared at Courtney in disbelief. "Oh?" Deedee was totally taken aback. She had mentored Courtney all through the startup and growing pains of the magazine, "Who's *George*?"

"A friend. He runs a hedge fund and is very successful. I mean *very*. He's agreed to help us financially and in every other way."

"Why didn't you tell us this before?" Ashley said, seemingly annoyed. "We're the editorial board. Heck, we're the *only* board. We're like your board of directors too. We need to know this stuff."

"Well, this is new," Courtney replied defensively. "It just happened a couple of days ago. I went to George to tell him of our predicament and he was more than generous."

"What predicament is that?" Deedee wanted to know.

"I needed the money to pay Billy. Billy said he would tell us what he knew if we paid him seventy-five thousand dollars. I got the money to pay him, and a whole lot more."

"From a hedge fund manager?" Bailey jumped in, suddenly concerned. "Courtney, did you sell us out? What did this guy get in return? Is this dirty money?"

"No, no, nothing like that. You're making a mountain out of a molehill. George is just a close friend. He wants to help us. He wants us to succeed."

"So what did he get? A part ownership in the magazine? Courtney, you can't just go and sell our stock to some guy without consulting us. This is a *women's* magazine, by the way. We don't want any man poking his nose under the tent." Bailey's eyes flashed. The other two board members were becoming increasingly concerned also. Deedee especially.

"So what *does* George get in return for this million dollars?" Deedee demanded. "Are you screwing him?"

"Of course not. How could you say such a thing? He's just…just a friend."

"So why is he so interested in us?" Bailey wanted to know.

"Alright I'll tell you. I went to him after I learned about the Army program and told him what I knew, which wasn't very much at the time.

I thought this could be the answer to our prayers: that men would stop being men and start acting, well, *reasonably*. Like us women. George was very sympathetic and agreed to help us. He immediately wired a hundred thousand dollars to our account and said he was good for up to a million. That was yesterday."

The women at the table were stunned. Bailey managed to say, "Again, what does he want for his million dollars? Courtney, we don't want to pry into your private life, but are you selling us down the river? If a guy so much as takes you out to dinner, he wants something in return. You know that. We know that. That's how it works."

"We're just friends. Honest." Courtney was beginning to resent her board members' suspicions. And she was not about to reveal her secret. Not to anyone, even to her mentor Deedee. "You have to believe me. George is not getting stock or anything *else*." She emphasized the word "else."

"He just donated the money to the magazine because he loves to help women," Deedee said sarcastically.

"Something like that." Courtney looked at Deedee blandly, trying to hide her deception.

"*Right*." Deedee signaled she knew it was a lie.

"So we got the money," Bailey interrupted. "Let's move on. Shall we vote on doing this story or what?"

"I'm against it. We're not that kind of muckraking magazine and, in any case, we're sure to be sued because the information is classified," Deedee insisted. "We're out seventy-five thousand bucks, I know, but we should take our lumps and walk away."

"Like I said, I'm for it," Ashley countered. "It will make our magazine."

"I'm for it too," Bailey added. "Though I'm not so sure why this Army project is relevant to our mission as a magazine. Can someone enlighten me on that?"

"I'm not so sure either," Deedee said. "The breaking news would sell magazines. I suppose that's a reason to publish it, but what does that have to do with our legal and moral rights as women? Nothing that I can see. If pressed for a vote, I would have to say no."

The three women turned their heads to Courtney. She was the swing vote, and they knew it would be a yes. It was a decision that would forever change the character of the magazine to which they had devoted so much of their time and effort. They would be on a different path now. Courtney looked soulfully into the eyes of her editors, each in turn, and then spoke from the heart.

"My dear friends, I have known and loved each one of you for a very long time. You have helped me as a publisher and as a person more than you can ever know. I owe whatever little success I have had in my career to you. I owe the existence of this magazine to you.

"As you know, we are together on a mission to change the world. We think – in fact, we *know* – that this world would be a better place if men would treat women as their equals, but they just don't. It is therefore our desire to create awareness among our peers thinking that, with our collective will, we can lift ourselves up. We have not wished to push men down, only to lift ourselves up but, try as we might, we have not been able to obtain a handhold. In fact, I would venture to say that this problem has existed ever since man first walked the earth thousands of years ago, and it has continued unabated to this day.

"Now it appears we have been handed a weapon that can change all that. If I understand correctly, the aim of this Army project is to cause a man to think, feel and act like a woman. If it achieves that, and you all heard Billy tell us that it does, its deployment would go a very long way toward bringing equality to the sexes. Life with the male gender would no longer be a constant battle. Men, who right now are our oppressors and are constantly creating havoc in the world, would be just like *us*.

"Bailey, you asked why our magazine, *Women Rising*, should be the publication to announce the dawning of this new age of enlightenment. Did you know that Roger, the brains behind this bioweapon, calls it 'Project *Nemow*' which is 'women' spelled backwards? Billy calls it '*Ballzoff*' because that's just what it does. It takes away the thing that runs them wild."

Chapter 19

There is nothing more horrible to watch, except possibly the vicious, intentional murder of a fellow human being, than the willful and wanton rape of a woman. Unfortunately for George Cleary, he witnessed such a rape at the tender age of nineteen and the memory of that scene became permanently seared into his brain. On the darkest of nights, when sleep eluded him, his runaway mind would play momentary flashbacks of that fateful evening while at college. He heard screams in one of the bedrooms at Psi Delta Fraternity House and opened the door.

He was at a party late in his freshman year. The fraternity had the reputation of being the most joy-seeking, wildest residential community on campus and George desperately wanted to be a part of it. He knew he wouldn't fit in at first, but he thought – he hoped against hope – that if he were able to become a member of the fraternity, its spirit would rub off on him and he could lift himself up by the bootstraps. He knew he was a nerd. But, being bright, he believed he could better himself by being friends with the big basketball bullies who balled the babes of Barnard: the honored heroes of the Columbia Lions who hailed from the halls of Psi Delt.

The room was confusion to him at first. Two boys were standing in front of the bed and blocked his view but the noises were unmistakable. All he could see were legs at the end of the bed, a boy's and a girl's. An inner force drove him to move closer for a better look. He did not know why. Had he instantly run from the scene and called the police, as he knew he should have, he would have been spared a lifetime of regret. There on the bed was the girl he would see again and again in his nightmares: Courtney Stillwell, her dress torn asunder and with one of her onlookers pressing his hand against her mouth to stifle her cries.

Much later George could recall the faces of the three boys involved. When asked to do so by the campus police, however, his mind was blank. He could not, or would not, conjure the images of those beasts. But now, in the safety net he had created for himself, he saw them clearly. He had recognized their faces in the college yearbook and knew who they were.

He had not been able to join that fraternity, nor did he want to. He remained a nerd all through college, partly because that terrible party continued to plague him, but he vowed to rid himself of what he considered a flaw in his character by making money – lots of money. His strength was in his ability to understand numbers. Mathematics came as naturally to him as music to Mozart.

As with most great composers, Mozart not only heard the music in his head, he could see it. It was the same way for George and his mathematical compositions. He could see the math, not as a jumbled white board of symbols and a series of formulae, but as landscapes, buildings, machines and events as if they were of some other dimension playing out in his mind. While still in college he became so familiar with complex systems and mathematical models that he could move to any part or level of such a system and *see* the internal relationships and understand the effect of one small change of any parameter or formula.

After college, he applied his talents to making money for the prestigious banking firm of Goldman Sachs. He was a quick study and within two years had explored his way through the ins and outs of the financial system and had received enormous bonuses for his work. By then he was already rich beyond his wildest dreams and was just getting started.

After five years, he felt he had learned everything Goldman Sachs had to teach him so resigned his position and started trading on his own. It had become for George a simple matter to understand the elements of one segment of the stock market and pull the strings to make it dance to his tune. He became fascinated with the way some financial instruments seemed to have a relationship with each other and he developed an entire system of algorithms to emulate it. It took more than a few sleepless nights and gallons of coffee, but alone in his room with his whiteboard he uncovered and discovered intrinsic truths about these stochastic processes. The initial rush of the realization that the models were working was almost overwhelming. He came to the giddy realization that he had his fingers on strings that could quietly pull an entire segment of the market of trading derivative instruments the way he wanted the segment to go. Almost unbelievably, he could *control it*.

Fortunately for him, the regulators were holding off from interfering for fear of unleashing consequences they had no way of understanding or predicting. In fact, other than George, very few people truly understood how derivative securities actually worked and, probably for this reason, they were allowed to continue, unrestricted and unregulated. They remained as a mysterious "black box" within the financial markets for hedge fund operators to experiment with. By the time the regulators finally realized what was happening, these securities had become an integral part of the complex system and it was too late to act. All the federal officials could do was to hope against thin hope that the market would regulate *itself* and continue to grow and thrive.

George had found his place in the universe. He focused his attention on the derivatives segment of the investments marketplace and started playing with simulations to test his new theories. In truth, he needed the freedom to wield his new algorithms without interference. He had nothing but scorn for the regulators in their inability to even conceive of the complexities of the market power he was controlling. And the exhilaration he felt from his mastery over market was addictive. He truly *was* a master of the universe.

Granted there were a few missteps in the beginning. He watched a few million dollars and once even ten million evaporate several times in the span of seconds but that was just another algorithm problem to overcome with a tweak here and there. Over a course of years he had smoothed out the wrinkles that inevitably came as the market naturally morphed and changed with global economic waves, but eventually his confidence grew and, so he thought, he had managed to morph *himself* into a new and stronger personality.

Competitors in the derivatives marketplace had no idea what he was doing or how he was doing it. Their algorithms predicted one direction for the market, but within microseconds, George's system took an entire section of the market in a different direction. He was implementing strategies that left his competitors without oxygen; he was sucking the air out of their investor's hard-earned retirement funds. As far as his competitors were aware, the market was just fickle and subject to unpredictable shifts that no math model could adequately follow despite the seemingly predictable way the laws of nature seemed to work. But George knew otherwise.

George was in control of an unregulated small corner of the vast investment-trading universe and was becoming secretly and abundantly wealthy at everyone else's expense. Like his algorithms, he had methodically built a complex set of rationalizations for what he did, adding all the more to his growing confidence and feeling of dominance. The more money he made, the more it seemed to feed his greed.

An ordinary mortal would find this activity sinister and even frightening. If the global financial system were compared to an old house, built to provide safety and security for the people inside, George's algorithms were like termites and carpenter ants, continuously eating away at the structure. While the occupants of the house slept inside, oblivious to the danger, these unseen creatures were working day and night, eating away at the beams, bite by bite, making the structure weaker and less able to provide shelter from the wind, the rain and the cold.

It was at this point that George Cleary received the email from Courtney, the girl who was raped at that fraternity party while he stood by and watched.

Chapter 20

The dinner with Courtney had awakened something within George, something that up to now was entirely missing in his life: the possibility of a relationship. Achieving mastery of his universe had required almost total concentration and focus, to the exclusion of those pleasant diversions that make life worthwhile: a dinner with friends, a stroll along a country lane, attending the theater, a concert, an opera, a ballet or even just a movie, not to mention a vacation trip to some faraway place. George could, of course, afford any or all of these things. He could have built himself a huge mansion on his very own island with a hundred foot yacht moored alongside, had he desired to do so. But none of these interested him. He did own an airplane – quite a large one in fact – which he flew himself. But after all was said and done, nothing was more interesting than making *money*, and lots of it.

But that evening spent with Courtney had been nothing less than a jolt to his soul. He found her looks delightful and her voice musical. Her strawberry-blonde hair cascaded over her shoulders, framing her face with her light blue eyes and pleasing smile. It was a vision he wasn't at all familiar with, nor was he prepared for its effect on him.

As he sat across from her that evening at Daniels he found himself falling under her spell. It wasn't so much what she said, although for the first time in many years he found he cared to really *listen* to someone; it was how she said it: with a charm and sophistication that was almost magical.

"I'm at the point," she was saying, "where I need some financial backing. There is this business opportunity I can't pass up."

"Your email called it a 'proposition.' I never got one from a woman before."

"This is not what you think. It's strictly business."

"I understand." George was instantly sorry he used the word "proposition."

Fortunately, Courtney pressed on. "There's this important story I learned about. It will make news and I want my magazine to take the lead in reporting it, but we can't afford to."

"Afford what? Pay for printing?"

"To pay an inside source. He wants seventy-five thousand dollars, cash."

George didn't even blink. Seventy-five million might have given him pause, but his hedge fund made at least a hundred thousand every hour of the day. "Why so much?"

"He's signed a non-disclosure with the government. And this story is classified as Top Secret."

"Is he willing to go to jail?"

"No. That's just it. No one is supposed to know who he is. I won't reveal his name."

"So *you're* willing to go to jail?"

"I don't think it will come to that, but yes. For my magazine I'm willing to face jail if that's necessary to protect my source. Besides, when I tell you what I know, you'll have to agree it's an important story. It has to get out there." Courtney looked deeply into George's eyes and his heart skipped a beat.

"You had me when you said 'Courtney' on the phone," was all he could think to say.

"It's a secret Army program," Courtney continued. "They have developed a new weapon that will—" she paused. "It will turn enemy soldiers into 'friends.'"

"Into what?" She was causing George to melt. She was such a determined woman, earnestly pleading her cause. It was difficult for George to pay attention to what she was saying.

"I've heard they are making men into... I don't know...so they behave more like *women*."

"And so? How is that a good thing?" George checked himself and was sorry he said that as soon as he'd said it. He hoped against hope she wouldn't take it the wrong way.

"When they use it on the battlefield, the enemy won't want to fight." Courtney had glossed over his remark, thank goodness. "It's a biological or chemical weapon. I'm not sure which," she added.

"And you want to publish an article about *this*?"

"About turning men into women. Yes."

"Won't this jeopardize our Army's use of the weapon? If you tell the world about it?"

"It might, yes. But don't you see? The world will be a better place if everyone could use it. The government wants to keep it a secret but we desperately need it. It would reduce crime and could even end wars in the future. Men have made such a mess of things. They create most of our problems," Courtney pleaded, "and now we'll have the ability to do something about it."

George thought a moment, trying to figure out just what she was talking about, but it was difficult to sort out. Finally, he cocked his head and smiled at Courtney. "Tell you what," he said. "I'll give you a million dollars to spend any way you want. No strings attached, except... I just want to see you again."

Courtney leaned back in her chair and almost gasped. "I'll drink to that," she said finally. She raised her glass of wine, George did the same and they clinked glasses. "No strings attached," she reminded him.

By the end of the evening George Cleary was smitten.

Chapter 21

It was the end of the day and General "Tommy-gun" Mason was in no mood for his usual evening delight. He sat at his desk and wondered what was happening to him. His female orderly opened the door and peeked in, smiling knowingly. "No more appointments, *Sir*." She emphasized "Sir" as if to mock it. "Everybody's gone." She stepped into the room, quietly closing the door behind her. The top three buttons of her military shirt were unbuttoned, against military regulations, revealing a deep curl of happiness. "I'm comin' in," she added."

General Mason stood up. "Not today, Eve. I'm going home."

"What? Had a hard day at the office? Here, let your baby help you take the strain off." She came forward while at the same time undoing two more buttons on her shirt. Her breasts ballooned upward, the latest in pushup bra technology doing its work. Mason refused to notice as Eve put her arms around his neck and pulled him in close. "Me, Eve," she talked baby talk. "You, Adam. God made Eve for Adam's enjoyment."

"I have to get home."

"Not without having your daily dessert. Here, let me give little Tommy a hand." She reached down and began to massage the lump in Mason's pants. Mason tried to deflect her hand but she quickly unzipped his fly and reached in. "Oooh, he's soft," she said. "Let me take care of my friend." She pulled little Tommy out of its tight-fitting package.

"That's enough." Mason angrily yanked her hand away from his private parts. "I'm not in the mood."

Eve pulled back, seemingly shocked. "What's the matter, baby," she purred in her best sex-kitten voice. "Li'l Tommy's been cooped up all day. He wants to come out and play."

"No he doesn't. And you get control of yourself, Eve," Mason snapped. He zipped up his fly and stumped sullenly over to the wall closet to retrieve his jacket and hat. "I'm leaving now. I've had enough of this playing around. Today or ever." He stormed out of his office, leaving Eve standing there in a state of partial undress.

Driving home from his office, General Mason took stock of his miserable marriage. Admitting his errant ways, he made himself a vow to make amends with his wife. He parked in the driveway in front of his garage. In full uniformed regalia he stepped out of the car and walked briskly up the path to the front door of his house. He was surprised the door was locked – not his wife's usual practice – so he pulled out his keys and opened it.

Stepping inside he heard noises upstairs. He stopped in his tracks, thinking the worst of what it might be. To avoid detection he quietly closed the door behind him and stealthily walked up the stairs, step by careful step, until he reached the top landing. Following the sounds he came to the master bedroom and threw open the door. There he saw what he thought he was hearing, but dreaded confirming that it was true: His wife Beth lay supine in bed with her legs held high while a man he had never seen before was on his hands and knees above her. Both were in the buff and both were clearly oblivious to the presence of the General.

"Beth!" Mason shouted in his most commanding voice.

The two lovers immediately interrupted what they were doing and took corrective action. The man jumped out of bed, grabbed his clothes and ran to the bathroom. Beth grabbed a pillow and attempted to cover herself. "This is not what it *seems*," she screamed in a panicy voice.

General Mason did a double take. Was he playing the cuckolded husband in a movie? No, this was *real* and, unbelievably, he had just seen his wife in bed with another man. He felt anger welling up. His face quickly reddened, his head nearly exploded and he screamed to no one in particular, "What is *happening*??" Then he checked himself and noticed he was still in control. Quite unlike his usual self he realized.

"Beth, what *are* you doing?" he demanded. He still couldn't believe what he had just seen but was determined to handle it appropriately.

"I was doing what you do every evening: You bang that little slut who works in your office."

"*But*—" the General was thrown off guard for a moment. "But I'm a *man*. That's *different*."

"No it's not! And by the way, when a man loves a woman, he's supposed to worship the ground she walks on. Instead you think you can fuck any young slut with a skirt. You *bastard*."

"Why are we even talking about this? *You* are the one who was fucking that…this *man*. And who the hell was he anyway? If he's a soldier his life is *over*. I'll bring criminal charges against him so fast he'll wish he'd never been born."

"Well, he's not. So you can't touch him."

Just at that moment the man, now fully clothed, opened the door to the bathroom, zoomed past the General and disappeared out the door of the room.

"Who the fuck *is* he anyway? I'll kill him *myself* with my bare hands."

"I'm not saying."

"*Tell me!*"

"All right, if you must know, he delivers my groceries."

"The *grocery guy*?" This day was becoming more surreal by the second. "You fucked the *grocery guy*?"

"Well I can say that to you too. You fucked the *orderly* in your office?"

"What if I did? That's no big deal."

"Well, what if I fucked the grocery guy. That's no big deal either."

"Yes it is!"

"No it isn't."

"It is."

"Is not."

"Is."

"Not."

The General was beginning to get the point. "All right then. Let's you and me stop screwing around, *right now*."

"*You're* the one who's been screwing around. You started it, and I'm not letting you off the hook. First, I'm going to keep screwing whomever I want and then, when I'm satisfied that I'm finally *even*, I'm going to file for divorce."

"*Divorce*?"

"You bet. And when I'm finished charging you with adultery, you can kiss the rest of your damn military career goodbye. This is going to get really ugly, really fast."

"You wouldn't *dare* divorce me. You've got it too good; people sucking up right and left as the General's wife."

"You think so? Just *watch* me."

"Okay, *okay*. Beth, you've got me by the balls. Just don't squeeze them, *please*."

"Now you're making some sense. You realize I'm deadly serious, right?"

"Stop. I give up. You nailed me good."

"You're never, *never* going to screw another woman?"

"I *promise* I won't. I'll be your *sex slave* if that's what you want. I'll do anything. I just want to stay married. To *you*."

"Then take off that uniform, General, and fuck me like you *mean* it. You're mine, I'm yours, and we're going to *keep it that way*."

The General ripped off his uniform and went to work. He didn't even notice that he had difficulty getting it up.

Chapter 22

The phone rang at three in the morning. General Mason was sleeping soundly after spending what little mojo he had saving his marriage. It took four rings but he managed to roll over and lift the red receiver at his bedside.

"Uh...hello? This had better be important—"

"Hold just a moment for the Chairman of the Joint Chiefs..." The General was jolted instantly awake and sat up in bed.

"General Mason? General Thomas Mason?" came an authoritative male voice.

"Yes, Sir. I'm here."

"We have a crisis on our hands. Is it safe to talk?"

"Yes, Sir. I'm on the secure line at my home. My wife is asleep. No one else is here."

"Alright then. Listen carefully. We've received the regular reports about Project Nemow. Understand the tests went well. Is that correct?"

"Y...yes Sir?" General Mason couldn't recall reading any such reports. When he saw "Top Secret" stamped on the cover, he must have filed them away as soon as those damn things landed on his desk. He didn't need or care to know about them.

"That Director Thornwood really knows his stuff. He's a crackerjack. The Army is lucky to have him."

"Yes, Sir." The General's mind was foggy to be sure. It was three in the morning for God's sake. But for the life of him he couldn't remember much at all about 'Nemow.' Luckily he and Roger had that talk just a few days ago or he would have been caught completely flat-footed.

"Things are not going well in Syria. The President wants to deploy Nemow. It's ready, right?"

"The P...President?"

"Yes. POTUS. Are you awake General?"

"Yes, Sir. I heard what you said. But that's against the Geneva Conventions."

"That may be true, General. But we have to deploy."

"Are you sure about this, Sir? I have strict orders not to make Nemow available to anyone. Only the President can order its use."

"The President gave the order. This morning."

"How can I be sure—?"

"Good answer, General. I'm glad you said that. You can't be too cautious. You're not even sure I'm Chairman of the Joint Chiefs, are you?"

"Well, no Sir. As a matter of fact, I don't recognize your voice."

"Would you recognize the voice of the President?"

"Yes, Sir. I would of course, Sir."

"I'll have him call you." The line clicked off, went silent for a moment and then went to a dial tone. The General returned the red receiver to its hook at his night table but the phone rang again, almost immediately, and he picked up.

"Please hold for the President of the United States…" General Mason almost dropped the receiver but he managed to hold on, his eyes widened.

Beth stirred on the bed beside him and looked up. "Who is it, dear?" Her husband put his finger to his lips to shush her. A second later an easily recognizable voice came on the line: that of the POTUS who was heard almost every day on radio and television.

"General Mason, I presume?" His voice was unexpectedly cheery. "I understand you're our man in charge of Project Nemow. Is that right?"

"Yes, Sir. That's right. I—."

"Well, then. I want you to deploy it. Our troops need your help. *We* need your help."

"B…But, the Geneva Conventions."

"I know. I know. But these are desperate times, General Mason. Desperate times require desperate measures."

"Yes, Sir."

"You got it?"

"Yes, Sir.

"Good. I was sure you'd understand. You're smart, General Mason. If this Nemow thing helps us to dodge this bullet, you may be looking at another star on your shoulder."

"Y…yes, Sir."

"That's settled then. Let's go with it."

"Yes, Sir. I—" The line clicked off.

A moment later the phone rang again. "Please hold for the Chairman of the Joint Chiefs." Then "General Mason? It's me again."

"Yes, Sir."

"Did you receive the call from the President?"

"Yes, Sir."

"Any questions?"

"No, Sir."

"Good. I'm sending a car to pick up Director Thornwood at zero eight hundred hours this morning. Call him and tell him to be ready."

"Ready for what?"

"Were sending him to the theater overseas. With four Navy SEALs and a whole lot of Nemow."

Chapter 23

Roger looked through his front window at precisely eight in the morning and saw a black SUV draw up in front of his house and stop. He grabbed his duffelbag and stepped out the front door. He turned back to pull the door tightly shut and locked it; he then walked down the short path to the street where two servicemen stood waiting, both dressed in Marine uniform. He didn't know where he was going nor how long he would be away, but he was ready. Dressed in starched fatigues and polished combat boots, he looked forward to this new adventure.

One of the servicemen loaded his duffel into the rear of the vehicle while the other opened the rear passenger door and stood at attention as he climbed in. In less than a minute they were on their way to Andrews Air Force Base in Washington, D.C.

Roger had left instructions with his research team at APG to make ready a suitcase-sized package of white powder for pickup by another military vehicle. His administrative assistant informed him that the transport arrived at seven-thirty in the morning and was already on its way.

To say that Roger was excited would be an understatement. His heart was pumping adrenalin-spiked blood. This was the moment he'd anticipated and had hoped for each and every day for the past five years. He had succeeded in creating the biochemcal weapon he had been tasked to develop, and now the U.S. Army was about to test it on the battlefield. He didn't seek fame or fortune – no one without a need to know was supposed to be aware of this weapon's existence – but he was proud of what he had achieved and he was glad the Army had asked him to be present at its first deployment overseas.

At Andrews, he was driven up to a compact jet aircraft waiting expectantly on the tarmac. It was a corporate jet, customized for fast movement of elite troops and/or military brass. Fueling was in process and uniformed members of a small ground crew hustled about checking the craft's vitals and loading bags and cargo into the hold. When Roger stepped out of the car, a well-decorated Naval officer came forward and introduced himself. He told Roger his name was Jim and said he was in charge of the mission. Following Jim's lead, Roger climbed up the airstairs to the side door of the aircraft and entered its darkened interior.

Roger's eyes took a moment to adjust. When they focused, he saw a row of seats on each side of the cabin, facing inward, with three soldiers already strapped in on one side. He took a seat opposite them next to Jim and fastened his seatbelt. The aircraft's engines spooled up and within ten minutes they were on their way.

"What's the plan?" Roger asked Jim once they had reached altitude and the engine noise subsided somewhat.

"We're landing in Israel where we're meeting a couple of agents and will await clearance to proceed. We've mapped out a strategy to access the water supply for the city of Aleppo. We'll have a Blackhawk helicopter at our disposal and whatever small vehicle we'll need to get in there and get out fast."

"Aleppo? Why not Damascus, the capital?" Roger asked.

"Aleppo is the largest city in Syria. It's caught in the middle between troops of the Bashar al-Assad regime, rebel forces against his regime, and the insurgents of ISIS. The Assad guys are besieging the rebels with a scorched earth, take-no-prisoners policy, while the ISIS Jihadi fighters are trying to impose their radical worldview by suicide bombings, torture and beheadings. It's an absolute nightmare."

"So how do we deploy our Nemo?"

"The city water comes from Lake Assad, a manmade reservoir created back in the seventies by building the Tabqa Dam on the nearby Euphrates River. We'll be going in to the main filtration plant under cover of darkness and will substitute your stuff for the sodium fluoride powder they use for fluoridation. We'll take out any resistance we find, but we hope to pull this caper off in complete secrecy without loss of life. With a bit of luck, your Nemow will be flowing in the water system of Aleppo within two days and no one will be the wiser."

"What do you want *me* to do?" asked Roger.

"You'll be joining the SEAL team to make sure your stuff is deployed correctly. We're not certain what we'll find so we want to be ready for any contingency."

"Will the mission be dangerous?" Roger wanted to know. He had never done anything like this before and felt a sudden surge of fear – fear of the unknown and fear for his *life*.

"Damn straight it's dangerous. You'll be wearing a flak jacket and a helmet. You never know where a stray bullet might come from."

"Oh, well *that's* reassuring." Roger looked at Jim with a slight lump in his throat. "Are you sure I need to come along?"

"We need to be sure there are no mistakes in the deployment. Don't worry, we'll make a hero out of you yet," Jim replied with a wide grin.

"But I don't want to be a hero. I'm just an ordinary, humble stay-at-home guy."

"Inside every stay-at-home guy there's a hero waiting and wanting to come out."

To Roger, Jim didn't seem at all concerned about his safety. Roger didn't say anything for a while but sat silently, trying to imagine what the mission would be like. There was nothing to draw on in his experience to aid his thinking. He could only imagine the worst, what with the scenes of ISIS torturing and beheading people and Assad's bombing of his own Syrian citizens on the television news every other night. Roger finally turned to Jim and asked, "How many men will we have with us?"

"You're looking at 'em," Jim replied, pointing to the three soldiers sitting calmly opposite him, animatedly talking with each other and laughing as if they were on their way to Disney World, not one of the most dangerous hotspots on the globe. "They're the best of the best. If you're in a bad situation, and we might well be – you never know – there are no folks I'd rather have with me to have my back than these men. We're going to be fine. You'll see."

Roger was not so sure, but his thoughts were interrupted by the appearance of a male flight attendant who came forward from a compartment in the rear of the plane. "Gentlemen," he announced, "now that we're at cruising altitude, the galley is open for business. It's a long flight so sit back, relax and enjoy the ride. We've got some great food and drink on board and I'm here to make it happen."

Roger did just that. As the jet plane flew across the Atlantic and over Europe into the very heart of the roiling Middle East region, Roger and the few soldiers in whom he would put his trust ate well, drank well, though not to excess, and enjoyed each other's company. They all arrived at Tel Aviv Airport in a jovial mood but, as they climbed deftly down the airstairs onto the tarmac in the darkness of night, still laughing at each other's jokes, their mood changed abruptly. They were met by two members of the Israeli Special Forces, known as Sayeret Matkal, who did not take kindly to their interference with the violent actions taking place in the nearby country of Syria.

One of the two agents made it very clear: "We don't want you mucking things up so don't count on us to help you. You Americans have no idea what you're dealing with."

Chapter 24

"Why's he got such a bug up his ass?" one of the Navy SEALs asked Jim as they were shuttled by van to temporary quarters at a U.S. facility on the airport grounds. "Yeah, what's his fucking problem?" asked another. Roger, who was more shocked by the jarring reception than he cared to admit, listened quietly but intently from the back seat. Everything about this trip was new to him and he was not sure he fit in. In fact, he was becoming more and more convinced that he was out of his depth.

"The Israelis have no problem with the fighting in Syria," Jim said. "In fact they don't want the fighting to *end*. It keeps the bad guys busy so they pretty much ignore Israel, although both Assad and ISIS would like nothing better than to blow this little country off the map. Israelis are therefore against anything that might interfere with the fighting. Although they don't know the specifics, they think that includes us."

"That makes a lot of sense. They'd rather have people shooting at each other than shooting at them," the first SEAL commented.

"Who would have thought?" remarked Roger. "I figured we were on the same side as the Israelis."

"They won't admit it, but they don't see much downside to the warring going on," Jim explained. "You won't see them involved in this conflict and won't see any Syrian refugees here in Israel. This country sits right next to all that bombing and destruction in Syria where those people fighting don't give a damn about the collateral damage. The refugees all go to Jordan or Turkey because Israel blocks its border and won't let any of them cross. From Jordan and Turkey these refugees walk for hundreds of miles with what little they can carry, sometimes in bare feet, and take rafts or rickety boats if they need to, to get to Austria, France, Germany, Hungary, Italy, Spain and Sweden. A few of them have even tried to cross over to England from France. That keeps the pressure off Israel."

"Damn," the second SEAL said. "If our mission is a success we're gonna really shake things up."

"It should move the needle in the right direction," Jim said. "And if this Nemow stuff really works, we might even have a shot at bringing peace to the Middle East. If we put it in the water here in Israel, they might stop posturing and finally sign a peace accord with the Palestinians. Make everybody happy."

"I have a question," interjected the third SEAL who had been quiet up to now. "You think the Israelis have any idea what we're up to? This is a top secret mission."

"That's bothering me too," the second SEAL said. "I thought only the President and the Chairman of the Joint Chiefs knew about this mission. And of course Roger here."

"We had to file a flight plan with the Israeli government to fly into Syria, so they know we're up to something." Jim replied. "All I can say is, this government is damn well connected in America."

"They wouldn't spy on us," the third SEAL countered. "We're supposed to be bosom buddies. They support us and we support them. The U.S. gives Israel over three billion dollars a year of foreign aid."

"Ever heard of Jonathan Pollard?" Jim asked.

"Okay, he was a spy. He got caught and went to jail a long time ago."

"Don't think for a minute there aren't others. Israel has more ears inside our government than the FBI."

Jim and the three other Navy SEALs went quiet for the rest of the ride to the bachelor officer's quarters.

Listening to this banter while sitting in the rear of the van, Roger began to feel courage and determination seep into his psyche. He was sure Nemo would work, but he had not fully understood or appreciated what his development could do to alleviate human suffering. Jim's words echoed back and forth several times in his mind, each time reinforcing the idea and the promise of a better world. By the time they arrived at their sleeping quarters, Roger was no longer an ordinary, stay-at-home guy. He had shed some of the fears of the unknown and was starting to think positive thoughts, if not like a Navy SEAL, then at least like what some women might call a *real man*.

The travelers had arrived in the dead of night and were tired from the trip. Roger was the last to climb out of the van in front of the BOQ. His two bags were brought in and deposited in his room. One of the bags contained the white powder that they were delivering to install in the water filtration plant for the city of Aleppo. It was packaged in an aluminum suitcase that looked conventional enough, however it weighed nearly one hundred pounds. This amount of Nemo, fed slowly into the water system of Aleppo, would last about a month – long enough for a true test of its effect on that war-torn city. Such a valuable substance in his suitcase made Roger concerned, but as Jim had told him, he knew the safest way to transport this package was to keep it "inconspicuous" in plain sight.

Roger fell asleep as soon as his head sank into the soft pillow and he slept, on and off, for nearly twelve hours. It was near noon when he finally woke with a start and looked at his watch. He had made no arrangement the night before to meet Jim and his small band of compatriots when they awoke so he was not at all surprised when the phone rang next to his bed.

"Okay, sleepyhead," came Jim's commanding but at the same time calming voice. "It's *show time*. We're heading out tonight."

Chapter 25

Emily Platt, editor-in-chief of *Cosmopolitan* magazine, was having a bad day. As she did every month just before the publishing deadline, she terrified her all-female staff in a manner no male boss could possibly get away with. Today was no different. The November issue was not coming together as the blowout issue she had imagined and planned for.

This issue was to be about women getting what they wanted, from *men*.

In point of fact, *Cosmo* magazine was *always* about getting something, and usually from men. Every month *Cosmo* came through for single women, age twenty-five to thirty-five, with tips on keeping oneself gorgeous and flaunting it.

It taught girls how to become *women*: What make-up would work and what wouldn't work for them; what clothes to wear to the office, to a party and when out on a date: the important first date and the all too important third date. How to improve those special relationships with other women and, most significantly, how to create, keep and care for what all women strove for: a relationship with that fascinating but elusive and maybe even doesn't exist, *Mr. Right*.

Once they found their guy and married him, Emily's readers would almost always say "*bye bye*" to the magazine. At least for awhile. They were no longer interested in *Cosmo* for a year or two, or maybe even three or four if they started a family. But most women came back. The magazine was there for these readers too, helping them re-imagine those exhilarating years when they were young, ripe and *randy*.

The November issue was supposed to prepare Emily's "*Cosmo* girls" for the real world of competition that was getting stiffer every year. A hard man was easy to find, but a good man was like a precious stone among the many rocks. You knew he was there but he didn't just jump out and grab you. You had to find your guy and grab *him*.

At the moment, Emily was on the warpath. For one thing, *Cosmo* was all about the cover and the cover wasn't right. Not right at all. It had to stand out among all those other mags and rags on the supermarket rack. It had to attract potential readers' eyes by their natural instinct to look at a pretty woman, and then draw them in by that even more basic instinct: sex.

The most important word in the English language, "SEX," had to appear in bold letters somewhere on the cover, preferably in the upper left corner below the title word "COSMOPOLITAN," the letters all crowded together to fit on one line in that famous *Cosmo* logo.

The image on the cover, the "cover girl," had to exude seduction without a hint of porn. She had to be wholesome, yet imply she was ready to romp. She was the girl next door or down the street who would like to be your friend for a night or, better yet, for a lifetime. Her hair, her eyes, her smile, her lips, her breasts, her dress, her posture, all had to be just right.

And there was always the background color. It had to match the dress *exactly*. Not be the same, but to *match* in a way only a woman would understand.

And most of these things were just slightly *off*.

Emily would get it right. The magazine was her domain and she was famously the *Queen Bee*. She dictated and demanded absolute perfection. A new photo with an airbrush here, a small crop there; a color change of the word "SEX" to a particular shade of pink; a new blend in the background color. Her staff worked feverishly around her, doing her bidding like worker bees in a hive.

She scanned the lead article by Veronica Miller one more time. Emily had edited out the reason Veronica's biker boyfriend didn't come on to her: that Top Secret government program she called "Balzoff." Emily had substituted a new kind of marijuana, organic or synthetic it didn't matter. It was fake anyway. The article was just about perfect now. Veronica should be proud. She could call herself a writer. Emily would make her a *star*.

Emily had fashioned the entire issue based on Veronica's article. The upper left corner of the cover bore the legend:

SPECIAL ISSUE:

WHAT IF YOUR SEX MACHINE SAYS 'NO'?

The word "SEX" was in bright pink.

Nearly all the other articles in the issue dealt with this same subject: What to do if your man isn't interested in sex. What if he won't or can't get it up? What if men stopped being like men? God forbid this could happen in real life. It would *ruin* her magazine.

Suddenly concerned, Emily's thoughts turned to Courtney. What if she were able to start a women's movement, demanding that men drink the Balzoff KoolAid? Courtney was passionate about her point of view and she was very persuasive. She might even start a religious crusade for heaven's sake.

Emily went back to work and finally signed off on the cover. The insides of the magazine were primarily ads, and they could take care of themselves. They were professionally done and most of the artwork was drop dead gorgeous. The artwork supporting the articles and sidebars not so much, but she didn't mind. Women, and some men too, bought the magazine because of the cover.

With the November issue put to bed, Emily speed-dialed Courtney. "It's me. Emily." She got right to the point. "What happened to that breaking news story about Nemo? You killed it, right?"

"Kill it? Where'd you get that idea? You don't have to spy on me. Just call."

"Spy on *you*? Don't flatter yourself. Just answer the question."

"You know me better than that, Emily. I'm going to create awareness. When I'm done, women will be screaming for men to get off their high horses and act with tact and decorum. We'll expect no less."

"That's a pretty tall order. I don't think you'll find many converts among the male population."

"I'm all set to do battle. We'll be firing the first shot with our next issue that comes out next week. Hold your breath."

Emily cringed inwardly but kept her cool. "Can you send me an advance copy?" she asked coyly.

"No can do, my friend. You'll see it when everybody does."

"Oh? Why not?"

"Let's just say you didn't make it to the top at *Cosmo* without breaking a few chops. And I'm not giving you a chance to piss me off."

Chapter 26

For the rest of the day, Roger and the Navy SEALs prepared to go into Syria. Jim held a meeting where he spread out several maps of the Aleppo area as well as detailed plans of the water treatment plant on the side of Lake Assad. One of the SEALs was an expert helicopter pilot who paid special attention to the geography, terrain and the trees in the vicinity of the plant and decided where and how to set the craft down. A large "X" was drawn on the map delineating the exact area and the orientation of the helicopter when landing. The landing spot was over a mile away from the plant so Roger, Jim and the two remaining SEALs would ride there together with their equipment and the package of Nemo powder, in an all-terrain, four-seat vehicle that was carried beneath the helicopter, held fast by a cable with a winch. When they returned to the waiting craft the ATV would be lifted by the winch and again held fast for its return flight to the base in Israel.

That evening they all suited up, ready for whatever action lay ahead. Jim gave the little band a final pep talk, encouraging his men to turn in their best professional performance in the task ahead. Roger felt the rush of excitement as he climbed into the open door of the helicopter, its engine humming and its blades swishing overhead. When all were aboard, Jim gave a hand signal to the SEAL pilot. The engine noise level increased, the rotating wings beat loudly against the air, and the craft rose upward into the transparent black sky.

The flight to Aleppo would take approximately one and a half hours. If all went well they would spend one hour on the ground to execute the plan at the water treatment plant and then fly back, so that the entire mission was to take no more than four hours. They planned to be back by three in the morning.

Strapped into a rear seat of the helicopter, Roger imagined himself a full member of the team. He wasn't truly a member, he knew, because he lacked the expertise, the training and, most of all, the *macho* of a Navy SEAL. He considered himself a valuable addition, however, because the team required his scientific expertise and his particular knowledge and know-how about the white powder they were bringing with them.

Eventually, the roaring sound of the helicopter engine eased off and Roger knew they were approaching the landing site. Jim had asked the pilot to throttle back the engine as much as possible when they flew in to avoid alerting anyone at the water facility. By coming in high and then descending sharply the chopper could effectively autogyro its way down with minimal power. What this meant to Roger was that they would be landing very soon, and his anxiety level shot up fast despite his efforts to keep a tight grip on his emotions. He kept repeating the mantra, "I hope I don't screw up," over and over, to take his mind off the dangers ahead.

No more than a few minutes after the power cutback the helicopter touched down with a jolt on hard ground. Roger felt the tremor in his seat and an instant later heard the side door slide open. Jim and his two comrades in arms jumped down and immediately started preparing the ATV for travel. Roger was still in the process of un-strapping himself and climbing down from the craft when Jim pressed a button and lowered the ATV with the winch. The major supplies, guns and ammunition, as well as the Nemo powder, were already loaded and held fast to the back of the small vehicle, but a few preliminaries still remained. Jim grabbed the electronic navigator from inside the helicopter, affixed it to the vehicle dash and switched it on. The navigator's screen came alive and displayed a map. When ready, Jim signaled his crew to climb aboard, Roger first and then the two other SEALs, followed by Jim himself in the driver's seat. Roger was just getting situated and secure in his seat when Jim turned the key to crank the engine, gave a quick hand salute to the pilot who remained in the helicopter, pulled down his night goggles over his eyes and headed off in the direction of Aleppo's water source.

The ATV bumped and bounced over the rough terrain. Roger began to feel somewhat queasy sitting in the rear seat but it was nothing close to needing a barf bag. He flexed from side to side to be at one with the vehicle as best he could, and he tried to understand where they were in relation to where they were headed.

Eventually the ATV reached a dirt road and Jim turned to follow it, speeding up slightly as he drove on this less rugged, though still uneven, surface. Within a minute or two, Roger could see a dim light far up ahead which he took to be the water treatment plant. His excitement level escalated another notch at this point. For Roger it was time to earn his right to be riding along on this adventure.

Jim drove only a short distance up the road before making a broken U-turn and stopping the ATV on the shoulder, facing back in the direction from which they had come. He shut off the engine, leaving the key in the ignition switch, and said to no one in particular, "We walk from here." All four climbed off and collected their gear. Jim took a pistol and released the safety before holstering it at his side. Each of the other two SEALs grabbed an automatic rifle and inserted a magazine to make it ready. They pocketed some extra ammunition as well as several grenades before they closed the visors on their helmets and checked their communications gear.

Meanwhile Roger unhitched the heavy suitcase with the Nemo powder from the ATV and secured it with straps to a small rugged dolly with two wheels. He too closed his visor and adjusted the com volume to hear the three SEALs speak to each other. As Jim had explained to everyone back at the base, their communications could not only be heard by the helicopter pilot waiting anxiously for their return to the landing site, they were being monitored by the Chairman of the Joint Chiefs and possibly also by the POTUS himself, the Commander-in-Chief.

"All right, let's do it," Jim said, and they started walking quietly up the path toward the light. Roger walked and pulled the dolly along behind the three other men. As they came closer they could make out shapes in the darkness. The three SEALs pulled their night goggles down over their eyes to see infrared and suddenly stopped in their tracks. Roger stopped behind them and heard Jim say, "This place is crawling with soldiers."

Chapter 27

Jim motioned silently for Roger to stay back on the road and for the other two SEALs to fan out ahead. Jim's path was to be straight up the middle while the other two were to enter the woods on both sides to cover the flanks. When all three were in position they were to walk separately, but as a unit, toward the building up ahead to ambush the soldiers.

Roger felt a full rush of fear for the first time since he had left the comfort of the United States and arrived at this distant and foreign land. Who knew what dangers were up ahead, lurking in the dark as well as those one could see in the light? Agreed that those soldiers were probably the enemy, but we were really the aggressors. Whatever killing we did would not be just. The soldiers were there to protect their water supply, nothing more. They were doing their job to provide security for their people.

These thoughts raced through Roger's mind as he watched the SEALs prepare for the attack. It suddenly occurred to him he should say somethng, although he wasn't at all sure it was his place to do so. His small team of SEALs were already committed and ready to proceed with what they had been thoroughly trained to do. They were a killing machine and he had no doubt they would dispatch every last soldier if they had to to complete the mission. He hesitated, thinking that perhaps his concerns were foolish or, even worse, born out of fear. Further, Jim might view any such action as insubordination. But Jim should value his constructive suggestions, and it took courage to speak up, didn't it?

Roger heard himself speak into the intercom. "Just a minute, Jim. There's another way."

"What?" came Jim's voice. It was not as calm as usual. It sounded annoyed.

"I need to tell you something, before you go farther."

"All right, what is it?" Jim's voice revealed his impatience.

"Come back here. We need to talk."

"Not now. We're going in."

"Yes, *now*." Roger insisted. By now he felt more sure of himself because he was committed now and only following through. "Come back, before the enemy sees you."

Jim barked an urgent command to the two SEALs at his flanks and they headed back toward Roger. When the three of them arrived, Jim lifted his shield and glared at Roger. "*What is it?*" he demanded in a low tone to avoid being heard.

Roger stood his ground and whispered, "Instead of you going in there, guns blazing, you should divert them away, long enough for me to do my job. Give me a half hour in there and I'll substitute my powder for theirs. When I'm done we can meet back here at the ATV and take off. They won't know what we did and nobody will think to check the water."

"Can you believe this guy?" one of the other two SEALs said. "You gonna listen to him? Change our plan?"

"I think what he says makes a lot of sense," said the second, and they all looked at Jim.

"A half hour? You sure you can do it in a half hour?" Jim asked Roger.

"Positive. Probably won't take that long."

"I agree then. That's a better plan," Jim said gruffly.

"This way, we might keep this mission secret," Roger added.

"When you're right, you're right. Okay then, new plan: We'll swing around to the other side of the treatment plant, continue on for a mile, and then set off first one grenade and then another. That will draw them out. When you hear that, Roger, you go in there and do your thing. Here," Jim drew out his pistol and handed it to Roger, "take this. You might need it. They might leave someone behind when they leave to find us."

"No, no. I don't want it. I've never shot a gun." Roger raised his hands in the air in protest. The very idea of shooting someone was abhorrent to him.

"I insist. You can do it if you have to. When it's either you or the other guy, you'll shoot."

Roger dropped his hands and gingerly took the gun. He looked at it and shoved it in his belt behind his back.

"All right, men? We good to go?" Jim scanned the faces of his team. The other SEALs nodded.

Before leaving, Jim walked quickly to the back of the ATV and grabbed an assault rifle and a magazine. Shoving the magazine home into the weapon, he said, "Remember everyone: Look at your watch when the first grenade goes off. Be sure to be back here in a half hour."

"Roger that," whispered one of the two SEALs.

"Roger too," replied the other, acknolwledging Roger with a nod and a quick smile.

Roger stood alone next to the ATV and waited for what seemed like a very long time. Five minutes. Ten minutes. He kept looking at his watch. About twenty minutes after the SEALs had left he heard the explosion. It was a small, almost insignificant "boom" muffled by trees and the underbrush. He checked his watch again to note the time and started out.

He pulled the dolly with the heavy suitcase along the gravel road as fast as he could go. He didn't make an effort to keep quiet this time because he assumed the soldiers up ahead had deserted the facility to find the source of the sound. As he moved along, however, looking far up the road he saw a soldier standing guard in front of the open door to the building. He quickly moved to the road's edge, out of direct sight from the building, and waited for another explosion. When he heard the muffled sound he stepped back onto the road again. Looking ahead he saw the soldier leave. This was his queue.

He hurried forward dragging the dolly behind him. Coming up to the building he looked warily around but saw no activity. He entered the open doorway and stood there, shocked.

The large equipment room appeared undisturbed but on the ground lay an attendant in his work clothes, motionless and in a pool of blood.

Chapter 28

Roger realized instantly what had happened. The soldiers were not there to secure the facility; instead they had made a surprise raid to take over the place. But why? Why would they kill the attendant on duty? There was no possibility at all that he could resist. Why not just tie him up and gag him? What was their objective?

Roger scanned the room for clues. Everything seemed to him to be in order until his eyes fell on a square glass bottle. It was out of place, sitting on the floor next to a jungle of pipes and valves of the water treatment system. He looked at the large lettering on the side of the jug but couldn't make it out. It was in Arabic. He examined the jug more carefully and saw a white label on the back near the bottom. The writing was in English. It said, "DANGER, DEADLY POISON" in prominent capital letters. Beneath that were the words "80 % Dilute Botulinum Toxin." Roger knew instantly what it was. A few drops of this deadly liquid could kill an elephant. He checked the lid on the bottle and saw it still bore a plastic seal. The soldiers at the facility were there to poison the water.

Looking around again Roger spotted the tank for the fluoridation powder used in the system to fluoridate the water. He flipped open the top of this tank and looked in. It was near empty. This was a stroke of good luck because otherwise he would have to take the tank off from its mount to remove its contents. He took hold of his suitcase, brought it up close to the tank and opened the top. Inside was the plastic package containing the Nemo powder and a large measuring scoop. He grabbed the scoop and started carefully ladling the powder from the package into the tank, making sure the powder was level to the top of the scoop and counting out the number of scoops.

While he was working he heard gunshots in the distance. He hurried with transferring contents of the package into the tank as fast as he could and then, after quickly examining the plumbing, adjusted two valves to meter out the proper level of Nemo.

He closed the suitcase, strapped it onto the dolly and, grabbing the dolly handle, headed for the door. Before leaving he stopped and looked back. He heard gunshots again and this time they seemed much closer, but the jug of poison sat there on the floor like an evil menace from the gates of hell. He yanked at his dolly, pulling it with him back to the jug, undid the suitcase, lay it flat on the floor and opened it again. He carefully placed the jug down in the empty space, closed the top and, after strapping the suitcase to the dolly again, drew the dolly behind him out of the building.

Once outside, he heard men shouting in Arabic deep in the woods. They must be the soldiers, he thought, who came to poison the water. He ran headlong down the road toward the ATV with the dolly bumping and banging along behind him on the rough gravel.

Roger was panting for breath by the time he reached the ATV. Ignoring his exhaustion, he placed the dolly with the suitcase on the baggage rack in the back of the vehicle and strapped it tight. As he was finishing, a soldier came out of the woods on the opposite side of the road, holding an AK-47 rifle pointed straight at his head. Roger held up his hands and froze, his mind racing to assess his options. Try as he might, he couldn't think of any possible plan that seemed at all viable.

The man was dressed all in black from head to toe. He didn't wear a facemask, as some ISIS soldiers do, so Roger was able to see his expression. It wasn't pretty. The man seemed anguished and tortured about something which did not bode well for a good outcome. He shouted at Roger in Arabic. His voice sounded high, like that of a man in his late teens.

Roger asked, "Do you speak English?"

Surprisingly, the soldier not only answered "Yes" to this question, but he also had an American accent.

"My name's Roger. Roger Thornwood. What's yours?"

The man ignored the question and shouted, "What are you doing here?"

"I'm an engineer. I came to inspect the water supply." What Roger said was true, at least up to this point. "Make sure the water's safe to drink."

"I don't believe you. Why would you come now? In the dark. In the middle of the night."

"I…I'm an American. It's dangerous to be here. I thought it would be safer—."

"You're an American? Then why do you care about the water?"

"We've heard about what's happening in Aleppo. It's absolutely horrible. The U.S. government sent me here. I'm an engineer and we want to do what we can. To help you."

"Have you been up there? To the treatment plant?"

"No, not yet. I was about to go up there." Roger understood that if he told the truth, the soldier would know that he'd seen the attendant who was shot and perhaps also the poison.

"Then don't. We don't need you. Go!" The young man motioned with his weapon for Roger to get on the ATV and leave immediately. Roger sensed the man's nervousness but tried to keep calm to prevent the situation from escalating.

Roger needed to keep the man talking long enough until the three SEALs returned. He knew that everything he said was being transmitted by his com, not only to the SEALs nearby but also to the helicopter pilot and maybe even to the Chairman of the Joint Chiefs. He managed a weak smile and tried to engage the man in conversation. "Don't shoot. I'm going." He got into the driver's seat and turned the key in the ignition switch. The engine started up, raced briefly then backfired and died. "It'll start in a minute. It must be flooded." Roger looked at his adversary and noticed his hand shaking, ever so slightly. It caused the muzzle of his weapon to wobble. "Please bear with me."

"You'd better go *now*. If the other soldiers with me see you here, you're a dead man."

"Where are they?"

"They're coming. I'm calling them *now*." The man reached into his pocket with his right hand for a mobile phone while holding the gun with his left.

"Wait. Please don't. Americans don't mean you any harm. We want to help you."

"You have no idea. You're not worthy. You're all *infidels*." The young soldier waved the weapon menacingly. His eyes flashed. Roger shuddered but tried to hide it.

"Come with me. Come back to America where you belong."

"America is the enemy. I want death to all Americans."

"It's not an enemy. America is your home. You can come back."

"They'll put me in jail. Or kill me. So *go*."

"That doesn't have to happen," Roger assured him. "If you cooperate, if you tell the authorities everything, you can start over. You don't have to be a nomad, without a life."

"Don't make me shoot you. Either you leave *now* or you will die."

Roger understood his present danger, but he also sensed this could be a turning point. He wanted desperately to reach out to this young man and he stood his ground. "*Stop*. I'm going to stick by you," he said. "I'm not leaving you. You made a mistake by joining these fighters. They don't care about you. They want you to die for their cause. I want you to *live*."

"It's so much *crap*." the man said but at least he stopped counting. He brandished the gun again, pointing it at Roger's head. "*Leave now or die*."

"I know why you're here," Roger said bravely.

"*Why*?"

"To poison the water. To poison everyone who drinks it."

The man suddenly wavered. "Yes," he said, his voice falling slightly.

Roger sensed the man was on a knife-edge and would make a decision: Either to shoot or stand down. The longer they talked the more empathy Roger felt for this young ISIS recruit, if that was what he was. Apparently an American.

"Do you really want to kill innocent people?" he pleaded.

"They're not innocent. They're infidels."

"Children too? When do little children become infidels?"

"I...I don't know."

"You want to kill children?"

"No."

"Then don't. Killing is not the answer."

"I didn't sign up for this." The man let the muzzle of his weapon droop slightly.

"What's your name?" Roger asked for the second time.

"Jamal. My name's Jamal."

"Is that your American name?"

"No, I changed it. In America I was called all kinds of names because I'm a Muslim."

"Well, you're Jamal now. And that will be your name in America too. So let's go home." Roger shot Jamal a warm smile and the young man actually seemed to make a move toward the ATV. His facial expression lost some of its fierceness and his shoulders drooped ever so slightly. Until a shot rang out in the woods and he suddenly slumped to the ground.

Chapter 29

Roger stared aghast at the sight, then looked up to see who had fired the shot. Jim came toward him from the woods on the other side of the road followed by the other two SEALs, all holding their rifles at the ready.

"We heard you talking over the com. Sorry it took so long to get here."

"You didn't have to *shoot*." Roger protested. He ignored the SEALs and clamored down from the ATV, rushing to aid Jamal who lay on the ground, sobbing.

"He'll be all right. I just shot him in the butt." Jim said, looking at the man with disgust. "From what I heard over the com, he had the drop on you."

"We've got to help him!" Roger screamed, seeing Jamal's blood seeping into his clothes. "Come here and help me carry him."

"Carry him where? Leave him there. We have to go."

"You just *shot* him. *He's hurt*." Roger was almost beside himself with concern for Jamal.

"He's a hostile. What are you *nuts*?" Jim waved his hand, motioning for everyone to get onto the ATV, and he climbed into the driver's seat himself. He turned the switch and started the engine, which revved smoothly.

"We have to take him." Roger shouted back, kneeling next to the stricken man. "If his own soldiers see him, they'll know we were here. They'll look at the water supply and find the Nemo."

"If we take him prisoner, they'll know anyway." Jim argued.

"Maybe *not*. He's an American. They'll think he deserted."

Jamal, who was clearly in pain, looked up at Jim with moist eyes and pleaded, "Take me with you, *please*. They won't miss me. They'll think I ran away."

"All right then. New plan," Jim commanded. "We'll take him." All three SEALs jumped down off the ATV and ran over to Jamal. They carefully lifted and brought him to the vehicle, easing him into place, stretched out on the two back seats, face down. "Hold on to the rack," Jim told the two other SEALs. "You, Roger, get into the front passenger seat and make sure this guy doesn't jump out. Use your pistol if you have to."

Roger climbed aboard. "He's not going to jump," he assured Jim. "He wants to come with us." The SEALs stepped onto the back of the vehicle and held fast to the bars on the rear deck.

Jim drove the vehicle back down the road from where they came, dodging rough spots in an attempt to keep it from jostling up and down. He stayed on the road as long as he could and then crossed over through the wooded, rugged terrain to the waiting helicopter. The vehicle bucked and clamored, causing Jamal to cry out in pain, but eventually they reached the aircraft, its engine slowly rotating the vanes overhead.

One of the SEALs jumped down from the ATV and yanked a gurney from inside the craft. Jamal was quickly transferred to the gurney, face down, and his wound was bound to stop the bleeding. The gurney was lifted and placed on the floor of the helicopter. Roger climbed in after and took his former seat in the rear. Jamal lay cross-wise on the floor in front of him. The SEALs made quick work of connecting the ATV to a cable and winching it up tight to the aircraft's underbelly, where it held fast. The bottle of Botulinum Toxin remained secure and out of sight in the suitcase on its luggage rack. Their work finished, the SEALs all climbed aboard, closed the side door, and the craft lifted off.

"How'd it go with the Nemo?" Jim wanted to know, sitting across from Roger, his back to the two pilots on the flight deck.

"It went okay. It's being metered into the water right now." Roger replied.

"We still have a few worries." Jim noted. "I can't figure why so many soldiers were there guarding that place."

"They weren't there to guard the place," Roger told him.

"What do you mean?"

"They were there to put poison to the water." Roger told Jim what he had seen when he entered the water treatment plant, starting with finding the attendant who had been shot. "We stopped them from poisoning the water supply," he said finally.

Jim stared at Roger, instantly annoyed if not angry. "And you didn't tell me? You should have *said* something. That's what the com is for. You could have jeopardized the whole mission."

"What would you have done if I told you? Killed all the soldiers? ISIS would have sent more soldiers to take their place. And the new soldiers would bring more poison."

"Well, thanks to you, the soldiers are still there. They're probably poisoning the water for Aleppo right now."

"No they're not."

"No? And how do you know that?" Jim said angrily.

"Because I brought the bottle of poison with us. It's here on the helicopter."

"You did *what*? Where is this poison?"

"I put the bottle in my suitcase. Right now it's strapped onto the ATV."

Jim seemed stunned and said nothing in reply. As far as Roger could tell he had accepted the situation. It was what it was.

Finally, Jim spoke with a sharp edge to his voice, "So now we're carrying one of those killers *and* the poison? Tell me why ISIS won't realize we took it from them."

"Because they will think Jamal took the poison when he deserted. Not everyone is up for killing innocent men, women and children. They'll think he carried off the bottle of poison and emptied it somewhere to avoid having this horrible murder on his conscience."

"So what? They'll just get more poison to replace it."

"That's not easy to do. The poison they're using is hard to get. If these soldiers tell their commander that one of their men ran off with the poison, they would probably be shot for allowing that to happen. My guess is they'll go back and tell their commander they did their job. They lost a deserter, but that's all."

"You have it all figured out, don't you?" Jim replied cryptically. Although apparently still annoyed with Roger, he had to be glad their mission had been achieved in spite of what ISIS was up to. In fact, the added complication made for a better report to his commanding officer. They had accomplished the goal of their mission, albeit a secret goal known only to very few; they had taken a prisoner whom they could interrogate for information about the enemy *and* they had prevented a mass murder of innocent civilians.

For the flight back Jim had ordered radio silence until they reached the Israeli border. While still flying over Syrian airspace Roger watched as he typed a message into his tablet computer reporting the success of the mission. Jim pressed "Send" only when his pilot told them they were in the clear.

When the "all clear" signal came, Roger sensed a sudden relief among the SEALs. They immediately changed from an attitude of "all business" to an almost joyous mood, smiling and shedding the gear that they wore. The mission was over and they were all going home to America, Jamal included.

Except that, Roger knew, the mission had been all for naught. The enemy would be drinking water from another source, believing the tap water in Aleppo contained their own poison. Only the innocent local citizens who drank the tap water would be affected by Nemo.

Chapter 30 ▬▬▬▬▬▬▬▬▬▬▬▬▬▬▬▬▬

Courtney saw her quest clearly now. She was going to make this movement bigger than the big battle to beat breast cancer. Help was finally on the way to bring an end to that age-old problem in the battle of the sexes: a problem to which Courtney gave the name "Male Madness."

Courtney sat at her desk computer, typing a draft of an article that, she thought in her heart, would rouse her women and call them into action. Male Madness, women would soon realize, was a scourge that needed to be addressed and brought under control.

Statistics proved it, Courtney knew. Male Madness is a *real* phenomenon. Male Madness is when a man or a boy (it's almost *always* a male) takes a gun and starts shooting students in school. Remember Columbine? Remember Sandy Hook School in Newtown? Remember Virginia Tech? A girl wouldn't even think of doing such a horrible thing.

Male Madness is when a *serial killer* shoots one innocent person after another. Ninety-eight percent of serial killers are men.

Male Madness is when an *active shooter* enters a workplace and shoots as many people as he can. Ninety-seven percent of all active shooters are men.

Male Madness is when a *mass murderer* kills more than five people at a time. Ninety-two percent of mass murderers are men.

Male Madness is when a spouse or significant other has been beaten or killed. Remember O.J. Simpson? Virtually *all* spouse abusers are men.

Male Madness is when someone blows up a building with children in it. Remember the Federal Building in Oklahoma City? Those that do things like that are *always* men.

Male Madness is when a politician advocates the "use of force" against another country or group of people. Such posturing politicians are invariably male.

Male Madness is with us every day as we women try our best to forge ahead in our careers and reach an invisible barrier. There is inevitably a man who stands in our way, and he has male friends who encourage and support him.

Men tell us what we want to hear. They'll say, "equal pay for equal jobs," but they really believe that their jobs are more difficult or more complex than ours, so they should be paid more.

Some men say, "Women don't have the strength to do our work," but the jobs that require physical strength are usually the lowest paid. Then how come the average income for men is far higher than it is for women?

"*What is it with men?*" Every time Courtney thought about it, it made her face flush. "Why do they have to be such *bastards*?" Throughout history women have had to put up with Male Madness. With great effort over time they had managed to have laws enacted to provide some measure of protection, but the laws did not help. It's in a man's nature to be violent and, despite these laws, their outrageous behavior has reamined unchecked.

Now *finally* there was a way to *stop* this madness. It was "WOMEN" spelled backwards: "NEMOW," or "Nemo" for short. Courtney liked the name "*Balzoff*" but she knew better than to call it that. She didn't want to emasculate men; she just wanted them to act more like the fairer sex. That would make for a much safer and more civilized world.

Courtney sat at her desk and, for a long moment, stared at the business card that Roger had given her, screwing up her courage to call him for information. She gritted her teeth, lifted the phone and dialed his number. The call went immediately to voicemail. She left a message with her phone number asking him to return her call as soon as he possibly could. "It's *urgent*," she added. She was sure he'd call back, if for no other reason than to demand once again that she not publish any information about Nemo.

However, she was in a rush. *Women Rising* was going to press in the following week and she had to cover all her bases before the shit hit the fan. She noticed from his card that Roger was located at the Aberdeen Proving Ground in Maryland. She Googled the APG and obtained a phone number: 410-306-1403. Searching further, she found the APG web page - apg.army.mil – required a password for entry. She shot off a brief email to Roger at his address on the card, requesting that he contact her right away, and then dialed the phone number.

A chipper Latina female voice answered the call on the first ring. *"Aberdeen.* How may I direct your call?"

"Hello, my name is Courtney Stillwell. I'm a reporter calling from New York City. I'd like you to put me through to Dr. Thornwood."

"Who did you say?" The voice was so cheerful it was almost sing-song.

"Dr. Thornwood. Dr. Roger Thornwood."

There was a pause on the line before the female voice came back and said, "I'm sorry. I have no one here listed by that name." Still cheerful.

"This is Aberdeen Proving Ground?"

"Yes, Ma'am. It's the right place but the wrong party. Would you like to try someone else?"

"No. I want Dr. Thornwood."

"But he's not listed, Ma'am." The voice was no longer so chipper.

"I'm holding a business card from Dr. Thornwood right here in my hand. It says 'Roger Thornwood, PhD. Director, Bioweapons Research. United States Army.' It gives APG as his address."

"Don't be curt with me, Ma'am. We don't have a Dr. Thornwood here at Aberdeen." Definitely not chipper.

"I don't believe it. Let me talk to your supervisor."

"Oh, yeah," came the voice, inflecting a mild hint of sarcasm, and even some snarkyness as if to say, "You're out of line, you Bitch." What the voice really said was, "My supervisor? You want to speak to my supervisor?" in a way of laying down a challenge.

"That's what I just said. Your *supervisor.*" Courtney was getting quickly annoyed herself.

"You don't have to raise your voice with me, Ma'am. I heard you the first time. I'll put you through to the Post Commander's office. Our General, he knows *evveerything.*" The voice stretched out the word "everything." Courtney thought it odd, but ignored it.

"The—." Courtney was cut off mid-sentence and heard a ringing sound.

"General Mason's office. Eve speaking." Another female voice. This time soft and a bit southern.

"Eve, I've been trying to reach Dr. Roger Thornwood. I left a message on his phone but it's very urgent. For some reason your telephone operator is telling me he's not at Aberdeen but I know he is. He's head of bio-research there and I need to speak with him."

"There's nothing like that here at this facility."

"I know there is." Courtney was becoming quite exasperated at getting the run-around.

"We test ordnance. That's about it."

"Let me speak to your supervisor."

"The General?"

"Whomever."

"What did you say your name was?"

"Courtney Stillwell. I'm a reporter from New York." Again Courtney used the word "reporter" which was technically incorrect but it seemed more fitting.

"All right then. I'll see if he's available." The woman didn't seem too hopeful.

Courtney waited for what seemed to be several minutes before a rough male voice came on the line. "This is General Mason. I understand you're looking for Director Thornwood."

"Yes, I need to speak with him." At last someone admitted he was at APG. "It's very urgent I'm afraid."

"Oh, really? What's this about?" The General demanded.

"I'm going to publish a story next week about a new bioweapon he calls 'Nemo.' I want to give him a heads up and ask him some questions."

The General didn't say a word for the longest time. So long, in fact, that Courtney thought he had disconnected. She was about to hang up the receiver when he spoke to her with a strong but even-tempered tone of voice: "Whatever it is you intend to publish, Ms. Stillwell, *don't*. If you decide to go ahead, you'll find yourself in jail."

If there was anything that could get Courtney's back up, it was a man who told her what to do. When she heard what she perceived as a command over the phone, she instantly went on the defensive. The General represented everything *male* that Courtney was fighting against.

Of course, neither Courtney nor the General himself knew that, as he spoke, Nemo was flowing through the man's veins.

Chapter 31

Eve burst into General Mason's office as soon as she saw the light on her phone console blink off.

"What did that cunt want? She claims she knows about Thornwood."

"Yeah. Thornwood warned me about her," he said, sitting behind his big desk looking glum. "She's about to blow the lid off of the Nemow project. The President gave the green light to use Nemo in a Syrian war zone. If news of that gets out there, the Pres'll be sucking air. We've got to stop her."

"Wouldn't be good for you either. It would kill your chance to get that shiny new star." Eve reached over and pretended to wipe the dust off the star on Mason's right shoulder. "What are you going to do?"

"I don't know." Mason thought for a moment. "I've got to report this. Let me think… Not many people know about Nemo… Okay, step one: I need to call the Chairman of the Joint Chiefs."

"Yes, Sir. Good idea," Eve said, realizing the urgency. That's what she liked about this man she was fucking, until recently at least. He was strong and he was decisive. She ran back to the office and quickly placed the call. When the Chairman came on the line she said, "Please hold for General Mason—," and pressed the button to connect him to Mason's line.

* * * *

Mason picked up, took a deep breath, and began by saying, "Good morning, Sir. I have—," but he was immediately interrupted.

"Mason, I was about to call you," the Chairman said effusively. "I have some good news. Nemo is flowing in the water of Aleppo as we speak. Our guys went in, put the stuff in place and got out. No one knows they were there except one guy who they took prisoner. Turns out he's an American turncoat to ISIS and they're drilling him for intel now. I wouldn't want to be that sorry son-of-a-bitch."

"That is very good news, Sir."

"You bet it is. The President's pleased as punch. He's going to bring you, me, those Navy SEALs who ran the mission, and also that Dr. Thornwood to the White House for a congratulatory handshake. It'll be off the record, though. Just private between us. We need to keep this program totally under wraps. The President's ass is on the line with this one."

Mason knew this was not a good time to tell the Chairman, but he had no choice. He took a deep breath and announced, "Well Sir, that was the reason for my call. Some woman reporter in New York has learned about Nemo and she's going to go public with the story."

"She's *what?* Did I hear you right, Mason?"

"Yes, it's true. I got off the phone with her a few minutes ago. She was trying to contact Thornwood here at APG, so I took the call. I told her to button it up or she'd find herself in jail."

"So? Is she a real threat?"

"I'm afraid so, Sir. She's got the bit in her teeth. I don't think even a preemptive lawsuit would have much effect."

"Jesus! We've got to stop this. If any word of the program gets out, the media will go absolutely *nuts*. We'll have an international incident on our hands."

"Yes, Sir. You're right, Sir."

"Does Thornwood know about this?"

General Mason was now in a dilemma. If he told the Chairman that Thornwood knew, the next two questions would surely be, 'When did Thornwood know and when did he report it to Mason?' Mason would have a hell of a time explaining why he didn't immediately report this problem up the line. Mason, always one to bob and weave to avoid the punches, responded, "Thornwood told me about this a couple of weeks ago, but we thought we had the problem contained. Thornwood told her that if any news about Nemo leaked out, Nemo would be useless as a weapon or for anything else. What the woman really wants is to get hold of the stuff so she can stop men from doing the things men do..."

"What do you mean? What kind of things?"

"I don't know. She's some kind of a feminist. Has a magazine called *Women Rising*. Violence against women, I suppose."

"A lot of guys out there are way out of line, Mason. We know that from experience here in the military."

"We figured she'd want to keep Nemo under wraps too." Mason finally got to the point. "Once men know about it, you can bet they'd all start drinking bottled water."

"Not only that, Mason, but there's another thing—."

"What's that?"

"We could never make enough of that chemical for everybody. It's damn expensive. We might want to deliver the stuff to prisons to keep the violence down in there, but that's about all."

"You're right, Sir."

"I assume we're dealing with a very smart woman here. If so, she can't realistically think she can change all men by spiking the water."

"But she's seized on this as a teaching moment for women. To point out men's bad behaviour."

"I can see what she's up to. Still, we've got to stop her."

"So what should we do?"

"First thing is to call in Thornwood. He's back now and he can tell us what he knows about this woman. Next thing is to talk to her. Give her what she wants and, in return, she gives us what we want: Absolute silence about Nemo."

"We can do that."

"So handle it. I'm counting on you, Mason. You can't fail us on this."

"Consider it done, Sir. But…just one thing—."

"Yes?" By the tone of his voice the Chairman of the Joint Chief's made it clear that this conversation was already over.

"What do you suppose the woman wants?"

"What all women want, Mason: Control over the men in their lives." The Chairman disconnected, and a moment later Eve rushed back into Mason's office.

"What did he say?" she asked excitedly. "Is he going to stop that woman?"

"He wants *me* to handle the problem."

"How are you going to do that?"

"I haven't the slightest idea."

Chapter 32

General Mason dialed Thornwood's cell number without waiting for Eve to get back to her desk, completely focused on containing the problem with Courtney.

"Director Thornwood? This is General Mason—." There was a pause. "We have a big problem. That Courtney person, who has that bitch magazine, *Women Rising*? She's going ahead with publishing an article about Nemo. Just like you said she would. It'll come out in the magazine *next week*."

Mason listened impatiently for a moment, then barked, "What can we do? We're going to stop her, that's what. We're going to New York, together, to talk to her... Tomorrow...Debriefing?...That has to wait. This is more important. Meet me here at zero eight hundred. That's a direct order, Director." Mason slammed the receiver down.

He looked up and saw Eve staring at him inquiringly. "We can do this," he barked. "Set up the appointment with this woman. Twelve noon. We'll drive up there and take her to lunch. Where do you suggest?"

"Remember when you took me to New York? We stayed at the Hilton and had dinner at Ruth's Chris? How about going there? Sure worked for *me*. We fucked our brains out that night."

The memory made the General wince "No," he said. "That's much too heavy. This has to be a prissy 'ladies' lunch'."

"A 'ladies' lunch' you want? Hmmm. Okay how about The Palm? The one on the West Side. Went there for lunch once, before a Broadway show. It's real nice."

"Book it. Go."

Eve scurried out and made the calls, first to Courtney and then to the restaurant. In less than ten minutes she came back and told Mason, "You're all set. Noon at The Palm. Courtney will be there."

"Good. We'll take my car. Alert Sam, my driver."

"Can I go?"

"Hell no. What're you nuts? We have work to do."

"You and I could stay overnight in New York. Just like before."

"Cut it out, Eve."

"Why not? Li'l Tommy-gun wants to come out and play. I heard him calling to me." Eve leaned in and reached for his member but Mason pushed her hand away.

"Stop it."

Eve made a pouty face. "You don't love me anymore," she said pretending to whine.

"Those days are *over*. I must have been out of my mind. I'm *married*, damn it, and I'm going to stay that way."

"Married? So what? That never stopped your li'l Tommy-gun from shooting before."

"All right. I don't feel like it. Is that a good reason? And anyway my marriage is more important to me now."

"How can you say that? You've *changed*, like from one day to the next. You're the one who came on to *me*, remember? And now you're hanging me out to dry, you bastard."

"So I've changed. So what? Get over it."

"It's like you've been drinking that Nemo KoolAid. You were hot, and now you're not."

The General thought a moment. "You know, maybe you're right. I do feel different than I did before. Just last week…I wonder…No, that can't be—."

"Can't be what?"

"My wife. She can't be spiking my drinks. She wouldn't *dare*."

Eve shot a coquettish look at the General's face and purred, "Maybe she did. You never know what a woman will do when it comes to a man—."

"No, that's ridiculous." The General shook his head. "She doesn't even know about Nemo."

"You should ask her."

"I don't believe it. And she'll deny it if I do. Anyway, I have more important things to worry about right now. Did you tell Sam to pick me up tomorrow morning?"

"Not yet, but I will. I'll tell him to pick up Thornwood first and then stop at your house. Eight o'clock. Be there, and don't fuck your wife. Save li'l Tommy-gun for *me*."

Chapter 33

General Mason rode together with Roger Thornwood in the back seat of the Army limousine as PFC Sam Watson, Mason's driver, headed north to New York on the New Jersey Turnpike. Small flags on the two front fenders of the car bore the star of the Brigadier General.

When Sam first picked them up, Mason was eager to learn from Roger what had happened on his trip to Syria. Roger gave him a blow-by-blow, telling of their successes, but then concluded by saying that he thought the entire adventure "was a bust."

"Those ISIS soldiers in Aleppo think they poisoned the water, so they're not going to drink it," Roger explained. "But they'll soon be surprised when not one person in Aleppo dies, or even gets sick. I'd give it a week before they realize the water's clean and start running tests. They'll find there's no poison."

"You think they'll find the Nemo?"

"Probably not. Depends on what they test for, but you have to know what you're looking for."

"Assuming they don't, how long will the Nemo last?"

"I put in enough to last at least a month."

"Hmm, the General murmured and then fell silent for much of the trip, thinking about what consequences Nemo might have. As they approached New York, Mason turned to Thornwood and finally broached the subject of their meeting with Stillwell. "Okay, here's the plan. We know the objective. We have this one shot to make it work. If we can't get her to stop the presses, we might as well hang it up with the Army and look for other jobs. Our asses are on the line here."

"I really don't think she'll budge, Sir. I've been over this with her and she's determined."

"I'm hoping she'll get the message when I show up. It isn't often a woman sits down with an Army General in uniform." Mason grinned and held his hands out to show off the graffiti on his chest and the stars on his shoulders. "Impressive, huh?"

"I'm impressed, General Mason. But she's…uh, *different*. She'll think you're pompous. She has her own agenda."

"So what agenda is that?"

"She wants men to be more like women."

"We've got to find her weakness and play on that, Thornwood. Should be easy. She's a woman, after all. Can't be that tough."

"Because she's a woman?"

"Sure. Women are pushovers. I've never met one I couldn't control. It's men you have to watch out for."

"That's precisely her point, Sir. She thinks men don't give women their due."

"Whaddaya mean? As long as they stay in their place, they get plenty of doo. And by that I don't mean 'shit.' Men suck up to them all the time. It's what we do."

"We do it when we want something from them."

"I know what you're thinking, Thornwood. We suck up to them when we want sex. Go ahead and say it. They hold the cards in that department. Gives them power."

"Like I said, General, she's different."

"Yeah, I know. She was gang raped. Men are really shits sometimes."

"That's a big deal. It changes everything."

"Women make a bigger deal of it than they should. Blow it all out of proportion."

"You don't mean that, Sir."

"Maybe I do, maybe I don't. That gives me an idea, though. Most women are looking to hook up with a man. Maybe she's attracted to you. You could…you know, oblige her."

"You can't be serious—."

"Dead serious. If there's one thing I've learned about women, once you've get them in bed they're pretty much yours to do with what you want. They call it love. It's in their DNA."

"You really think I should hit on Courtney Stillwell?" Roger was incredulous.

"Wouldn't hurt to try. Take one for the team, Thornwood. If you get in her pants it'll be a home run. Mission accomplished."

"Well, count me out."

"You're about the same age as this woman, right? I'm old enough to be her father and anyway, I'm *married*. Now I know a lot of women go for older men and I've—." Mason broke off suddenly. "Anyway, it'll be interesting to see which one of us she—."

"That's off the table, Sir," Roger insisted. "We can't do that."

"All right. I figured I should bring it up anyway. Can't fault me for trying."

"No Sir."

"There's got to be another way. I'm sorry though, but I'm at a loss—."

"I have a suggestion, but you may not approve."

"*Me* not approve? I'll go to any length to get this job done. My fucking career depends on it, damn it."

"All right then. Let's say we offer to deploy Nemo in her behalf."

"Deploy Nemo?"

"Completely in secret of course."

"Why? What for?"

"She might want to see what happens. As a kind of test maybe, but we know that Nemo works—."

"What do you propose to do? Spit it out, Thornwood."

"Put it in the drinking water of anybody she designates, within reason of course."

"She designates? Like who? Who would she designate?"

"The men who raped her."

Chapter 34

When General Mason and Roger entered The Palm on 50th Street and Eighth at five past twelve, Courtney Stillwell was already there, wearing a cotton print dress that hugged her curves, standing and speaking with the concierge. She recognized Roger when the men walked in and turned toward them. "So nice to see you again, Dr. Thornwood," she said stepping forward and offering her hand with a warm smile.

Roger shook her hand and gave an introduction to Mason. "I'd like you to meet General Mason. Thomas Mason. The Post Commander at Aberdeen Proving Ground where I work." Mason was in full Army uniform and the stars on his shoulders glinted in the overhead lighting.

"So you're the big boss," Courtney said with an apparent mock deference to his male authority while holding her hand out to him, but this time without a smile.

"Well, not exactly. It's complicated." Mason replied. "Army stuff." He beamed at the young woman with a high wattage grin. Taking her hand he held it a bit longer than he should have. He couldn't help noticing that she looked smoking hot with her strawberry blonde tresses, her cute countenance and her bountiful boobs, but he felt no sexual urge whatsoever. For a split second he wondered if something might be wrong with him and fleetingly recalled what Eve had said about his drinking spiked water. However, he brushed the thought aside thinking maybe he was getting more sex than he could handle from his horny wife, as if that were ever possible.

Since she was an attractive female, he nevertheless did what he always did in such situations: He turned on the Mason charm. "It's a great pleasure to meet you, Miss. I understand you publish a very important magazine for women."

"Mizz."

"Uh, what?" Mason didn't expect this response.

"It's Mizz, not Miss."

"Mrs.? Are you married?"

"No, are you?"

"Why, yes as a matter of fact. Happily so. Why do you ask?"

"Your title, 'General,' doesn't exactly convey whether you're married or not."

Mason was having trouble following. "I don't understand. The word 'General'—."

"Never mind. It's not important. Should we sit at a table or in a booth?" Courtney waved her hand in the direction of the restaurant tables. Mason surveyed the layout and noticed the cast of hand-drawn caricatures that grinned at patrons from their places along the walls. There were also framed photographs of celebrities who had been at the restaurant.

"I think a booth would be best. Don't you?" he replied. "Would give us an intimate place to talk."

"A booth it is then." Courtney nodded to the pretty female concierge and she led them to a quiet booth on the side of the main room. Mason motioned for Courtney to sit on one side together with Roger while he sat on the other, facing her. Another pretty female took their order for drinks and disappeared.

Mason immediately took charge of the conversation. "'Women Rising.' That's a nice name for your magazine. Your idea?"

"It's my magazine. Yes, I thought up the name. I think it conveys what we're doing."

"Which is?"

"Creating awareness that women should rise. Lift themselves up. We've been stuck on a lower rung."

"Do you really mean that? I see my women up on pedestals. Way up there." Mason pointed skyward.

"*Your* women?"

"The ones I deal with. You know what I mean." Mason was becoming slightly flustered.

"No I don't, General. Did you know that a recent study found storms with female names like "Katrina' and 'Sandy' were taken less seriously than the ones with men's names, like 'Adolf' and 'Andrew'? Why do you suppose that is?"

"Because women are nicer than men? Women should be proud of that."

"Maybe it's time we stopped being nice. Men take advantage of it all the time so we women have a lot to be angry about."

"Whoa." Mason raised his hands to stop the flow. The conversation was not going as planned. It had turned adversarial. He took another tack and tried to lighten it up.

"Thornwood tells me you know the editor of *Cosmo* Magazine, what's her name? Emily something?

"Emily Platt. What of it?"

"My secretary has a subscription. She gives it to me when she's through reading. Great pictures of women." Mason sensed this was the wrong thing to say as soon as he had said it. He saw Courtney cringe and Roger rolling his eyes.

"Oh? Pictures of women? So you like to stare?"

"Well, yes. What man doesn't? That's why God made you look so damn—," he couldn't think of any other word that wouldn't be offensive except "pretty." He would rather have been able to say "sexy" but this woman was much too touchy.

"I wouldn't know. I don't look at women that way. And I don't think men should either."

Oops. Mason had to try still another tack. Roger was staring blankly at him, not helping at all. He decided to just get down to business. There was no charming this woman no matter how great she looked. "Courtney, do you know why we're here? Why we're having this lunch?"

"Yes, I think so. Is it because you've discovered a way to make men nicer and I'm about to publish an article to tell the world all about it?"

"You can't do that."

"Yes I can, and I will. The story's coming out in my magazine next week."

"No it's not. You'll go to jail if that happens."

"I shouldn't need to remind you, this is a free country."

"Not where national security is involved."

"Perhaps, but your Balzoff is useless for national security. It's outlawed by the Geneva Convention. That takes national security right off the table in this case. Sorry."

"It's a weapon, and we'll use it if we have to. And by the way, it's Geneva *Conventions*, plural. There are a number of treaties."

"You don't have a legal leg to stand on. I'm going to press, General, and you can't stop me."

"We'll get a court order. Tomorrow. If you violate the order, it's jail time."

"I'm willing to do that. The publicity would be good for my magazine."

"We'll close the magazine down."

"No you won't. It's set to publish automatically. Online."

"Okay, just for argument's sake, let's say we don't go to court. Let's make a deal."

"What kind of a deal?"

"How would you like to see Nemo in action?"

"What do you mean?"

"I mean Thornwood here can arrange to have Nemo put in the water of any guy you name and turn the bastard into a Mama's boy. You know what I mean. Nemo can do that. All we ask is that you keep it confidential."

"Are you bribing me, General?"

"You can call it a bribe; I'll call it a deal, fair and square."

Courtney thought a moment. Mason and Roger looked at her and held their collective breath.

"I'll tell you what," Courtney said finally. "Can either you or Dr. Thornwood present the deal to my editorial board tomorrow morning?"

Chapter 35

General Mason and Roger remained at the luncheon table a short while longer to discuss strategy after Courtney excused herself and left for her office. Mason, explaining that he and Stillwell "just didn't hit it off," told Roger to stay the night and attend the board meeting alone. "I'd be like a bull in a China shop," he admitted. Roger, who would have preferred to have the General at his side at the meeting, grudgingly agreed.

"I'm counting on you," General Mason said. "You had better bring home the bacon, Thornwood, or both our asses are grass."

Using his cell phone Mason called Sam to pick him up and take him home. Roger gave a parting salute to his commanding officer as the Army sedan drove up and Mason climbed into the back seat. Mason opened his side window and gave Roger a final pep talk: "Take the train to Baltimore and Sam will pick you up. And Thornwood, don't you come home without a deal."

Anxious and worried, Roger walked slowly north on Seventh Avenue the five blocks to Fifty-fifth Street and checked into the Dream Midtown Hotel. He went to his room and spent the afternoon and evening in a deeply troubled state of mind. He was not at all sure he could prevent the public disclosure of the new biological and chemical weapon he had developed. The media storm that could arise from this might eventually lead to a reveal of its use on the battlefield in Syria. Not only would the entire program be jeopardized, but this violation of the Geneva Conventions would surely do damage to the U.S. relations with other governments. And it could even bring down the Presidency.

* * * *

At precisely ten o'clock the next day, Roger took a deep breath and knocked on the office door. Courtney opened the door and, without speaking, she motioned for him to follow her and led the way to the conference room. As he entered he saw three women sitting at the conference table.

"Meet Dr. Roger Thornwood," Courtney began as Roger stood there next to her. "Dr. Thornwood, I won't bother you with their last names because you won't remember them anyway. Going clockwise around the table, we have Ashley, Bailey and Deedee." As each person's name was called, that woman responded with a friendly smile. Roger nodded, looking squarely at each one in turn, trying to make a connection with these women whom, he understood, would be deciding his destiny.

"Dr. Thornwood is the brains behind Project Nemow," Courtney continued, "and would like to speak with us about keeping it secret. You know that our lead article next week will tell the world about this government program. I called you all and asked that you interrupt your busy lives to come and listen first-hand to what he has to say. Then I'd like us to make a democratic decision today on whether or not to publish the article.

"Why don't you take a seat over there, Dr. Thornwood." Courtney pointed to the seat at the far end of the table. "I'll sit at this end." She took her seat but Roger did not. He walked to the far end of the room but remained standing.

"I'd rather stand," he said, "if that's okay."

"Suit yourself," Courtney replied. "You have the floor, Dr. Thornwood."

Roger eyed the four women before him and began, somewhat hesitantly at first, but then warmed to his tale. "My name is Roger Thornwood. Please call me 'Roger.' Everyone does. Everyone, that is, except in the military. I work for the Army as a scientist. Everyone calls me 'Thornwood' there, but I much prefer 'Roger'."

"All right," Courtney spoke for the group. "'Roger' it is."

"For the past four years now I've been heading a skunkworks in the Army to create a new kind of biological and chemical weapon that will neutralize men who are fighting against our country. I'm based at Aberdeen Proving Ground. It's the home of the Army Ordnance Corps and is known for testing conventional weaponry: handguns, rifles, artillery, armor-piercing projectiles, mortars, that sort of thing. Guns and ammunition. So no one would normally think there's a bio-research lab there.

"The program was, and still is classified as Top Secret. That's the government's highest classification for secrecy. But I understand from Courtney that you have somehow learned about it through a breach in our circle of confidentiality.

"As you know, the idea was to develop something we could put in the water to make men less prone to violent behavior. This was basically brain research. We first had to understand why men act out the way they do and then find a biological or chemical substance that altered this state of mind.

"We didn't want to do the obvious: provide a vehicle that would effectively 'castrate' men, because this would be noticed by the enemy, although we certainly could. They would immediately take steps to block or even reverse the effect. Very soon in the development, however, it occurred to me that our aim should be to make men more like women.

"There is a kind of a transgender scale from left to right, with femaleness on the left side and maleness on the right side of the center. No person is all the way to the left or to the right, you understand. All men are positioned somewhere to the right of the center on this scale but none of us are *all* male. What I realized, however, was that the more to the right a man was on this scale, the more he was prone to violence. The objective, then, was to find a way to move men toward the left, in the direction of femaleness, without going all the way past the center."

As Roger spoke, Ashley and Bailey stared at him, eyes wide, as if transfixed. At this point Ashley raised high her right hand and wiggled her fingers to gain attention.

"Yes, Ashley?" Courtney moderated.

"Dr. Thornwood. You mean to say that all of us women here are at different places on that scale? Somewhere on the left side, I would assume." There was a light titter in the group. Bailey even stifled a laugh.

"Call me 'Roger' please," Roger pleaded. "Good question and I'd have to say that's exactly right. Some of you are farther to the left than others," He responded as pleasantly as he could considering the sensitivity of the answer. The women looked at each other, seemingly wondering who could be considered the most 'female'.

After a pause, Roger continued. "In our research we studied the work others had done, mostly in the field of mental disease. We learned how the brain responded to different chemical stimuli and different biological substances, such as foods from different cultures. It was a long and tedious process, but we gained some interesting insights and made a few discoveries. We found connections among the effects on the brain of different compositions, both chemical and biological. We tried synthesizing some of what we thought were active ingredients and experimented with rabbits and rats. As you can imagine, there were false starts and a lot of dead ends. Something like Thomas Edison's quest to find a filament for the incandescent light. We were frustrated by our lack of progress at first but we pressed on, trying to understand the mechanism in the brain that makes a man a man and a woman a woman. Finally, after three years of this intense research we made a breakthrough. We created a substance which could be delivered either as a dry powder or as an aqueous solution that moved mammals to the left on the transgender scale."

Ashley's hand went up again, this time even more urgently than before. Roger stopped again to take her question.

She asked, "If you put this new stuff you came up with in the water, let's say, will it move *both* males *and* females farther to the left on the scale?"

"The answer is 'yes'," Roger replied. "Nemow will have that effect if it is ever deployed. However, you'll be glad to know it has no effect on children because they are gender neutral until they reach puberty.

Chapter 36

Having answered the questions truthfully, Roger had no idea whether he had helped or made it more difficult to halt the public disclosure of the development of Nemow. There was nothing else he could do but to press on. He looked for a reaction from the board members but could see none, so he continued.

"Since our idea was to move men to the left on the transgender scale so as to make them more like women, we called our discovery "*Nemow*," which is women spelled backwards. It's an awful sounding name though. I prefer to call it "Nemo," as in *Finding Nemo*--you know, the animated movie?" Roger looked for a response to this funny name he came up with, but saw none. Somewhat uncomfortable now, he cleared his throat and continued.

"After three and a half years of research and development and also testing with animals, we had to try Nemo out on humans. This was the big moment. We had been working toward this for years, but when the testing came close I almost got cold feet. It's one thing to conceptualize and come up with the idea of making men think like women; it's quite another to actually have the means in hand that might do just that. It was like when they tested the atom bomb for the first time after years of work on the Manhattan Project. They were sorely afraid of what the consequences would be."

Roger took a breath during which he again tried again to discern the reaction of his audience sitting around the table. The four women looked up at him, apparently still interested in what he was saying, but he had no idea what they were thinking. So he pressed on.

"We needed to try out Nemo on some men at the very right side of the scale and see if we could move them to the left. We also needed to find out if there were any harmful effects, or lasting effects, of this drug, because that's what it was: a drug. We needed honest feedback from our test subjects to fully evaluate Nemo and to understand how it worked.

"This testing phase, we felt, would be the most challenging part of the development. What 'real man' would want to take part in such an experiment? And even if we could talk him into drinking our concoction by paying enough compensation, what tough guy would be honest in telling us his innermost feelings. As I'm sure you women know, 'soul searching' is not a thing that men normally do."

Roger finally got a rise out of those at the table. They rolled their eyes and nodded knowingly, as in "been there, seen that" in men. As far as these women were concerned, the characteristics and qualities of a so-called "real man" could be left in the trash bin of evolution.

Roger realized he should tread with care. If he touted Nemo as effective in emasculating men, these women would be motivated all the more to tell the world about this startling development. He decided to take a different tack.

"As it turned out, we needn't have worried," he continued. "At first we were going to recruit some random Army men to conduct our tests but then, I thought, these normal men were not the types we wanted to change. We needed to try out Nemo on the baddest, most violent-prone, trigger-temper men we could find. So I started asking around.

"I spoke to the commander of an Army prison facility about selecting men with violent tendencies; I talked with a number of Army psychologists to learn the dynamic of violent gangs; and finally visited a number of police departments and asked law enforcement officers who they thought might fit the profile. Almost everyone suggested the same thing: Men in motorcycle gangs. Not only were these gang bangers violent, they were easy to find because of their bikes. You could tell they were at one of their hangouts when you drove by because their bikes were parked outside.

"So, with a few tips from the police, I got in the car and started to drive. Within a few hours I found my men. I'm sure you heard the rest, from Billy. That guy you have been speaking to. What did you pay him to break his confidentiality agreement? Twenty thousand dollars? That's double what he got from us."

Roger stared at Courtney expectantly, knowing that she had paid him *something*; he just didn't know how much.

"Seventy-five thousand," Courtney replied blandly.

"*What*? Seventy—." He broke into a grin. "Well I'll be… No wonder he caved. I would have been tempted too for that amount of money. And here I thought that Billy gave up our government secrets because he didn't know wrong from right."

"All right," Courtney said, appearing annoyed. "We paid him. So get over it. Tell us what you came here to tell us. Let's move on."

"Long story short, we ran the tests and the results were better than we ever expected in our wildest imagination. We moved these men almost a third of the way to the left on the male-female scale. Our program was an over-the-top success. Our Nemo was *real*." Roger ended on this up note with a smile and surveyed his audience again. This time most of the women seemed at least mildly pleased. All seemed to be with him except Courtney, who still wore a frown. It was time to focus in with a plea for their support.

"So we now have this additional weapon in our military arsenal that can bring fighting to a halt or at least damp it down. But Nemo won't work if the enemy knows about it, or even suspects it. If they do, they can deploy the simplest of countermeasures. They can stop drinking water from the public water supply."

Roger let that message sink in for a moment, and then added, "The publication of your article about this program would ruin everything. I need to tell you to stop. Our country finally has a secret weapon that could give us a significant edge against our foreign enemies, while at the same time reducing the violence of war. Your publication would destroy this advantage, not to mention the four years of effort it took to develop this weapon. As I'm sure you can understand, secrecy is key."

This time, Deedee raised her hand. Looking over to Courtney, she asked, "What are you going to do to us if we publish?"

"Once the existence of our weapon is known, it will be too late to collect all the bees and put them back in the hive," Roger admitted. "But there could be some major jail time as a warning to others."

"So at this point it's basically an honor system?" Deedee asked. "We're supposed to be good girls why?"

"For the reasons I gave, and because your government requires you to."

"Am I hearing this right? We're supposed to just do the right thing and salute the flag?"

"Something like that. But there is one more thing—."

The women looked at Roger as if he'd asked them to attend the funeral of someone they didn't know or care about. "Oh, what's that?" Deedee asked, her voice filled with her skepticism against stopping the presses at this late hour.

"The public disclosure of Nemo would not serve any purpose at all. The substance of Nemo is, and will stay, a well-kept secret. As long as the formula for Nemo is locked in the vault, no one can reverse engineer it. It will never see the light of day."

The four women had apparently not considered this possibility and appeared somewhat stunned by Roger's announcement. They sat there for a moment, reflecting on the situation and saying nothing. Roger went in for the one-two punch. "There is also something I can offer you," he added.

The women looked at him questioningly, waiting to learn what further cards he had to play.

"Now we're getting to it," Courtney commented. "What have you got?"

"I've spoken to General Thomas Mason and he has authorized me to make you this one time offer: If you will stop publication of the article and agree to forever maintain the secrecy of this military weapon, subject to the severe penalties accorded acts of treason, we will agree…," Roger took a breath and the women leaned in to catch every word, "… to deploy the weapon, in total secrecy you understand, against any man that you name."

Chapter 37

"Let me get this straight," Courtney replied after a long pause. "You want us all to sign some kind of a paper agreeing never to reveal anything about Nemo?"

"Yes," Roger nodded in affirmation.

"And if any word about Nemo slips from our lips, we can be sent to jail for a long time without so much as a trial?"

"You would be in breach of contract not to mention in violation of our national security laws. A trial maybe but, yes, you'll be sent to jail without even passing go."

"However, in return we get to pick some man whom you will 'Nemo' for us?" Courtney asked, confirming her understanding.

"Yes, that's it. In total secrecy, of course. No one will ever know we have deployed Nemo."

"Well that's the craziest thing I've ever heard," Deedee remarked.

"Crazy like a fox," Bailey remarked brightly. Bailey had said little since Roger arrived but Roger saw that a plan was formulating in her mind.

"That's my offer," Roger confirmed. "And I must ask you to make a decision on this right away. Before I leave here today."

"Why don't we caucus?" Bailey suggested. "Let's send Dr. Thornwood out of the room and talk about it."

"That's just what I was going to say," Courtney agreed. She stood up from the table and looked at Roger. "Would you mind?"

"Not at all. I can wait right outside if that's all right. Will you take long?"

"I don't really know," Courtney answered. "This could take just a minute, or it could take all day."

"Well, I'll wait for a bit. If you think you will take longer just let me know and I'll go to a museum or something."

"That's a good plan. We'll let you know."

Roger walked out of the room and Courtney shut the door behind him. Turning and standing in front of her board members she cocked her head and asked the big question, "So what do you think?" Three women looked back at her but didn't say a word. Courtney had the fleeting thought that this was quite unlike her editorial board. She usually had trouble keeping their girl-talk in check so their meetings could end before midnight.

Courtney sat down again at the head of the table and began the discussion in her usual manner. She started at the top of the alphabet, with the youngest member of her board, by turning to Ashley. "Ashley, what do you think?"

Ashley thought for a moment and began philosophically, "We members of the board are all your friends, Courtney. We are here for two reasons: to support your magazine and help it to grow and also, perhaps more importantly, to support *you* and help you to grow. We three are aware of what happened to you back in college, and we know there is some kind of connection between your travail and your starting this magazine. It was a horrible thing, and those bastards should be made to pay. Perhaps this is a way—."

Courtney smiled in acknowledgement, but did not reply. She simply said, "Bailey."

"I think this a no-brainer. We get something for nothing. As Dr. Thornwood pointed out, we shouldn't be publishing the article anyway. And he, and whomever he works for, are willing to use Nemo against whomever we say."

"That's a 'yes' then?"

"I don't want to be greedy, but how about also asking for the seventy-five thousand dollars we paid Billy for information. That's money thrown away if we don't publish."

"That's very true."

"I find this entire situation just incredible and amazing. We kind of lucked into it, but here we are. We brought the U.S. Government to its *knees*. They are *begging us* not to publish and they're willing to pay us for that. I say go with it, but ask for the seventy-five thousand."

"Deedee," Courtney said finally, turning to her close friend. "There are two out of four board votes in favor so we need your sage advice now. I'm willing to publish if you are. I think Nemo can work a sea change in how women view men. We need to know your take on all of this."

Deedee, the senior member of the editorial board, surveyed the other women at the table. Her thoughts, based on her many years of experience in the field of publishing, counted for much more than her single vote. She was the conscience of the board and, as such, she held a special place as second in command and a mentor to Courtney. In this role and capacity she was rarely overruled. All eyes were on her as she spoke. "I don't know about you," she said, "but I think this Dr. Thornwood is *cute*. If I were twenty years younger I'd make a pass at him."

Courtney blushed bright red. After a long pause she managed to stand and, without speaking, walk to the door. She opened it and Roger stepped in. "Please have a seat," she said and motioned toward the empty chair at the opposite end of the table. This time Roger did as he was told and sat to face whatever music he was going to hear.

Courtney also sat down in her chair and, looking at Roger meaningfully, she announced, "We have come to a decision." Roger appeared to cringe, which was just the reaction Courtney hoped to elicit. Although she had been overruled, this was her moment and she was enjoying it. "We want more. We want a refund of the seventy-five thousand dollars we paid Billy. Other than that, we accept your offer."

Roger blanched visibly. It was as if he had been holding his breath and then released it. He rubbed his face and, with a slight smile, he mumbled, "I'm very glad. We can do that."

"We haven't discussed or decided where we would like you to use Nemo," Courtney continued.

"Yes, we have." Ashley broke in.

"Oh? What? Where?" Taken aback, Courtney shot a stare at Ashley.

Deedee exercised her prerogative and spoke up for the group. "There are three men we know who did violence to Courtney, and who never had to pay. We would like you to Nemo *them*." Deedee looked Roger in the eye for emphasis as she said this.

"The effect will be only temporary, you understand," Roger said.

"Okay, how long?" Deedee asked.

"One week."

"Make it a year," Deedee countered.

"No. But I can maybe go to two weeks."

"That's not going to work. These men have to be taught a lesson."

"Okay, I can do four. That's the absolute maximum. And no one is to know what we're doing, you understand."

"We can live with that. If you agree to Nemo these three men for one month, and pay seventy-five thousand dollars, we'll sign anything you put in front of us."

"All right then. I'll prepare a written agreement, just between us. We can't get lawyers involved in this because no one else is to know. In the meantime, you'll pull the article about Nemo?"

"Yes," said Deedee. "That's the deal, and word about Nemo will never leave this room."

"Good. So let's talk about deploying Nemo in the water for the men you spoke about. You said there were *three*? That may pose a logistics problem, but who are they?"

Deedee looked at Courtney expectantly. Only Courtney knew the names of the men and Courtney had not said anything yet. She had not even said these were the men she would choose. However, everyone at the table knew she would.

"There *is* this little problem," Courtney said.

"What problem?" Roger asked. "There's nothing we won't try to do to uphold our part of the bargain."

"I know where these men live," Courtney replied. "I have an interest in how those SOB's are doing so I've been watching them. From afar. They have really fancy homes. They're like fortresses with a lot of security. There's no way you'll be able to get inside to add Nemo to their water."

Roger hadn't thought this through yet, but he was willing to explore all possibilities. "If they're connected to a public water supply we can use that. But this means we need to put Nemo in the water for a whole town."

"Three different towns?" Deedee asked.

"No, they all live in the same town. With their wives and kids. Very happily I would assume, " Courtney added.

"Well that's a plus." Roger noted. "What town is that?"

"Chappaqua, New York."

Chapter 38

Roger frowned and uttered "Uh-oh," almost to himself.

"Is that a problem?" Courtney asked, looking suddenly worried. The three other women also looked concerned.

"Isn't that where Bill and Hillary Clinton live?" Roger asked.

"They have a home there, yes, but I don't think they actually live there much."

All four editorial board members looked at him with pleading eyes. Roger paused for a moment as he thought through the possible consequences of adding Nemo to the water in this suburb of New York City. Then his face slowly broke into a mischievous grin. "It'll move them both to the left on the male-female scale," he said. "It may stop Bill's philandering, for a month at least, and it should soften up Hillary. She might even enjoy being more of a girly-girl."

The Alphabet Soup suddenly appeared visibly to relax and devolved into nervous laughter. "We might just save them from themselves." Deedee quipped. "When can we start?"

"Very soon." Roger said, as he stood up. "But you understand that the Nemo effect is not permanent. In fact, it will go the other way for awhile after the month is over. It should shake things up in Chapaqua." Roger grinned and walked around the table, shaking everyone's hand. "I'll need to do a bit of research on the Chappaqua water system, but we can do this thing. It will make for an interesting experiment."

Courtney led him out and said goodbye at the office door. Before pressing the button for the elevator in the hallway, Roger pulled out his cellphone. He could hardly contain his elation as he typed out and sent a text message to Mason: "We did it! We stopped the publication."

* * * *

As Courtney walked Roger from the conference room to the door, she felt something stirring within her that she couldn't identify. She brushed it off as a wasteful emotion, but it briefly improved her mood. She was surprised to feel a modest pang of joy. At the door she looked Roger in the eye, shook his hand again, and thanked him warmly for coming. She then returned to her waiting board members in the conference room.

"Well, that's that," she said almost jovially as she walked into the room. "I'll pull the article. But what do we have to replace it? Anyone have an idea?"

"I have it. Why don't we go with my original idea?" pressed Bailey. "Jennifer Aniston cheating on Brad Pitt. We demonstrate that infidelity is doable for women who want to scratch an itch. What's good for the gander is good for the goose."

"Yes, but *her* goose was cooked remember," Deedee noted. "Brad Pitt left her."

"Plus we women have our standards to uphold," Ashley added. "We shouldn't be wading into that slime pit along with men."

"I agree. The story's trashy," Deedee said with finality. "We're not that desperate as a magazine. Not yet anyway."

"Okay. How about this," Courtney began. "I've been thinking for some time now about doing a series on rape. I have some preliminary ideas and I think I can flesh them out if I just start writing—."

The three other board members looked at her, startled. Courtney was certainly one who could write from personal experience but they never expected she would lay bare what had happened to her. "Whether we publish it or not, your writing about rape might be therapeutic," Deedee said sympathetically. "But you should be careful, Courtney. The scars are still there. Your writing may instead set you back."

"I don't think so. I should make a start at least, and see where this leads me."

"But the next issue is due to come out next week. You won't have enough time," Ashley argued.

"You're probably right," Courtney agreed. "Any other ideas?" She surveyed her board members but saw only blank faces. "Well there must be something out there we can use. I'll circle back with Veronica and see what she has up her sleeve."

"She's about to go on the cover of *Cosmo*," Ashley commented. "Not her picture; her article."

"Yes, and I got her up there," Courtney reminded the group. "She owes me."

"Sounds promising," Bailey said. "I like her stuff. She writes about her life in the gutter." She smirked. "That should spice up this magazine."

"A bit trashy is okay, but not *too* trashy," Deedee reminded everyone.

As the women stood and were walking out the office door after bidding each other goodbye, Courtney remarked casually, "I'm having second thoughts about killing the story. It could be the biggest news of the year, or maybe even a decade, and we're letting it slip right through our fingers." The three women stopped and stared at her, aghast. "I'm just *kidding*," she told them. "Jeesh."

When her board members left, Courtney went into her office and immediately phoned Veronica.

Ronnie picked up on the first ring. "Courtney, what a surprise. I was just going to call you," she said breathlessly.

"I'm thinking you owe me a story," Courtney got right to the reason she was reaching out. "Now that you're going to be breaking out of anonymity with your big article in *Cosmo* – an article which I placed for you, don't you forget – I want to be first in line to buy the very next article you write. We desperately need something to fill a hole in *Women Rising*, and we're going to publication *next week*."

"Really? Well that's serendipitous or something. That's why I was going to call. I just finished another story."

"You did? What's it about?"

"Well you remember that Ballzoff stuff he was taking that made him, uh, impotent?"

"Of course I do. That's what your article in *Cosmo* is all about."

"Yeah, well, he stopped taking it you know. And I figured things would get back to normal. One fuck a day like."

"It didn't? What happened? *Tell* me." Courtney checked herself. Surprisingly, she felt a sudden pang of prurient interest.

"Its like he bounced back and went right off the scale. He's horny all the time now. He can't get enough of me. He has to fuck me two or three times a day."

"Is that true? And you think that's because of the Nemo?"

"Definitely is. He said it must be a side effect or something. His biker gang friends all feel the same way. They're fucking like rabbits. Anyway, I wrote an article about this. I'm having the opposite problem from before. It's a wet dream."

Courtney was stunned. Her mind raced as she thought through the consequences of this new development. "Did you or any one of Billy's friends tell Dr. Thornwood?"

"Hell, no. Why would he care? I know how touchy you are about Ballzoff so I didn't mention that at all. I just wrote what it was like when your man wants desperately to fuck you. All the time. I found that it gives you tremendous *power*, provided you don't get raped, that is."

"That's *too* weird," Courtney said. "But it might work. You're article in *Cosmo* says your boyfriend doesn't want sex, and we publish another that says he wants too much. Both articles in the *same month*."

"You got it. Shows how good I can write. I'll be famous. You want to know the title?"

"Sure…" Courtney was already thinking how this new angle might rattle the cage of her magazine. It would spice it up, surely, and it might shed some new light on male-female relationships.

"'**MY BIKER BOYFRIEND IS MY PERSONAL SEX MACHINE**'."

Chapter 39

At eight-thirty the next morning Roger walked into the outer office of the Post Commander. Eve looked up from doing her nails and eyed him quizzically. "Well?" she asked. "How'd it go?"

"How did what go?" Roger didn't know whether Eve was supposed to know anything about Nemo.

"You know….that woman, the one who's going to spill the beans."

"Oh, well there's good news and bad news. I need to brief the General."

"You can tell me. I'll find out anyway."

"I'm sorry, I—."

"I know, I know. Top secret stuff." Eve shook her head in mock disgust. "The games you men play. We women aren't supposed to know anything but we do. How do you think we keep this country running? Nothing happens around here without us."

"I guess that's true, but—."

"Never mind. Let me tell the General you're here." Eve lifted the phone and buzzed him. "Dr. Thornwood is here to see you…" She looked up at Roger. "You may go right in." As Roger walked passed her desk she gave him a conspiratorial wink. "Good luck with him. He's kind of, uh… *changed* recently."

Roger opened the door and walked in. General Mason remained sitting at his desk but acknowledged Roger's presence by nodding and said, "Close the door and have a seat." Roger did so. "Thanks for the message, but how'd it go?"

He'd just heard that same question from Eve, Roger realized, so he gave much the same answer. "There's good news and a bit of bad news, Sir."

"I know the good news. You stopped that bitch, right?"

"Yes, Sir. She agreed to pull the article. She agreed not to disclose anything about Nemo. Ever."

The General visibly relaxed in his seat. "Good going, Thornwood. I knew you could do it. What did you have to do? Screw every one of those damn women on her editorial board?"

"Well, no, but—."

"I know, of course not. You wouldn't do such a thing. But I said you could offer to use Nemo on some rapist bastard. Is that what happened?"

"Yes, Sir. But it's not just one man. It's three."

"You agreed to three?"

"Yes, Sir. Three men for one month."

"A *month*?" The General eyed Roger critically as if Roger's brain had just blown a fuse.

"And there's more—."

"*More*?"

"They want seventy-five thousand dollars."

"Seventy-five thou—?"

"Yes, Sir. I assumed we could afford that, but there's a catch.—"

"A catch? There's a *catch*?"

"Yes. These guys get town water, so we'll have to put Nemo in the public water supply."

"The public…? *God damn it,* Thornwood. We can't do *that,* I was thinking you could do what you did to *me.* Go in there and install a water filter or something in those bastards' homes."

"Like I did to—? You… you know about that?"

"Of course I know, Thornwood. My wife told me you paid her a visit and I figured as much. At first I thought of having you arrested and court-martialed. But if what you did ever got out, it would be like airing our dirty laundry, not to mention endangering the secrecy of Nemo. And I figured, shit, you saved my marriage, so what the hell. We'll just keep it between ourselves. Right?" General Mason's eyes bore down on him and Roger withered. He felt like sinking through the bottom of his chair.

"Y...yes, Sir."

"So, what do we have here? Three men for a month? Right?"

"Yes, Sir."

"All right. The public water supply. Three public water supplies. There's a tremendous risk that someone will find out. We can't possibly do that."

"Only one, Sir. One water supply. All three men live in the same town."

"Three men? Same town? What town is that?"

"Chappaqua, New York."

General Mason looked at Roger in disbelief. "Chappaqua? You mean where the Clintons—?"

"Yes, Sir, the same."

"Well, I'll be damned." Roger watched as General Mason's face slowly morphed from an angry scowl into an expression of wonder and, for the first time he'd ever seen it, an actual smile. "We can keep this a secret, right?"

"Yes, Sir. We did in Aleppo."

"Well, that's a hoot. I *like* that idea."

The General's intercom buzzed and he pressed a button on his desk. "Eve, I'm in the middle of something. What do you want?"

Eve's voice came loudly over the speaker, "The Chairman of the Joint Chiefs is on the phone, Sir."

"Oh, well that's different. Put him on." His phone beeped and General Mason lifted the receiver. "General Mason speaking…Yes, the problem has been contained, Sir…My goodness, really?" The General listened for what seemed to Roger to be several minutes and then the General said, "Very good Sir. Understood. We'll be there. Fifteen hundred hours… Thank you."

General Mason hung up and stared at Roger with a dazed look. After a moment to process what he had just heard, he reported, "The President would like to meet us at three o'clock this afternoon and thank us for what we've done. Nemo is starting to do a job for us over there in Aleppo. It seems no one knows you put it in the water."

Chapter 40

The Chairman of the Joint Chiefs of Staff, General Thomas Mason and Dr. Roger Thornwood waited in an anteroom of the White House and, at the appointed hour, were ushered in to see the President. Roger felt as if he didn't belong with these other dignitaries and was merely along for the ride, but he told himself he should try and enjoy the experience as much as he could. He was dressed in his dark Sunday suit, which he wore only to weddings and funerals, and had picked out his best blue and red striped tie to go with his white dress shirt. He looked like he belonged and that's all that mattered, he thought. Anyway he didn't need to say anything, so that made it easier.

The POTUS welcomed them and shook each person's hand, in turn, starting with the Chairman. A photographer was present in the Oval Office and unobtrusively took pictures during the first five minutes or so that they were there. Roger could not help thinking that the experience was surreal. He was in the office and the presence of the most powerful man in the world; he was alive and would be able tell about it. Wow!

When it was his turn to take the President's proffered hand, the President paused in his welcome routine to look at Roger warmly, saying, "So it was you who went over there and installed your new weapon in the water. That was very brave, Dr. Thornwood. Our country owes you a lot."

"Thank you, Mr. President," Roger managed to mumble. He had heard that very same phrase many times on radio and television, but it felt strange to say it.

"More than that, Dr. Thornwood. You may just have come up with the right stuff that can end this conflict we're having in the Middle East...maybe even the conflict between the Israelis and Palestinians, although that will probably take a little longer. But before I explain what has happened over there, I want to take a minute and present an award."

The President then turned to General Mason and said, "General, I told you that if this new weapon turns out to be effective, you'd be first in line for a promotion. In behalf of the United States Army, the Chairman of the Joint Chiefs and I have the distinct honor and pleasure to present you with this new star as a symbol of your commission as Major General."

The Chairman handed the President a small package containing two sets of two stars, one set for each shoulder. The President took the package and presented it to General Mason with his left hand while he shook the General's hand with his right. It looked like General Mason's knees would buckle beneath him. It was his turn to mumble, "Thank you, Mr. President."

"As you know," the President said, "we normally ask our officers to have their spouses join them when we make such an important award, but you'll understand why we didn't do that in this case when you hear what I have to say. The entire Project Nemow must be kept under the strictest secrecy. Not even our wives are to know about this program."

The President then stepped back and motioned to the two facing couches that formed a small comfortable social area away from his imposing power desk. This was a signal for the photographer to leave the room and he quietly did so. "Have a seat here, gentlemen, and I would like to say a few words about Nemow." General Mason and Roger instinctively took the couch on the left while the President and Chairman of the Joint Chiefs sat down on the right one, facing them. Roger still felt uncomfortable with the experience he was having, but he mentally told himself to take it all in and record it in his memory so he could relive and savor it later, as many times as he wished. He was in the Oval Office sitting on a couch right opposite to the *President*.

"I have been receiving reports from our men on the ground in Syria," the President began. His voice was even in tone and didn't reveal or anticipate at all what he was going to say. Roger couldn't help noticing he was a master at masking his thoughts. You were either born with this ability or you acquired it over time if you were going to succeed in politics, Roger assumed.

"Some strange things are occurring in Aleppo," the President continued. "Peace seems to have broken out. No one can explain it, but everyone in that city is suddenly playing by the rules. Instead of fighting they are actually talking to one another.

"That's not to say that it's *Kumbayah* over there. The Assad regime is still turning the screws and denying the people their basic right to a free society, but the rebels appear to be realizing that dying for their cause is counter-productive. By dying they have not advanced their cause one iota so it appears they may have turned a corner. They are trying peaceful resistance and non-violent civil disobedience, like Mahatma Gandhi or Martin Luther King, and that strategy seems to be working. They are gaining the understanding and the sympathy of the local media. And best of all, the idea seems to be spreading. The brave folks in Aleppo are becoming a model for people in other cities.

"Now the four of us in this room know why this is happening, and I'd like it to continue. But we would be doing so at great risk. If the media ever found out that we spiked the water over there, that would surely sink our administration and other countries not so friendly to the United States would have a field day. The reputation of America as a guardian of the free world would be forever tarnished. No one wants their food adulterated, much less their water.

"So as far as the public is concerned, Nemow doesn't exist. Not now; not for the foreseeable future; possibly not ever. Do you understand me?" The Chairman, the Major General and Roger all nodded their heads in the affirmative. "We can't breathe a word of this to anyone: not to our closest colleagues or even our spouses. We must keep it under wraps until Nemow has been deployed in the battlefield for so long that no one can say there is any conceivable downside to using it.

"You'd think if we discovered the fountain of youth or the elixir of life, no one could possibly complain. But they would and they do. And since the buck stops right here in this office, it would be all my fault. I'd be vilified in the press, and for sure some crazy nut would try to shoot me, thinking he had justification."

The President stood up and assumed an erect, presidential posture. Roger and the other two men jumped up as well. "I'm not afraid, you understand. I just wanted to explain to you how I see this. I'm willing to take the risk of putting Nemow in the water but you have to do it very, very carefully so it remains a secret. We can do a lot of good if this miracle stuff you've come up with works as well as it appears to be working now.

We can really bring about a change, both at the level of the ordinary citizen and on a global scale. Just think of what we could have done about dictators like Saddam Hussein, for example.

"If we'd had Nemow way back in 1935 we might even have avoided World War II and the Holocaust for heaven's sake.

"And for this, we have you to thank, Dr. Thornwood. You have made it possible for us to create a better world." The President locked eyes with Roger but, instead of enjoying the moment, Roger felt even more uncomfortable.

It was clear that the meeting was over. The Chairman and General Mason started to leave but Roger hesitated. The President noticed this and shot him an inquiring look. "Did you want to tell me something?" he asked.

Roger had trouble getting his mouth to move because of what he felt was a shining light in front of him. He began to mumble something no one could hear. "Dr. Thornwood? Are you all right?" the President seemed suddenly concerned.

"Ye...yes, Sir," Roger stammered. "I...I just wanted to say that we need to try Nemo out in a town here in the U.S. Would that be okay with you?" Roger surprised himself he was able to ask that, but realized instantly that his diction left something to be desired.

Roger became semi-aware of General Mason who shot him a fierce look that screamed "*Stop.*"

"A town? Here in the United States?" the President asked.

"Yes, Sir."

"What town? And why?"

"It would be a way to closely monitor the effects on both men *and* women," Roger heard himself saying, not knowing what else to give as a reason. "We need to study this 'miracle stuff' as you call it, a bit more so that we fully understand the biological mechanism at work. We are tinkering with the basic mammalian constructs and—."

"I don't need to know the details," the President interrupted Roger, yet intensely interested and trying to get quickly to the point. "What town do you have in mind?"

"Chappaqua, New York."

The President did a double take, and then burst into laughter. "That's where the *Clintons* live."

"I'm afraid so."

"Are you sure you can keep this experiment completely under wraps?"

"Absolutely, Mr. President. No one will know."

"Then I say go with it," The President replied mischievously. "If Nemo works on them, we might try using it Syria again. This time on Syrian President Bashar al-Assad."

Chapter 41

Courtney was in her office making the last editing touches to Veronica's article when her phone rang. She didn't recognize the number but she picked up anyway.

"Hi," a male voice said. "I've been meaning to call you for weeks. It's been hectic."

"And you are?"

"George. George Cleary. The one who sent you that check?"

"Oh, I'm so sorry. I didn't recognize your voice. George how *are* you?"

"I've been fine but, frankly, I've had to dodge some financial bullets. The market's been uppity lately. That often happens in October for some reason."

"You still a millionaire?"

"Billionaire, but yes, I'm okay. Can't say the same for some other guys though. Where there are winners there have to be losers. That's the game we play."

"I'm happy for you." Courtney's sarcasm letting slip a negative attitude about what he did for a living.

"I've been meaning to ask you for the longest time," he continued, ignoring the dig. "How about dinner together?"

"I hope you're not asking me out on a date, because if so—."

"No, no." George didn't let Courtney finish the sentence. "I just want to get to know you. You're a fascinating woman, in case you don't know."

"Well, I'm not sure, George. I don't want you to get the wrong idea. I'm not exactly dating material."

"That can change, you know. Give life a chance."

"You think one dinner is going to make a difference?"

"One small step for a man—," George said, paraphrasing Neil Armstrong. "Unless you want to make a giant leap and spend the weekend with me."

"No, I couldn't ever do that."

"Why not? Vermont is great this time of year. They say the fall foliage up there is the best it's ever been."

"I don't know, George. Right now I'm focused on getting the magazine out the door and into the hands of my readers."

"I almost forgot. This is the big one, right? The one where you go public with that story about the bioweapon?"

Courtney suddenly realized she hadn't told George what happened to that story. He had paid the seventy-five thousand dollars needed to pay Billy and also a lot more, which she had poured into the magazine to pay debts and solicit subscribers and advertisers, but in her haste to prepare the October issue for publication she had failed to inform him of her editorial board's decision to scuttle the article.

"I'm sorry, What did you say about Vermont?"

"The fall foliage. It's in full—."

"I've always wanted to go to Vermont in the fall." Courtney blurted out, seemingly gushing. She was thinking that maybe, just maybe, she could explain to George what had happened during a peaceful walk in the woods. That way only she and the birds would hear his angry screaming.

"Really?"

"Yes, really, but I never seem to have the time, or the money, to go way up there and stay overnight." Courtney was being honest now, but she didn't relish spending the night with a *man*, even this man who had been so kind and generous to her.

After a beat, George replied, "Hmmm, your magazine's coming out next week. You can take a break before you have to start on the next issue, right?"

"Yes, but—."

"You owe it to yourself."

"I know, but—."

"When do you publish?"

"We're like *Time Magazine*. We finish putting the finishing touches on it on a Friday afternoon and *Women Rising* comes out over the weekend with Monday's date. Only once a month though. We're not a weekly magazine, *yet*."

"Will you be finished by five on Friday?"

"We have to. I need to press the button on the computer and send the magazine to the printer by five."

"All right then. Bring a pair of jeans and sneakers, and pack your toothbrush. I'll have a limo waiting for you on the street outside your building at five. Leave the rest to me."

"Are you…sure?"

"Absolutely. Allow me to be your guide for the weekend."

"I don't know what you mean by 'guide,' but I'll accept." When she finally put down the receiver after she and George said their goodbyes, she couldn't help thinking, "Oh my God. What have I done?" The phone call had whizzed along so fast she hadn't had time to think. Now she was committed to spend the weekend with a *man*? A man she hardly knew. In fact, the very man who stood and watched as those other men—.

She had to phone George back and call this whole thing off. *No.* He was her benefactor and had been a perfect gentleman up to now. He must still feel guilty for not rescuing her from her rapists. Yes, she was sure about that. That's why he gave her the million dollars, right? No man would ever give it up without some good reason like that. No, she would tell her friends she was going with him to Vermont. If anything happened, at least they would know where she went.

She lifted the receiver again and speed-dialed Deedee's number. Deedee picked up on the first ring.

"How's Ronnie's article about life in the gutter?" Deedee asked without so much as saying 'hello'.

"It's actually pretty good," Courtney admitted. "Better than I expected. It asks the question, what would we women do without men?"

"Same thing we always do. We run the show. Only men won't steal the credit for our creativity and hard work."

"Her point was a bit more complicated than that, but that's not why I called. I just want to tell you, I'm leaving for Vermont on Friday evening, with George."

There was a pause before Deedee answered. "I'm sorry, Courtney. Did I hear you right? You're spending the weekend in Vermont with *George*. George Cleary, the billionaire?"

"Yes, the magazine will be put to bed by Friday evening, so I thought—."

"But with *George*?"

"Yes, what's wrong with that?"

"He's a *man*. Have you ever spent the weekend with a man before?"

"No, but—."

"You know what this means? He'll expect…you know, payback."

"I don't think so. Unless proven otherwise, I'll assume he's a gentleman."

"There is no such thing as a gentleman when it comes to men's urges. You should know that more than anyone, my dear sister. *Think of what you've been through.*"

"I know, I know. But that was so many years ago. I'm trying to get over it as best I can."

"I wish I could come along and be your guardian angel, but I can't. You'll have to go it alone. You have no idea what might happen. Are you… prepared?"

"You mean am I on the pill? Of course not."

"No, I mean you'll need to be absolutely firm and just say '*no.*' Can you do that?"

"I think so. You know me. Tough as nails."

"Where are you staying?"

"I don't know."

"Where in God's name are you going?"

"I don't know."

"How are you going to get there?

"I don't know."

"*What*? Well, then God help you. You'll have your cellphone with you?"

"Yes, I will. I'll make sure of that."

"All right. Call me the instant things get out of hand. And believe me, they will. Promise me you'll call."

"All right, I promise to call."

"Good. I'll alert the rest of the Alphabet Soup. We're all there for you, Courtney."

"Thank you, Deedee. All I can say is that you and my dear Alphabet Soup are a great comfort to me. When I get back I'll tell all of you what happened," Courtney said, and then added cryptically, "Hopefully *nothing*."

"Goodbye and good luck, my dear friend. I hope you have a *wonderful* time in Vermont."

Chapter 42

The next Friday Courtney sat in her office reviewing the pages of her magazine one last time. As she scanned through, she could not help smiling to herself; it was a work of art that was as beautiful as it was persuasive of her cause. Women needed to rise up and seize this moment in the United States of America. They had an opportunity to remove their shackles, encrusted as they were with years of history, and go about their daily lives, free and filled with hope, in full equality with men.

Ronnie's second article about her biker boyfriend fit right in. If you want a friend, it should make no difference whether the person is male or female; if you want a stud muffin, you should be able to get one and enjoy that too without being called a "slut."

At five minutes to five, Courtney pressed the button on her computer and sent the entire magazine, page by page, zinging through the Internet to a first vendor who printed ten thousand copies on glossy paper, bound and bundled it, and then loaded it on a truck for delivery to a second vendor who applied labels, mailed copies to subscribers and delivered packages of five, ten and fifteen copies each to newsstands, hotels and any other outlets that requested it. Satisfied that this month's effort was put to bed, she let her trusty computer go to sleep, grabbed her valise and switched out the light as she walked out the office door. She was ready for her weekend in Vermont.

Courtney stood an unusually long time in front of the elevator due to the rush of clerical workers heading home. She stared blankly at the door, trying to imagine what George had planned. The anticipation excited her senses but, at the same time, she was not entirely comfortable not knowing what he had in store. She hadn't even been on a date with a man since her college years, and now she was spending an entire weekend with the very man who had—. She quickly pushed that horrible image out of her mind.

She had called George back to ask him what clothes to bring, but he had not been fully forthcoming. "Just bring what you would wear around the house," he'd said, "and maybe a jacket in case it gets cold at night."

Of course she packed a bit more than that, but she had taken George at his word and made choices as if she were going for an overnight in the country with a female friend.

The elevator arrived, half filled with several young women and two men in suits, and she stepped in, rolling her bag over the threshold sufficiently so that the doors could close behind her. When they reached the lobby Courtney walked out to the street and looked for George. He was nowhere in sight. She felt annoyed as she stood there, holding the handle of her small suitcase as people rushed by on their way to wherever they needed to go to pursue their busy lives.

"Courtney Stillwell?" She heard a male voice and looked about, at first not knowing who spoke. Then she noticed a tall young man with a black suit and black cap, looking at her inquiringly.

"I'm Courtney."

The man beamed a warm smile and stood at attention. "I'm your driver. Call me 'Isaac.' George Cleary asked me to pick you up and take you to Teterboro."

"Take me where?"

"Teterboro Airport in New Jersey. That's where he keeps his airplane."

"An airplane?"

"Yes, it's a twin engine Beechcraft. Seats 10. He flies it himself."

"Oh."

"May I take your bag?" Isaac nodded toward the suitcase Courtney was holding.

"Yes, of course." Courtney let go of the suitcase and Isaac briskly hoisted it to his shoulder.

"Follow me," he said, walking between the parked cars to a black limousine, double- parked on the street. He put the suitcase down and opened the rear door for Courtney. She climbed in as gracefully as she could, but not without nearly bumping her head. She awkwardly grabbed a strap that dangled from inside the door jam and held on tight as she eased herself in.

Isaac carefully closed the passenger door and stepped to the rear. Courtney heard him open the trunk, place the suitcase inside and close it again. He then came around the opposite side and climbed into the driver's seat. He placed his cap on the front passenger seat and looked in the rear view mirror to check Courtney. "All set?" he asked.

"Yes, thank you."

"Then here we go."

Isaac drove across town to the West Side Highway and joined the stop-and-go traffic heading north. Courtney asked Isaac some brief questions, but it was clear that he preferred to devote his full attention to driving. Courtney eventually fell silent and sat comfortably in the rear, lost in her own thoughts. She learned from her few questions that Isaac worked exclusively for George as his personal driver and "man Friday," and he also doubled as his personal trainer and security guard, although security was not considered to be of much concern. George's business was confidential so no member of the public knew enough to be a threat. George took great pains also to keep his competitors in the dark about his activities while he surreptitiously picked their pockets.

When they arrived at the airport, Isaac drove up to a gate and held out his pass. The guard obviously recognized him and waved him through without examining it, and Isaac proceeded along a side road past some buildings and onto the tarmac. Courtney's curiosity peaked as they headed past several tethered aircraft and Isaac stopped close to one of the sleeker ones with two engines and two large propellers. Standing next to it, smiling broadly, was George.

"Just a moment, Miss Stillwell," Isaac said as he jumped out, grabbing his hat. He moved swiftly around to the right side of the car to open Courtney's door. Courtney had the feeling of being some sort of celebrity as she placed one foot then the other on the ground and stood, with Isaac waiting at attention and George coming forward to welcome her.

"It's wonderful to see you," George said, lightly embracing her by the shoulders while gently kissing her on the cheek. "I have a very special weekend planned for us."

Isaac retrieved Courtney's bag from the trunk and carried it over to the aircraft.

"Just leave it right there, Isaac. Thank you. I'll let you know our ETA on Sunday evening. You're free to go now. As of this moment, you're on your own time."

"Very good, Sir," replied Isaac. "Nice meeting you, Miss Stillwell." He tipped his hat and returned to the car. Courtney watched as he drove away leaving her alone on the tarmac, except for George and one large airplane.

George took her bag and pointed toward the narrow stairs that led up to an open side door of the aircraft. "Let me go first if I may. Just follow me." He walked ahead and carried the bag up the steps into the aircraft. "We have a special hold for baggage, but it's quicker to just place it under one of the seats." Courtney climbed the steps behind him and watched as he dropped the bag between two passenger seats and then returned to offer her a hand. "Come on in. If it's all right with you, I'd like you to sit in the cockpit with me."

Courtney's eyes opened wide as she looked forward and saw all the colorful instruments arrayed in the flight deck. "Are you sure it's okay?"

"It's not only okay, I want you to help me fly this thing. You sit right there and get comfortable. I'll close the side door." George pressed a button on the wall, and the door, with the steps on one side, pivoted upward about its hinge at the base of the cabin and locked itself closed with a "thunk." He then came forward, slid into the left seat of the cockpit and buckled himself in. Noticing this, Courtney found her seat belt and did the same.

"Welcome to my world," he said. "At least some of it anyway. I love this plane."

Although overwhelmed, sitting in the lap of technology, Courtney kept her composure and said, "Seems nice," with a smile.

"I've done the walk-around already and everything is ship-shape. So let's get started."

George looked out the window to the right as he pressed a button, causing the left engine propeller to rotate. The engine caught and the propeller spun up, becoming quickly a circular blur. George then looked right and repeated the process with the right engine. Courtney felt the aircraft vibrating comfortably beneath her, in tune with its two humming engines.

George reached back and took down a headset from the wall behind him. Holding it he turned to Courtney and spoke loudly above the engine noise. "There's a headset for you too if you'd like to use it. That way you can hear the chatter with the controllers and it will be easier to talk to each other." Courtney followed his lead, unhooking the headset, pulling it over her head to cover her ears and adjusting the pencil microphone. Immediately she could hear someone talking rapidly in the background. It was a new world for her: a strange one she had never experienced before.

She heard George's voice through the headset although she could barely see his lips moving behind his microphone. "This is November Alpha seven-two-three-one at Westair. Ready for taxi."

Courtney heard a series of replies, words she barely understood, something about atmospheric conditions, and then a further exchange with the ground control.

"Two-three-one take ramp two-A to runway six."

"Two-three-one."

George placed his hand on the dual throttles and moved them slowly forward, causing the engines to rev slightly. The aircraft hesitated at first and then began to roll. Courtney heard continued chatter in her headset but it was all mumbo-jumbo so she ignored it. George guided the craft to the runway and braked short of the black and white stripes. Holding the brakes fast, he looked at the gauges while doing a brief engine run-up and made a final check of the wing surfaces while moving the hand controls. Courtney watched, amazed by the apparent complexity of this take-off procedure and the amount of knowledge a person needed to fly a plane.

"Two-three-one, take position and hold."

George revved the engines once more. The aircraft crept forward and lined up with the runway. A moment later the earphone voice barked, "Two-three-one, you're clear for take-off. Left turn out and then switch to ..." Courtney could not understand the rest.

George pressed the throttles all the way forward. Courtney silently grit her teeth. The engines roared and the propellers took hold. They literally gripped the air and pulled the plane down the runway. Within a matter of seconds, Courtney realized they were airborne and saw the ground fall away.

In the distance as they rose she could see New York spread out before her, the windows of the skyscrapers reflecting the evening sun with spots of gold here and there. The plane turned slightly left as she gazed out her side window in wonder. The panoramic view of the city was breathtaking.

Through her headphones Courtney heard George's voice, "So how do you like my favorite 'man-toy'?"

"I could get used to it," Courtney allowed herself to say, though a bit wistfully, still looking out the window as the gray and brown of The Bronx morphed into the green of Westchester County. Turning her attention back to George she asked, "By the way, where *are* we going?"

Chapter 43

"We're heading northeast to Lebanon, New Hampshire."

"I thought we were going to Vermont."

"We are, but we'll land in Lebanon. It's right near the Vermont border. From there we'll rent a car and drive west across a bridge over the Connecticut River that separates the two states."

"How long is our flight?"

"About an hour. If we drove up there, it would take four or five. We're flying right over the Friday evening traffic."

Courtney looked down and saw Interstate 84 clogged with cars and trucks heading east toward Hartford. The vehicles, so small from the air that they looked like colored ants, were bumper to bumper and hardly moving. She couldn't help feeling a pang of sympathy for the poor people down there, trying to get home or wherever they needed to go, creeping along on the clogged roads. She looked over at George but had the distinct impression he didn't share the feeling. Wound tight from the stress of her busy life, she began to let go.

"Time to navigate," he exclaimed enthusiastically. "Let me show you." He pressed some buttons on the glass window centered on the instrument panel in front of them and the image on the screen changed to a map. He typed in the letters L-E-B and the map highlighted the location of the airport. "It's like the navigator in your car, except much cooler. It tells you exactly where to fly in three dimensions: what azimuth, what altitude, and what areas to avoid. It's a lot easier than navigating used to be, back in the day when I learned to fly." He demonstrated the technology by pressing some more buttons on the screen and the map images changed, indicating the route to LEB.

Courtney tried her best to show an interest, but the whole situation – the plane, the trip to Vermont, the time she would spend with a man she didn't know very well at all – suddenly seemed strange to her and unreal. To make small talk, she agreed that finding their way seemed easy, but her odd mood persisted until George asked her to fly. From that moment on her dark clouds lifted.

"Our heading to Lebanon is zero two-six. Watch, I'll turn a slight right and line us up with this angle on the compass." George banked right for a moment and leveled out. "We're cruising at one hundred seventy-five knots at fifty-five hundred feet." He pointed to the altimeter on the instrument panel. "Now, take the controls and fly the heading, straight and level."

"*Me?*"

"There's no one else here. Just you and me."

"I mean, I don't know how to fly."

"I'll teach you. It's easy as one-two-three."

"So many numbers. I'm not sure I can."

"Grab hold of your controller and I'll let go."

Courtney put her hands on what looked to her like a piece of a steering wheel but was afraid to move it.

"Now pull back." Courtney did so and the plane nosed up abruptly. "Not so much." Courtney pushed on the wheel and the plane lurched downward. "Too far forward." Courtney immediately put her hands up, letting go of her wheel. George grabbed his controller and leveled the aircraft. "Small movements like this." George demonstrated. Courtney tried again, this time pulling back on the control, very slowly and gingerly, before letting it move back to its normal position. The aircraft responded by nosing up slightly and then leveling off. Courtney couldn't help smiling a little. She looked at George for approval. "Now turn right," he said, "*slowly.*" Courtney did so, and the aircraft banked to the right. "Straighten it out. This is not like a car; you don't have to keep turning." Courtney evened the controls but the aircraft stayed in a banking turn. "See what I mean? Now rotate to the left. Not too much." The plane leveled off and Courtney felt proud of herself. She was beginning to feel an elation she had never experienced before. She felt she could *fly*.

"I think you've got it," George said encouragingly. "Now you can have a little fun. Fly any which way you want."

Courtney looked out through the windshield and focused on the horizon. She pulled back and went up. She pressed forward and went down and then leveled off. She banked to the right and banked to the left. She could sense her natural fears evaporating to the point where she imagined she was a bird on the wing. George was sitting right next to her and wouldn't let anything bad happen, right? She began to throw caution to the wind and make bolder maneuvers in the sky. She forgot where she was and where she was going. She became almost giddy with this new kind of freedom.

For the next half hour Courtney soared in the sky. She forgot about George; she forgot about *Women Rising* and her many deadlines; she lost herself to the feeling of flying.

She returned reluctantly to reality when she heard George call over the radio, "Lebanon Tower this is November Alpha seven-two-three-one. Ten miles out to the southwest. Request permission to land.

* * * *

Roger sat with Jim and his three Navy SEALs in an office at the Pentagon in Arlington, Virginia. They had spent several hours working out how best to infiltrate the Highway and Water Department in the Department of Public Works in the Town of New Castle in New York State. They needed detailed plans of the water facility for Chappaqua, one of the hamlets in New Castle, and approached the problem in the same meticulous way they had done for the city of Aleppo in Syria. If they could secretly and successfully install Nemo in that water facility, they could certainly do so at a site in the U.S. where no terrorism was expected. Trouble was, such site plans were nowhere to be found, even using their sophisticated technology for snooping the Internet.

"We'll have to break into the office of the Water Department," Jim said. "They must have those plans on file there somewhere."

The other SEALs looked at each other and grinned. This was just the kind of clandestine caper they had signed up for but never got to do. Their leader, Jim, had agreed to this task to help Roger and, as before, the existence of Nemo had to remain Top Secret. The SEALs were definitely operating outside their military authorization, which was always on foreign soil, but they rationized that their actions were required to maintain the circle of confidentiality. Only those who already knew about Nemo were permitted knowledge of this effort to salt the water supply.

"No need to carry any guns this time," Roger informed them. "We're not going into enemy territory or anything."

"We always carry guns when we're on a mission," Jim replied. "You never know when you might need them for self-defense."

"But we'll be trespassers. We'll be the bad guys. You can't shoot people for trying to protect their own water system."

When their plan was finally hatched and the precise timing worked out, they went their separate ways but agreed to meet the following evening at APG. From there they would drive north to Chappaqua under the cover of darkness in two black Chevy vans, bringing with them a large supply of Nemo.

Roger was not looking forward to executing the plan. If anything went wrong there would be hell to pay. He slept fitfully that night and was not himself all day, worried about how the coming night would play out.

At nine o'clock in the evening, the SEALs picked up Roger and loaded two large plastic containers with the concentrated Nemo powder. They then drove north on the Jersey Turnpike and, after crossing the George Washington Bridge to New York City, dropped down to the West Side Highway going north. This road merged into the Saw Mill River Parkway and took them directly to Chappaqua.

Turning off the Parkway at the Chappaqua exit, the two vans proceeded straight ahead off the ramp onto Hunts Lane. A short time later they pulled up in front of the address, number 280: the location of the Department of Public Works. No lights were visible. They pulled to the right into a parking slot.

"Let's roll." Jim commanded and climbed out of the driver's seat of the lead van. Roger, riding shotgun, did likewise. Dressed all in black and wearing black face masks, looking for all the world like the ISIS Terrorist from Hell, 'Jihadi John,' they moved stealthily toward the back of the building.

Chapter 44

The sun had recently descended below the horizon in front of them as George drove west on Interstate 89 over the Vietnam Veterans Memorial Bridge toward Vermont. The clouds above reflected golden sunlight forming a panoramic painted sky. Illuminated by the evening sunset, the leaves of the trees on the bank of the Connecticut River glowed bright yellow and orange with remaining patches of green here and there.

After arranging with the FBO at Lebanon Airport to take care of the plane, George had rented an SUV and loaded their bags in the rear hatch. Courtney had not said very much at all since that experience of flying, allowing the spell to linger in her memory, but she felt glad to be safely grounded now. She rode in the front passenger seat and admired nature's final curtain call of the season before ordering the leaves to fall from the deciduous trees in preparation for winter.

George took the ramp off the superhighway at Quechee and followed Route 4 south for several miles into the town of Woodstock. A quintessential New England town with red brick buildings with white trim, Woodstock was just beginning to turn on its streetlights as darkness fell. George drove around the village green and pulled up in front of the Woodstock Inn, a delightfully large, white clapboard, colonial building with black shutters on its many windows. "We're finally here." he said excitedly. "Let's go check in. I've reserved two rooms."

Hearing this, Courtney felt relieved she would not have to insist on her own room. George had done the gentlemanly thing and arranged for a private room in advance. It boded well for a cordial relationship with George as a friend that would allow her to enjoy her brief visit to Vermont. The last thing she wanted was for this weekend to turn into a nightmare of wrangling over where she would sleep.

In fact, George could not have chosen a nicer place to stay. The Inn was as lovely on the inside as it appeared on the outside, and the service was friendly, yet with a touch of local reserve. Courtney felt comfortable with this provincial New England custom, thinking she could keep a respectful distance from the people around her, including her companion

George. As they rode up to their rooms in the elevator, George asked her to meet him in the lobby at eight-thirty, explaining he had previously made a reservation for dinner at a nearby restaurant.

Courtney hurried to make ready for dinner. She showered, taking care not to wet her hair, and donned the one dress she had brought with her. Doing her best to look presentable in the time allotted, she combed out her hair and put on her favorite lipstick. The color almost matched her hair: strawberry blonde.

Promptly at eight-thirty she rode the elevator down to the lobby. She had almost forgotten to be nervous about venturing out alone with a man: her first since that horrible night so many years ago. What made this a particular milestone for her was that she was having dinner with George.

George stood waiting and smiled as he came over to her. "You look lovely," he said with a slight bow of the head. "I am so happy you could come with me this weekend. I haven't made any plans, really, except for dinner tonight. We can talk about that over breakfast in the morning. For now let's walk just a few blocks to one of the best restaurants in all of Vermont. It's called the 'Prince and the Pauper'."

Courtney took George's arm and they set out. There was a chill in the evening air, but the night was still pleasant as they strode along past some government buildings on Court Street, crossed over the village green, walked a half a block to the right on Main Street and took a left on Elm. On the sidewalk ahead she saw a pole with a colorful sign on top that read:

The Prince
& The Pauper
Fine Food & Spirits

In the center of the sign was the picture of a table being served by a Renaissance-style waiter. There was a prince on the left and a pauper on the right having dinner together. That's appropriate for me, Courtney thought somewhat amused. Compared to George, I'm certainly a pauper.

The concierge led George and Courtney to a table for two by a window. It had a clean white tablecloth, a silver service and crystal glasses. A young waitress in colonial dress with a white cap lit a candle on the table and poured ice water into two of the four glasses. "I'm Bessy," she said. I'll be serving you this evening. Can I get you something to drink?"

Courtney looked at George for a cue and George asked her, "Would you like wine?"

"A glass of white would be nice," Courtney replied.

Bessy waited while George quickly examined the wine list and selected a German Riesling.

Bessy left and they examined their menus. After some discussion they decided they both liked the same selection: a country pate for an appetizer and a rack of lamb for an entrée, with spinach, mushrooms, puff pastry and sauce Bordelaise.

Bessy returned with the bottle of wine and poured George a small amount to taste before half-filling the remaining two glasses. "You're going to like this wine," George said to Courtney and then placed their order for dinner.

"Very good, Sir," Bessy commented. "That's our specialty of the house."

When she left, George raised his glass. "To your magazine," he said. "May *Women Rising* change the world as we know it."

Courtney followed suit. "Let's drink to that, and to women everywhere." She took a long sip of the wine. It tasted somewhat sour but it helped her to relax as she sat there facing her wealthy patron. "George, I've been meaning to tell you about what's happening at the magazine. Is now a good time?"

"Of course. I'm anxious to hear. I think you are on to something. Something very important that needs to be said."

"Well, it's like this," Courtney said, a bit hesitantly. She didn't know quite how to tell him what happened to the article about Nemo. She had asked George for his money to help her research the story, and he had given her much more than she asked for, but now she had traded her right to publish it for…for what? For adding Nemo to the water in Chappaqua?

She decided not to tell him that. Anyway, she was sworn to keep that a deep dark secret.

"I met with our editorial board," she began. "We decided, for reasons of national security, not to publish the article. I'm sorry." There goes a million dollars, she thought to herself. He's going to stop the funding and he'll ask me to pay back the money I spent already. What am I to do? She grit her teeth and waited for his wrathful boot to drop.

"You didn't publish a word about it?"

"No, we didn't," Courtney admitted. "We thought it best—."

"Well, that's *good*," George responded quickly. "You did the right thing. You could have damaged the reputation of our country as the law-abiding leader of the free world."

"Wa…wait a minute. That's what you think?"

"Yes, and you could have also ended up with a very expensive lawsuit. It could have ruined your magazine."

"You thought that?"

"Yes, I was concerned about you, believe me."

"Then why did you give me the money?"

"There were two reasons. First I wanted to give you a chance to make a reasoned decision about this. Use your own judgment, free from any monetary restrictions."

"Really? You mean you gave me the money as some sort of a test?"

"You can look at it that way if you want to. I would rather you consider it a gift to give you more opportunities. Anyway, if it was a test you passed with flying colors."

"Okay, so what's the second reason?"

"Second reason?"

"Why you gave me the money."

"Oh, well, this is really the main reason. I'm intrigued by you. You're one heck of a woman, and I want to get to know you better."

Chapter 45

"You're kidding of course; but I want you to know, I've already used a good quarter of the money so you can't get it back."

"It's a business expense. I don't want it back. I just want you to use it wisely. You made a good judgment call not publishing that article."

Courtney didn't let on that she probably would have published the article had Roger not offered to infuse the water system of Chappaqua, New York, with a dose of Nemo. "Whew. I guess I dodged that bullet. It's a good thing you're rich."

"You have no idea."

Courtney took another sip of the wine and asked, "Just how *do* you make your money?"

"I suck it out of the stock market."

"How much do you make doing that?"

"A million dollars a day roughly. Sometimes more, sometimes less, but that's about the average."

Courtney was holding her wine glass and almost dropped it. Instead she took another sip of wine to stall for time while she got her head around that amount of money. It felt warm going down and tasted better this time. "Uh, a million... So it only took a day to earn the money you gave me."

"Invested."

"Invested? But you never asked for any stock in my company."

"I invested in *you*."

"Me? You invested in... Now wait just a *minute*."

"I didn't mean it that way. I believe in your enterprise, because you own it and make the decisions."

Courtney looked at George critically, wondering if he really meant what he just said. He looked sincere enough that she let the thought pass. In fact, with his dark hair and horn-rimmed glasses she felt he could almost be considered handsome.

After a beat she replied, "Okay, I'll accept that, for now. But tell me: How do you manage to suck all that money out of the market? And why doesn't everyone do that?"

"Because they can't. They don't have the equipment or the software. I've got a system that cost me some big bucks to give me an edge."

"Where does the money you get come from?"

"It comes from other people of course. But they don't know I'm picking their pockets. The market goes up and it goes down, but on the average it's up. Other people in the market are making a small profit so they think they're doing okay. They're not aware of the money I'm taking out. They'd be making a lot more if I, and other hedge fund managers like me, weren't skimming the cream."

"Doesn't that bother you? Taking other people's money I mean." Courtney couldn't help realizing she was taking *his* money which he had taken from the "other people."

"No. Not at all. It's legal."

"But is it fair to those other people?"

"'Fair'? I don't understand."

"You know, it's like you're cheating them."

"No I'm not. Like I said, it's legal."

"Well, I think there ought to be a law against it."

"That'll never happen."

"Oh? Why not?"

"We pay our Congressmen way too much money."

At this point Courtney realized she would get nowhere in trying to change George's point of view. She filed the colloquy away in the back of her mind and moved on to change the subject, although she still felt torn by the knowledge of where her million dollars had come from. It helped that Bessy arrived with the country pate' for two and a basket of fresh bread. Bessy placed them on the table between them saying, "You two are going to enjoy this. All the appetizers here are great, but this is my favorite." She picked up the wine bottle and filled the two glasses. "Would you like another bottle?"

George looked at Courtney inquiringly and followed her cue. "No, I think we'll pass for now." Courtney was not about to let herself go in the presence of this man. When Bessy left, she took another, this time small, sip of wine and continued the conversation.

"I liked flying your airplane."

"I'm glad. Fewer women fly than men."

"Why am I not surprised?"

"Women could become pilots if they wanted to. Apparently they don't."

"I'm sure there's a sexist reason in there somewhere."

"Now, Courtney, don't be so cynical. Not everything is a man's fault."

"You have to agree, men cause most of the world's problems."

"Men also try to fix the world's problems. Many men have died to keep our country free and preserve our way of life."

"They wouldn't have to fix the problems if men didn't create them."

George raised his hands in mock surrender. "Maybe we should talk about the weather."

Courtney raised her glass, and George followed her lead. "To Vermont," she said. "This is a lovely place. Thank you for asking me to come with you." Courtney took a draught and held the glass against her cheek to cool it. She was starting to feel a glow but didn't want to let George know she was not in complete control. "Why don't we try the pate'?"

Courtney and George spent the rest of the evening enjoying their dinner as well as each other's company. Courtney made an extra effort not to speak ill of men or of anything else and, for his part, George kept the conversation going by telling stories about flying, starting from when he first got his pilot's license to the time when he visited the Beechcraft factory in Kansas to watch his new airplane being built. There had been a number of close calls, especially at the beginning when he was low on the learning curve. George told his tales well and Courtney found herself fascinated by the lure of the sky. "Once you're up there and things get dicey, you can't just park at a curb until you can think things through or wait until help arrives."

One story that Courtney particularly liked concerned the unexpected arrival of inclement weather. George had been taking flying lessons in a small, two-seat Cessna at Suffolk County Airport at the eastern end of Long Island. After shooting a few, very shaky, touch-and-go landings, George's instructor, whose name was Arne, told him to land and taxi over to the terminal.

"After about a month of flying lessons, and about a hundred tries to land the plane, Arne told me to head for the terminal, I figured that was it. He was throwing in the towel. As a student pilot, I was just too dangerous for him. Instead, he told me I was ready to fly *solo* and he quickly jumped *out*. Before he bailed he told me I should fly over to Brookhaven Airport thirty miles to the west on Long Island, land, and then come back to Suffolk. I sat there, really worried about flying without an instructor, and yet feeling oddly elated at the same time. I was free to *fly*.

"Weren't you scared?" Courtney asked, following every word of the story. "You knew you'd have to land eventually."

"Scared is an understatement. I knew I'd have to deal with that, but right then I didn't really need to land at Brookhaven. I could cheat and just go there, make a U-turn and fly back. That's what I did.

"On the way back I tuned to the tower at Suffolk Airport. I still remember hearing that voice because it was a woman. Believe it or not, most aircraft controllers are men. She announced that the airport was closed for VFR traffic. Oh my God, I couldn't *believe* it. But I looked out and right away I saw why. A thin layer of clouds had come in from the east underneath me. When I looked straight down I could see the ground, but when I looked diagonally down all I could see was a white haze. *No airport*. I was up in the sky and couldn't see where I could come down. And even if I saw it, the airport was *closed*."

"Were you panicked?" Courtney wanted to know.

"I was terrified. I didn't know what to do at first."

"I can't imagine you that way," Courtney commented approvingly. "It turns out you have feelings after all."

"I don't do death easily. So I keyed the mike and called the tower. I simply told the woman I wanted to land. Didn't know what else to do. And she replied with some tower jargon like, 'Are you declaring an emergency and requesting special VFR assistance because you're too stupid to know how to deal with your situation up there by yourself?' I didn't understand half the gobble-de-gook she said, but I replied '*Yes*.'

"Well, apparently that was the *magic word* because she found me on the radar screen and told me to fly at such-and-such an azimuth until I was right over the airport. I lined up with that angle on the gyrocompass and, sure enough, within a few minutes I could look straight down and see the runway

"When I taxied up to the terminal, cut the engine and climbed out of the airplane, I was tremendously relieved but still shaking. Arne came running out to greet me. He had heard the whole thing on his pocket radio listening to the tower so I didn't have to tell him what happened. Instead of a scowl, though, he was grinning from ear to ear. He said. 'When you saw the clouds coming toward you, you should have just turned around and landed at Brookhaven. You were in an airplane, stupid. *It can go faster than the clouds.*'"

"That was some adventure," Courtney said, beginning to feel a bit of admiration for this man who sat opposite her and kept her entertained with tales of his exploits. "I'm sorry I don't have a story like that to tell."

"I'm sure you do. Whatever you've done and wherever you've been, I'd like to hear about it."

"I've led a very sheltered life."

"We have the whole weekend. I'm all ears."

"You'd be bored to tears."

"Try me."

"Okay, I just might."

After dinner the couple strolled back to the Woodstock Inn. The night air was bracing and Courtney felt the chill on her face. The moon shone brightly and bode well for a bright clear day on Saturday. As they approached the Inn, Courtney wondered what she should say if George tried to up their new, friendly relationship to a male-female level. He had been a perfect host and gentleman thus far and she hoped he wouldn't spoil it by making embarrassing moves. But, surprisingly, he didn't. When they exited the elevator on the fourth floor where their rooms were, George ended the suspense by saying, "It's been a long day for me. If you don't mind, I'd like to retire early and get a good rest. We need to be fit tomorrow to hike the Appalachian Trail."

"Sounds good to me. I'll check my email messages and then go to sleep too. I look forward to tomorrow." Courtney gave George a quick kiss on the cheek and entered her room for the night.

Chapter 46

The next morning the sky was clear blue and the sun seemed to be shining brighter than ever as Courtney and George stepped out of the Inn, pulling their luggage behind them. They had enjoyed a sumptuous country breakfast together and, after returning briefly to their rooms to use the bathrooms and grab their suitcases, they had checked out. George paid for both rooms. He had apologized to Courtney that he had to fly back early that evening to attend to his business "that never quits, even on a Sunday." She had pretended to be disappointed but was secretly glad to return to the comfort of her own home.

They loaded their bags in the back of the rented SUV and drove in a northwesterly direction on Route 12, following signs toward a Vermont town called Barnard. After passing through farmland on a level stretch, the road began a long climb upwards into wooded hills, following the course of a narrow river. Courtney watched carefully for a road sign or some other indication for the Appalachian Trail which crossed this road at some point according to the map. After traveling some fifteen miles, constantly uphill, she spotted the trail. On the left side of the road, on the bank of the river, she saw an outdoor message board with various papers tacked to it. Next to the board was a small footbridge across the river followed by a path leading south.

George pulled over to the right side of the road and stopped. Courtney got out and walked across to the message board. "This is it." she shouted, seeing a trail map and various messages posted on the board. George maneuvered the car and parked as far off the road as he could. Climbing out he asked, "Which way should we go? North or south?"

Courtney surveyed the landscape and decided, "Let's go north. The path is uphill in that direction. We'll probably be tired on the way back but we'll be walking downhill."

"Good plan" George agreed. They were soon on their way. Courtney grabbed her sweater, George took a jacket out of the car and they started walking. The sky was still clear except for a thin haze that had crept in, and the sun's rays lit up the leaves in the forest canopy overhead. Some of the leaves were still green but most had turned yellow, orange and red and reflected the light onto the trail with a golden glow. Suffused with bright spots in this way the path through the woods was enchanting at every turn. Wildflowers could be seen among the ground pine on both sides of the path. Courtney spotted several wild azaleas that were still blooming and even a jack-in-the-pulpit, which she enthusiastically pointed out to George. George reached down and squeezed the little plant with his fingers, pressing on both sides of the "pulpit," and Jack the minister preached a soft "squack."

Every so often, a dead tree lay on the ground on the side of the trail, probably having fallen during one of the Nor'easters that ocassionally came through Vermont, Courtney thought. Some of the tree logs were rotting; others were still solid but had holes in them, sometimes covered with crawling black ants that had made them their home. Now and again she could hear a rustle and looked to see an occasional chipmunk or squirrel scurrying across the ground or up a tree. Courtney was reminded that the woods were alive with crawling insects and small animals, an environment she was only passing through but that was hearth and home to wildlife.

Courtney and George walked the path for awhile as it zig-zagged uphill for awhile and then followed the crest of a mountain ridge in a northeasterly direction. At about one o'clock Courtney noticed the sunlight in the forest had dimmed significantly. She looked up and saw that clouds had rolled in while she and George were walking and enjoying the wild. Eventually she alerted George. "It's getting darker," she said, with mild concern in her voice.

"Let me check the weather," he replied calmly and took out his smartphone. "There's no phone service around here but there's always a satellite."

George pressed the screen a few times and stared. "Oh, oh," he said. "We'd better head back."

"What's the matter?" Courtney asked.

"Thunderstorms are heading our way."

"*Darn*. We've walked a couple of miles already. Let's hurry."

Courtney and George retraced their steps on a near run. The distance that had taken them over four hours at a leisurely pace took only two on the way back, but by the time they started descending toward the road where the car was parked they could hear the raindrops begin to pitter-patter on the leaves above them. When they finally had the road clearing in sight, the wind had picked up and was shaking tree branches, at first calmly and then occasionally violently. The shaking was accompanied by a noisy rustling sound and leaves were falling and swirling all around them. "Oh my gosh," George shouted. "We need to find shelter." He dashed ahead to the car and opened the door for Courtney as the rain started coming down hard. She climbed in as quickly as she could, her hair drenched and her face dripping. George slammed the door behind her and ran around to his side of the car. Seconds later he climbed in beside Courtney and pulled his door shut, safe from the rain and the wind outside. He took a deep breath and exhaled. "Wow. I sure didn't see that coming."

"What shall we do?" Courtney asked.

"I don't know," George replied. "I've long since earned my instrument rating," he added, causing Courtney to recall his story about flying VFR, "but I can't possibly fly in this kind of weather. There must be a front passsing through that will ground us for hours."

"We can go back to Woodstock," Courtney suggested. "Check in again at our Inn."

"There's a town up ahead called Barnard. Why don't we continue on and see if there's a place we can stay."

"I'm for that. I'd like to get out of these wet clothes."

"I think we're very close to this town. Let's go and explore."

Courtney took a handkerchief out of her purse and wiped her face. "I must look a mess." She looked at George so he could see how wet she was.

"You look like a drowned rabbit." His face was also dripping. They couldn't help but burst out laughing.

George started the car and headed up Route 12 toward the town of Barnard. "Barnard, Barnard, rhymes with barnyard," George said aloud as he drove, peering past the windshield wipers that clattered rapidly back and forth. "Where are you, Barnard?" In a little over a mile they saw a hanging sign on the right side of the road that read:

Barnard Inn

1796

and had a small sign hanging below it:

Restaurant

&

Tavern

In spite of the storm they could see a red brick colonial house with a white porch and green shutters. "What luck," Courtney shouted. "Good for you, George."

"I'm not so sure," George said. "These small country inns don't have many rooms and it's the height of tourist season here in Vermont." George pulled into the driveway. "Stay here. Let me go in and see."

Courtney nodded and watched George brave the storm, which was continuing by the minute to worsen with strong gusts of wind and an occasional flash closely followed by a thunderclap. George opened and then closed the car door behind him and ran to the side door of the Inn. Courtney waited. As the time stretched out she began to lose hope that there were rooms available. Finally she saw George emerge from the same door and run towards the car. He immediately jumped in and slammed the car door shut, but that brief dash didn't save him from getting thoroughly wet. He was drenched to the bone but nevertheless grinning. "There's no room there," he said, but I had the proprietor call ahead. There is one room left at a bed and breakfast just down the road. He reserved it for us."

"Anything. Just to get out of this storm," Courtney agreed.

"But I managed to make a dinner reservation at the restaurant. They had a cancellation."

"I'm not surprised." Courtney replied looking out as the rain pelted the windshield.

"We'll go get settled first and then come back."

George backed up the car and headed out, turning onto Route 12 again, and followed the road for another half mile until they saw a white wooden fence. They could barely make out a sign: "THE MAPLE TREE INN." "That's it." George said, and turned just before the sign onto a long driveway. Up ahead in the distance they could barely see a huge front porch gracing the front of a seemingly new gray house with white trim. George drove up and parked next to a small cluster of other cars and turned off the engine. "We're here," he said with a sigh of relief.

The storm was raging now as the two jumped out, grabbed their suitcases from the trunk and carried them on the run up the steps to the porch. They stood on the porch for a moment catching their breath, dripping wet, when the door in front of them opened. "Come on in," said a nice-looking man with a friendly voice. "We've been expecting you."

Chapter 47

"My name's Mike. My wife, Nelly, is in the kitchen baking cookies. And this is Becket our bulldog," he said, reaching down to pet his pooch who had run up to the door to see who was there.

George introduced himself and Courtney, his "significant other," and followed Mike upstairs, carrying both their suitcases up to the landing. Mike pulled a key from his pocket and unlocked one of the doors facing the hallway. Each of the doors had a small brass plate with the name of the room. The one Michael unlocked bore the words "Cupid's Retreat."

"This is our largest guestroom," Mike said proudly, opening the door and handing over the key to George. "Nelly and I live downstairs, so if you have any questions or need anything, feel free to knock on our door. Nelly's cookies will be ready in a few minutes. Breakfast is from seven-thirty to ten tomorrow." George thanked him, picked up the suitcases again and entered. Courtney followed him into the bedroom.

The room was indeed large, dominated by a king-sized, four-poster bed with a majestic colonial headboard against one wall. The bed was adorned with luxurious-looking pillows and a puffy white down comforter. A fireplace with split logs on the hearth graced another wall. The storm, howling outside, could be seen and heard through the colonial-style windowpanes. It made the room seem all the more cozy.

Courtney went straight to the bathroom and dried her face and hair with a towel. She then came out and unpacked her suitcase. Finding the dress she had worn the evening before and a clean set of underwear, and grabbing her toiletry kit, she returned to the bathroom and made herself ready for dinner. George had changed his shirt and pants and donned his jacket in the meantime. When Courtney was finished he spent five minutes in the bathroom before emerging, ready to go. "I'm really sorry about the weather," he said. "I should have checked."

"That's all right," Courtney replied. "I'm sorry I'm wearing the same dress as last night. I only brought one."

"You look terrific, Courtney. You're one in a million."

"All right then. Let's make a night of it."

"That we will. And the night starts right now. Let's go to dinner."

Having cleaned herself up Courtney felt in a better mood than when they had arrived. Her only concerns involved the sleeping arrangements, but she brushed them aside. George was a gentleman she assured herself.

George borrowed two umbrellas from Mike and they each held one upright as they raced to the car. Once inside the car they caught their breaths and enjoyed the short trip through the wind and rain to the Barnard Inn restaurant. They were one of the first guests to arrive and the maitre D' showed them to a table in a private corner by a window. The table was adorned with white tablecloths, sterling silver tableware and crystal glasses, seemingly fit for royalty. Courtney looked around and didn't see any other table set this way.

The waiter arrived and introduced himself. "My name is Harold," he said. "I will be serving you tonight. I know who you are, Mr. Cleary, and I feel honored to be at your service."

"Thank you, Harold. My friend and I are looking forward to a wonderful dining experience."

"You are both in for a treat. We have a new chef who performs absolute magic in the kitchen. After you select a wine I'll go over the specials with you." Harold handed Mike a leather-bound wine list.

"Would you care for a wine?" George asked Courtney politely.

"Yes, please. I would love a red this evening." Courtney's mood was light, in anticipation of a delightful dinner.

George ordered an expensive cabernet sauvignon.

"Excellent choice, Sir." Harold bowed and left.

Courtney stared at George. "That man knows who you are?"

"I don't know how come he made such a big deal of it. I did give the restaurant my name when I came in to make the reservation, but..." George held up his hands in a gesture of not knowing. "Well here we are again, having dinner together. I must say I enjoy your company very much."

"I'm having a wonderful time, George, in spite of the rain. Thank you." Courtney held out her hand across the table and George took it.

"I feel the same way," he said. "With or without the rain, it doesn't matter."

Harold proved to be a perfect host. He was helpful but not hovering. As the evening progressed Courtney felt her mood mellow while keeping herself fully under control. Unlike the previous evening when George did most of the talking, she carried the conversation and held him spellbound, so it seemed to her, with tales of her life since college. When she and George emptied the bottle of wine he ordered another and they emptied that.

"I'm so glad you came on this weekend trip with me," George said. This triggered something in her mind and Courtney replied, "There was a time when I couldn't have taken this trip. You know the reason."

"The greatest regret in my life is that I didn't come to your aid when you needed it most, Courtney. I think about this almost every day and wish to God I could have a do-over, but I can't. What I *can* do is try to make it up to you."

"You know that I've not been with a man since that...that time," Courtney told him, surprising herself that she said this.

George just gazed at her with a look of sympathy and understanding. Tears welled up in his eyes. "I'm sorry," he said.

"Don't be. I'm a big girl. But sometimes I think I'm missing out."

"You'll have a lot of catching up to do."

"I guess so. I wouldn't know."

Harold came and presented the bill. George paid it with cash so that they could leave immediately. They drove back to the Maple Tree Inn in silence and went straight to their room. Courtney took a white bathrobe out of the closet and disappeared into the bathroom.

Chapter 48

It started with a kiss. Courtney allowed George to kiss her when she came out of the bathroom dressed in her robe and underwear. He was still fully dressed but had shed his sport jacket and shoes. She closed her eyes and felt the sensation of his lips against hers. He pressed his tongue against her lips and she parted them, letting him in. It was a natural progression after that.

She felt her robe slip to the floor as her lips remained locked with his and he explored her mouth with his tongue. His hands, which had deftly removed the robe, squeezed her thighs and pulled her tightly against his body. She felt a lump against her lower abdomen and realized it was his manhood. She didn't care. She didn't stop him. She let herself go because at this point it was too late. "The place" between her legs already felt warm and wet.

George's hands slid up her back and unclasped her bra. Courtney felt her breasts swell as the bra released its pressure holding them in. Her nipples felt sensitive to his touch. George's hands came forward and lightly squeezed them between his fingertips. She could not help noticing her breasts did not feel this way when she undid the bra herself.

Still kissing, Courtney felt his hands slide down and tug at her panties, pulling them down and exposing her sex, which by this time was fully aroused. Letting go of her mouth and dropping down, George buried his face in her breasts for a moment and then continued sliding downward, tracing his tongue along her belly until he reached her pubic hair. He knelt before her, holding her thighs between his hands and plunged his face into the outer lips of her vagina. The sudden pleasurable sensation caused her to arch her back. She felt herself falling backwards against the bed. Reaching behind her she caught her fall and eased herself down onto the soft white comforter. She lay on her back and her legs parted, letting George's tongue find her private parts. A part of her wanted to concentrate on the pleasure she was having but she struggled hard to remain in control. But the arousal constantly distracted her thoughts. The warmth of George's breath proved maddeningly exciting.

He teased the dewy lips of her cleft until she felt almost dizzy with the need to climax.

"My *clit*," she uttered. "Tongue my clit."

George understood her urgency and went on to find her clitoris. His tongue slipped to the top of her sex and stroked the pulsating bud of her arousal. The sensation was enough to make her groan. Courtney stuffed the back of her hand against her mouth to stifle a scream of delight. She pressed her shoulders back against the bed and thrust her pelvis upward toward him. The urge for release had been strong before; but now, as his tongue drew circles around the throbbing bead of her clitoris, she realized she was only moments away from ecstasy. Knowing she had to show some restraint and determined that George would not reduce her to a quivering wreck of satisfaction, Courtney steeled herself against the pleasure and managed to say, "Now, tongue *inside*. Please."

He was more obedient than she dared to hope. His tongue slid slowly down from her clitoris and eased itself inside between her labia. The warmth was divine. The intimate penetration was so intense that Courtney had to grip the comforter with both her hands to maintain her show of equanimity. His tongue slid deeper into her vagina while at the same time his mouth sucked her clitoris, transporting her to an even higher plateau of unparalleled delight. She felt the heat within her core float her upward, like the flames blowing into a hot-air balloon, until she could no longer hold herself back. Her inner muscles began to spasm, followed by intense spontaneous convulsions. The shock of the searing pleasure was so strong she wanted to scream. Only her deep inhibitions prevented her from becoming completely undone by the actions of this man.

And in a moment, the feeling was over.

Courtney composed herself as she lay on her back, at first breathing heavily and then catching her breath. She imagined briefly she was floating on a cloud in heaven, but quickly came back to earth realizing that George was about to mount her. Her orgasm had aroused him so that his organ had grown enormous and ramrod stiff. She rolled to one side to avoid penetration by his menacing manhood, but at the same time understood that he could not easily be deterred. She had to quickly do something to protect herself from this love situation that was fast escalating out of control.

Although she had never touched nor even seen a penis before, she instinctively knew what to do. She quickly sat up on the bed, reached over and grabbed hold of it. She squeezed it tightly and could feel it throbbing, seemingly with a life of its own. She deftly massaged it twice up and down and felt it convulse. She saw it explode in her hand and spit semen halfway across the bed onto the comforter. George uttered a primal gasp and his knees gave way. He sank suddenly to the floor.

Courtney sat there stunned, amazed at the power she felt. She had used her wits and diverted the dangerous situation. She had been vulnerable in allowing herself to orgasm to the point of almost losing consciousness, but she took back control and avoided what at that moment appeared to be an inevitable relinquishing of her privacy and primacy. She had retained her dignity and self-respect. Paraphrasing the infamous words of the then President, William Jefferson "Bill" Clinton, she could in all honesty say to herself, "I did *not* have sex with that man."

Chapter 49

The rain stopped overnight. The storm ran its course and moved on, sweeping the clouds with it and leaving the sky crystal clear and deep blue. Courtney and George awoke with the sunlight streaming in through the windows. They showered, dressed and went downstairs to enjoy a delicious four-course breakfast served up by the proprietors of the B&B. Courtney had felt awkward sharing the room, and she hardly spoke to George except when necessary to coordinate their use of the bathroom and ask important questions such as:

Courtney: "Have you seen my underpants?"

George: "I think they slipped under the bed."

After breakfast they returned to their room, packed their bags and came downstairs again to check out and be on their way.

Curious, Courtney looked over George's shoulder as he paid the bill with his Amex card. After they had said their farewells to Mike and Nelly and they were walking to the car with their luggage in tow, Courtney commented, "That bill was awfully expensive, don't you think? It's like the hotel prices in New York City."

"It's the height of the season," George replied without seeming concerned. "I can afford it and we were lucky to have a room here at all."

"Well, thank you for a lovely evening, and a lovely weekend in fact. I'll always remember this."

"I hope we can do it again soon. If you're willing to join me, there's no place we can't go. I have an airplane you know."

"Can you fly it to Paris?"

"I'll rent a Learjet."

"No, no, George. Don't do *that*." Courtney laughed. "I was just joking."

They drove back to Lebanon Airport, making only limited small talk on the way. George drove a different route back than the way they had come so he could show Courtney the red covered bridge in Taftsville. As the car clattered through the tunnel-like passageway of the wooden structure, Courtney felt conflicted, wondering whether she should thank

George for going out of his way to show her the sights. She still felt awkward about the night before and just wanted to get home to the safety and solace of her apartment in New York.

The flight back was uneventful, although Courtney did enjoy the view. When they landed, Isaac was there to pick them up. He held open the right rear door of the car for Courtney as George climbed in on the left side. On the way George used his iPad to connect to the Internet and conduct some urgent business. Courtney watched him, wondering what it was like to have so much money. When they arrived at her apartment, she begged George not to get out. He obliged her, yet took her hand and kissed her on the lips. She felt uncomfortable with that, but she tried not to show it by fending him off. By agreeing to join him on this trip to Vermont and allowing him to become intimate with her, she had led him on, she realized. She would not let it happen again.

"Thank you again, George." She forced herself to appear warm and appreciative, but she could not help being perfunctory. She wasn't sure why, but something just didn't feel right. She squeezed George's hand and opened the car door before Isaac had a chance to come around. As she took her suitcase from Isaac and walked into her apartment building she felt a distinct sense of relief. For the first time in two days she could again be her private self and live in her own separate world among her women friends. Men were such *animals* she thought. Women were too, if they allowed men to lead them on. She shuddered and let the idea slip from her mind.

Chapter 50

The SEALs used burglar tools to unlock the back door and slipped inside of the Department of Public Works in Chappaqua. Roger followed them up to the second floor and entered the Highway and Water Department. No one was there, not even a night watchman. They scanned the walls and ceiling for video surveillance cameras and found none.

Using their flashlights, they started a search for plans of the water treatment plant. They located two file cabinets marked "Water" and picked the locks. Roger joined the SEALs in opening drawer after drawer and walked their fingers through the tabs on the hanging files. They took out a few papers and photographed them, but none provided the needed diagrams for the system of filtering, flocculating, oxidizing and fluorinating the water. What they did learn was that the treatment plant was in Millwood, three miles distant. It obtained raw water from the Catskill Aqueduct System on the other side of the Hudson River, and it served nearly seventeen thousand people in New Castle with about 5300 metered customer connections. It pumped four million gallons a day to meet the needs of the residents of Chappaqua, Millwood and Mount Kisco, as well as wholesale customers like IBM.

"Look at *this*." Roger pulled out a sheet of paper and showed it to Jim. "They just recently installed a new security system."

The sheet gave only cursory information about the system itself but it had detailed figures on the cost. The security equipment had been extremely expensive to install and was costing enormous sums of money to monitor and maintain. "Whew," Jim whistled under his breath. "That's not good."

The water facility was located near the site of the old railroad station in the hamlet of Millwood. It was operated under contract by "Suez," a water company based in New Jersey and owned by a multinational corporation by the same name, based in Paris. "Let's get out of here. We're in the wrong pew," Jim said when Roger finally finished combing through the files and found nothing further. Careful to leave no trace of having been there, the men departed the building, climbed back into their vans and took off for Millwood.

They exited Hunts Lane and followed the directions of their navigator to Millwood. Entering the town they took a left on Station Place, named for the railroad station that once stood there. The railroad bed was now a bike trail and the center of the community had moved to a nearby shopping mall. This part of town had become solely industrial.

"We'll do a drive-by and look for surveillance cameras." Jim's voice was heard in the other van directly behind via their secure communication system. "Then we'll park up the road apiece and walk back."

The two vans pulled into a nearby supermarket parking lot and stopped at an empty far corner. The men donned their black hoods and backtracked on foot in the dark night.

In addition to guns, the men carried black backpacks filled with various tools of their trade. That included burglar tools as well as hypodermic injection capsules to quitely neutralize the unsuspecting security guards.

Walking cautiously to avoid being seen, two of the SEALs snuck up beneath a pair of surveillance cameras and ignited firecrackers, one on each side of the front door. Jim and the other SEAL waited, out of sight, for security guards to appear. Roger stayed behind and watched from a distance.

Sure enough, the door opened and out came two uniformed officers to investigate what caused the noise. They walked around the building, looking everywhere, including up at the surveillance cameras which had shown them nothing.

The two SEALs came up from behind, out of sight of the cameras, each grabbing one of the guards in a chokehold, and drove their hypodermic needles home. The guards slumped to the ground.

Meanwhile Jim entered the building with a remaining SEAL, guns drawn and ready for action. Right ahead of them in the lobby was a security desk with a startled security officer sitting in front of a bank of video screens. He held up his hands.

"We won't hurt you," Jim barked sharply, holding his gun on the man. "We're here to inspect your facility."

The man grimaced. "Really?"

Jim's accomplice approached him while he was still sitting and jammed a hypodermic into his arm. He grabbed him as he slumped and lowered him to the floor.

"That's three," Jim said. "Let's see if there are others."

Before calling in the men from outside, Jim reached down on the control panel and pressed a button marked "RECORD." A red light, indicating surveillance videos were being recorded, toggled off.

"The path is clear," he announced over his com. "Come on in."

The two remaining SEALs came into the lobby from outside, followed by Roger.

They found no other guards were present so Roger went to work investigating the plumbing of the water treatment plant. He located the tank that held the fluoridating compound and looked inside. It was nearly half-filled with white powder.

Meanwhile two of the SEALs ran back to the supermarket parking lot to retrieve the vans. They drove them around to the rear of the building, backing the one that held the Nemo powder toward the loading dock. Both men got out and lifted the plastic containers with Nemo onto the platform. They also grabbed an empty container and a large ladle for emptying fluoridating powder from its tank. They brought these inside to Roger who set about replacing the fluoride with Nemo. He scooped white fluoride powder into the free container and refilled the tank with the Nemo powder. Roger could only estimate that this was about a one-month's supply for twenty thousand people.

When he finished loading the Nemo, Roger re-adjusted the plumbing valves to cause the right amount to flow steadily into the water system. Jim stood by, prodding him to hurry by pointing to his watch.

"Those guys are going to wake up. If they see us here, they'll remember us."

Roger nodded that he was done, and they all left through the rear of the building. They climbed back into the vans and headed out in the direction from which they came. As they drove by the front of the building they looked over and saw the two guards in front trying to stand on wobbly legs. They zipped past in the dark and headed to the Saw Mill

River Parkway entrance at Chappaqua for the long drive home. Dawn was just beginning to lighten the eastern horizon as they headed south toward the George Washington Bridge.

"I'd love to be a fly on the wall when those guards fully wake up," Roger remarked with a grin.

"They won't remember a thing," Jim replied. "That military drug we gave them not only puts them out, it erases their memory of what just happened."

Chapter 51

When Courtney returned to her office on Monday, she found a message on the office answering machine. It was from Roger.

> *"Courtney, this is Roger Thornwood. I just want to bring you up to date on Nemo. We've made some progress on what we talked about. I'd like to have a meeting with you as soon as possible to discuss how we can monitor the effect on people. Please call me back, anytime day or night."*

Courtney stared at the machine for a moment and thought about what to do. She had intended to call him to express some of her concerns about "salting" an entire community with this new military weapon. In the meantime, Roger had gone ahead and done exactly what he had promised. Her idea for exacting revenge and retaliation against her rapists had suddenly become very real and she was feeling the weight of responsibility for anything rash that might result.

She called Roger and asked that they meet the very next day.

She then sat down at her computer and composed an email to the Alphabet Soup – her editorial board.

> *"Dear Ashley, Bailey and Deedee:*
>
> *"Our new issue of Women Rising will appear today in the newsstands and in our subscribers' mailboxes.*
>
> *"I would like the editorial board to meet tomorrow at one o'clock sharp to discuss the media buzz about this issue and to plan for our issue next month.*
>
> *"I have also asked Dr. Roger Thornwood to join us at two o'clock to bring us up to date on Nemo.*
> *"As always, Courtney."*

The women assembled in the conference room at the appointed time the next day. Having been alerted by Deedee, all of the board members knew about Courtney's trip to Vermont. As soon as they took their seats the questions started coming.

Ashley led off with, "How was Vermont?" She gave Courtney a sly wink at the same time, communicating the clear message that she didn't expect her to spill her beans. She assumed that 'what happens in Vermont stays in Vermont.'

"I can honestly say it was wonderful," Courtney responded. "The fall foliage up there takes your breath away."

"You went up there with George Cleary, right?" Bailey asked inquisitively.

"Yes, I did."

"Isn't he the one who's invested the money in *Women Rising*?"

"Yes."

"How much was it, exactly?"

"A million dollars."

All the board members fixed stares on Courtney. "Whew. That's certainly a lot," Bailey commented.

"Well, this puts us on a surer footing. I'll be asking you soon how best to spend what's left." Courtney said, then added, "I'd like to use the money for marketing mostly."

"Did you go up there alone with him?" Bailey pressed her.

"Yes. We went in his private airplane and he let me fly it. It was just *amazing*."

Deedee appeared somewhat disturbed to hear this but kept quiet.

"He owns an airplane? Really?" Bailey remarked, even more curious now.

"Yes, and it's pretty big. It has two engines, seats about ten people and—."

"Wow." Ashley blurted out. "This George is a good man to know."

"He's all right," Courtney said as matter-of-factly as she could. "He and I go way back. I met him in college."

The room fell silent for a moment while Ashley, Bailey and Deedee digested this information.

"Where did you go in Vermont?" Deedee asked.

"Woodstock."

"Woodstock? I thought that was here in New York, where they had that wild music festival back in the day."

"There's a Woodstock in Vermont. It's an idyllic New England town."

"You stayed in a hotel in Woodstock?" Deedee probed.

"Yes, in fact it's called the 'Woodstock Inn'."

"Did you have separate rooms?" Ashley threw discretion to the wind and dove right in to elicit the juicy details.

"Yes, we did. And if you must know, George was the perfect gentleman."

"He didn't kiss you?" Ashley asked incredulously.

"He kissed me on the cheek." Courtney feigned mild indignation.

Deedee looked askance at Courtney, as if something was amiss but she couldn't quite place it.

"Well, I guess that's that," Ashley concluded. "Nothing happened." She eyed Courtney to give her one last chance to say something. "We're all Sisters here."

Ashley and Bailey seemed satisfied. Deedee, not so much. She continued to frown. Courtney could sense Deedee suspected there was something left unsaid.

Courtney looked sternly at her board members and changed the subject. "So let's move on, everyone. Get down to business. Roger will be here in a few minutes and I want us to be prepared. He's going to tell us what's happening with Nemo."

Ashley did a double take and broke into a broad grin. "That's *funny*. All those people up there in suburbia, they won't know what hit them."

Bailey and Deedee also appeared amused. "I can't imagine." Bailey said breezily. "What will happen to Bill Clinton when he can't get it *up*?"

"Hillary will say, '*Thank God*.'" Deedee replied. "She'll say, 'Bill is *finally* over the hill and I can trust him with other women around.'"

"That's just the kind of thing we have to find out," Courtney commented. "Maybe we can use our nose for the news and root out stories for the magazine."

"Do you think that's wise?" Deedee tried to elicit a serious discussion. "This thing could blow up in our faces. We could be held responsible as co-conspirators for breaking all kinds of laws."

"Co-conspirators with the government?" Ashley wondered allowed. The others looked at her questioningly. "Just asking," she added.

"Remember the stuff is called 'Ballzoff'," Bailey interjected. "How bad can it be?"

Courtney called for order. "Clearly we have some issues here. But remember why we asked him to do this. In exchange for not running our article about Nemo and to get back at those awful men who…who—," Courtney couldn't say it. The memory of her ordeal suddenly came flooding back and moved her akmost to tears.

Deedee quickly got up from her chair and came over to Courtney. She knelt next to her, put an arm around her shoulders and held her close. "We'll get back at those bastards," she said tenderly but with firm conviction in her voice. "Let's talk to Roger about what we can do to deliver a bitter message to those men."

Courtney sniffed and blew her nose with her handkerchief. "I'll be all right." Deedee handed her a tissue. "Thank you, Deedee." She looked at the others in the room. "And thank you all. I…I'm sorry. I guess I'm just not over this."

Courtney almost missed the soft knock on the door of the outer office. She looked at her watch. "Oh, my goodness, it's two o'clock already. He's *here*."

Deedee went back to her seat while Courtney dabbed her eyes with her kerchief. "How do I look?" she asked. Every one of her board members nodded approvingly.

Courtney rose, smoothed her skirt, and left to open the door for Roger.

Chapter 52

For the second time in as many weeks, Courtney presented Dr. Roger Thornwood to the Alphabet Soup. He stood in the doorway for a moment. "I'm back," he said with a shy, endearing smile and gave a small wave. "It seems you can't keep me away." The seated women all smiled approvingly and warmly welcomed him into their little reactionary conclave with the common charter of changing the world for the better. Courtney invited him to again sit at the head of the table and went around to take her seat at the opposite end. "Dr. Thornwood, …I mean Roger," she began, "please tell the editorial board what you told me…about Nemo."

"The first thing I need to say," Roger cautioned, "is that in addition to you five people, only about twenty others in the whole world know about this new experimental weapon, and we absolutely have to keep it under wraps."

All four women nodded in agreement.

"All right then. Now that I've told you the bad news, let's get on with the good: As of two days ago, Nemo has been flowing in the water pipes of Chappaqua. By now the people there are starting to experience its effects. Consider it a noble scientific and social experiment. We'll be able to see what happens in a community when the line on the transgender scale has been moved a couple of notches to the left in the direction of femininity."

"An experiment? I thought you knew what the effects will be." Ashley said indignantly.

"We know how Nemo affects men. It makes them softer, less prone to acting out. But we don't know how it affects women. And for sure not a whole community of men and women together."

Deedee was the one who seemed most concerned. "Could that be a problem?"

"No. It's only for a month. After that, the effect will wear off."

"Won't those people figure it out?" Deedee pressed. "They'll realize they've been drugged or something and they'll start to investigate. They will find out what's going on and start suing everybody."

"Not if we don't tell. You can't test for it unless you know exactly where to look and what to look for. The effects are subtle and if they notice any change at all, they'll never figure out it was the water they drank. If they eventually suspect anything, the month will be up and the Nemo will be long gone."

"Will it change people's minds about…things?" Deedee wanted to know. "If they're racist, say, will they start treating black people…uh, fairly?"

"They might. That would be a very good thing, wouldn't it? But when the effects wear off, my guess is they'll return to their old ways of thinking. Maybe even more so after having left their comfort zone for awhile. Billy did, you'll remember."

"*Their* comfort zone, not mine."

"Will the men be…uh, *potent*?" Bailey wanted to know. She wasn't married but she was smack in the middle of her child-bearing years.

"Nemo doesn't affect a man's equipment," Roger explained. "It may make him disinterested in sex, but it certainly doesn't make him impotent. The same applies to women. They can still have babies and there's no way that babies can be affected. It doesn't work that way. What we don't know is how it may affect the relationships between men and women."

"*That'll* be interesting," Bailey commented with a wink.

"The point was to make men less violent. That is the purpose of this bio-weapon and we have achieved that."

"But it could affect women you said. Make them more feminine."

"This will be the first real trial with women," Roger admitted. "But that's why I'm here. To ask you to go up there and find out what's happening."

"You want us to do *what*?" Deedee demanded.

"Investigate. Do it for your magazine. Find out what's going on in the community. Write a story. Just don't make any mention of Nemo."

"And how do you expect us to do that?" Courtney asked. "Just go there and talk to people? Are you kidding? No one is going to tell us anything."

Roger held up his hands, palms out, to stop the questions from coming. "Wait, wait," he said. "I have a plan. Hear me out."

The board members halted their chatter and let Roger speak. For the next ten minutes he lay out a detailed plan for investigating and rooting out the sexual mores and attitudes of the Chappaqua community in the presence of Nemo. The women listened intently and intrigued, nodding their heads in approval as he spoke. When he finally finished, the women looked at each other and came to a quick consensus.

"That's a great plan," Courtney spoke for the board. "Let's *do it*."

"May I suggest you send in your youngest investigators?" Roger added.

"You're absolutely right," Courtney agreed. "Ashley, how about it?"

"I'm your man." Ashley volunteered, grinning from ear to ear.

"Also, how about Veronica?" Roger suggested. "I'm sure she can relate to those teens up there and she will know what to look for."

"My gosh, I almost forgot about her," replied Courtney, getting more excited by the minute. "She wrote the lead article in *Cosmo* this month." She reached for her phone and dialed a number, then lay the phone on the conference table and pressed "Speaker." Veronica picked up on the first ring and said, "Hello?" In the background they heard loud noises that sounded for all the world like an office party.

"Ronnie, it's Courtney. I'd like to commission you to write an article for *Women Rising*."

"I don't know, Courtney. I'm writing for *Cosmo* now. Just a minute. I'll hand my phone to Emily. Talk to her. She's my new boss."

Ten seconds later Emily Platt came on the line. "Courtney? I can't believe that you called just now. We're having a celebration in honor of Ronnie. Her article was a *huge* hit in our magazine. You should come on over and join our party."

Chapter 53

Courtney noticed a number of things that were out of the ordinary for her as she entered the *Cosmo* offices a half hour later, followed by Roger and her entourage of board members. First, except for an occasional gay-looking man, all of the partiers were women. Second, except for Emily who spotted her entrance and headed her way from the far side of the reception area, all of the women appeared younger than she. And third, all of the women were perfectly made up and drop-dead gorgeous. You could almost smell the estrogen in the room.

Veronica was over at one side of the space, surrounded by a bevy of women who listened adoringly as she spoke, although it was difficult to hear over the high-pitched sounds of the many female voices in the background.

"We're very proud of Ronnie," Emily practically shouted over the din when she finally made it through the crowd. "Courtney, we sold more magazines this month than ever before. Ronnie's article must have hit a nerve."

"You owe me." Courtney said in reply, also almost shouting above the din.

"Excuse me," Emily brushed past her when she spotted Roger and swiftly came up to him. "Welcome to *Cosmo*." She grabbed his hand and pulled him behind her to the center of the room. "Quiet everyone." She clapped her hands twice. Like magic, the many voices suddenly stilled. "I'd like you all to meet Dr. Roger Thornwood. It's not every day that we welcome an attractive, down-to-earth *single* man in our midst. I can assure you ladies that he's the real deal. Go for it." Emily gave Roger a quick peck on the cheek and spoke close to his ear, "I thought I told you not to come here. Most men can't manage this menagerie. Now you must take your medicine." Emily walked away, allowing women to close in around him like piranhas to a piece of raw meat.

"Now, Bitch," she said to Courtney when she returned to her side, "Let me greet your women friends."

Ashley, Bailey and Deedee were at the reception desk of the *Cosmo* offices that was doing double duty as a makeshift bar. A male bartender, dressed in tight jeans, a lavender shirt and a black bow tie, was making cocktails for everyone when Courtney and Emily walked up. The young man winked knowingly at Emily. "You can have any cocktail you want here," he told the Alphabet Soup of women with an amused look, "as long as it's a Cosmopolitan." He had lined up a row of funnel-shaped glasses on the front surface of the desk and was filling them, one after the other, with a pink elixir from a large glass pitcher.

"This is Chester," Emily explained. "He's one of our most knowledgeable fashion mavens."

"At your service, dear ladies," Chester said, passing the first filled glass to Courtney. "Try this. It will melt away your inhibitions," he gave her a coy look and added pointedly, "if you have any, that is."

"Chester, this is Courtney Stillwell," Emily chirped. "Unlike us, she publishes a *serious* women's magazine called *Women Rising*. We're definitely *not* in competition."

"*Women Rising*. Hmmm," Chester scratched his head, feigning ignorance. "That's a switch. I've seen *men* rising, but how do you women do it? I'd like to see that."

"We *won't* do a demo," retorted Emily. "Not on my watch, anyway."

Courtney held up her glass and signaled for her board members to do the same. "To *Cosmo*." she toasted, "and to the woman who runs it like a dominatrix. Emily, these are my lifelines at my magazine. Ashley, Bailey and Deedee. Stick my name right in the middle and we're the first five letters of the alphabet. Easy to remember."

Emily greeted and warmly welcomed Courtney's three women friends. "Don't let her fool you. I'm really a pussycat. She's the one we call the 'Bitch'."

The women smiled sweetly and took sips of their cocktails. "Man, this is *strong*." Deedee said, making a face. "After a couple of these I'd be an easy lay."

"We aim to please," Chester grinned.

"Let me tell you about Ronnie's article," Emily said. "The minute *Cosmo* hit the newsstands, we started getting calls and emails. Tweets up the whazoo. Women are looking to have sex. We knew that, but what's new is that a lot of them aren't getting enough. Ronnie wrote a terrific exposé that helped those women understand they're not alone out there. It's kind of a taboo subject for women but we're bringing it out into the open. Thanks to Ronnie, now women are talking about it."

"Do you have plans for Ronnie?" asked Courtney. "To write another article like that?"

"Of course. She's hot at the moment and a good writer to boot. I have you to thank for that, Courtney. You discovered her."

"What she was writing didn't exactly fit our mold. I'm happy you can use her, but that's why I'm here. I want to her work for me for a month."

"You want to what?"

"I need to borrow her back. For a month."

"But you just said…Her writing doesn't fit…"

"Can we talk privately? What I have to tell you is highly confidential."

Emily looked around and let her eyes fall on Roger. He was surrounded by admiring females and, surprisingly, seemed to be holding his own. Courtney followed her eyes and saw it too. She felt an unfamiliar feeling of jealousy seep into her psyche, like the wetness of rain soaking into her clothes. It felt uncomfortable so she dropped her eyes. "How about my office?" Emily suggested. "It's quiet there."

Courtney nodded, excused herself from her board members, and followed Emily. They exited the reception area and walked down a long corridor to another large open space, this one filled with low partitions that formed individual workplaces containing secretarial desks with desktop computers. Emily led Courtney through this maze to an office in a far corner with wall-to-wall windows facing south and west with majestic views of New York City. Courtney was instantly drawn to the panorama of skyscrapers and walked up to one window. It extended from ceiling to floor and, as Courtney looked down, she could see cars and people inching along on the street seventy stories below. "Wow." She caught her breath. "I forgot you had this specatular view."

"You can get used to it," Emily said and added, "unfortunately. When I first moved in I couldn't stop looking out the window. But after a week or two the novelty wore off and now I'm jaded."

"It sure beats my little old office on forty-fourth Street. Maybe if I work hard and my magazine grows I can aspire to this. That'll be awhile."

"You started something. That's very difficult." Emily said sympathetically. "I came into a thriving business with a great brand."

"I'm not sure I could ever do what you do. Your magazine has so many moving parts. We have a single focus and I'm sticking to that."

"So let's talk about Ronnie."

"Okay, here's the thing. I agree you have a great brand. *Cosmo.* Everyone's heard of it. I need to build my brand too and I've been working on a plan to do just that. I'm going to go on a talk circuit and give speeches to young women. And I mean *young* women, like girls in middle school and high school. I want to reach them before they give in to the current culture and start cozying up to men as if they were indispensable to a satisfying, happy life. I want them to realize the dangers posed by the masculine gender so they can stand on their own *terra firma* and negotiate from strength with the men in their lives. I'm going to tell them what my magazine tries to tell them every month, month after month; namely, that it's time for us women to rise up and demand that men stop the violence, the rapes, the beatings, the killings and, yes, the wars that they fight, always standing on principle, self-righteous and assured that they are doing the right thing when, in fact, they are the cause of practically every one of the problems we have in this world."

"My goodness, that's a mouthful." Emily commented. "So where does Ronnie fit in?"

"When I give a speech in a high school I want to start a movement, kind of like a club, where the girls who are interested get together and write stories for the school newspaper. I want Ronnie to work with me to coach these females on the power of the pen and of the press. I need a team of young women like Ronnie, and also Ashley whom you met, to infiltrate the school after I give the speech and get to know the girls, earn their trust and lead them in the right direction."

"Whew, that's quite a plan. Sure you haven't studied Scientology or something? You're really serious about starting a movement, aren't you?"

"Yes, I am. And I need Ronnie to help me with it. It's kind of an experiment. I'll give it a go for one solid month. If my sparks can't light a fire within that month, the experiment will have failed and I'm off to do other things. I don't want to waste my time trying to buck male and female nature when that's simply not possible, but if I can make a difference with my efforts, the time is *now*."

"Okay, okay. Enough said. I capitulate." Emily threw up her hands. "You can have Ronnie for a month. Just one month, and then I want her back. She's a diamond in the rough and I'm going to bring her in from freelance. I want her on staff."

"That's a deal. I promise."

"So where are you going to start? Your first speech? With this trial balloon of yours?"

"The plan is to start at Horace Greeley High School in Chappaqua, New York."

Emily gasped. "Really? Chappaqua? That's where they train those teenage girls to be Stepford wives."

Chapter 54

Just before six Emily ordered in food, light sandwiches and diet soda, from a nearby gourmet deli. Pizza was never on the menu for the *Cosmo* women who had to be constantly vigilant about their weight.

Roger made his excuses and left at seven, saying he had a four-hour drive to get back to APG. Courtney and Emily walked him to the door and gave him hugs before he left. "I'm amazed at you," Emily told him. "My girls are not easy to impress but I could see they took to you like kids to candy. Don't be surprised if you get a few calls from them, asking when you'll next be in New York."

After he left, Emily paused a moment and stared quizzically at Courtney.

"What?" Courtney asked.

"He's a keeper, you know."

"I'm not dating. You know that."

They walked back to join the party with Courtney's mind still occupied and excited by her plan for creating awareness among girls. She spotted Deedee deep in conversation with Chester and went over to join them.

"Ahem," remarked Chester with a wink. "I sense something goin on." Deedee put her finger to her lips to shush him and brought Courtney into the conversation.

When the party was over the Alphabet Soup, including Courtney, left together and squeezed into the elevator with a number of *Cosmo* models. They appeared somewhat less gorgeous in the harsh light and after the long day that included partying at the office. Nothing was said until they walked out of the building and stood on the street where they hugged and kissed each other and gave their goodbyes. It had been a long day for them too, but with a surprise happy ending.

Deedee stayed behind with Courtney waiting for the other women to walk away. When they were finally gone, she asked, "Your place or mine?"

"Your place is much nicer than my mousy apartment." Courtney gave Deedee a knowing look.

They walked at a rapid pace the entire twenty blocks to Deedee's apartment building. Deedee fumbled with the keys to the deadbolt on her apartment door but finally got it open. They rushed in, slammed the door behind them and kissed, Deedee's tongue sliding deep into Courtney's mouth and doing a dance inside.

"I want to play doctor," Deedee ordered, when they came up for air. "I'm the doctor and you're the patient."

Somehow they managed to make it to the bedroom, groping and taking each other's clothes off as they traversed the distance. Deedee pushed Courtney forcefully down onto the bed and commanded, "Stay there. I'm going to examine you."

Courtney centered herself on the bed but then lay still, flat on her back and stark naked, as she watched Deedee go around to the other side of the bed and open a drawer in her nightstand. Deedee reached in and took out a vibrator, an appliance with a handle and a short protruding stub. Next she grabbed a rubber disk from the drawer and pressed the back of it onto the stub, fixing it in place. Holding the device in her left hand she pressed a switch and it began to hum, causing the disk to vibrate. Still holding the vibrating device she reached into the drawer again and took out a small ball. After placing it on the nightstand she sat on the side of the bed and turned to Courtney. "I'll examine you now," she said with a very professional look on her face.

Courtney felt Deedee massage her feet, first with her right hand and then with the vibrator. It tickled at first but she quickly let her muscles relax, absorbing the vibrations and allowing her senses to awaken. She felt a heightened awareness of her body as the vibrator moved slowly upward along her legs, with Deedee examining every inch and pressing the vibrator against the curved surfaces to excite each and every individual muscle as it went. Courtney closed her eyes and followed the flow, feeling a pleasant warmth extend slowly upward until it reached and focused on her core. She could sense an arousal between her legs and as the vibrator came closer, it tingled.

Deedee allowed the vibrator to float of its own weight as she passed it up over Courtney's mound of Venus, and moved it upward to her tummy, examining and pressing the vibrating disk against her belly button and the soft skin on either side. Courtney shuddered as the device came in contact with new areas of her body and finally arrived at the base of her breasts. Instead of using the vibrator, Deedee held the vibrator steady with her left hand while lightly but thoroughly massaging Courtney's now heaving breasts with her right. Courtney felt her take one nipple between her thumb and forefinger and move the two fingers back and forth, lightly twisting the enlarged tip. She did this with the other nipple too as Courtney floated on an imaginary cloud, her eyes closed but nevertheless seeing puffy white billows where she lay.

While still holding the vibrator against her belly Deedee lowered her head and took Courtney's left nipple in her mouth. She sucked tenderly, drawing not only the nipple but also the surrounding breast inward while titillating the nipple with her tongue. At the same time Deedee moved the vibrator downward, passing it back and forth on her tummy, lower and lower, with each pass coming tantalizingly closer to her vagina. Courtney could feel the pleasure building between her legs and the area becoming saturated with her wetness. "Lower," she murmured, and Deedee complied by allowing the disk of the vibrator to roam downward and press against her labia. "Harder," Courtney moaned. Sensing that Courtney's feeling was becoming intense now, Deedee massaged the area with the vibrator, pressing harder and harder with each stroke. Courtney moaned louder and rolled her head on the pillow from side to side. She urgently needed release from this searing delight but Deedee lifted the vibrator from her body each time the pleasure peaked and allowed the feeling to briefly subside.

Courtney was just about to grab hold of the vibrator herself and press it hard against her vagina when Deedee turned her back and took it away. Courtney was about to protest, "What are you *doing*?" but was glad that she hadn't because Deedee quickly produced the vibrator again, this time with the disk replaced by the small round ball.

Courtney could feel Deedee spread her labia with her fingers and insert the vibrating ball between them. The ball glanced by her clitoris and she nearly exploded with pleasure as her legs stiffened and her toes curled tightly. She could feel Deedee move the ball up and down between her legs, each time coming close but not touching the sensitive source of the feeling, until she could stand it no longer. "*Now,*" she screamed and grabbed the vibrator herself, forcing it tightly against her pleasure spot. A shockwave of ecstasy shot through her body and for a second she blacked out from the intensity of the orgasm. The last thing she remembered were the convulsions of her vagina before the extreme delight swept her consciousness away.

"Okay, okay," Deedee said impatiently after a long moment. "Get up and get to work. It's *my* turn."

Chapter 55

Courtney sat in the office of the HGHS Principal, Barbara Westerhoff, flanked by her two young writers, Ashley and Ronnie. It had not been easy to make the appointment. Horace Greeley High School was in full session, with all its many clubs, sports and after-school activities in full swing, and Principal Westerhoff had her hands full. She was not about to allow just anybody to address her student body in the auditorium.

On the principal's desk in front of her were three back issues of *Women Rising* that Courtney had FedEx'd in advance after her preliminary telephone call. After sending the magazines, Courtney had called again to explain why she wanted to meet. Westerhoff had been intrigued enough with what she said to put the meeting on her schedule.

"Our magazine has been out there about one and a half years now," Courtney was saying. "Our mission is to create awareness in young women that men pose a threat to us, and to society in general. Not all men, mind you, just certain men who are prone to violence. It's a statistical fact that virtually all violent crimes are perpetrated by men."

"I can agree with you there," Westerhoff nodded in agreement. With the Principal being a professional woman, and an attractive one in her early fifties at that, Courtney felt she was speaking to the choir. Westerhoff surely understood more than most what women were up against in a man's world.

"I'd like to speak to your student body," Courtney continued, "and explain some of these statistics. They are scary and I think your students will get the point. I'm not here to sell magazines. In fact I won't even mention *Women Rising* at all if you don't want me to. My thought, now that the magazine has started and is showing some success, is that I should get out there and spread the word as a public speaker. I have created a program, with two of my young writers here, Ashley and Ronnie, where we spend a whole month at your school. I give an initial kickoff speech and then make myself available to speak privately with any girls who come forward. They may have issues with boys that they don't want to tell their parents. In the meantime, Ashley and Ronnie will volunteer their time to work with the students on your school newspaper, in a hands-on experience of investigative journalism, to assist in writing stories about student life that are germane to the topic."

"The *Tribune*." Westerhoff said.

"Tribune?"

"The name of the school newspaper is the *Tribune*. The *Horace Greeley Tribune*."

"Oh. Well, all of this will be at no cost to the school by the way, and you can monitor us every step of the way. In fact, I'm sure some of your women teachers will be fascinated to hear what we have to say."

"I don't see how I can say 'no' then, as long as you're not too graphic about the male violence. I dare say this type of real-world awareness is needed and long overdue."

"You'll be a pioneer," Courtney exclaimed. "This is a pilot program, you understand. We'll be learning ourselves as we go. It will be interesting to find out what questions your female students may have, and what stories they're willing to share."

"Yes, interesting I'm sure. I'll be present to introduce you when you give your speech, and to explain the program to the students. After that, as you say, I'll monitor you very closely. Nothing goes out in the *Tribune* without my initial review and I'll censor anything I find offensive."

"Agreed," Courtney replied. "I'd like that. There's no telling what we'll come up with, and we may not realize just how offensive it may be."

"Well, that's it then. You're good to go. I'll have to pass this by the Superintendant, but that should not be a problem. We have an open assembly for the entire student body every Wednesday morning at ten. I'll schedule you in."

"Any Wednesday would be fine. Oh, and one more thing. My writers here would like to infiltrate your student body and become eyes and ears to their student life. We would be particularly interested in having them present in the cafeteria at lunch time and in joining your cheerleaders as they train."

"The cheerleaders?"

"Yes, we understand you have a separate group for each of your major boy's sports."

"We do, but why the cheerleaders?" Westerhoff asked.

"We think the social attitudes at the high school start with the cheerleaders. They're usually the hottest girls that the boys want to impress. If we can get the cheerleaders to understand what the boys are after, we've planted the seed. Their attitudes will be picked up by other female students."

"You think so?"

"It's a theory, anyway."

"It should be interesting to find out."

"We're particularly interested in the basketball cheerleaders." Courtney continued. "Only because I was a basketball cheerleader back in the day."

"I'm sure you were a good one. You look pretty hot yourself for a career woman." Westerhoff shot her a knowing wink.

"No, I'm not." Courtney protested.

"Well I won't debate *that*," Westerhoff chortled. "You're welcome to your opinion. But yes, you can speak to the Chappaqua cheerleaders. They even have a website. They meet for practice after school in the gym at the same times the boys practice basketball. It's kind of a 'team effort' you might say."

"How about the *Tribune*? When do they meet?"

"They put out five issues a year As a matter of fact, they're almost ready to publish their first issue this year. They meet after school in one of the English classrooms. I'll give you and your writers here each a visitor's badge after we do take your fingerprints and do background checks. Security stuff." Westerhoff pressed a few keys on her computer and glanced at the screen. "The *Tribune's* in Room 522. Here's a plan of the high school buildings and grounds." She pulled out a folded brochure from a bottom desk drawer. "It will help you navigate."

"I can't thank you enough," Courtney stood. Ashley and Ronnie also thanked Principal Westerhoff, and they all shook hands before leaving.

On the way back to Ashley's car, an aged Rav4 Toyota that was in somewhat better shape than Ronnie's old junker, Ronnie said, "This is going to be fun. I can't wait to teach these privileged teenage bitches a thing or two about real life."

Chapter 56

When she returned to her office Courtney set about preparing for her speech to HGHS. In doing so she realized that her message was especially meant for girls, and that boys would surely object to hearing that their attitudes and antics, which since time immemorial were tolerated under the maxim "boys will be boys," were no longer okay with the opposite sex. Courtney feared the boys might disrupt her talk with jeers and catcalls in an attempt to make a mockery of what she had to say.

The girls, not wanting to assert their independence from the very boys they wished to befriend, would eventually side with the boys in laughing her off the stage. It was in a girl's DNA to want a boyfriend at this age, and they were not about to jeopardize their quests for male-female companionships by antagonizing them.

After some careful thought along these lines, Courtney lifted the phone on her desk and called Principal Westerhoff. She tapped in four different numbers in response to voice prompts before Westerhoff came on the line. "Barbara Westerhoff. speaking." Her voice was cheery.

"Ms. Westerhoff, this is Courtney Stillwell."

"Yes, of course. You're coming in on Wednesday. We're looking forward to your talk."

"That's what I want to discuss with you, Ms. Westerhoff—"

"Call me 'Barbara.' Please. Only the students have to call me Ms. Westerhoff."

"Barbara, then. Thank you. Please call me Courtney. Most people don't even know my last name."

"That's a nice name, Courtney. It's old school. Blue stocking, like the name 'Hannah.' Very sophisitated, yet friendly.There's a lot of meaning in a name, you know. How may I help you?" Westerhoff said all of this as it it were one sentence.

"I'm preparing for my speech on Wednesday. I'm wondering if I shouldn't give it just to the girls. The boys are not going to like it and won't agree with it, I'm sure."

"You know, I was actually thinking the same thing when we talked in my office. Maybe your subject is better directed only to the distaff side. It might be a bit disarming to the boys."

"That would be a relief to me, Barbara. That's all I can say. I was becoming concerned there'd be a backlash from the boys."

"Understandably. Don't we know it: 'Boys will always be boys.' You can count on that." Westerhoff said this with a distinct tone of disapproval, as if she were talking about some smelly underwear. Courtney knew at this moment she had a solid sister in Barbara.

"I'll tell you what," Westerhoff continued. "We'll divide the Wednesday Assembly into two half hours: a first half for the girls and a second for the boys. We've done that once before. You can take the first half; I'll find someone appropriate to talk to the boys. Some sports figure, or maybe someone career-oriented."

"Career oriented?"

"You know, like a CEO of a corporation, a male figure who can inspire the boys to go to college and work hard."

"How about a hedge fund manager?" Courtney asked timidly.

"Sure. That would fire them up. You know someone?"

"As a matter of fact, I do. His name is George. George Cleary. He's invested in our magazine."

"That sounds ideal—," Westerhoff paused. "Just a minute. Let me look him up." Courtney waited for nearly a minute before hearing Westerhoff's voice on the phone again. "We have to vet our speakers very carefully," she said when she returned. "You wouldn't believe how well we looked into your stats. I was very impressed, by the way...Okay now, I'm not seeing a lot of information about this guy. He seems to be running some kind of millisecond stock trading operation. I'm aware of their type. They steal from the rich and give to themselves. Not exactly positive role models. Can you vouch for him?"

"I've known him since college, and he's made himself *very* rich. He makes more money in a day than most people make in a lifetime."

"I don't know if that speaks well of him or not, but I'll take your word that he'll make a good presentation to the students. We'll need his fingerprints and do the usual background check, but I'll want to see a synopsis of his talk before we let him go on."

"Understood. I'll call him and, if he agrees to present to the boys, I'll have him call you."

"Good," Westerhoff said. "Well, I guess that's it then. Anything else?"

"No. I'll email you my own synopsis later today. You didn't ask for it, but I'm sure you'd like to see what I'm going to say."

"That would be best. Yes."

The two women exchanged email addresses and said their goodbyes.

Courtney hung up and immediately dialed George's number. She heard three ring sounds before he picked up.

"Courtney. What a pleasant surprise," George answered, clearly delighted to hear from her. "I've been meaning to call you but, to be absolutely honest, I've been having trepidations. I was hoping you enjoyed our weekend but I wasn't sure. You seemed so…so distant when we parted."

"It was memorable, George, believe me, and I had a very good time. Thank you. Now I'd like to ask a favor."

"Sure, *anything*. Your wish is my command. Fire away."

"I wonder if you would join me in giving a speech to the high school students in Chappaqua, New York. I'll speak to the girls and you speak to the boys."

"In Chappaqua? Why way up there?" George asked.

"I chose it because it's where those horrible men live that—." Courtney suddenly felt uneasy talking to George about this.

"Oh God, Courtney. That's, uh—." George paused. "I kind of see the point. But what would I talk about?"

"I volunteered to give a speech about *Women Rising* to the girls, but they need someone to speak to the boys about…about what it's like out there in the grownup world. Someone and something inspiring."

"Yeah, I guess I can do that. Should be fun."

"Really?"

"Of course. That's a piece of cake. And for you I'd do anything. You know that."

"*Yes.* I'm so glad." Courtney couldn't help smiling to herself. "You need to speak to the school principal right now. Her name is Barbara Westerhoff. She's expecting your call."

"Okay, done. Now how about another date?"

"Not right now, George. I need to prepare my speech. We're scheduled to present next Wednesday, by the way."

"Okay, I guess I can wait that long. Can we go up there together? I can have Isaac pick you up."

"That would be nice, except I'm going up with a couple of my writers. We're a tag team. That would be too many to fit in the car."

"Nonsense. I'll have Isaac take my stretch limo. I can sit in the back with you too. There'll be plenty of room."

"How can I refuse?"

"You can't. We'll pick all of you up early Wednesday morning and drive up there. It's only an hour ride. I've been there many times on business."

Courtney clicked off and sat motionless for a moment, thinking about how easy that was. It was nice to have a man at her beck and call. If only it wasn't George. He carried so much baggage.

Chapter 57

Courtney had told Ashley and Ronnie to meet in the office on Wednesday, at seven in the morning. These two late sleepers protested but Courtney prevailed, saying that this was the one and only time they would have to do this. For the rest of the month they could leave much later to cover the lunchroom and the after-school activities.

Isaac called Courtney from the street and they all came down. For many years, during the time when E.B. White wrote *"Talk of the Town,"* Courtney's office had been home to the venerable *New Yorker Magazine.* Still well preserved, the building now housed an eclectic variety of small businesses, from two-man law firms, to engineering consultants, to literary agencies. *Women Rising* was the only magazine tenant, all other magazines having long since vacated the Fifth Avenue area for nicer digs on high floors in shiny new towers on Sixth.

Isaac stood erect holding open the rear side door of the long black limousine. The car was double-parked, but had it found a place at the curb it would have taken up two parking places. Courtney climbed into the dark interior, followed by her two writers. She settled in to the rear seat next to George, who welcomed them all as they entered. Ashley and Ronnie found comfortable places on the bench seat that extended along one side of the space behind the front chauffeur seat. Neither of these two women had ever ridden in a stretch limo before and they gawked at the lavishly appointed interior. It had a writing table that sported a lamp with a cute lampshade, a fully stocked bar with a built-in wine cooler, a refrigerator, a coffee-maker and even a TV. They both looked at Courtney with an expression that asked "Who is this guy?" Courtney shot back a stern look that said, "Be appropriate. It's just a guy, so deal with it."

"Is your speech all ready?" Courtney asked George, mainly to break the ice. "Did you send a copy to Ms. Westerhoff?"

"Yes, and yes. I'm all set. How about you? Are you ready to knock 'em dead?"

"I think so. I'm still a little nervous, to be honest, but it's a little late to back out now."

"You'll be fine, once you stand up there and face the audience. Those girls will love you and what you have to say. It's high time somebody said it, by the way. Boys have been getting a pass for much too long."

"You think?" Courtney was glad to hear that George might be catching on. She was indeed nervous, but she was finally on her way to tell young teenage girls to stand up to men and demonstrate their independence.

Not much more was said as Isaac drove up the West Side Highway in Manhattam, crossed the toll bridge over the Harlem River into the Riverdale section of The Bronx, and merged onto the Saw Mill River Parkway that passed through Yonkers and continued north. The Saw Mill was named a "parkway" because that's just what it was: miles and miles of parkland on both sides of the divided highway and, as it passed through Chappaqua, for a long stretch of woods between the two lanes.

After traversing this section with the park in the center, Isaac turned right onto Readers Digest Road and followed the winding highway up the hill where DeWitt and Lila Bell Wallace, founders of The Readers Digest in 1922, built the majestic, brick-colonial Readers Digest Building. Reaching the top, Isaac turned right at the sign "HORACE GREELEY HIGH SCHOOL" and entered the high school campus grounds.

Isaac opened the side door for his passengers as a few stray students who happened by did a double take stare at the imposing automobile. Courtney led the group inside to the high school office to meet the principal.

Barbara Westerhoff came out of her inner office to greet them, all smiles and perky as she was introduced to George Cleary.

"I'd like you to stay in my office, Mr. Cleary, while Courtney gives her speech to the girls. Then, when the girls have left the auditorium and the boys are assembling, I'll come and get you and then introduce you as the speaker. They're a tough crowd, these boys, so you can expect some interesting questions. I'll stay with you the whole time to keep them in line in case you need it."

"George," George said.

"What?"

"Please call me George."

"All right George. I will. Now Courtney, are you ready?"

"Yes, Ma'am."

"The girls can be a tough crowd too, believe me. I'll go first and introduce you three as the editor and writers for *Women Rising*. I'll settle the crowd down and then you go on."

Courtney took a deep breath and followed Barbara Westerhoff out the door with Ashley and Ronnie in tow. They headed down the hall to the school auditorium.

Chapter 58

"Quiet down everyone." Principal Barbara Westerhoff clapped her hands twice and the large auditorium, half filled with chattering teenage girls, slowly calmed down and became still. "I have a special treat for you this morning."

There were four chairs on the stage. Courtney, Ashley and Ronnie occupied three of them and sat primly erect, facing the audience, while Principal Westerhoff spoke.

"Today I have the pleasure of introducing a truly remarkable woman, Courtney Stillwell. On the day she graduated from Barnard College she began her career as an investigative journalist." Principal Westerhoff glanced down at her notes. "In her first job out of college she did a stint with *Vogue* Magazine as a researcher, fact checking stories before their publication. After serving two years at this editorial desk and learning the basics, she jumped ship and became a free-lancer on a mission to uncover, and write about, *skullduggery*. Digging deeply to unearth the secrets of corrupt politicians, the fraudulent schemes of lawyers and businessmen and, though less often, the sexual proclivities of media celebrities, she wrote stories that got real results: A number of powerful men were cut down to size and some even spent time in jail.

"Courtney became a Master – or should I say, a *Mistress* – at finding out whatever she wanted to know. Once she is on the trail of something wrong, she works the *what, why, where and when* of the story, the four W's of journalism, until she roots out the truth. Then, and only then, she writes about it."

From her seat on the stage, Courtney could see that the audience was entranced. Not a single girl looked at her smartphone or talked to her neighbor. They stared attentively at Principal Westerhoff as she prepped them for what they were about to hear.

"About two and a half years ago, Courtney started a magazine, called *Women Rising*, to tell teenage girls and young women like yourselves about the dangers lurking in the big world out there." Principal Westerhoff lifted a copy from the podium and held it up, cover facing outward.

"You need to *read* this. It comes out every month. It has important information you need to know." Principal Westerhoff put the magazine down and turned around to look at Courtney. Courtney stood up and walked toward the podium as the audience clapped politely. Principal Westerhoff continued, "It is a distinct honor for me to present to you, *Courtney Stillwell.*"

Courtney gave Principal Westerhoff an appreciative nod for the kind introduction and stepped up to the podium. She took a deep breath, smiled at the audience, and began.

"Good morning, students. Today I want to talk with you about using your power."

The audience, prepped and intent on listening, tittered when they heard the topic. They glanced at each other excitedly, then focused in on Courtney. She already had their avid attention when she had said, "Good morning."

"I'd like to amend that slightly. I'm going to talk about using your power when negotiating with *boys.*" The word nearly electrified the room. If it were possible, the audience focused in even more intently.

"Now bear with me a moment while I explore something with you. How many of you in the audience like to buy clothes. Raise your hands."

Nearly two thirds of the audience raised their hands.

"How many like to buy shoes?"

Seeing where this was going, three quarters of the audience raised their hands.

"How many are looking forward to going to the Junior Prom next year?"

About half the audience raised their hands.

"How about the Senior Prom."

Again, half the audience raised their hands. Some of the hand raisers were the same as for the Junior Prom, but most were different.

"What is it you like most about going to a prom? It's dressing up, right?"

Nearly the entire audience raised their hands in approval.

"It's all about the hair, the make-up, the dress and the shoes, right?"

The audience was totally with her now. Some shouted, "*Yes*." Others cheered.

"Would you be surprised to learn that most boys don't like to dress up at all?"

Nearly all the girls in the audience shook their heads 'no'. Someone shouted, "*We know*." Another shouted, "Boys are such *slobs*."

"What do you think boys are interested in? Anyone. Shout it out."

"Girls." came an answer, instantly.

"Well, yes. But other than girls."

There was silence a moment while the girls thought about this.

"What are their hobbies?" prompted Courtney.

The auditorium remained quiet until one girl raised her hand and said, "My little brother plays with his electric trains." That opened the floodgates. Another said, "My brother rides his bike everywhere." Still another shouted, "Cars."

"You're onto it." Courtney shouted back. "You're getting warmer and warmer. It's a statistical fact that girls like clothes, and boys, at no matter what age, like *planes, trains and automobiles*."

Courtney stopped for a moment and let that message sink in. The girls started talking to each other and continued talking as Courtney stood there calmly, saying nothing. Since the talking didn't seem to settle down, Principal Westerhoff stood up from her chair and glared. The auditorium became instantly quiet and Courtney continued.

"Now let's assume that's true, and see where it takes us. Suppose, just suppose, your father had a set of model trains. Suppose it was a wonderful set, with tons of track and switches and locomotives and train cars. Your father had his train layout in the cellar when you grew up, and he played with it every minute of his spare time when he wasn't off working hard to feed his family. And let's just suppose you didn't have a brother so when your father died, bless his soul, he bequeathed the train set to you. He was hoping you'd like to play with them too but you have no interest at all. Now you have a model train set you don't want." Courtney paused again to let her audience catch up.

"What do you do with it?"

The audience seemed stumped again for a moment. Courtney probed, "Do you play with it anyway?"

The girls shook their heads 'no'. "*Sell it.*" someone shouted.

"Exactly." said Courtney. The sound of her voice from the public address system reverberated throughout the hall. "But who's going to buy it?"

"*Boys,*" came the answer, almost in unison.

"Now here's the teaching moment. You have something that most boys want. You have it and they want it. That is *power.* If they want to get it, they'll have to satisfy *you.* Pay you money or do your bidding in some way." Courtney let that sink in, and then dropped the bomb. "The same concept applies to *sex.*"

The auditorium erupted with female voices, all talking at once.

"You have something that boys want badly," Courtney thundered over the high-pitched voices that filled the space. "If you hold off giving it to them, that's *Girl Power.* More power than you can ever imagine. *So don't give them what they want.*"

Chapter 59

"Any questions?" Courtney looked at her watch and noted it was nearly ten twenty-five. Principal Barbara Westerhoff stood up from her chair and came forward to join Courtney at the podium. Principal Westerhoff leaned into the microphone and said, "We have time for two questions, girls, so make them count."

The room was a hubbub and several girls raised their hands, some more urgently than others. Principal Westerhoff picked out a girl in the third row, waving her hand wildly over her head. "Okay, Karla," she called on her by name. "What's your question?"

"What if we already choose not to have sex? Where's the power in that?"

"What's the answer, Courtney?" Principal Westerhoff asked, stepping back and offering Courtney the microphone again.

"You're not *supposed* to have sex. That's a good thing because the power comes from *not* giving the boys what they want. The instant you give it to them, the power is gone. *Poof.*" Courtney waved her hands in the air to indicate the power evaporating.

The girls in the audience sat stunned for a moment and then started raising their hands again. "We have time for one more question," Principal Westerhoff said after again stepping up to the microphone and scanning the crowd. "Bernice. Have you got a good question for Ms. Stillwell?"

A well-endowed young girl, seemingly mature for her age, stood up and said, "I think so. Ms. Stillwell, in your example with the trains, the girl didn't really want to play with them herself. That gave her power over the boys who wanted to have them. What if we want to have sex as much as the boys do?"

"Whooo." The sound came from other girls in the audience. All the girls looked expectantly at Courtney who returned to the mike.

"That's a very good question. It's been a best kept secret of women since the days of Queen Victoria. Everyone was told it didn't happen until you were a little older, but it does. Back in the day they gave it a nice, euphemistic name: they called it "romance." Girls were supposed to learn all about sex by reading romance novels, or by watching family TV shows and plays and movies about coming of age. Well, the truth is out now. We know better, don't we?

"All I can say is, you're in the envious position of having power over the opposite sex because they want it and they think you don't, or maybe shouldn't. In fact, you probably have more power over them right now than you'll ever have again, later in life. So go ahead and take advantage. Feel free to *use it.*

"But let me close with a word of caution to you all. Some men don't take 'no' for an answer. They want to rob you of your power to say 'no' and, given half a chance, they will. They believe they're stonger than you are and, in Neanderthal their way of thinking, might makes right.

"That moment may come for some of you and, if it does, stand up and *fight back.* Never—," Courtney paused for effect and made eye contact with as many girls in the audience as she could. "Never, *ever,* let a rapist go unpunished."

Courtney gave a little wave to the girls, signaling she was finished and Principal Westerhoff took her place at the podium. The audience began to clap and then all the girls stood up and continued with a thunderous applause. Courtney gave them a broad smile and returned to her seat. After a beat, Principal Westerhoff announced, "Before you leave, I'd like to say one more thing. Ms. Stillwell brought with her two of her best writers at her magazine, *Women Rising.* They are, left to right, Ashley and Veronica. Veronica calls herself 'Ronnie.' Won't you stand, young ladies?"

Ashley and Ronnie both stood and gave a brief bow.

"I have given them permission to meet with you, as a resource, for the coming month. They can give you insight into a possible career in journalism, especially those of you who are working on the *Tribune.* They can also mentor you as 'big sisters' who have taken the next step in life. Ask them questions, about anything. This is a kind of experiment in social science so I'll keep close tabs on it, but I'm sure you'll find them interesting to talk to. They'll be available in the cafeteria at lunchtime and during your activities after school."

Principal Westerhoff turned and shook hands with her three women, then returned to the microphone. "Well, girls, that's it. File out in an orderly fashion and return to your classrooms as quickly and as quietly as you can. The boys are waiting to come in here for their Wednesday Assembly."

With that, Principal Westerhoff walked off the stage, followed by Courtney, Ashley and Ronnie. Before Principal Westerhoff headed back to her office to get George, Courtney asked if she and her two colleagues could sit in the rear of the auditorium to hear George's speech. Principal Westerhoff readily agreed.

* * * *

The boys entered the auditorium and took their seats. They were much quieter than the girls who had just left, although they were jabbing each other and making sarcastic jokes as they filed in. Principal Westerhoff led George to the stage and motioned for him to sit on one of the empty chairs until he was introduced. George appeared calm, Courtney thought, as she watched from the back. He was dressed in a dark gray suit but had on a red sweater vest that made his outfit less formal.

Principal Westerhoff quieted the audience and gave the introduction. George had sent her a C.V. which she read aloud and then encouraged the boys to "welcome him warmly." They clapped enthusiastically as he stood and came forward to the podium.

"Young men," he began. "How would you like to get rich? I mean *really* rich?"

From the getgo he had their attention. George told the boys how he got started in the world of finance and where he was now. He was likeable, and his audience clearly enjoyed listening to him talk. He had lilting rhythm in his manner of speaking that was endearing to the boys at first, and also to Courtney. She knew most of what he had to say, yet she was as fascinated as they were to hear his presentation.

Nevertheless, in her mind the entire premise of his profession, to take money from the retirement savings of others, was a moral dilemma, and the fact that George failed to see this dilemma was more than troubling to her. She had long harbored doubts about George, and the more she learned what he was about, she more she wondered if she could trust him.

Although the crowd was eager to hear his story, they also appeared to become increasingly restless as George told them how he made his money. Having reservations about this same issue herself, Courtney watched with interest as the young men become more and more unsettled and anxious to question him.

When Principal Westerhoff stood up to signal the allotted time was coming to a close, George called for questions. The Principal didn't take over the Q and A this time, as she had done for Courtney. She deferred to him, perhaps because he was a man, Courtney thought, and trusted him to keep the crowd under control.

However, as the questions began to come, Courtney realized that Principal Westerhoff had made a big mistake.

Chapter 60

George took the first question from a boy in the back of the room. He stood up and asked, "How does your hedge fund work exactly?" Then remaining standing for a moment he added, "My father says it should be illegal," and sat down.

"It's complicated," George began. "Very complicated. The term 'hedge' originally referred to a line of bushes around a house or a field, but it has come to mean placing limits on risk. Originally, hedge funds sought to hedge their risk against market fluctuations by shorting some of their investments. My fund hedges risk too, but not in that way. Let me explain it with an analogy:

"When I was in grad school I took a vacation in Europe and stopped in at the casino in Monte Carlo. Before going, I read up on strategies for playing roulette and decided to use this simple one. You hedge your bets by placing a chit on both red and black at the same time. If the ball lands on black, you win two chits back: the one you played and a bonus chit. But you lost the chit you placed on red, so you're even. You hedged your bet, but you haven't made any money. To make money, you play again, this time doubling your bet and adding a chit on red. That's three chits on red and one on black. If the ball lands on red this time, you'll get your three chits back plus three chits as a bonus, but you'll have lost the chit you placed on black. If you quit now you'll have five chits - six chits from red but you lost the chit on black – for an initial investment of two. *Not bad* for two turns of the wheel. It turns out if you continue to play this way, doubling and also adding one each time on the color that didn't come up, when you finally end the game you'll have made one chit for every turn of the wheel."

Hands went up, waving furiously. George picked a boy near the front. He stood up and asked, "You mean it doesn't matter whether red or black came up, you'd still always win?"

"That's right. That system makes money, day in and day out, no matter what."

The boy remained standing and asked a follow-up question even though other hands were waving wildly. "In Monte Carlo, the casino allowed you to do this?"

"They did back then." George replied, looking past the boy to choose another waving hand.

"What do you mean, 'back then'? They don't allow it now?"

"Well, no. They changed the rules to increase the odds in their favor."

George pointed to another boy, but that boy immediately pulled his hand down, deferring to the first one who remained standing and asked another follow-up question, "How did they change the rules?"

"It used to be," George said rapidly, trying to brush this line of questioning aside, "that if the ball landed on green, they would leave the red and black chips on the table. They changed the rule to take those chips away too."

Satisfied he made his point, the boy sat down and the boy he had chosen stood up. "Your hedge fund works like that?" he asked. "Isn't it like stealing money from the market?"

"Not at all. It's *earning* money from the market," George replied and looked around for another boy.

"But you haven't really earned it. You just took it. You didn't do any market research or anything." Having made his point, this boy sat down.

George seemed flustered, Courtney observed. She wondered what he would say to this comment. However, he ignored it and quickly picked another waving hand.

"What good are you doing for the economy?" this boy asked. "Isn't the stock market supposed to support the economy by investing in successful businesses so they can succeed and grow?"

"No, not at all. Once a company, like Google or Facebook has done an IPO, they don't care what happens to their shares, whether they go up or down. The original investors have made their money." Courtney could see George was becoming defensive. It didn't look like he fully believed in what he was saying. George turned to look at Principal Westerhoff, but she held up her two hands, indicating he was on his own. He picked another boy.

"What about the people, like our parents, who have retirement accounts invested in the market? Isn't that where your money is coming from? Aren't you stealing from them?"

George became red in the face. He was not used to being challenged in this way. As Courtney watched him squirm she thought she was beginning to see his true character. He was a taker. From the boys' questions she realized that his hedge fund had no useful purpose other than to reward him handsomely.

The questions continued and became even more critical. Through them Courtney understood that Congress refused to change the rules to make the system more fair, because hedge fund managers, some of the most highly compensated individuals in America, contributed heavily to Congressional campaigns.

She also learned about the tax breaks these managers enjoyed. Instead of their professional fees being taxed as ordinary income like that earned by ordinary citizens in America, their income was taxed at a reduced rate as a "capital gain," which in itself was an enormous tax loophole for the rich. A capital gain was considered "unearned income" and, because it was *not* earned, it was somehow taxed *less*.

It was an unfair world these men had made, and George was an integral part of it. Instead of being a part of the solution, he was part of the problem. She wondered why women had stayed in the background for so long and had allowed such a system to continue. Courtney could feel her resentment rising and she regretted having accepted his money as an investor in her magazine.

Principal Westerhoff let the Assembly go overtime into the eleven o'clock hour, allowing the teaching moments to continue, but she eventually stopped the drop-by-drop blood letting by coming forward to the podium and thanking George for his presentation. Courtney could see the relief on his face as he shook her hand. He took out a handkerchief from his pocket and wiped his brow.

"All right boys," she turned and spoke directly into the microphone to broadcast her voice. "I hope you all learned something this morning. Now give it up for Mr. Cleary with your enthusiastic applause. Show your appreciation for his coming up from New York City to speak to you."

The applause was less than deafening, but George managed a broad grin and waved an acknowledgment.

In the rear of the room Courtney stood up and quietly left the auditorium with Ashley and Ronnie. They headed for the main door of the school to wait for George. Courtney knew the ride back to the City in his limousine would be extremely awkward.

Chapter 61

As Isaac drove them down the West Side Highway, George tried to pin Courtney down on a date for dinner. She demurred, saying she would have to check her schedule at the office, hoping he'd take that as a signal she wasn't interested. She felt hemmed in but there was nothing she could do about it. He had invested a million dollars in her magazine so the least she could do was to take his calls.

After Isaac drove off in the long limo with George in the back, leaving Courtney and her colleagues off on Forty-Fourth Street, the three women lingered on the sidewalk to talk about their morning.

"He asked you for a *date*," Ronnie gushed, eyeing Courtney enviously. "He's a multi-millionaire. He could *change your life*."

"That's nothing," Ashley told her. "George and Courtney already spent a weekend in Vermont."

"You *did*?" Ronnie's mouth curled into a smirk. "You randy lady. I knew you had it in you."

"Nothing happened," Courtney said flatly, embarrassed because she knew it was a lie.

"Jeez, well *go* for it. If you don't, I will. It would sure be a step up from Billy, 'cause he's no fun any more. Good for is sex, maybe, but not much else."

"Pardon my saying so, Ronnie," Ashley said, "but you wouldn't stand a chance. There's a difference between being randy, like Courtney here, and raunchy like you."

Courtney shot the two women a serious frown and protested, "*Nothing* happened. Now can we get off this subject? We need to talk about what we do next, up in Chappaqua."

"I believe thee protests too much," Ashley told her, and added, "A weekend in Vermont together? What are you, a Mennonite?" Courtney felt the sting of sarcasm although she knew it was just in jest.

She tried to move her colleagues off the Vermont weekend to the subject at hand. "Now that I've broken the ice at the high school, it's time for *you* to have some fun," she said with an upbeat tone she didn't feel. "You have a month to go up there, get to know the girls, tease out what's happening because of Nemo, and write up a report for Roger. Make sure you keep Principal Barbara Westerhoff in the loop, and me too. But remember, you're undercover. No one knows about Nemo and no one should ever know. If the word gets out, the whole special weapons program will be exposed and we'll probably end up in jail. Roger too. His rear is on the line with this, and it will be because of me."

"Because of *you*?" Ronnie wondered. "What do you have to do with it?"

"I suggested Chappaqua. Don't ask me why."

Ashley, who was present at the board meetings when the decision was made, signaled Courtney with her eyes that her lips were sealed. She asked, "Should we go up there every day?"

"I don't know. See what you can find out. You need to be there enough so the girls feel comfortable confiding in you. You're their Big Sisters, remember."

"Yeah," Ronnie smacked her lips. "I can't wait to learn what my little sisters are up to. I'll bet they have a few secrets to share."

* * * *

The next day Ashley and Ronnie sat together at a table on one side of the cafeteria and observed the lunch crowd. They had taken pains to dress the very same way as the girl students. They had hit the mall the previous afternoon to buy new outfits. They both had on UGG boots, designer jeans, factory faded and torn in just the right places, and fluffy white blouses. They wore lipstick, just the right amount and shade so as not to look too slutty, and had their hair pulled back in a ponytail. They fit in perfectly.

As they watched they saw the social gatherings in action. The girls and the boys always ate at separate tables, except in one instance where two good-looking boys were allowed to sit at the table with three great-looking girls. Even though the boys had joined them, the girls ignored them. One of the girls pretended to be messaging with her iPhone.

For the first hour Ashley and Ronnie sat alone together but eventually, as the tables filled up, a couple of girls scanned the room, holding their trays, and came over.

"Can we sit here too?" asked one of them, carrying a bowl of salad and a bottle of water on her tray. "There's not much room left."

"Please," Ashley replied as Ronnie eyed them critically. They weren't the hottest of girls, but it was a start Ronnie thought.

The two girls sat and eyed each other uncomfortably, obviously wondering whether they could continue a private talk they were having, until one of them asked, "Weren't you at the Assembly yesterday?"

Ronnie shot her a saccharin smile and replied, "Yes, that was us. We're here to be Big Sisters to you guys."

"Big Sisters? What do you mean?" Both girls appeared dumbfounded.

"You know, answer any questions you might have."

"What kind of questions?"

"I don't know. About boys, for example? About real life when you get a bit older? Whatever. The Principal here is conducting a kind of experiment and asked us to mentor you guys. If you want to be mentored, that is."

"Oh." The girl looked at her companion and they both stifled a small giggle.

"So what did you think of Courtney's speech yesterday?" Ashley asked in an attempt to start a conversation. "My name's Ashley by the way. And this is Ronnie."

The other girl, who had been silent up to now, opened up a little. "I'm Betty. This is Mary Kate." She nodded toward her friend. "We liked it."

"The speech?"

"Yes."

"Do you think it was helpful?"

"Not really."

"Why not?"

"Power over boys? I don't think so."

"You don't agree?"

"Boys aren't even interested in us."

"You'd be surprised," Ronnie interjected. "For every girl there's a boy who wants to get into her pants."

The two girls looked at each other and stifled another giggle.

Mary Kate, the more forward of the two, said, "The boys go for the hot girls. Like the ones over there." She half pointed to the table of girls that had allowed the two boys to sit with them.

"That's a problem, I know," Ronnie replied sympathetically. "There's always competition, no matter how good you look. But eventually you'll see. If you have a good heart the boys will find you."

"Yeah, *right*. They can look right through us and see our hearts. What do you think, they have x-ray eyes like Superman?"

"I'll tell you this: You'll have better hearts than those girls over there. Hot girls get spoiled by all those suck-up boys. It's kind of a curse. Ruins them for life."

"That's a curse I'd like to have," Betty commented.

"What if we told you that within a month you're going to have boys look at you differently? Guaranteed." Ashley leaned in close so she could lower her voice for emphasis. "And they'll appreciate who you really are."

"You make it seem so simple. It's not." Betty said, somewhat sadly.

"Trust your Big Sisters," Ronnie urged earnestly. "We've been around the block. We know what's coming."

"We'll help you," Ashley added.

Betty and Mary Kate looked at each other. For a moment it seemed too good to be true, but then they looked back at their new mentors.

"What the heck," Mary Kate said. "We'll give it a try. We've got nothing to lose."

Finished with their lunches, the two girls got up from the table, looked hopefully at Ashley and Ronnie, and took their trays.

"Hope to see you tomorrow," Ronnie called as the girls left. "Same time, same table." When they were out of earshot she turned to Ashley and lowered her voice. "Nothing to lose but their virginity," she said with a smirk.

Chapter 62

Ashley and Ronnie had previously agreed to split up the afternoon school activities. Ashley would take cheerleader practice in the gym while Ronnie lent a hand at the *Tribune*, the school newspaper. They cooled their heels in the school cafeteria until the academic classes let out for the day. "Knock 'em dead, Kiddo," Ronnie said as they parted ways. Ashley punched her friend in the arm.

Ashley found the gym without difficulty and entered a side door, carrying a small duffel with her gym clothes. The space was enormous, enough for two basketball games to go on at the same time, with extra space for cheerleading practice over at the far end. Bleachers lined one side. Ashley walked over to where the girls where assembling in groups to practice in several different teams, and introduced herself. "Hi. I'm Ashley. I've been asked to be a Big Sister and help you guys out."

The few girls who were there by this time stared at her as if she were from some foreign planet. They wore tight-fitting T-shirts with the word "*basketball*" on the front. Two other cheerleading squads were assembling nearby for other school sports and a female coach was moving among the three groups of girls checking names with a clipboard. Ashley gave her name to the coach when she came by and, to her surprise, the coach had her name on the list.

"We don't need any help," snapped one of the girls when the coach stepped away. She stood out as the tallest and sleekest one of the bunch. "Go away."

"Whoa." Ashley responded. "If you don't want my help, that's okay. Mind if I watch though?"

The girl who had spoken glanced at the other girls for their tacit agreement. They nodded; she answered, "No. This is private. We're practicing our moves. We don't want *spies* watching us."

"Were you girls at the Assembly yesterday? Maybe you didn't hear. Your principal would like me to observe what you're doing. I'm not a spy."

"A spy for *her*," came the reply. "That's just as bad as for another school."

"All right. Let's start over again," Ashley suggested. "I think we began on the wrong foot. I used to cheerlead when I was at college. I was pretty good in fact."

"Oh, yeah? So you think we care? Now *leave*."

"I could teach you a thing or two; if you'd give me a try."

"Wait just a minute," one of the other girls broke in. "Let's see what she's got."

The first girl, who had done all of the talking, was about to rebuff her but thought better of it and snarled, "Alright. Go ahead."

Ashley had not been bluffing when she said she'd been a cheerleader. "Just a moment," she said evenly. "I'll be right back," she grabbed her duffel and quickly disappeared to a secluded area behind the bleachers. She came back a few moments later wearing a T-shirt instead of her blouse and sneakers instead of the UGG boots. The girls stood eyeing her critically as she stepped out onto the floor.

Ashley went through a routine of somersaults she had learned while at college. She had lost some of her edge but she was still fit, due to her daily workouts, and her performance was far better than what these high school girls were used to. As she performed, more girls dribbled in to join cheerleading practice and also stood watching, as did the faculty coach who at the moment was with another cheerleader group on the other side of the gym.

"She's good." remarked one of the girls who just arrived. "Who is she?"

"She's one of Principal Westerhoff's spies. She was there at the Assembly," replied the mean girl who had been the spokesperson for the group thus far. "The bitch is trying to butt in, but I told her to butt out."

"We could use some help," said the other girl. "We've been fucking around and we're disorganized. The coach isn't helping us and she looks like she knows her stuff."

"Fucking around? You think we've been just fucking around?"

"Yes, as a matter of fact I do. Have we been getting better? Have we learned anything new?"

"The season's just started, dumb-ass."

"Let's take a vote," the new girl suggested to everyone as Ashley finished her moves and walked up, breathing hard. "All in favor of having her stay and work with us, raise your hand."

A good two-thirds of the girls raised their hands. The mean girl grunted, "If she stays, I'm going."

"You're having your period, right? What makes you so high and mighty all of a sudden?"

"She's pouting. Her boyfriend dumped her. I saw it," one of the other girls said.

"He did *not*," the mean girl protested. "I dumped *him*. That bastard."

"Now wait a minute," Ashley broke in. "I can help you with this." She addressed the mean girl. "Trust me, I've had a lot of experience along these lines, with boys acting up. What was the problem…uh, I don't even know your name."

"Muriel. Muriel Benjamin."

"Muriel. Do you want your boyfriend back or are you sick and tired of him?"

Muriel stared at the ground and spoke with a whining voice, "I want him back."

"Well then, let's do it." Ashley was enthusiastic now. "One of the ways you can win him back is to really get good at cheerleading. That will get to him at the place where it counts: his *prick*. So let me show you girls how."

Ashley spent the next half hour working with the cheerleaders and drilling them while the school cheerleading coach watched from a distance. They were willing subjects and, because of their efforts, they made some real progress in improving their flexibility and style. They could see that the workout was paying dividends and in the end they appeared to feel good, although exhausted. They were all smiles when it was time to go and they credited Ashley for taking them in the right direction.

"You're a keeper," one of them said. "Can you come back tomorrow?"

"I promised your Principal I'd spend a month with you."

"Hooray." The cheerleaders cheered; the practice hour was over all too soon.

When Ronnie left Ashley she headed straight for the room where the *Tribune* staff met after school to prepare and edit the school newspaper. Holding a plan of the building in her hand she navigated her way to an upstairs classroom. The door was closed so she knocked twice, opened it and walked in. The *Tribune* staff turned and stared at her, like deer caught in the headlights. A male teacher sat at a desk on the far side of the room, apparently busy with reading and grading student papers.

"Hello, everybody." Ronnie exclaimed cheerfully. "Ronnie's here to teach you a thing or two about journalism." She reached into the handbag that hung from her shoulder, pulled out a copy of *Cosmopolitan* magazine and held it up, cover facing out. "No, that's not me on the cover. But that's my lead article there." She pointed to the headline on the cover. "When I'm through, you'll all be better writers."

The staff consisted of three girls and two boys. The girls were cute, in a studious sort of way; the boys were gangly and pimply. Ronnie figured they'd signed up for the *Tribune* to get close to the girls. Not a bad strategy, she knew.

"Who's Editor in Chief?"

The teacher at the desk pointed to one of the girls and she raised her hand. She looked more mature than the others. Probably a senior, Ronnie thought. Having done his job to point out the Editor, the teacher went back to grading papers.

"My name's Zoe. And you are?"

"Veronica. Call me 'Ronnie'."

"And why are you here?"

"Were you at the Assembly yesterday?"

"No. I was here working on the newspaper. We've got to get it out tomorrow, Friday. We're panicking."

"Were any of you there?" Ronnie looked at the others. The other four staff members all raised their hands and nodded their heads affirmatively. "I was sitting on stage, remember? Well, for the first half anyway. The Principal introduced me?"

The two girls nodded.

"I'm on loan from *Cosmo* Magazine for one month. I'm an investigative journalist. Here to teach you the ropes."

"We don't have time," Zoe said. "We have to get the paper out."

"Tell you what. I'll just be a fly on the wall for today and tomorrow. I'll read your stuff and make a comment or two, but that's all. When you're done with this issue and you can take a breath, let's get to know each other and have some fun doing the next one.

"That's not until Christmas," Zoe replied. "We only do five issues a year."

"So much the better. That'll give us more time. You want to learn journalism? I'm here to help."

The staff seemed to like that approach. With a nod they went right back to work, editing and pasting the pages into a computer-generated mock-up for publication. Ronnie saw paper copies of articles lying on the table and two of them caught her eye. She picked up one with the headline:

W.A. GIRLS HEAR MAGAZINE MAVEN
Secrets of Girl Power Revealed

She read through the article and was impressed. The author had absolutely nailed Courtney's speech at the Wednesday Assembly. The byline gave the name "Yvonne O'Mally."

"Which one of you is Yvonne?" she asked. "This is *great*."

A dark-haired girl looked up and raised her hand. "You think so?" she replied timidly.

"Yeah. You mind if I do a few text edits? I won't change the content. Promise."

Yvonne smiled. "Sure. Maybe you can make it better? As long as there's time. We're in kind of a rush."

"I'll do it now with my pen and give it right back. You can reject all the edits if you want. Your call."

"Okay with me. Okay, Zoe?"

Zoe, annoyed at being interrupted in her work, grumbled her assent. Ronnie went to work and line edited the article. "Here," she said, handing the papers to Yvonne. "Take a look."

Yvonne took about as long to review the edits as Ronnie did to make them, then looked up. "These are *good*," she said. "I'll make them." She brought up the document on her computer and started making the changes.

Ronnie then scanned the table for an article about the boy's session at the Wednesday Assembly. She spotted an article with the headline:

HEDGE FUND MANAGER ON W.A. HOTSEAT
Defends Sucking $$$$ from Financial Markets

It bore the byline, Victor Menendez. "Who's Victor?" she asked.

"Vick," one of the two boys said. "That's me."

"Mind if I read it?"

Vick thought a moment and seemed about to say no, but then apparently thought better of it. "Okay," he said. "But I don't like anyone changing my stuff."

Ronnie read through the article and saw several statements she thought were wrong. The article was a hatchet piece, it seemed to her, which exaggerated the negative and didn't give George Cleary credit for any of his accomplishments. If it were so easy to do what George had done, earning how many millions of dollars, more people would have done it. George was a brilliant financier, Ronnie felt, but the article didn't give him any quarter. She didn't want this report to publish this way and she told Victor so.

"This isn't fair," she protested, pointing to the page. "Reading this you'd think that George Cleary was a criminal or something. He's not. He's a legitimate businessman."

"I call it the way I see it," Vick said. "Who are *you* to put it down?"

"Just saying. I don't think you should put an article out there that's supposed to report the news when it's really an opinion piece. That belongs on the editorial page."

Zoe looked up from what she was doing and frowned. "Let me see that."

Ronnie handed it over and Zoe took a moment to review it. Victor was not happy, but there was nothing he could do. By this time the other staff members, including Yvonne, had stopped what they were doing and were watching Zoe with baited breath, as if she were *Alexa Hente* drinking the coffee.

"This is shit," she announced flatly. "Walter, you take over. You redo it, and do it right."

The other boy, whom she called "Walter," groaned and took the paper from Zoe. "I've got enough to do. Why don't you have *her* write it? She was there. I saw her sitting in the back. Let 'Miss Know-it-All' here fuck it up."

"I'll do it," Ronnie said brightly. "But I'm not supposed to write for you guys. My name's not going on this. I'm writing anonymously."

"Suit yourself," Zoe said. "But we need it this afternoon."

Ronnie sat down at one of the computers in the room and composed the perfect newspaper article. It took her just an hour. The headline read:

W.A. BOYS HEAR MASTER OF THE UNIVERSE
Secrets of a Hedge Fund Revealed

Zoe placed the two articles about the Wednesday Assembly on the front page, side by side. Despite his objections to having a ghostwriter, Ronnie gave Victor the byline for the boys' article so the front page would appear to readers to be a competition between a boy and a girl staff writer. What no one knew, other than Ronnie and the newspaper staff, was that a girl had already won.

Chapter 63

Ashley and Ronnie walked out of the school building at four o'clock and headed for Ashley's Toyota in the parking lot. It was a clear, late October day and the women both donned their tinted glasses to shield their eyes from the bright afternoon sun. They could see girls practicing lacrosse and boys practicing football on the fields in front of the school building.

"Let's go watch for a minute," Ronnie suggested.

"What? Lacrosse practice?"

"No, silly. The football. Those hunky boys."

They strode over and as they came close they could hear the coach screaming, seemingly enraged about something the boys were doing, or not doing.

"Block him. Block that play," he was shouting. His ruddy face was flushed and spittle coated his lips. As the girls walked up he checked himself and stood erect, acknowledging their presence.

"Is there a problem, coach?" Ashley asked pleasantly. She was still dressed in her cheerleading gear and carried her duffel so the man would naturally think she coached some girls' team.

"Naw. Just trying to fire these boys up. They've been getting slower and slower this week and we have a game with Port Chester on Saturday."

"The usual time?" Ashley asked casually. She didn't want to reveal she didn't know the game time, but needed to know when it was.

"Yeah, at three. We'll be lighting the bonfire after the game."

"We'll be there," Ronnie exclaimed, immediately picking up on Ashley's train of thought. "Good luck."

"Looks like we'll need it," the coach said, allowing a dubious tone to creep into his voice.

When they got in the car and started their drive back to New York City, Ashley used the Bluetooth connection between the car and her cellphone to call Courtney. Courtney picked up on the first ring. "Ashley. I've been wondering about you guys. How was your first day of school?"

"You're on the speaker, Courtney. Ronnie and I are in the car on the way back."

"Hi Courtney. It's me, *Ronnie*." Ronnie was her usual upbeat self.

"Hi Ronnie, I'm all ears. What's the report?"

"It started out pretty rocky for both of us," Ronnie replied. "But we turned it around. We're now *in like Flynn*."

"Really?"

"Yes. And I think your strategy's working," Ashley said. "We're covering the lunchroom at noon and both cheerleading practice and the school newspaper after school. Oh, and we walked over to football practice. Turns out, there's a game on Saturday, with a bonfire. We should go."

"That's wonderful." Courtney's enthusiasm spilled out over the speakerphone. "Roger called this afternoon to find out what was happening. He's treating this as some kind of science experiment. He said that Nemo should be kicking in right about now and we need to track its effects."

"We haven't seen anything unusual," Ashley said. "But your two spies are on the case. We'll keep our eyes out."

"Good. I'll tell Roger."

"We did hear one thing," Ronnie broke in. "The football coach was pissed because he said his boys were slacking off. He was worried about the game on Saturday."

"Really? Maybe then I should go. Roger too. What do you think?"

"That would be great," Ronnie replied. "How about asking George?"

"George? I'm not so sure. He and Roger never met—." There was a pause before Courtney continued and said, "No, I don't think so."

"Why not? I think he's cute."

"He knows about Nemo but he doesn't know that Roger put it the water in Chappaqua. Besides, I don't want to encourage him."

"Encourage him? You went to Vermont with him, for God sakes. I'll bet you got laid. You can't undo that."

"Yes, I can. And if I want to I will." Courtney suddenly realized she might have acknowledged something had happened.

"All right. But I can't see what your problem is. He's like this perfect specimen. Rich too."

"The game starts at three on Saturday," Ashley chimed in. "I'll pick everybody up at your office, Courtney. Have Roger meet us there."

"You heading up there tomorrow?" Courtney asked.

"Of course. We're now Big Sisters to these girls in Chappaqua. We can't let them down."

"Good going. Well, goodbye then." Courtney said.

"Bye."

Ashley clicked off and the two rode for awhile in silence. Eventually, Ronnie interrupted the somber mood by saying, "I really like him."

"Like who?"

"George."

"Sorry, Ronnie. He's way out of your league."

"I know. It sucks."

* * * *

On Friday the two women drove to Chappaqua again and arrived just in time for lunch. They went through the cafeteria line and took their trays to the same table where they held court the day before. Betty and Mary Kate joined them again and they sat together, taking in the social scene as it played out before them.

"That's Muriel Benjamin," Betty indicated without pointing. "She thinks who she is."

"Do the other girls like her?" Ashley asked.

"She has her little clique. She's really mean to everyone else, though, with the exception of some of the cute boys. She thinks she's so hot but she's not."

"Does she have a boyfriend?"

"*She* thinks so. John Baker. He's captain of the football team."

"I've seen them together," Mary Kate added. "They're always holding hands. It's disgusting. They do it to make everyone jealous. Like Hollywood celebrities or something, they're play-acting to show off."

"I heard he dumped her," Ashley said. "Have you seen them together recently?"

The two girls looked at Ashley with their mouths open. "OMG. Really?" Betty asked, a smile curling up on her lips. "Serves her right."

"I don't think it will last. Muriel's too smart for that."

"You're in on the dirt?" Mary Kate asked, leaning in. "Tell us."

"I don't really know anything, except Muriel is trying to get him back, and she will eventually. Don't get your hopes up."

"How come you know so much?" Betty demanded.

"I was at cheerleading practice yesterday. She's a head cheerleader."

"The *bitch*." Betty was not at all happy to hear this latest gossip.

"Do you think John Baker has been in her pants?" Ronnie asked.

Mary Kate fielded this question and made an attempt at answering it. "The way he acts he's been into every girl's pants. But my guess is 'no'. Like you said, Muriel's smart. She's a prick tease and she knows if she lets him have what he wants, he'll think she's a slut."

"That's like the Girl Power that lady was talking about at Wednesday Assembly," Betty added. "She uses it, *big time*."

"We'll see about that," Ronnie commented slyly. "Things may be about to change."

"What do you mean?" Betty asked.

"Just a guess. An educated guess. We'll soon see if I'm right."

"What about you?" Ashley asked Betty. "How is *your* love life coming along?"

"Funny you should ask," Betty replied. "The boys seem…I can't explain it…more friendly. Not so uptight. I find I can even talk to some of them."

"See. Give it time. Like I said before, the boys will go for the good heart, not the hot looks. What about you, Mary Kate?"

Mary Kate could hardly contain herself. "Me too. This cute boy came up to me and started talking, just like *that*. I couldn't believe it. We actually had a *conversation*."

Ashley and Ronnie looked at each other incredulously. "It's working," Ronnie said.

"What's working?" Mary Kate asked, picking up on what was said but totally confused.

"We are," Ashley answered. "Your Big Sisters are here to make everything right."

Chapter 64

Ashley and Ronnie stayed in the cafeteria observing the social scene, as they had done the day before, until the final bell rang, then left for their student activities: cheerleading practice for Ashley and the *Tribune* for Ronnie. They received a much warmer reception this time and during their sessions were able to garner further the friendship and confidence of their student "charges." They kept on the alert for scuttlebutt about the social scene and, on their trip home in Ashley's car, shared together the gossip they had gathered.

"We had a party today," Ronnie gushed. "The gang finished putting together the newspaper and sent it to press. The English teacher who's in charge? He doesn't do shit but he brought in some wine and cheese. He pulled down the shade and locked the door then let the staff have at it. Said it was part of 'learning the newspaper business'."

"Now *there's* a good teacher," Ashley commented sarcastically. "Did he drink too?"

"Oh, yeah." Ronnie said, rolling her eyes. "And you won't believe this, but I could see his little wheels turning. He wanted to come on to me but he didn't dare do it in front of the students. I got out of there as soon as the party was over."

"Did the kids have a good time?"

"Well, there's these two guys and three girls. The guys are not so great looking so you just know they signed up for the newspaper so they could meet girls. No problem there, but the funny thing was that it was backward this time. The girls were all over the guys and it looked like they didn't give a shit. The girls were flirting away like crazy and the boys just wanted to talk shop. It was the damndest thing."

"Nemo, you think?"

"Must be. It reminded me of my ex-boyfriend Billy."

"*Ex*-boyfriend? I thought you were tight, especially after he stopped drinking the Nemo."

"It was good for awhile. He was hot to trot, but that wears thin over time. I think I can do better."

"I think you can too, Ronnie," Ashley said appreciatively.

"You want to hear the funniest thing?" Ronnie said, not responding to Ashley's comment. "The names of these guys that that do the newspaper. First of all, I found out the teacher's name. It's 'Uwe'. Uwe Czybulka. Polish or something."

Ashley smiled. "Funny name."

"That's not the end of it. The two boys are called 'Victor' and 'Walter'. So that's 'U-V-W'. Get it?"

"No, I don't really follow."

"One of the girls is named 'Xaviera'. 'Exsie' for short."

"Odd name."

"So we have 'U-V-W-X.'"

"Don't tell me,,,"

"You guessed it. The other two girls are Yvonne and Zoe. You can't make this shit *up*."

Ashley laughed out loud as she drove. "That is so funny."

"Weird, huh? So tell me. Can you beat that?"

"Muriel was a little less testy today," Ashley reported when she calmed down from laughing. "She actually apologized for her attitude yesterday. She seemed…" she groped for just the right word, "…almost *feminine*."

"Any news about her boyfriend? What's his name? John something?"

"John Baker," Ashley said. "Yeah, things are moving really fast on that front. Apparently they're on speaking terms again. She calls him her 'pussycat' but says they're going 'platonic' right now. Her words. That's not like her, though. I couldn't believe it."

"No 'holding hands'?" Ronnie asked with a snarky tone in her voice.

"Nope. Apparently that's out for now at least. Muriel says John is under a lot of stress because of the game on Saturday. Seems the football coach comes from Port Chester. He grew up there and played football when he was in high school. He lives there still but now he coaches Chappaqua and gets paid the big bucks."

"They're playing Port Chester on Saturday, right?"

"Yeah. It's a rivalry against the coach's old team and he desperately wants to win. It's a matter of pride, and also reputation."

"Remember yesterday? The coach was screaming at the boys." Ronnie recalled. "That kind of explains it."

"You're right. And you know what? With Nemo kicking in now, it must be driving him *crazy*." Ashley said, trying to stifle her mirth.

"And John's turned into a *pussycat*." Ronnie smirked.

"And he's the team *quarterback*."

Barely able to contain herself, Ronnie tried to hold back a laugh as she connected the dots. "The coach is from Port Chester you said? He's not drinking the Chappaqua water."

"No Nemo for *him*," Ashley looked over at Ronnie as she drove, and the two women completely broke down and howled.

* * * *

The group assembled at one o'clock on Forty-fourth Street in front of Courtney's building. Roger arrived on time and, since it was Saturday, he found a parking spot in her block. He was getting out of his car as Ashley drove up with her Toyota and double-parked next to him.

Courtney was there, waiting, when Roger and Ashley drove up, and she greeted them each warmly. A minute later Ronnie pulled up in her junk-mobile and stopped right behind Ashley. Courtney made a quick decision about the travel arrangements and asked Ronnie to park in Roger's spot. She asked Ronnie to ride along with Ashley so she could ride with Roger. This way she and Roger would have a good chat, she thought, and work out the next steps in their plan. She still had to deal with those men who had raped her while at college.

As they drove up the Saw Mill River Parkway, following Ashley and Ronnie, Courtney broached the delicate subject. "What happens next?" She had already spoken to Roger on the phone and told him that the Nemo was taking effect and working to change the social dynamic. "What about the three men we talked about at the board meeting? Now that the Nemo is flowing, what can we do?"

"I've been working that out in my mind," Roger explained, thoughtfully, as he stared ahead at the road, driving. "I have this idea for teaching them a lesson. Let me pass it by you, and Courtney. be honest. Tell me what you really think. If you don't like it we'll try something else."

"Okay. I will." Courtney promised.

Roger proceeded to lay out a plan. As Courtney heard him relate it, she became more and more enthused. It was brilliant, she thought, and felt honored to have a man like Roger in her corner. It had a lot of moving parts and required many others to cooperate, but it was a daring strategy that, if carried out successfully, would exact a most perfect revenge.

By the time they reached Chappaqua they had worked out the logistics in great detail.

Chapter 65

Roger and Courtney in one car, and Ashley and Ronnie in the other, arrived early enough to find empty spots in the school parking lot. It was a homecoming game and nearly all the school parents were expected to be there, in addition to the school faculty and administration, not to mention the opposing team and their entourage from Port Chester. Needless to say, spaces in the parking lot were at a premium so many of the motor vehicles were shunted to a nearby playing field.

Roger and the three women walked over to the football field and found places in the stands on the home team side, not very far from the fifty yard line. The best seats were taken up by the high school marching band with all their instruments.

The little group would later take turns making runs to the concession stands for food and drink and to the strategically placed porta-potties to pee.

The excitement in the air was palpable. The crisp air was abuzz with people meeting and greeting each other, chatting, calling to friends, shouting encouragement and watching their children playing on the grass in the sidelines, and just generally having a good time.

The kickoff came at precisely three o'clock. Chappaqua lost the toss so they kicked off to Port Chester. Everyone in the stands stood up and roared as the ball flew through the air. A Port Chester team member caught it at their eighty-yard line. The fans held their collective breath as the boy started running forward, his burly teammates clearing a path in front and on either side.

What happened next set the tone for the game that followed. Instead of running down the field toward the oncoming enemy, the Chappaqua team stood in place and watched the green uniforms of Port Chester charge toward them. Big and brawny they came and when they collided, the Chappaqua boys were mowed down like lightweight bowling pins. The running back with the ball kept right on going as his teammates blew a hole in the Chappaqua defensive line. With a fellow teammate on his right and one on his left, the young man ran through the opening and continued the remaining fifty yards to reach the goal line. He turned and looked out toward the Port Chester families in the stands on the opposite side of the field, holding the football high in the air like a trophy. Courtney could hear the loud cheering from across the field, as she was sure all the houses in the surrounding neighborhood could also.

The Chappaqua coach, shouting from the sidelines, was nearly apoplectic. Courtney thought he would have a heart attack then and there, his face becoming beet red and puffy as he shouted at the top of his lungs, chastising his team on the field.

For their part, the Chappaqua football team members picked themselves up and just stood there, looking embarrassed, yet required to stay on and continue to play.

The Chappaqua football cheerleaders, a different group from the basketball cheerleaders Ashley was coaching, immediately went into a sexy routine that diverted attention from the poor showing on the field. All eyes were fixed on them for the next few minutes as the Chappaqua band, sitting centrally in the stands, played the Chappaqua fight song and the cheerleaders jiggled their T and A. Few noticed as Port Chester kicked the extra point.

"Some fight," Courtney commented, speaking directly in Roger's ear to compete with the din. "You think that's because of Nemo?"

"Probably," Roger shouted in return. "Is Chappaqua normally this bad?"

"I don't know. Let me check the program."

Courtney looked through the small pamphlet that was handed to her when she climbed on the stands. It listed the names and showed pictures of all the team players and gave a history of the rivalry between Chappaqua and Port Chester. "Nope. They won last year and the year before."

"That's our Nemo then. They have us to thank," Roger admitted.

Courtney needled him. "But we're not talking."

Port Chester kicked off and Chappaqua let the ball bounce on the ground before pouncing on it. The Port Chester team ran down the field and set up their defensive line.

Chappaqua snapped the ball back to John Baker, the quarterback, who stood there motionless for a moment, looking for a teammate to throw to, while his offensive team was annihilated in front of him. Port Chester quickly broke through the line and headed straight for him. He backed up several steps and, seeing the inevitable, sat down on the turf to avoid getting hit. The opposing fans in the stands stood up and jeered. "*Boo.*"

Baker sat on the ground, looking up at the Port Chester bruisers who surrounded him, hugging the ball like a little brown teddy bear.

"That poor kid," Courtney said, sympathetic to the boy's plight in spite of her elation that Nemo was clearly working. "He'll be the laughingstock of the school. He's never going to live this game down."

"Yeah. Everyone's taking pictures. Not good," Roger replied.

"I wish there was something we could do." Courtney made a squeamish face. "This game is going to be *awful.*"

"I think there's a way," Roger said hopefully. "I thought this might happen."

"What do you mean?"

Roger turned to Courtney and spoke directly into her ear. As she listened her face brightened. She looked at him and nodded. "It's certainly worth a try."

"You go talk to the coach. I'll run back to the car and get my backpack." Roger told her.

Courtney turned to Ashley and Ronnie, who were sitting right behind her, and asked them to save their two seats. She and Roger stood up and eased their way sideways toward the aisle in front of the people in their row, then walked down the steel steps to the field level. Roger turned to go to his car while Courtney headed for the coach. She tried to think of a plausible approach to him but was not at all sure what to say. It was a tricky situation because she couldn't let the coach know why his team was playing so badly and letting him down.

As she walked up he was actually sitting, stunned by what was happening on the field. She took a seat next to him on the bench and started talking. At first he didn't listen at all but, as she started repeating herself, he took notice of her presence and stared at her. His forlorn face reflected the humiliation at losing to Port Chester, the arch rival of Chappaqua.

"Coach," she began "I see your boys are having a really bad day. I think I can help. I have a friend with me who's a doctor." That was not a lie because Roger was in fact a PhD. "He's been watching the game and has a good idea of what's wrong. He has seen this problem with young men before and knows how to treat it." The coach was ignoring her so she repeated the essence of what she had said. When he turned to listen, she continued. "My friend's gone out to his car to get something your boys might take. It's not a drug or anything like that. It's really water, but if you tell them it's a special potion, they might just get their mojo back."

The coach brightened slightly but didn't say anything. He looked at Courtney, not knowing what to do with this strange person and this strange request. Courtney was about to speak again when he said. "I'm at my wits' end. I'll try anything."

Roger arrived five minutes later with his backpack. In the meantime, the Chappaqua offense had made another play and had gotten pushed back another ten yards. It looked as if the Chappaqua boys were playing touch football while the Port Chester team was playing tackle.

Roger opened the backpack and, together with Courtney, started pulling out water bottles. Roger had about twenty bottles, enough for every member of the team. The coach watched what they were doing, his interest growing, as he saw the bottles of clear water.

"You're sure it's just water?" he asked.

"This is the doctor," Courtney dodged the question and introduced Roger. "His name's Dr. Thornwood."

The coach looked at him and nodded perfunctorily. "Coach Sanders, Doc."

"Give a bottle to every player," Roger told him. "Just between us it's a placebo, but if you can can convince them it'll work, you'll see a difference right away."

The coach took one of the bottles in and twisted the cap to open it. He took a sip, smacked his lips, and looked at the bottle in his hand. "Tastes okay to me," he said after a beat. "Okay. I'll do a time out and give it to the boys. We've got nothing to lose but this damn game."

Chapter 66

The boys walked off the field for the time out and joined the defensive players surrounding Coach Sanders. He appeared haggard, although no longer desperate, as he gave them a pep talk. "I want all of you to drink this," he said, holding his water bottle high to show the team. "Everyone take a bottle."

The boys all stared at the water bottle dubiously but did as they were told. They lined up and, one by one, picked a bottle out of Roger's satchel.

"It's a powerful steriod," Coach Sanders told them. "It will make you more *macho*." The alliteration of "m's" rolled off Sander's tongue and added mystique to the message. Believing it to be an illegal drug the coach had smuggled in for them, every team member took a deep draught and then some. They were desperate to avoid an embarrasing loss and trusted their coach to make that happen.

"Now, Baker," the coach said, addressing the team captain. "We're in a deep hole. Rather than punt, I want you to throw. Play number seventy-seven."

The boys all looked at each other as if the coach had called for a miracle.

"Got it, coach. I'm for that," John replied, his self-confidence quickly building. "What do you think guys?" he held out his hands in a gesture of query and scanned the faces of his teammates.

To a boy they nodded their assent and shouted, "Let's *go*." Their mojo was in the ascendance.

"*Okay*. Let's *do* it then." John exclaimed with conviction in his voice and led his offensive team back onto the field.

It was a crucial and risky play. If it didn't work, the ball would stay on Port Chester's twenty and the Chappaqua rivals would either land another touchdown or at the very least score a field goal. Play number seventy-seven was a complicated new tactic they had learned and practiced over the past three weeks, but they had never tried it during an actual game. That meant that Port Chester had never seen it, nor could they anticipate the moves. On the other hand, it required a thirty-five yard throw by the quarterback to a particular spot on the field, and required a receiver to be at that spot at the precise time the ball made landfall to catch and run with it.

It boosted their cockiness when the defense team saw the next play would not be a punt. They took their positions on the line with an intimidating snarl at the Chappaqua linemen. John Baker called for the snap and received the ball. The big Port Chester coursers charged forward but were blocked by a blank brick wall of the offense. John stepped back three paces and launched the ball into the air at a forty-five degree angle. It looped forward and upward in a ballistic trajectory, rotating in a smooth spiral and falling downward to land exactly thirty-five yards ahead toward the Chappaqua goal. A Chappaqua runner appeared out of nowhere to snatch it out of the air in the nick of time. Grabbing the ball tightly he turned one hundred eighty degrees and headed straight down the field with three Port Chester team members in hot pursuit. He eluded the clutches of two of these pursuers as they lunged forward at him but was brought down by the third as he got within feet of the end zone. Falling forward, he held the ball out in front and managed to have it clear the goal line before slamming it down hard on the turf.

The Chappaqua fans went absolutely bonkers, cheering and screaming ecstatically with joy on the top of their lungs. The band took up playing the school marching fight song while the cheerleaders jumped up and down, shaking their blue and white pom-poms with excitement. The tide had suddenly turned in Chappaqua's favor.

"What the heck was in that water?" Courtney asked Roger when the crowd calmed a bit.

"It's just plain water. Honest."

"A placebo?"

"Yup. And to my surprise it could counteract the effect of the Nemo."

Chapter 67

As the game continued it was clear that the two teams were evenly matched. From the score at this point, which stood at seven to seven, the jumbotron scoreboard tallied the numbers as they escalated, the teams alternating in adding seven points to the board on their respective Home and Visitor's panels until, at the final blast of the horn, they were tied at twenty-eight to twenty-eight. A "sudden death" playoff was announced, starting with another coin toss to decide which side would kick off.

Both teams were game weary by this time, and so were the fans. They wanted it to be over so they could get on with the partying. If Chappaqua won, so much the better, but that would be only the icing on the cake. This team had done well and had plenty to be proud of. The fans were exhausted from the excitement and screaming and wanted to light up the bonfire. They wanted to *celebrate*.

Port Chester won the toss again so Chappaqua kicked. The same player as before caught the ball for Port Chester and started his run. However, this time he was blocked and tackled to the ground at the sixty-five yard line: too far for Port Chester to kick a field goal.

The Port Chester team tried twice to run the ball forward but Chappaqua held them fast, blocking their advance. It was a struggle between opposing teams whose players were tired and couldn't maintain a sharp focus. To the fans in the stands it looked like beehive football.

On the third down, the Port Chester quarterback passed off to the side and the tight end ran forward eight yards before being pushed out of bounds. Port Chester needed one more down to make it to fifty-five and a first down.

The play was to be a wedge blast right through the center. The quarterback faked a pass and handed the ball to his running back as he zipped past and drove forward, straight into the Chappaqua defensive line. Chappaqua stopped him, but he gained a few feet of ground.

The ball lay on the grass at the point the runner had managed to reach when he was stopped cold. It was not clear whether Port Chester could claim the coveted first down, so the referees measured the distance the ball had advanced with a ten-yard rope between two poles. The ball, they found, was six inches short of the lead pole. The Port Chester players and the Port Chester fans all emitted an audible groan. The Chappaqua side stayed silent out of respect for the team's valiant effort to move the ball forward. It was now Chappaqua's turn to try.

Coach Sanders called a final time out and the players gathered around him.

"We have four shots to gain ten yards," he said, "but that's not nearly enough. We need thirty-five yards to get within field goal distance. I assume the other side's expecting us to try an end run on this first down. Let's surprise them again with play seventy-seven."

He made eye contact with his boys. They looked back at him blankly in their exhaustion, but they were clearly willing to try and "get it up" just one more time. Captain John still had some juice left and that's all that was needed. He gave a high sign, agreeing to make the pass. All the team members, offensive and defensive players alike, joined together in a mutually self-supportive, sporting cheer.

Out on the field again the offense lined up and snapped the ball. John eased back a few steps and tossed the ball, this time a little wobbly but nevertheless true. The ball sailed out through the air towards its target on the twenty-yard line.

The fans on both sides followed the ball with their eyes as it flew. They saw it loop high and descend in an arc. When it finally landed no one was there to make the catch. The ball bounced on the turf and went sideways, like a football is wont to do because of its shape. The closest player to the ball happened to be on the Port Chester team and he pounced on it, covering it with his chest. The player stood up with a smile, leaving the ball in place on the field. Port Chester had control of the ball again, but they had a long way to go before they could score.

As the ball lay there at Port Chester's eighty, players and fans on both sides stared at it without speaking, as if it were a small bomb about to explode. They waited with baited breath to see what would happen next.

Coach Sanders would have liked to win the game, but he had to admire the performance of Port Chester, the town he grew up in and their schools he attended through all twelve grades. After a moment of reflection, he raised his hand, interrupting further play, and walked straight across the field to the opposing side. He sought out and spoke to the Port Chester coach, and within ten seconds the two had struck an amicable bargain. They would end the game and call it a draw. Both sides would log it as a win and obtain their bragging rights.

When this deal was announced, a great roar of approval went up from the fans on both sides. It was the right way to bring this rivalry to a close.

Only Courtney and Roger knew why the boy on the Chappaqua team was not where he was supposed to be to catch the ball. Courtney winked at Roger; in response he leaned over and told her, "Just goes to show you can't rely on a placebo."

* * * *

The celebration started at dusk and would last into the wee ours until the bonfire was reduced to glowing embers.

Ashley and Ronnie sought out their friends in the basketball cheerleading squad and the *Tribune* newspaper. Ashley saw Muriel clinging to Captain John, the most popular boy in the school at that moment. She had her arm around his waist and leaned her head on his shoulder, making sure everyone knew they were still together. The other girls in her squad were standing together nearby, the better to catch the eyes of John's teammates. Nearly as much as for John himself, they treated his teammates like conquering heroes. Ashley watched as the boys savored their moment of fame, however clueless they were, she knew, that the high school adoration would fade in a month when the Nemo wore off.

Zoe had assigned Walter to write a sports column that would explain the football game from an insider's point of view. It would be challenging to describe the intricacies of the game to lay readers without undue detail and without losing the drama and excitement of the amazing storybook tale. Exsie and Yvonne both wanted to work with him, but Zoe nipped that opportunity at the bud and assigned Victor to assist. Because of the Nemo, Victor and Walter were not at all unhappy with that arrangement, but they didn't altogether spurn the attention of the two girls. It was all very friendly, without a hint of flirting, Ronnie walked over to Mr. Czybulka, the English advisor to the *Tribune*, and they made pleasant conversation without his making a single sexual innuendo or inappropriate advance. The Nemo was working now, and working nicely.

Courtney and Roger mingled with the adult crowd, not only the teachers but many of the parents as well. They dodged questions about why they were there at the game, while getting to know the vocations and avocations of the people they spoke to. They had to explain they were not a "couple" so many times that they eventually gave that up and allowed themselves to be pegged as such. Chappaqua was a couple-oriented community, but no one seemed to care whether they were married or not.

Food and drink were catered, with liquor sold only upon proof of age. As the evening wore on Courtney and Roger both noticed that the men and women socialized easily without coalescing into separate groups, male and female, as often happened at parties. This was borne out and made especially poignant when a small group of revelers broke into song and the entire community eventually joined in, their faces illuminated by the warm glow of the firelight.

Let there be peace on earth
And let it begin with me.
Let there be peace on earth
The peace that was meant to be.
With God as our Father
Brothers all are we.
Let me walk with my brother
In perfect harmony.

Let peace begin with me,
Let this be the moment now.
With ev'ry step I take
Let this be my solemn vow;
To take each moment and live
Each moment in peace eternally.
Let there be peace on earth
And let it begin with me.

After singing this song around the bonfire the feelings of peace and serenity were so pervasive, among the young and old alike, that folks were reluctant to leave. Roger, however, said his goodbyes to Courtney, Ashley and Ronnie, explaining apologetically that he was facing a four-hour drive to return to his home in Aberdeen, Maryland.

After he left the three women continued to participate in the celebration. They enjoyed the Chappaqua warmth and euphoria which, they knew, was at least partly due to the effects of the Nemo. The usual tensions and stresses of everyday life appeared to be missing from the revelers around them and enhanced their own serene mood until, suddenly, as they mingled with the crowd Courtney saw *them*: the three evil men from her past, reflected in the firelight while they stood together talking.

Courtney froze. When she eventually got a grip on herself she said hurriedly to her two friends, "We have to go now. I can't stay here any longer."

On her way back to the City a short while later, Courtney sat in the back of Ashley's car and reminisced about this nice day with Roger. Not only was there something calming about him that soothed her restless spirit, but he would soon become her knight in shining armor in her quest to seek revenge on the three men who had raped her.

Chapter 68

Two weeks later as the sun was setting, a long black limousine slipped quietly up a long paved driveway to a large home in Chappaqua. It came to a stop in the porte-cochère and an overhead light came on automatically. Isaac, dressed in a black suit and sporting a limousine driver's hat, alighted, walked forward around the front of the car and up the steps to the colonial entranceway, and pressed the doorbell button. His passenger, Roger Thornwood, remained comfortably seated in the luxurious space in the rear of the car.

Inside the house a dog began barking angrily while outside a carriage light came on adjacent the front door. Within seconds a young-looking woman opened the door and peered out. She held tight to the leash of a fullgrown black Labrador retriever who eyed Isaac critically but stopped making sentry sounds.

"You're here for Alex, I know," the woman said pleasantly. "He'll be down in just a minute. Won't you come in? There's quite a chill in the air this evening."

"No thank you Ma'am. I can wait in the car."

As Isaac turned to go, a man came bounding down the stairs carrying a small duffel. "I'm all set, Susan. Is this my ride?" He shot Isaac a quick look and gave his wife a peck on the cheek. "Don't wait up for me."

Isaac walked ahead of the man to the car. He opened the rear passenger door and held it as the man climbed aboard with his duffel. When the man was settled Isaac took his place behind the wheel and started the car.

"Hello. I'm Roger Thornwood," Roger introduced himself to the new passeger who was now seated in the back. Roger sat facing the man with his own back to the driver's seat. Alex eyed Roger and acknowledged his presence with a perfuntory nod and a query, "And you are?"

"I'm a doc," Roger explained. "I've been asked by Columbia to accompany you just in case there are any medical issues. You men tend to overdo it during these alumni basketball games."

"I work out at the Mount Kisco fitness center. I won't have a problem."

"You're what, thirty-three?"

"That's right."

"Your two colleagues here in Chappaqua, they're about your age too?"

"We were all in the same class together at Columbia. How'd you guess our ages?"

"The school sent me your alumni stats. I need to be ready for any emergency."

"Well that's pretty cool. The old school didn't tell me they're sending a physician along to the game."

"I do sports medicine. You can't be too careful. I can also help you win by the way." Roger shot Alex a wink.

"Oh, yeah? You can?"

"We'll talk about that later when we're on our way."

The limousine went on to pick up the two other Columbia Lions team members from their respective homes. The first of the two homes was of average size for the town of Chappaqua, worth roughly a million dollars because of its location. The second was considerably larger, worth several million and by any standard it could be called a "mansion." Bradley ("Hello. I'm 'Brad', Rhymes with 'bad'.") lived in the modest home while Carl ("That's me, Red Ryder. Rhymes with 'snarl'.") owned the mansion.

The three men sat comfortably together on the rear bench seat of the car as Roger explained the program for the evening. As he talked the limo sped south along King Street toward Armonk with darkening woods on both sides of the road interrupted by the occasional light from a suburban home.

"Traffic on I-84 to Hartford is always backed up on a Friday," Roger said. "The school knows you'd never get there in time if you went by car, so they sprung for an airplane. We'll fly up to Windham Airport, just a few miles away from the UConn at Storrs."

"Sounds good. As long as Columbia's paying," responded Brad.

"Private planes are pricey," Carl noted. "But they're a great way to travel."

Alex spoke up. "I wonder who's going to be there from the Yale team. I hope not that tall black dude. He crushed us on the court."

"We have one more chance to beat those fucking Bulldogs," Brad said. "Let's make it count and cut 'em down to size."

"Yeah," Carl agreed. "Those SOB's made us look like shit in the playoffs. We've got to square things up."

"Did you know that the Columbia Lions have been fighting the Yale Bulldogs since 1900?" Alex commented rhetorically, mostly for Roger's benefit. "It's the oldest rivalry there is in college basketball."

"How'd the Lions do?" Roger wanted to know.

"Not too shabby. The Lions held their own over the years but in our senior year the team fell apart. We lost big time," he replied.

"It was a horrible game," Brad added.

"We've gotta *fix* that," Carl said. "This is our one shot to save face."

"If you really want to win," Roger said, "I have something that can help you."

All three men stared at him, eyes wide. "Oh yeah?" probed Carl. "Whadda ya got?"

"I'll explain when we get in the air," Roger replied.

The limousine arrived at a clearing by a large reservoir, turned right for a brief stretch along the shore and then turned left again, following King Street as it traced the Connecticut border briefly before reaching a main crossroad with a traffic light. The car turned left at the light onto the access road to Westchester Airport, known by the letters "HPN" -- an acronym for the nearby City of White Plains. Before reaching the terminal building it turned right at the sign for "General Aviation," slowed at a gate for identification by a guard, and was waved through.

The limo drove out onto the tarmac in front of a large hanger and came to a stop next to a sleek Beechcraft King Air 250. The side door of the airplane was open outward and down forming airstairs that extended to the ground. In the doorway stood a woman, her curves forming an hourglass outline in the dim light of the cabin behind her. She smiled seductively as Isaac held open the passenger door and the four men stepped out.

Carl whisted. "She's a beauty,"

"Who do you mean? The girl or the aircraft?" Alex asked.

"The plane, stupid. Who does it belong to?"

"I don't know," Roger replied. "It's rented for the weekend. It'll get us there and back."

The four men climbed aboard. The craft interior was arranged with two large captain's chairs on each side of a center aisle and two seats in the back facing forward. The captain's chairs could be rotated one hundred eighty degrees to either face forward, toward each other or to the rear. In the front of the cabin, behind the cockpit door, was a WC on the left and a small galley on the right with room for passengers to stand and converse while enjoying the on-board amenities.

Ronnie warmly welcomed the three men and asked them to take seats in the back. They tucked their duffels under their seats and strapped themselves in. She offered them drinks but they refused, saying it was a short flight and they needed to stay alert for the upcoming game. They would celebrate with their teammates after they beat the Bulldogs.

Ronnie and Roger sat toward the front of the cabin, with their seats turned so they could face the three men. Before she sat down, Ronnie introduced herself. "My name's Veronica, but everyone calls me 'Ronnie'," she said. "Welcome aboard the UConn express. My aim is to make this flight as comfortable and as unforgettable as possible."

The three men looked at her and smiled. "Reminds me of the old days," Alex said, "when stewardesses were, you know, *stewardesses*."

"I hope you fellows win today. I really do," Ronnie continued, smiling sweetly. "You look like such nice men. I understand you're going to play at the Gampel Pavilion. Home of the Connecicut Huskies."

"Maybe the luck of those Amazon women will rub off on us," Brad said. "They sure can play."

"This is supposed to be a neutral venue," Roger reminded them. "So neither you nor the Bulldogs have an advantage."

"What about that *fix* you spoke of," Carl wanted to know, looking at Roger knowingly. "What have you got?"

"As a matter of fact, it's time to ask you guys," Roger replied. "I brought along something that will give you an edge." He reached over and opened a black briefcase next to his seat that the men now noticed for the first time. He lifted out three water bottles and held them up.

"A steroid?" Brad wanted to know.

"Partly. But also much more. It will boost your mojo."

"Any side effects?" Alex asked.

"None that I know of. It's like caffeine but a hundred times stronger."

"Give me a bottle," Carl growled. "I'll drink it."

"Me too. We need all the help we can get," Brad said.

Roger passed a bottle to each of the men.

"I'd better drink it too. We've all got to take it," Alex pointed out. "What about the other guys on our team? Do you have enough for them?"

"I'm sorry, but it doesn't work that fast," Roger replied. "I do have more stuff with me, but if they take it when we arrive there, it's not going to kick in until after the game."

"Fuck them. We'll drink it. We're the ones who spark the team," Carl said, opening the bottle cap and chugging its contents. Brad immediately followed suit but Alex was more cautious. He held the bottle for a moment and sipped its contents.

"Tastes something like licorice," he announced. The other two men looked at him, frowning. He quickly threw caution to the wind and drank it down.

Chapter 69

In the cockpit were the pilot, George Cleary, in the left seat and his co-pilot, Courtney Stillwell, in the right with her headphones on. When Roger signaled the cabin was locked and loaded, George went through his protocol to begin the flight, starting first the left engine then the right one, and radioed his intentions to ground control in the tower.

Looking out the right front window of the flight deck, Courtney could see Isaac look forlorn at the departing plane before returning to his limo. He climbend into the driver's seat and drove off.

Soon they were airborne. Courtney watched the altimeter wind clockwise until it reached five thousand feet, then hold steady for a moment as George banked to the left before continuing upward. When they reached cruising altitude, George pulled back on the throttles slightly, causing the engines to soften their sound from the somewhat angry whine to a more comfortable, steady hum. Looking over at Courtney he grinned and said, "We're up there." He scanned the instruments again for the up-teenth time. "Everything looks good. I'm switching the feed to our headphones so we can hear what goes on in the cabin."

"You have it wired for sound?"

"There's a mike with a recording device."

"Good *thinking*."

"You have Roger to thank for that one."

"I'm not surprised."

"Now how'd you like to fly it for awhile? I'll teach you how to keep it straight and level."

Courtney remembered her earlier experience at flying and jumped at the chance. "Sure. I'd love to."

"Okay. Take the controls." George raised his hands to show he wasn't touching the yoke. Courtney felt a flicker of panic, giving the yoke a slight jerk as she grabbed it, but she quickly got a grip and settled down, staring intently out the windshield into the darkness. As soon as her eyes grew accustomed to the nighttime view, she tried to discern the earth's horizon.

In the distance she saw lights flickering on and off but, try as she might, she couldn't see a clear demarcation of where the earth met the sky.

"It takes some getting used to," George remarked, "but you'll catch on quick."

Movement of the big needle on the altimeter caught her eye and she realized the plane was descending slowly. She pulled back on the controls and brought the altitude back up to eight thousand feet. She checked the gyrocompass and saw she was now off course, so she banked slightly to bring the azimuth back to forty-two degrees. She had to make these corrections several more times before she was able to maintain a steady course and altitude. After a half hour of this piloting experience, she began to gain confidence. She looked over at George and smiled to show her appreciation. "I think I've got it now."

"I think you do too. Keep it up. I'm going to go back there and say 'hello' to our passengers."

"*What*?" Courtney exclaimed, shocked by the thought of flying without his sure hand next to her. "Don't leave me here. I don't trust myself *that* much."

"Well *I* trust you. You've flown before. Just keep it at eight thousand feet with the heading at forty-two." He unbuckled his seatbelt and lifted himself up, turning as he did so to head back to the rear cabin. "Steady as she goes," he added. "Just watch that horizon and keep it straight and level." Out of the left corner of her eye, Courtney saw him move rearward, leaving her alone in the dimly lit cockpit. She gritted her teeth while holding the yoke tightly between her two hands.

Courtney stared out through the windshield and could finally see a faint line where the starry night met the black earth, with occasional lights here and there evidencing human activity. Moving the yoke stiffly at first, but then more smoothly with increasing confidence as the minutes wore on, she began again to feel the freedom she had previously enjoyed on her flight to Lebanon, New Hampshire. This time, she knew, the trip would take an hour or two longer, traveling the full length of the State of Maine all the way up to the northeastern-most tip of the United States. George had made preparations to land at dawn at a seldom-used, grass airstrip in Van Buren, Maine, called Bresette's Mountainside Airfield.

When George appeared in the cockpit doorway the three men looked up and reacted as if they had seen a ghost. George stared back at them. "Good evening," he said. "Remember me?"

The three stared at him, saying nothing, but it was clear that they recognized him. The problem was, it just didn't compute. What was George Cleary doing here? Was *he* the pilot on this flight?

"Do you know why he is here?" Roger asked the men.

The three together shook their heads "no".

"One word," Roger said, looking them with fire in his eyes. "It beings with an 'R'."

The men blanched.

"Do you know now?" Roger asked again.

They nodded "yes" this time.

"What?"

"The Barnard Club," Alex replied, wincing.

"The Barnard Club?" Ronnie asked, taking over from Roger. "What the hell is *that*?"

Alex looked over at his colleagues for help, realizing he may have revealed something he shouldn't have.

"What is the Barnard Club?" Ronnie asked again, louder this time.

The men remained silent and stared back at her.

George slowly reached back and pulled a knife from a sheath clipped to his belt. He held it up, its shiny blade glistening in the dim light, and grinned. "When we get where we're going, we're going to cut your balls off."

Roger held up his hand, face out. "Just a minute. Give them a chance."

"What is the Barnard Club?" Ronnie demanded a third time.

The men looked at each other, obviously worried, and Carl spoke. "It's nothing," he said. "We were keeping a list of the women we fucked."

"*Raped* you mean," Ronnie corrected.

"No *fucked.* It was always consensual."

"That's not true," George said accusingly. "You're a liar, Carl. Ronnie's right. You're a *rapist.*"

The three men looked up at him. George stared back at them, shaking his head slowly. "You three should have gone to jail," he said. "But it's not too late for you to pay for what you did."

Brad, who had not yet spoken, managed to say, "You were the one who was there. You stood at the door watching, you fucking voyeur. You'd make a piss poor witness to prove there was any rape. You didn't do shit to stop us, so you can't prove a thing. It's your word against ours."

"Really? So you're accusing *me* now?" George asked incredulously.

"There was no rape," Alex said flatly. "None. There never was."

"Courtney Stillwell knows differently. She'll testify against you."

"We're not worried."

"You sure?"

"If we raped heer, she would have gone to the police long ago."

If eyes were lasers, George's would have burned a hole in the man's forehead with his stare. "She went to the school officials, but they did *nothing*," he said.

"We know. Because it was three against one. We said nothing happened."

Roger, who had kept quiet during this exchange, pressed further about the Barnard Club. "This Barnard Club," he said. "Who was a member?"

The three men looked at him but said nothing. George walked toward them in the cabin to be within arms length. The men shuddered, clearly frightened now, but remained still, saying nothing. George held his knife in front of Carl's face. Alex and Brad stared, horrified at the threat. "Were you members of the Barnard Club?" George asked them with a threatening tone, this time looking directly at the man in front of him.

"Y...Yes. We all were," replied Carl.

"Was there anyone else?"

"No. It was just the three of us."

That opened the floodgates and the other two men came to Carl's aid.

"It was a game," Alex said defensively. "We got a point each time we scored with a coed."

George looked at him, fiercely. "Scored? *Raped* you mean."

"No, no. Most of them were good."

"What if they were not...*good*?"

"We didn't hurt them," Brad said hastily, seeing the danger of this line of questioning. "Sometimes we'd slip them a Mickey. They didn't even know what was happening."

"Who won?" George demanded.

"Won?"

"Won the game."

Brad immediately turned on Carl. "He did," he said, nodding in Carl's direction.

Carl looked at George in an attempt to gauge George's attitude toward the Barnard Club. "Alright, so what," he said hesitantly. "I was captain of the basketball team. That gave me an edge."

Ronnie eyed the man, shocked at what she was hearing. "How many did you get?" she asked, her voice dripping with disgust.

"Points? I got twenty-four. My friends here got sixteen each."

"I got sixteen," Brad said, somewhat less hesitant now to open up because their fate was already sealed. The three men had kept the Barnard Club a secret for so long it was almost cathartic to finally tell someone. "One more than him," he said nodding toward Alex. "He got only fifteen."

"How many points did you get for raping Courtney Stillwell?" Roger asked. Like Ronnie, he could hardly believe what he was hearing.

"One point each," came the reply. "It boosted all our scores."

There followed a loud scream from the cockpit, "*You bastards,*" and the aircraft lurched upward. George, who was still standing in the cabin facing rearward, turned and shouted "Courtney *no*! Don't pull up. You'll *stall*." He ran back to the cockpit, holding on to the tops of the seats as he went.

The plane nosed up and began to shake violently. The engines sounded differently as the propellers bit into the still air. George punked down in his seat, just as the plane nosed down, banked sharply to the left and began a sharp descent into a black oblivion.

Chapter 70

"Who the fuck was flying this airplane?" Carl screamed as the machine headed downward in a twisting tailspin.

All the occupants of the cabin braced themselves with fright. They stared out their side windows to see nothing but blackness at first but then, to their extreme horror, they saw faint lights on the ground rushing upward toward them. They closed their eyes and when nothing happened they opened them again. Meanwhile the twisting feeling stopped, although the nose of the plane was still aimed downward. Looking out again, this time they could see clearly that the ground was rushing up. They held their breaths and closed their eyes again. Slowly, as if in slow motion, the nose of the craft started to nudge upward, bit by bit, until the airplane finally leveled off and began to climb slightly.

The sound of the engines changed from a high whine to a deeper, less penetrating pitch. The sound remained steady for a few moments and then became louder as the engines exerted more effort with increased power and the aircraft headed skyward again.

The occupants of the cabin emitted a collective sigh of relief.

In the cockpit, Courtney had felt her heart stop and then start up again. Still shocked and upset by what she had overheard, she was totally shaken by losing control of the aircraft. In her anger she had pulled back on the yoke, then lost her orientation because she saw the blackness of the sky and couldn't relocate the horizon.

"That was totally my fault," George said, taking a full breath after averting the crash. "I shouldn't have left you alone in the cockpit."

"I'm sorry, I…I don't know what happened."

"What happened to you has happened to many other pilots before. It's a known problem, and I should have stayed in command."

"Known problem?"

"Remember John F. Kennedy, Junior?" George recalled.

"Yes. He died in a plane crash. With two women aboard."

"Right. He lost the horizon, just like you, and flew his plane right into the ocean."

Courtney shuddered. At least she was in good company. The unfortunate difference was that the young Kennedy had paid for his piloting mistakes.

* * * *

As they flew on, Courtney sat silently in her seat. Still recovering from the near disaster, she tried to distract her mind as they traversed the State of Maine by admiring the crystal canopy of stars in the halfmoon-lit sky.

"There's a landing strip up ahead," George said eventually, pointing slightly to the left of a small cluster of lights. "See it? To the left of the lights of those buildings."

Courtney strained her eyes but couldn't see anything but the blackness of woods at first. "I don't know—," she replied. She looked briefly on the map to get her bearings and then stared out the windshield again. "Wait. There it is. I *do* see it." It was a narrow strip of open area that blended in with the farmers' fields, all softly illuminated by the moon. There were no buildings or other landmarks next to it, but she noticed a white wind sock at the southern end of the strip. It hung down from its perch on a pole like a wet noodle.

George let their altitude bleed off and came in for a landing. He let the aircraft roll out to the southern end of the airstrip, then turned around and taxied back to the north end. Turning around once again to aim the craft down the runway, he cut the engines. The sudden silence, after hours of constant humming, felt strangely calming Courtney thought. She remained in her seat and adjusted the volume on her headphones to listen in to the cabin. Now it was showtime. Time to surprise the three rapists that sat in the back.

George got up from the pilot's seat and pressed a button on the cabin wall. Hydraulics hummed briefly as the door swung outward and down and came to rest on the grass below. Cold air filled the cabin, bringing with it the clean fresh smell of pine.

"Time to wake 'em up," he announced.

Chapter 71

Roger and Ronnie got up from their seats and stood over the three sleeping rapists. The sudden silence and the coolness in the cabin stirred them awake.

"Uh, are we there yet?" asked Carl. "I must have fallen asleep."

"Yes, this is the end of the line," Roger replied. "It's time to go."

Waking too, Alex glanced out the window and did a double take. "What? Where are we?"

Brad and Carl looked out too and saw nothing but blackness. "Have we landed at Windham Airport?" asked Brad, yawning and blinking his eyes.

"No," Ronnie answered. "You've been asleep for hours. We're no longer in Connecicut."

"Just a minute," Carl said, becoming quickly fully awake. "Where the fuck *are* we?"

"That's for you to figure out when you get off the plane." Ronnie replied with a grin. She was clearly enjoying the men's confusion.

"Weren't we supposed to play basketball?" Brad wondered allowed.

"Basketball? You guys are over the hill. You're has-beens," Ronnie joked.

"No, I mean the alumni game against Yale. We were supposed to play this evening," Brad insisted, still confused at what was going on.

"There was never any game," Roger explained. "That was just a trick to get you on this plane."

"You *son of a bitch*!" Carl's anger rising and making his face turn red. He tried to get up from his seat but Roger stepped in front and stared down at him.

"You mean the trip to UConn—?" Alex was still trying to understand the situation.

"You took the bait, hook line and sinker," Ronnie said gleefully.

"How come we fell asleep?" Alex wanted to know. "Did you give us something?"

"I gave you a Mickey," Roger explained. "Probably the same kind of drug you gave those girls. Remember the water you drank? You said it tasted like licorice."

Carl stared at Roger with contempt in his eyes. "So what happens now?" He snarled. "You know we're going to sue you bastards when we get back to Chappaqua. When we get through with you, you won't have two dimes to rub together."

"You'll feel a bit different when you get back to Chappaqua," Roger said mysteriously. "That's not going to happen."

Carl ignored the remark. "What are you going to do now? I'll bet there's an all-points bulletin out there to find us already. When they do, you'll go straight to jail. You bastards are so dumb, but not too dumb not to know what's coming."

"Apparently you haven't figured it out yet," Ronnie said. "This trip never happened."

"What?"

"We're just a figment of your imagination." Ronnie grinned.

"You idiot. You think we can't prove what you did to us?"

"Think about it. You can't prove you've been in this aircraft. You don't even know where we are right now."

"We're at an airport. There will be a record of that."

"Not true. This is not an airport," Ronnie told them.

"We can prove we've been on this plane."

"Not true either," Ronnie replied. "You don't even know the tail number."

"It's time to kick you off the plane," Roger said finally, "but before we do, we have a little surprise for you."

"Oh yeah? Don't think you'll get away with this. We'll find your ass and—."

Courtney removed her headset, got up from her co-pilot's seat and stepped out of the cockpit. "Hello," she said, looking fiercely at the three rapists. "We finally meet again."

As the men stared up at her, the color drained from their faces.

After a long moment, the three men simply stood and dutifully disembarked from the cabin into the freezing cold of northern Maine. They shuddered and clutched their duffle bags to their chests as they stared into the vast darkness. In the distance they could see a dim light flickering through the trees and headed in that direction.

Chapter 72

Courtney calmly took a seat in the cabin next to Roger and Ronnie. George pressed the button on the cockpit wall, causing the cabin door with the airstairs to rise and close itself. He entered the cockpit and within minutes he had the engines humming. He revved the engines and the airplane began to roll. With three less passengers and much less fuel in its tanks, the craft accelerated nimbly down the grass strip and, within seconds, took to the air. They were up and away, above the trees and climbing toward the moon and the stars in the night sky.

Courtney sat quietly a moment with a wistful smile on her lips, not unlike the Mona Lisa. Finally she said, "I'd love to be a bird looking down at them right now."

George scanned the fuel gauges every five minutes as they flew south, becoming more and more concerned as they came closer to landing in Lebanon, New Hampshire. He was about to warn the crew, who were celebrating their successful mission in the cabin behind him, but he thought better of it. There was nothing they could do about it anyway, so he kept the problem to himself. When he finally touched down and pulled up to the Granite Air Center and shut down the engines, the red warning lights were on. He could have landed in Portland, Maine, or anywhere else along the way, but the stopover in Lebanon made for an alibi just in case the three rapists claimed they'd been abducted and flown to a remote airfield. George had an account with the FBO because he frequently landed there, and he knew that if push came to shove these people would have his back.

The entire flight crew piled out of the aircraft and enjoyed an early breakfast at the airport eatery as the plane was being refueled. They were tired and weary from the hours of flying but were all in a jovial mood. They had carried out the plan without so much as a hiccup, except for the scary tailspin.

While they were there, George took Courtney aside and asked her if she'd like to stay overnight with him in Woodstock, Vermont, but she declined. She told him she had to get back to the City to attend to the magazine. He was an investor, she reminded him, and had an interest in her making the magazine the best that it could be.

When they returned to the refueled airplane, Ronnie asked if she could ride with him in the cockpit. George looked at Courtney questioningly and she nodded her approval. "That's a good idea," she said brightly. "Let Ronnie see what it's like up in front there."

"Okay, Ronnie. You're on," George told her.

"*Yippee.*" Ronnie clapped her hands. "I've never been in a cockpit before."

George directed her to the right-hand seat and asked her to strap herself in. Ronnie climbed gingerly into the co-pilot's position, trying not to disturb any of the controls or instruments, and tightened her seatbelt and shoulder strap. When ready, she looked over at George smiling sweetly while keeping her hands folded primly in her lap.

Once settled in, George set about starting the engines and taxiing out to the active runway. Receiving clearance from the tower, he revved the engines and, following a brief acceleration down the runway, he took off into the early morning sky. After climbing for ten minutes he reduced the power to a comfortable sound level, adjusted the heading by banking slightly to the right and set the autopilot to guide the airplane. "There," George exclaimed finally, removing his headphones. "We can relax for awhile."

"The view from up here is *fantastic*," Ronnie said excitedly. "I love this." She looked at George with a wide smile.

"I love this airplane," he said. "It's my only vice."

"Really? Only one?" she asked teasing. "I have to admit I have several."

"Let me guess. I'll bet it has something to do with your gregarious personality."

"Guess I'm guilty," she admitted. "But isn't that what makes life interesting?"

"Come to think of it, you're absolutely right."

"Guilty pleasures and all that come with it. The downside."

"Yeah," George agreed. "The downside. This plane is *expensive*. But I keep telling myself that I can afford it."

"You *can* afford it. I heard your speech at the Wednesday Assembly at Horace Greeley. I was impressed." Ronnie told him.

"Thanks for saying that. Those kids gave me a hard time, I remember."

"They're just kids," Ronnie said sympathetically. "They don't know shit. Take it from a girl who's been around."

Back in the cabin Courtney and Roger sat opposite each other in the captains chairs and reminisced about the night's exploits. "I'll never forget those looks on their faces when you appeared from the cockpit," Roger said shaking his head and grinning. "They were priceless."

"I guess they'd forgotten all about me," Courtney replied. "But I hadn't forgotten about them. Thank you, Roger, for all that you've done."

"Those men deserved it. I feel I was doing a public service."

"I doubt if they'll tell anyone what happened to them, but if they do it will stand as a warning to men. Retribution can come swiftly in the night when one least expects it."

"Why not write an article about rape for your magazine?" Roger asked. "That would get the word out."

"That's exactly what I've been intending to do all along, but I've been too close to it. I just couldn't put pen to paper."

"Do you think that might change some day?"

"I believe this trip has done me some good. At least I don't feel so bitter about what those men did. They've had their comeuppance now."

"Let me fill you in on a little secret. You know that water I gave them to drink?"

"Yes," Courtney answered, smiling. "Like those boys at the football game. They thought they were getting a steroid, but instead of a placebo they got a Mickey."

"They got more than that," Roger confided.

"What do you mean?"

"When I first started work for the government they asked me to come up with a formula that would make enemy soldiers passive on the battlefield. That turned out to be a tall order because, while they already knew how to make men eunuchs, they couldn't figure out how to make them passive for a *short time*, and then have them go back to being tough men again as if nothing had happened."

"They already had a formula that could make men *yooks*?"

"Yooks? What are yooks?"

"You know, *eunuchs*. It's just an expression I heard."

"*Oh*, I see." Roger smiled, and then continued. "The Army knew it wouldn't be right to turn enemy soldiers into *eunuchs*. That would be chemical warfare. So they asked me to come up with something new that worked only for a short time. Just long enough for us to negotiate a peace settlement with the enemy. And that way the stuff could be kept a deep dark secret."

"That's how you discovered *Nemo*."

"Yes. It took awhile, but I eventually developed a formula that works really well."

"Well, a month has gone by now, so the Nemo should soon be wearing off in Chappaqua."

"That's right, and no one will be the wiser. In the meantime, I believe it helped us keep the rapists under control while we flew them to Maine."

"I agree. I know those men too well. Without Nemo they could have been terribly dangerous."

"Courtney," Roger said, looking her in the eye. "There's one more thing I need to tell you."

"What's that?"

"I gave those rapists the original formula. Now they really *are* yooks."

* * * *

George was becoming intrigued by the young companion in the cockpit with him, a woman whom, he realized, he knew nothing about.

"What is it you do, exactly?" he asked Ronnie.

"I'm a writer. I write for *Cosmo* Magazine," Ronnie replied, trying to keep the pride out of her voice. She wanted to sound nonchalant, like it was no big thing. She then added, "I have the lead article on the cover this month."

"No *kidding*. Now *I'm* impressed."

"It was nothing."

"What was it about?"

"You really want to know?"

"Yeah, *sure*."

"It was about a problem I was having. No, no. I can't tell you," Ronnie said reluctantly.

"If you don't tell me I'll just get a copy on the newsstand. I probably will anyway."

"It's about what to do if your boyfriend stops wanting to have sex."

"*You* were having that problem? I can't believe it." George looked at her. Ronnie noticed he wasn't looking at her face.

"It's true. It does happen sometimes. A lot of women have that problem."

"So what did you do?"

"I kind of raped him." Ronnie blushed when she said that. She didn't mean to blurt it out.

"You did? How? How does a girl rape a guy?" George was clearly fascinated by the subject.

"I got him drunk and he passed out."

"An you, uh, got him going while he was out cold?"

"Yeah, in an off-handed way."

"He didn't even know?"

"No."

"Did he know when he woke up?"

"I think so. He had a big smile on his face."

"How about you?"

"How about me what?"

"Did *you* like it?"

"Sort of. I wanted to teach him a lesson." Ronnie blushed again. She was giving this man way too much information. She decided, probably too late to save her reputation, to change the subject. "We really socked it to those guys back there, didn't we?"

"Yeah. It was great. I never had so much fun."

"They deserved it, those SOBs."

"I agree. I was a witness to what they did to Courtney. It was *horrible*."

"I didn't know." Ronnie was surprised at this. "You were there?"

"Yes, I was. I should have done something." George shook his head, somewhat bitterly. "But I didn't. It's been haunting me ever since."

"Well, we sure made up for it. We nailed 'em, *big time*."

"Yeah. I feel a bit better about it now. I hope Courtney does too."

"There's nothing like revenge to soothe the soul."

George grinned. "I like that."

"Revenge therapy," Ronnie added.

"You're very smart, you know."

"Tell me more." Ronnie grinned in response.

"There's just one thing," George said, looking at her somewhat askance."What's that?"

"You said you raped your boyfriend. Isn't that just as bad as raping a girl?"

"Heck *no*. There's a huge difference."

"Oh yeah? What's that?"

"First of all, he's a biker. He can take care of himself. And second, like I said, he had a big fat smile on his face."

Chapter 73

Isaac was waiting with George's limousine at Teterboro Airport when George landed his Beechcraft. FBO personnel immediately surrounded the plane to set the chocks and to start the refueling and post-flight maintenance.

All four people alighted the plane and walked over to Isaac who stood by his vehicle. They said their goodbyes and headed their separate ways. Roger rented a car at the terminal and drove south on the New Jersey Turnpike toward his hime at APG. Courtney sat in the back of the limousine with George while Ronnie rode up front and got to know Isaac. Isaac, who was intensely devoted to George as his "man Friday," asked question after question about what they did from the time they left HPN to the time they returned to TEB. Ronnie kept him spellbound as she related their adventures with her sparkling enthusiasm. She related how Courtney took the plane into a tailspin and everyone on board thought they were going to crash and burn. Ronnie made it sound like the ride in Space Mountain at Disney World.

In the rear of the limo, George and Courtney were deep in conversation about the next issue of *Women Rising*. Courtney told him she would write an article about rape and, in reponse, George suggested the working title, *"Avenging a Rape."* Courtney felt she was ready to take on this subject, but said she was unsure what personal details she was willing to reveal.

"Perhaps you can write about the "Barnard Club," just in general, and see if it rings any bells. Maybe other women victims will contact you, realizing they are not alone. They may be willing to have you report on what happened to them," George suggested.

"I like the idea. That way the story doesn't have to be just about me."

"You might be able to post pictures of dozens of Barnard Club women on the cover, the way *New York Magazine* did for those victims of Bill Cosby."

"I need to pass this by my editorial board," Courtney said. "It's high time for a meeting anyway, to plan for next month's issue."

"Can I join you at the meeting? Just a thought. If you don't want me—."

"No, no. You should come. After all you're our main benefactor. It would be good for the board members to meet you. I should ask them about it first, though. I hope you understand."

"Of course. I don't want to be there if I'm not wanted."

"I'll set it up for tomorrow afternoon. Say two o'clock at the office?"

George briefly checked the calendar on his smartphone and nodded. "That's good for me. I can come."

"I'll let you know," Courtney promised.

"Now that that's out of the way, how about scheduling another weekend in Vermont? I'm still thinking about our last trip. Remember when we stayed at that bed and breakfast during the storm?"

The memory of that night of sex came flooding back and Courtney blushed. "Yeah, I do. But I don't think I'm quite ready for that again, George. Please give me some time."

"*Oh, oh*. I sense a problem."

"I don't know. It's just…I haven't dated at all you know."

"I do. Believe me I understand. It was that… that horrible night. I…I just froze. I couldn't move. I think of it all the time. If I could only turn back the clock and have a chance to do it over…to do the right thing by you, I would. But we don't get second chances."

Courtney looked at George and felt touched by the sadness she saw in his eyes.

"Well what you did last night…I am so grateful. With this behind us, and with your investment in the magazine, you have given me a chance to have a life. A real life."

"Revenge therapy."

"What?"

"Revenge therapy. That's what Ronnie called it. She said it soothes the soul."

"She said that?"

"Yes. She's a smart one, that girl."

"I know." Courtney thought for a moment, then asked, "Do you like her?"

"Sure. What's not to like? Say listen: For your article on rape, why don't you send her to investigate what happened to those men after we left them on that airstrip up there in Maine. She's a journalist. Right?"

Courtney looked again at George. In the back of her mind she thought the sexy young writer might just be turning his head, creating competition. After a beat she said, "You know, maybe I would like to go to Vermont with you again. Now that we know each other better I'm sure it won't be so awkward as last time. So let's *do* it."

"Next weekend?"

"You're on."

"I'll set it up, " George said with a smile, and he took out his smartphone again to mark his calendar.

Chapter 74

Courtney spent the next morning outlining her lead article for the next issue of *Women Rising*. She thought of a good title, *The Bad Boys' Barnard Club,* and imagined the magazine cover with college yearbook pictures of the three rapists. The words *"MEMBER"* would be printed in large capital letters, angled upward from left to right partly overlaying the boys' faces, as if stamped there by a Barnard Club official. The article itself would feature pictures of the men as they looked now as well as pictures of their homes in Chappaqua, especially the mansion of the ringleader, Carl, the one-time captain of the basketball team. She would rely on Ronnie to find out and report the latest information.

Courtney still had difficulty deciding how much to reveal about her own rape. She wanted to tell her story, but also she didn't. This was a dilemma that, she hoped, her Alphabet Soup could resolve that very day at their meeting.

At one o'clock in the afternoon the women assembled in the conference room. They took their usual places with Courtney at the head of the rectangular conference table. The door to the room and an empty chair were at one end. Ashley and Bailey sat on one side of the table with Deedee on the other. Courtney sat at the end facing toward the empty chair and the door.

The room was initially abuzz with several women talking at once. Everyone wanted to know what had happened the day before, but Courtney kept them in suspense until she finally called the meeting to order. "Let's get started," she said, clapping her hands. "George Cleary will be here in just one hour and I'd like to go over a couple of things having to do with the next issue of the magazine."

Ashley immediately raised her hand to interrupt. "We want to hear about yesterday first." The other women, except Deedee, nodded in agreement.

"Okay, okay. I'll do my best. Roger and Isaac, George's personal assistant, picked up those three…um, *bastards,* and drove them to Westchester Airport. George flew all of us in his own airplane up to the northern tip of Maine where we dropped them off at the end of an airstrip."

"In the cold?" Ashley wanted to know.

"Yes, and believe me, it was pretty cold up there. I'm sure they froze."

"How did they get back?" Bailey asked.

"I don't know and I don't care. We left in a hurry, so they couldn't see the tail number on the plane."

"It won't be hard for them to find that out. They knew George, right? And it was George's airplane." Deedee played the devil's advocate.

"Even if they suspect it, they'll have no proof." Courtney explained. "George will say they made up some imaginary story."

"Can they still be charged with rape?" Deedee asked.

"Absolutely. I've learned there's no Statute of Limitations for rape in New York."

"If you wanted to charge them, could you prove it?"

"I don't intend to, but yes. They admitted it while on the plane, and we made a recording. That's why they won't be suing us for what we did to them."

"Clever." Ashley exclaimed. "Who thought of all this?"

"That was Roger. He was amazing."

"Sounds like George was amazing too," Ashley added. "Flying you guys in his private plane."

"They all were. Ronnie too."

"She was with you?" Deedee's antennae went up.

"Yes. She wanted to do something to punish those men, so we asked her to come along."

Deedee frowned and looked at Courtney with concern. "Why would she join you? It could have been a dangerous trip."

"Now that you mention it, I don't really know. I wondered that myself."

"Did she do anything?" Deedee pressed.

"She helped a lot, in fact. I was in the cockpit with George all the way to Maine, but I listened in on the cabin with a set of earphones."

"How about on the way back?"

"Ronnie took my place in the cockpit."

"Umhmm," Deedee was not finished. "Courtney, let me ask you: Are you and George an item?"

Courtney blushed. "*No*, of course not."

"You spent a weekend with him in Vermont for goodness sake. Has he asked you out again?" All three women leaned in to hear what Courtney would say.

She looked back at them, somewhat embarrassed, and replied, "Well, if you must know, I'm going up to Vermont with him again this weekend."

Deedee stared at her blankly. A shadow of disgust darkened her face and then quickly passed. No one noticed it but Courtney.

Just then two light knocks were heard on the conference room door. The door opened and in stepped George.

"Hello," he said cheerfully. "I'm sorry to interrupt. I'm a bit early. May I come in?"

Chapter 75

"Please come in," Courtney replied, relieved by the interruption from the unwelcome probe into her personal life. "Here, take this seat." She stood up and offered him her own chair. He smiled warmly and came forward to shake her hand and turned to greet the other members of the board.

"I'm George Cleary," he said to them. "I'm glad to meet you all finally."

The three board women looked at him, somewhat in awe of his reputation, and two of them uttered a meek, "Hi."

George sat down in the chair that Courtney offered him; Courtney walked around and took the seat at the opposite end of the table, her back to the door.

"Well," Courtney began, assuming a prim and proper manner. "You have all met George now. As you know he's invested a substantial amount of money in our magazine. We all wish to thank you for that." Courtney started clapping and the other women joined in to show their appreciation. "I'd like each of you now to introduce yourself. Ashley, we'll start with you. Please tell George your name and a bit about your background."

Ashley nodded and started the introductions by telling her story. Courtney called on Bailey next and finally Deedee. Only Deedee was at all reticent about offering details of her life in the literary field. The other two spoke proudly about their impressive careers and, when the introductions were completed, George acknowledged the three women and thanked them appropriately.

"I guess it's my turn now," he said. "You probably want to know why I'm here and why I invested in your magazine."

The three board members nodded affirmatively. Courtney pretended she knew, but wondered what he would say.

"Has anyone here seen the movie *Jerry McGuire*?"

All of the women, including Courtney, tentatively raised their hands.

"Remember the scene at the end where Tom Cruise appears at the women's consciousness raising session and starts pouring his heart out, expressing his love for Renee Zellweger who sits there in stone silence?"

All of the women nodded "yes" and smiled recalling that touching moment in the movie.

"And at the end of this heart-felt rant he looks at Renee questioningly, hoping he didn't embarrass her but desperately wanting to know if she shared his feelings?"

The women were with him now, intensely curious about where he was going with this.

"And after an awkward and agonizing moment, Renee says to Tom, *'You had me at hello'*?"

Ashley was the first to speak. "Perfect ending to a great romantic comedy." Bailey and Deedee seconded the thought.

Deedee said, "I don't like the whole idea of a romcom, but I have to admit, this one was well done."

"You don't like romcoms? What's wrong with a romcom?" Ashley wanted to know, tossing her golden blonde tresses to emphasize her femininity.

"It stereotypes our roles as women. That we need a man to be a whole person."

"Now, now, ladies," Courtney interrupted. "We can all agree there is such a thing as romance. But let's not lose sight of the mission of our magazine. We're not against men *per se*. We're just against the terrible things they do. We want them to be more like *us*."

"Everyone *shut up*." Bailey exclaimed. "I want to hear what George has to say." She bristled and glared at the other women, who were shocked into silence by her brash remark.

"Okay," George continued tentatively. "As I was about to say, I've been in love with you, Courtney, ever since the first time I saw you back in college. I wasn't good enough to play on the basketball team so I consoled myself with the position of student manager. I took care of all the crappy details, like making sure the balls were pumped up, arranging for transportation to the away games, things like that. I didn't think I was good enough to even speak to you, so I kept in the background and you didn't know I existed. When that…*thing* happened, I froze. That was my chance to come to your aid, but I *couldn't*. I just couldn't. I don't know what came over me, but I have regretted it ever since.

"I never married because I didn't want my love for you to fade. I loved loving you. I treasured you in my heart. You were my motivation to focus on making money. I went to work and, sure enough, I made a lot of money. I made it for *you*.

"When I got that email from you, Courtney, I was astounded. It was totally unexpected. I thought 'this is my chance of a lifetime.' So we met and I agreed to 'invest' a million dollars in your magazine. It didn't really matter what the magazine was about. In fact, I thought it was a bit kooky, with all this feminist stuff, but I did it for *you*."

Ashley, Bailey and Deedee all stared blankly at George, their eyes wide. Courtney blushed bright red.

"And when I heard about your wanting to get back at those sons-of-bitches, I jumped at the chance. I helped out in the only way I could. I provided the transportation. It was a small part, I know, but it felt good to be by your side, getting back at those men.

"I'm hoping that you have feelings for me, Courtney, the way I've had feelings for you for all these years." George looked fondly across the table at Courtney, his eyes pleading for her to declare her love for him. He also looked at the faces around the table in hopes of some emotional support.

Courtney stared back at him but said nothing. There was a long awkward moment during which the board members looked expectantly at Courtney without speaking.

George also said nothing, but after the pause he blurted out meekly, "This is where you're supposed to say, '*You had me at hello*.'"

Chapter 76

When no response came from Courtney, Ashley's eyes flashed angrily, and she scolded her with an accusatory tone, "Courtney, the man is *waiting*."

Bailey prompted her, "Yeah, Courtney. What's the matter with you?"

Ashley added, clearly annoyed, "What else do you want? The guy clearly *loves* you."

Only Deedee seemed not to be upset with Courtney. She said, "Matters of the heart should be kept private. We don't need to hear this, Courtney. Maybe you can work it out with George during your weekend together in Vermont."

That calmed the mean feelings and even George seemed mollified, if not satisfied by Courtney's demeanor. "We can talk then," he said, giving Courtney a knowing look.

Courtney returned his gaze with deep sympathy in her eyes and said gently, "I'm sorry, George."

"Let's get on with the meeting then," Deedee said brightly. "We're here to discuss the next issue of the magazine. It will be about rape, I assume, including Bill Cosby and anyone else like him who's been in the local and national news. It's high time we devoted an entire issue to the subject. It's like gun violence. People are so used to it they don't even think about it any more, but when it happens to you as a woman, you're devastated. We need to wake our people up."

"It's the one male behavior that's most offensive to women," Ashley said. "But rape's a big subject. The main article should be about Courtney's experience. Don't you agree, Courtney?"

"I...I'm not sure. I don't really want to give details. It should be enough to say that those three men raped me. Can't we let it go at that?"

"Of course," Deedee replied sympathetically. "Maybe we should have someone else write the article. What do you say?"

"I want to do it. I'm thinking the article should be about the Barnard Club," Courtney said, "and I have an idea for the cover: Photos of the three men with the word "MEMBER" stamped over them in red letters."

"It'll be *breaking news*." George said. "That would sure sell magazines."

"The Barnard Club?" Deedee wanted to know. This was the first that she or any other board members heard of it.

"Yeah, what's that?" Bailey asked. Ashley seconded with a questioning look.

"The rapists confessed to Roger and Ronnie, on our to Maine, that there was something called the 'Barnard Club'," Courtney explained.

"So?" Bailey pressed. "What is it?"

"It's like the 'Mile High Club,' only it refers to Barnard women who were raped."

"*Really*?" Bailey was astounded. "Can we prove that?"

"It's on the recording we made."

"How many women were in the Club?" Bailey asked.

"I don't know exactly. It could be forty or fifty. Some were duplicates."

"Duplicates?"

"Raped by more than one of the boys."

The thought left a pall in the air. There was a long pause.

"Holy shit," Deedee exclaimed eventually, stringing out the word "holy." "And you're one of those women?"

"Yes. Unfortunately, I am."

There was another long pause.

"Maybe we should have Ronnie write the article," Deedee suggested. "You're too close to it, Courtney."

"You have a recording. One of *us* could listen to it and write the article." Ashley said. "That way we won't have to pay Ronnie. It will save money."

"But Ronnie was there," Deedee countered. "She has it first hand. She's a good writer, not that all of you aren't also. But I'd say let her write the first draft at least."

Everyone around the table looked at each other, trying to gauge each other's opinions.

"Don't look at me," exclaimed George, holding his hands up, palms out. "I'm not involved in editorial decisions."

The women looked at Courtney to see if she'd defer to Ronnie in writing the article. "I even have a title for the story," she said defensively. "'*The Bad Boys' Barnard Club*.'"

"It has a nice ring to it," Bailey agreed. "I like the alliteration."

"I don't," Deedee said. "The title doesn't say anything. No one will know what you mean by the 'Barnard Club'. They'll think it's a sorority or something."

"I'm with Deedee," Ashley said, nodding affirmatively.

"All right then," Courtney acquiesced. She felt the board was ganging up on her. "Let's decide democratically. All in favor of Ronnie writing the article raise your hand."

Three hands went up. George, who wasn't on the board, didn't volunteer a comment.

"I guess we should call Ronnie then," Courtney said grudgingly. "Can anyone think of another title?"

The women were silent, but after a beat George raised his hand. "I have a suggestion," he said.

"Okay?"

"How about '*Anatomy of a Rape*'?"

Chapter 77

General Tommy-gun Mason sat at his desk and thought about his career. He was a two-star general now and things were about to change. He knew he would have to shoulder more responsibility and he was waiting nervously for the shoe to drop. He liked the additional pay, the more frequent admiring looks of military females and the jealousy of his male peers – that was the best part of the promotion in his humble opinion – but he was going to lose his post as Commanding Officer of APG. He hadn't realized how good he had it here until the job was about to be taken away. The post was easy duty and it came with good benefits: his orderly assistant, Eve, had been one, for example.

At the moment Eve was sitting in the outer office doing her nails. Mason knew that, although he couldn't see her, because she groomed herself constantly when she was idle, which was most of the time. He didn't mind that at all because her work came in spurts: periods of high stress activity between long stretches of boredom. During the periods of boredom she used to urge him to "get it on" to brighten her day. However, those days were behind him. Genreal Mason was all business now and he aimed to keep it that way.

Eve was just getting up from her chair at the end of the boring day when the phone rang. It was the Chairman of the Joint Chiefs of Staff.

"Put the General on," came the gruff voice over the receiver.

"One moment, Sir." She put the call on hold and alerted Mason over the intercom. He felt like a bolt of electricity ran through him and immediately picked up the receiver. "General Mason, Sir."

"General," the Chairman began, "I have good news and bad news. The good news is that Nemo continues to work well beyond our expectations. Aleppo is practically at a standstill right now. No one there wants to fight. The bad news is that the war in Syria rages on. Their President al-Assad continues his attacks against his own people. We need to close him down, pronto."

"The POTUS has narrowed it down to two options: Bomb the shit out of al-Assad's palace or spike the water in Damascus with Nemo. He chose the latter."

"Huh…Yes, Sir. I understand. What do you want me to do?"

"Get your team together: That's Thornwood and whomever else in his Research Department that he needs, and meet me at zero eight hundred hours tomorrow with all the Nemo he's got. We're going to muster you out with the Navy SEALs tomorrow. You're heading for the theater in Syria and, General, *you're* in charge.

"As of now you're no longer responsible for APG. I'm giving you this new assignment. We're moving your wife and her household furnishings to officer's quarters here in Washington while you attend to the war over there. We want you to turn al-Assad into *mush*. We want him to sue for peace on a platter. That's your new job, General. Think you can handle it?"

"Yes, Sir," Mason said with seeming assurance he didn't feel. "I'll make you proud, Sir."

"That's the *spirit*, Mason. And remember, no one outside of our team is to know what we're doing. Not even your wife, understand? This matter is absolutely Top Secret and right now it's our nation's most important mission. *Make it happen*." The phone clicked off.

The General sat stunned as Eve, seeing the call had been terminated, rushed into his office.

"What's that about?" she demanded, seeing Mason staring blankly at the telephone instrument. "Is everything okay?"

"No. It's *not* okay. Just…just…I have to think a moment." The General tried his best to process the information dump. "I…I think…I know that it's over. I'm no longer in charge here. They're moving me overseas. *Shit*. Do you know what they say? Be careful what you wish for? Well, I should have listened to them, the *bastards*."

Eve didn't know whom he meant by "the bastards," whether they were the POTUS and the Chairman, or those people who made up aphorisms, whoever *they* might be. She came over to the General and started rubbing his shoulders. "Is there anything I can do?"

He waved her off. "Not that," he said absently, getting up from his chair. "There's so much to do. I've got to make a list. That's it: a list of things that need doing. First of all, go to your office and place a call to Thornwood. You know him. He's been in here several times. Put Thornwood on and I'll start packing my things. I'll need some cardboard boxes." He surveyed the office with his eyes. "About five, I think. Yeah, five. There's so much stuff in here. I don't know how I'll transport it all. After you get Thornwood, get me a driver and a three-quarter ton truck. Also get one for Thornwood and whoever he brings with him. The damn Nemo has to go too. We need to load the trucks tonight and head down to Washington at six in the morning. Go."

Eve scurried out and did exactly as she was told. She called Thornwood's landline number on the base but the call went to voicemail. She left an urgent message for him to call the General, then tried and reached him on his cell. She put him on hold and buzzed the General. He picked up immediately and pressed the button to make the connection.

"Thornwood," he said. "Wherever you are and whatever you're doing, *stop*. We've been ordered overseas to single handedly put an end to the war in Syria."

Chapter 78

General Mason stayed up all night with his wife, Beth, helping her decide what household things they should take to their new home near Washington. Beth couldn't stop harping that it was unfair of the military brass to so precipitously kick them out of their house. *"From one day to the next,"* she screamed. He assured her their new digs in Arlington, Virginia, would be newer and more spacious, so she should be more appreciative of the powers that be. He told her he had to go away for awhile so he couldn't help her pack, but he'd arrange for an orderly to assist her. To his surprise, this calmed her down and she stopped complaining. What he didn't know was the thought of working with a young orderly while he was away gave her something to look forward to. "What was good for the gander—."

* * * *

At six the next morning a panel truck drove up with Roger Thornwood in the front passenger seat and ten white plastic cases of Nemo in the rear. Roger brought only a suitcase filled with his clothes, shoes and his toilet kit because, unlike Mason, he had no orders to move his household to Arlington. For him this was supposed to be just a field trip.

No one in Washington was to know the purpose of the mission except the President of the United States, who ordered it, the Chairman of the Joint Chiefs, General Mason, Roger and the four Navy SEALs who would carry it out.

A military Gulfstream jet aircraft was on the tarmac at Andrews Air Force Base, fueled and ready to go, by the time Mason and Roger arrived. The two were first ushered into an outbuilding where they met Jim and the other three SEALs where Jim briefed them on the initial plans for the mission. Mason listened and nodded his head every so often to show he was interested. As before, they were to fly into Israel and take a chopper into Syria during nighttime hours two days hence.

Before they exited the building to board the Gulfstream, Jim said to Roger, "There's someone here I'd like you to meet."

"Who?" Roger asked.

"You'll see. Let me get him."

Jim walked out of the room and returned moments later with Jamal. Roger stood dumbstruck when he saw him, as his recollection of their original meeting in the dark Syrian woods came flooding back. After a beat, his face brightened into a wide smile and he held out his arms to the young man he captured there and whom he was able to convince to fly back with them to the United States. Jamal came toward him and they embraced each other tightly. It was clearly an emotional moment. Mason, standing nearby next to the SEALs, watched and wondered whom this young man could be. With tears in his eyes, Jamal recounted his rescue from having joined the ISIS terrorists at a very young age and related what had happened to him since his return to the United States.

As Jamal explained it, the CIA had interrogated him over a period of weeks. He had cooperated fully but the CIA kept asking more and more questions that he couldn't answer. He was able to provide some intelligence on ISIS operations, however, and eventually the CIA seemed satisfied and decided not to have him prosecuted for war crimes. The CIA finally found he had simply made a terrible mistake, Jamal said, after realizing he was a young Muslim who was bullied by his peers.

Notwithstanding the rough treatment he received at the hands of his interrogators, Jamal said he harbored no ill will because he understood the fault was his for joining the terrorist group in the first place.

"I've been so lucky," Jamal told Roger and the others. "I don't know what I was *thinking*. I can't explain it, but that's all behind me now."

"I could tell you weren't one of them," Roger said sympathetically. "You didn't have the anger and hatred that it takes to kill innocent people."

"Anyone else would have shot me on the spot out there in the woods. I owe you my life, you know."

"What are you going to do now?" Roger asked.

"My parents are here to take me home," he replied. "It's…well, different now with them. They understand why I left home and they want us to start over as a family. We have a lot of catching up to do."

"Where is your home?" Roger wanted to know.

"Not far from here. We live in Middleburg, Virginia, far enough away from Washington that they call it 'horse country.' We're the only Muslins out there, I think. My dad works for a military contractor in Herndon and bought a small farm there to calm his nerves. His job is really stressful."

"Are you going to keep the name 'Jamal'?"

"Yes. I'm Jamal now and I want to stay Jamal. My parents said it was okay with them, although they named me 'Jason' when I was born. I gave myself the name 'Jamal' so it's mine to keep."

"Are you ever going back to Syria?" Roger asked.

Jamal gave a nod to Jim and the SEALs whom he had gotten to know during his dangerous rescue and his return to the U.S. "You can guess that, I suppose. But I'm not allowed to say."

"Well, I wish you well, wherever you go."

Roger gave Jamal a goodbye bear hug and and told him he'd like to pay him a visit when he returned from this new mission. Jamal asked when that might be and Roger didn't answer, partly because the mission was secret and partly because he didn't know himself.

When Jamal left, General Mason came up to Roger and asked, "Did you really save that man's life?"

"I did just what anyone else would do."

"Knowing you, Thornwood, I'm sure you went the extra mile."

Grabbing their bags, General Mason, Roger, Jim, and the three other SEALs walked out onto the tarmac and climbed aboard the Gulfstream jet to fly out to an adventure in the Middle East.

Chapter 79

The seats were arranged in two rows with their backs to the walls and windows of the plane. Mason sat on a seat flanked by Roger and Jim. The other three SEALs sat opposite, facing them.

"What do we know about the water system in Damascus?" The General asked once the flight got underway.

"Information is scarce," Jim replied. "Most of the people in Syria get their water from wells and springs. Groundwater too in some cases. The city of Homs is supplied through a nine mile pipeline from Lake Homs, for example. The whole system is fragmented. That's our main problem.

"Another problem is that only Aleppo has an actual water treatment plant that we can tap into. In Damascus it's catch as catch can. But we do have one thing going for us. The Syrian government built a huge water tower near Damascus that supplies the president's palace and the nearby military base. If we drop our Nemo into that tank, we can knock out all the bad guys, including al-Assad, who are fighting the civil war."

"That would be interesting." Mason said with a sly grin. "The Syrian rebels are mainly from outside the city so they'll get to keep their balls."

"It would be a great test for Nemo," Roger noted. "We should be able to see what happens when two sides fight each other: one side with Nemo and the other without."

"In a fight like that," added Mason, "I'd want to be on the side with the balls."

"We have aerial photos of the water tower," Jim continued. "We can see it's heavily guarded. The only way I can see to access that tower is to cut a hole in the top so we can drop a hose down from a chopper. That way we can pour Nemo down that pipe, just like refueling an aircraft in flight."

"All of this in broad daylight?" commented Mason sarcastically. "Yeah, *right*."

"No, it's at nighttime, but it might as well be daylight. The Syrians will hear us and start shooting for sure."

"Not good. Bad plan." Mason said.

"I know," Jim admitted. "You have a better one?"

"Not me. I'm just the General in command here. I'm relying on you guys to come up with the ideas."

"Roger and I have worked something out," Jim said. "We're going to go in there undercover, like local citizens, and see what's what. We're going to try to add Nemo to the water right under their noses without causing suspicion."

"*Right.* We'll just start fixing the plumbing without anyone noticing. That'll happen," Mason was even more sarcastic now.

"No, no. We can't do it ourselves obviously, but we can hire a couple of locals with a panel truck to go in there. *We're* in the panel truck looking out with a three hundred sixty degree angle video camera on its roof, and we're telling our Syrian guys what to do."

"And where do we find these 'Syrian guys'? Look up 'plumbers' in the Yellow Pages?"

"The CIA has undercover spies all over the Middle East," Jim explained. "We'll give them a shout."

"You think they'll answer the phone? We can just call up the CIA and ask to borrow a couple of their spies in Syria?"

"I can't do that," Jim replied. "But *you* can. You're a Major General. That's why they put you in charge, Sir. You can get things done."

General Mason thought for a moment. He had almost forgotten the kind of clout he might be able to wield with that additional star the POTUS had given him. "Okay," he said brightly. "Glad to be of help."

The rest of the flight was uneventful. The Gulfstream landed in Tel Aviv in the late afternoon and, as happened during Roger's previous trip to Israel, it taxied to a special U.S. facility at a remote end of the airport. Unlike with the previous trip, however, this time the plane continued into the open bay of a large hanger. After the plane's engines shut down, the hanger door behind it moved slowly downward. Once closed off from view, the plane's side door opened outward and down, allowing both passengers and crew to disembark. A truck drove up to the rear of the plane to unload the baggage and the cases of Nemo.

The group was taken to a nearby hotel by shuttle bus with their baggage in tow. After settling into their rooms and a change of clothes, they convened again on the lobby floor for drinks and a four-course dinner, followed by the hotel's entertainment which included local stand-up comedians telling jokes about Israeli politicians and the ever-present Palestinians. "You have to feel sorry for Bibi Netanyahu," one of them said. "He's tried just about everything but he just can't make the Palestinians *disappear*."

* * * *

Courtney sat in her office and brooded over her forthcoming trip to Vermont with George. It was pretty clear that George was hers for the taking, but she was unsure of her feelings for the man. For reasons that possibly stemmed from that terrible night at college, she just couldn't imagine herself with him in a long-term relationship, much less a marriage. He was reasonably good looking, in a geeky sort of way. He seemed to be kind and was certainly generous, at least to *her*. And he was wealthy. *Very* wealthy. If she were to marry him she would never have to struggle financially, the way she had struggled month after month before he invested in her magazine.

With his investment she was able to give herself a small raise and her magazine, she hoped, was about to enjoy a big bump in circulation when the next issue came out. With this issue, the magazine would hopefully turn the corner, leaving her financial worries in its wake.

Wait a minute. She said the word *marriage*? What was she thinking? She had never thought about marriage before. She never even had a boyfriend really, except in high school when she had a crush on that nice boy who became valedictorian their senior year. Whatever happened to him, she wondered. Probably married with kids by now.

She was not getting any younger. Maybe it was time to think about marriage after all. Did she have some kind of aversion to the idea? Not all women wanted to be tied to a man. Was she one of those? She was not at all sure of her feelings on the subject. But first things first: She needed a man to love. If she could find a man who melted her heart, then this marriage thing might be an option. That brought her back to George. Why was she so unsure? Was it *him*, or was it *her*? What?

Courtney's cellphone rang and she picked it up. It was Isaac calling from the car, waiting outside to pick her up and drive her to Teterboro airport. She grabbed her bag and headed out, carefully locking the door of the magazine office before turning to go.

Chapter 80

Ashley and Ronnie drove north in Ashley's Rav4 for their last visit to HGHS. On the way they talked about the changes they had seen since their very first visit, nearly four weeks ago.

"The boys have certainly come a long way," Ashley commented. "I like what's happened to them. They're somehow more...," Ashley groped for the right word, "*human*."

"I can't agree," Ronnie replied. "They're *boring* now. They don't care about girls any more. All they do is talk about their damn *schoolwork*."

"That doesn't mean they're boring. They're just interested in something more important than the girls."

"I don't know. It's more than that. Like it was with Billy. They've lost their *mojo*. They sit around and talk. *Bla, bla, bla*. Like a bunch of old ladies."

The two debated the pros and cons of the changes brought about by Nemo for the whole hour it took to get to their destination. In the end, when Ashley pulled into the school parking lot, they had to agree to disagree. They both realized there was no right answer.

The two entered the lunchroom before the first students appeared and took their places at their usual table. Ashley went forward to the counter to get lunches for them both: two bananas and two small cartons of orange juice. The lunch break for the students was a full two hours, from eleven o'clock to one, with groups of students cycling through for their half-hour lunch. It was Ashley and Ronnie's routine to eat lightly throughout this period, going back to the counter every so often to buy some more fruit.

Students started dribbling in at eleven and by eleven-fifteen the room was full of activity. The two women watched carefully as the students arrived and made mental notes of their dress and their demeanor. Over the past month they had seen a sea change in their appearance. The girls had become much prettier in the way they looked and much softer in the way they acted.

They had shed their jeans and T-shirts for skirts and dresses with bright colored prints, and had dropped their ponytails for long flowing manes with pretty hair bows and headbands. Some of them, those with developed breasts, had revealing necklines that advertised their assets. They all seemed to have lost their brashness and appeared more demure.

The girls still sat at separate tables from the boys but they always left two empty seats at their tables, apparently in the vain hope that two brave boys would take these seats.

The boys, on the other hand, remained just as sloppily dressed as they ever were but, unlike before, none of them sat at a girls' table. They stayed to themselves in clusters and, as far as Ashley and Ronnie could overhear, "talked shop," which in this case meant the subjects they had been learning about that day.

The girls kept looking over at the boys, but were unable to make eye contact.

"See that?" Ronnie said to Ashley, nodding in the direction of Muriel's table. The girls there all looked like models... "It's *pathetic*. They're trying so hard to attract the boys, but nothing's going on."

"I see what you mean. They're very pretty though, don't you think? It's refreshing to see that."

"I prefer the bitches that they were. They're too prissy now."

"They're real girly-girls. They're *feminine*. I think that's a good thing."

Mary Kate and Betty arrived shortly after eleven-thirty and came over with their trays to join their two Big Sisters. They were not in a good mood.

"What's the matter?" Ronnie asked, noticing immediately that something seemed wrong.

The two girls sat down, somewhat glumly, before saying anything. Once they were settled, Mary Kate brushed it off. "It's nothing," she said.

"*Something's* the matter. That's pretty obvious," Ashley commented.

The two girls exchanged looks but didn't respond.

"Tell us. We're here to help," Ronnie urged.

The girls stared down at the table for a long moment, but finally Betty spoke up. "Remember month ago when we first saw you, you told us things would change?"

"Yes, and they did, right? They changed, just like we said." Ashley replied.

"Well, they did for awhile. The boys started talking to us. It didn't matter if we were hot or not."

"We're your Big Sisters. We wouldn't steer you wrong."

"You said, 'If we had a good heart, the boys would pay attention.'"

"I remember. And that's true, believe me." Ashley looked at Betty, trying her best to understand what was on her mind.

Mary Kate finally spoke too. "At first we thought you were right. We thought some boys were trying to get to know us. We had hope at least."

"What happened?" Ronnie asked. "*Tell* us."

Mary Kate looked at Betty, questioningly. Betty finally blurted out, "*Nothing* happened. That's the whole point. We're still *virgins*."

* * * *

Before leaving the school at the end of the day, after mentoring the cheerleaders and the staff of the *Tribune*, Ashley and Ronnie stopped in to see the principal, Barbara Westerhoff. They told the secretary in the outer office they were there to pay a courtesy call and say goodbye. When the secretary relayed this message, Principal Westerhoff immediately came out of her office and greeted them warmly. "I've been meaning to speak with you and with Courtney about your program," she said. "Come on in and let's talk."

Ashley and Ronnie entered the inner office and Principal Westerhoff closed the office door before taking a seat behind her imposing desk. She asked them to sit also and make themselves comfortable. "I'd like to spend a few minutes on this," she said. "First, I'm anxious to hear what you have been able to gather and learn from our students, and second, I want to share some concerns with you. There have been some very odd goings on that perhaps you can help me with."

Ashley and Ronnie shot each other a knowing look, as in "Oh, oh. Here it comes." They both knew they couldn't say anything about Nemo but feared that some damage control might be in order. Ashley responded with a tentative, "Yes?" For the moment, Ronnie stayed mute.

"For starters, why don't you tell me about the basketball cheerleaders, Ashley. I understand they've been having some difficulty lately."

"Difficulty?"

"I've heard rumors of some defections. Some of the girls don't want to work out. Do you know about that?"

"Uh,…yes I guess that's true. A few of the girls left because they didn't want to muss up their hair or break a fingernail. It's nothing to worry about though. Girls are girls."

"That's never happened in the cheerleading squads before. There has always been a waiting list for cheerleaders, and now there's not. You don't see a trend here?"

"No, no. I saw that when I was a cheerleader in college. Not all girls like to break out in a sweat."

"And the *Horace Greeley Tribune*," Westerhoff continued, turning to Ronnie. "I'm worried about that too. I hear Zoe wants to resign as editor. Says it takes too much time away from her social life. She's always been such a go-getter. I've just written the most glowing recommendation for her application to Harvard. I think she has a chance to get in, but now I'm not so sure—."

"I don't think that's a problem," Ronnie replied. "She just wants some down time from the rat race. We all do sometimes. Anyway, Victor and Walter are shifting in. The two of them together make a good substitute for Zoe."

"That's not the point. Boys have always taken the lead. I want a girl in that position and my girls are…how should I say it…not *pulling their weight* these days."

"We should let them be girls," Ashley said.

"What does that even mean?" Principal Westerhoff stared at her.

When Ashley didn't answer she said, "And another thing. My boys aren't doing too well in sports either. Our football team lost their last two games after squeaking out a tie with Port Chester. And don't ask me about the basketball team. They're total losers so far this year. It's the same with all the sports. The boys seem to have lost their fighting spirit."

"I heard the boys' grades have gone way up this month," Ashley commented brightly, trying to put a positive spin on the situation.

"As a matter of fact, that's true. I can't put my finger on what's going on. I don't live here in Chappaqua, but it's like there's something in the water—."

Ashley and Ronnie shot each other another glance and then stood up quickly, signalling they had to leave. "We'll be summarizing our thoughts in a report," Ashley said.

"I might even write an article about this time with your students," Ronnie added. Without naming names, of course. Ashley and I have had a wonderful experience."

"I'll want to see that before it goes out," the Principal said sharply. "It's been a very strange month, I must say."

During their drive home that evening Ashley and Ronnie relived and role-played their meeting with Principal Westerhoff and couldn't stop laughing.

Chapter 81

Courtney enjoyed the flight to Vermont. George again let her handle the yoke but this time she held it steady. She tried her best to maintain a constant altitude and heading but found herself drifting off course a number of times. She felt George's watchful eyes upon her the entire trip, on one hand giving her a sense of security, on the other unsettling her. It was clear that George had lost whatever trust he might have had in her natural ability to fly the plane.

As before, George took over the landing phase as they approached Lebanon Airport. After bringing the plane in, taxiing to the FBO and shutting it down, he assisted Courtney with her bag as she disembarked. George arranged with the FBO to park for two nights and rented a mid-sized SUV from Hertz. Courtney couldn't help thinking he was trying to please her at every step as he loaded her bag in the hatch and held the door for her as she climbed in. She made herself comfortable in the front passenger seat as he walked around to the driver's side and got behind the wheel.

"Here we go," he said with a smile and they headed west, crossing the Connecticut River into Vermont.

"Woodstock is so picturesque and authentically colonial," Courtney commented. "And I just *loved* the Woodstock Inn."

"Oh, didn't I tell you? We're going back to Barnard. I reserved at the Maple Tree Inn."

Memories of the sudden thunderstorm that brought them, chilly and drenched to the bone, to this warm and cozy bed and breakfast came flooding back. "That was a lovely place too," Courtney replied. "I like that. Thank you."

She also remembered the sexual experience that had surprised her with its intensity. She thought sex with Deedee was good, but this male-female encounter had awakened feelings she didn't know were there. In her mind the only thing that detracted from the experience was that, at the time, she didn't really care for George. Maybe this time it would be different, she thought.

When they arrived at the Inn George parked in the front driveway and walked around to the back of the car to retrieve their suitcases from the trunk. He carried both Courtney's and his own up the long path to the front porch. Mike, the husband side of the couple that owned and operated the B&B, came to his aid as he struggled up the porch steps. He took Courtney's suitcase and led the way into the house, his bulldog Becket jumping around at their feet to eagerly welcome the new guests.

As they passed by the kitchen on their way to their room upstairs, Mike's wife Nelly appeared in her apron and welcomed them also.

Mike led them to the same room in which they had stayed a month before and, after handing the key to George, he quickly took his leave, closing the room door behind him.

Alone in the room, George embraced Courtney and pressed his lips against hers with unsuppressed passion. Startled, Courtney pushed him away gently but firmly and stood there a moment, at first not knowing what to do. "I…I'm sorry George," she stammered, somewhat embarrassed by her own awkward response. "I was not expecting…such a kiss. Can't we…huh, go to dinner first? It's been a long day and I'd like just to relax a bit."

"Sure. Good idea," George hid any embarrassment he might have felt from kissing her. "Let's go back to the Barnard Inn just up the street. Like we did the last time."

"That would be lovely. We can unpack later."

"You got it. Let's go."

Courtney felt relieved as George called the restaurant to see if he could reserve for two. She wasn't in the mood for having sex at that moment and wasn't at all sure her mood would change. However, the Barnard Inn was considered to be one of the most romantic restaurants in Vermont and, with a little wine and some comfort food, she might be persuaded if George played his cards just right.

The main dining room had nothing available until ten o'clock but the concierge offered them a table in the tavern. Courtney learned that George had earlier made a reservation for ten o'clock, which he now cancelled in favor of a table right away. It was Friday night after all, and the restaurant catered to weekend visitors.

When they arrived they were shown to a small table by a window, quite remote from the loud activity at the bar. The tavern had the appearance and the scent of old oiled wood. It had probably been that way for some time, the house having been built nearly two hundred years earlier. Courtney relaxed and reviewed the menu as George scanned the wine list. "Would you prefer red or white?" he asked.

Courtney chose red because she intended to order one of the turf items on the menu. George ordered an expensive bottle of cabernet sauvignon. When the wine was served, George raised his glass and, gazing at Courtney, offered a toast to start their weekend. "There is no one I'd rather be with right now than you, Courtney," he said. "Let's drink to *us*."

Courtney did not think there was an "us" just yet, but nevertheless clinked her glass to his and took a sip. The wine was smooth, not acidic, and it warmed her throat. She held the glass and took two more sips before setting it down.

The waiter came and they placed their orders. George knew just what he wanted without looking at the menu; Courtney ordered a small filet.

"Did you like flying?" George asked, obviously just to get the conversation started.

"Yes I did. I was a little nervous though. Much more so than the last time we came up here. I didn't know then how easy it was to make a terrible mistake."

"That was all my fault," George said, again acknowledging his failure of supervision during their flight to Maine. "Instrument flying doesn't come naturally to anybody and I apologize for expecting you to do what takes hours of practice to learn. Maybe there's a lesson in there for us, though. Life is short and we should grab hold of it while we can."

"I thank you for being so understanding, but I still feel bad about it."

"We're here now, aren't we? That's all that counts. Let's drink to that." George held up his glass again and Courtney did the same. They both took another sip.

By the time the meal was served they had finished the bottle and George ordered another. With their delicious-looking dinners on the table in front of them, but before they tasted the food, George looked at Courtney fondly and said to her earnestly, "I'm looking forward to spending the night with you."

Courtney felt an inward shudder and replied in a soft voice, "Please be gentle, George. You know I...I have not had intercourse before, except..."

George nearly gasped. Not knowing what else to say, he looked at her and said simply, "Of course, Courtney."

"I'm sorry about the last time we were here," Courtney continued. "I was not expecting to spend the night with you."

"I understand," George said. "We were caught in the storm."

"It came out of nowhere. I couldn't imagine why they didn't predict that."

"Me neither," George replied quickly. "Whatever. But let's eat." He picked up his knife and fork and waited for Courtney to do the same before attacking his meal. As the evening progressed George drank nearly all of the second bottle of wine.

Courtney enjoyed her dinner and, as their dessert and coffee were being served, a feeling of anticipation mixed with anxiety welled within her. It would shortly be time to return to their room at the Maple Tree Inn.

Chapter 82

As they walked out of the Barnard Inn, George handed Courtney the keys to the car. "You drive," he said. "I've had a bit too much wine."

"Sure, I'd love to. I don't have a car so I don't get much chance to drive. Too bad we're not going very far."

In fact, it was less than a mile on a straight road to the Maple Tree Inn. As soon as Courtney parked facing the building, George got out and walked ahead, a bit wobbly to be sure, up the path and up the steps to the porch. Courtney followed close behind, her intent being to catch him as best she could if he were to fall.

George made it safely into the Inn, entering through the front door and turning right at the kitchen to climb the steps to "Cupid's Retreat" on the second floor. Courtney remained downstairs a moment, distracted by the cute items on display behind a pane of glass at the reception desk. There were coffee cups, egg cups, a salt and pepper shaker and even a Christmas tree ornament, all hand-made and embossed with a maple leaf and the name of the Inn. "Are these for sale?" she asked Mike, who was sitting in the closet-sized office behind the desk.

"Yes they are. They make great souvenirs. Memories of your stay here."

"They're beautiful. And useful too. I'll want to get something when we check out."

"No problem. We have several of each, all boxed and ready to go."

Courtney was about to head upstairs to join George, but then hesitated and said, "Mike, can I ask you a question?"

"Sure."

"How much does it cost to stay here?'

"About two-fifty a night on weekends. Less during the week."

"Oh." Courtney thought a moment and then said, "We stayed only one night the last time we were here. The charge was, like five hundred dollars."

"That was for two nights."

"But we stayed only one."

"We don't offer reservations on a weekend for just one night. If you want to stay over on a Saturday night you have to reserve for Friday too. We're oversold on weekends so you have to book two nights, sometimes far in advance. Especially in October."

"You…you had a reservation? I mean, George reserved the room for the weekend?"

"Yes. Friday and Saturday."

Courtney said nothing for a moment, confused, trying to understand what had happened. They had stayed at the Woodstock Inn the first night. In fact, they were supposed to fly back on Saturday afternoon but had gotten caught in the storm. How could it be that George had reserved at the Maple Tree Inn? Thinking this through, Courtney was thunderstruck. She thanked Mike and quickly ran up the stairs, reaching the top just as George managed to open and enter the door to their room.

Courtney stormed in behind him and closed the door, her face flushed with anger. "George, I just found out you reserved this room long before we came up here to Vermont last month."

"Uh, yeah. What of it?" George was still fumbling with his keys, clearly tipsy from the wine.

"You *also* reserved at the Woodstock Inn."

"I had to be prepared for any contingency. Like a storm, and it happened. You can't fault me for that."

"You thought a storm might be coming?"

"Well, if you must know…"

"Know what?"

"A pilot always gets a complete weather briefing before he flies an airplane."

"*What*? You knew that storm was coming?"

"Of course."

"And you pretended to find shelter for us, here at the Maple Tree Inn?"

"If I hadn't reserved here, there would have been no room."

"You did that to try to get me into bed. Didn't you?" Courtney shouted, accusingly.

"I have to admit, the plan worked pretty well."

"You *bastard*. You BASTARD!"

Courtney grabbed her purse and suitcase and stormed back downstairs. As she passed the kitchen and reception desk, her suitcase having banged and clattered down the steps, both Mike and Nelly appeared and watched with astounded expressions as she rushed by.

"Is anything wrong with the room?" Mike asked after her, clearly upset.

"Nothing's wrong with the room, It's *him*," Courney screamed as she left through the front door, leaving it to close itself behind her.

Courtney took the keys from her purse and unlocked the SUV. She angrily heaved the suitcase into the back seat and climbed in the front behind the wheel.

She drove nearly half the distance to New York City before she calmed down. When Courtney finally thought she was able to think straight, she fished her iPhone out of her purse with her right hand while steering with her left, found a phone number among the "*Recents*" and pressed "*Deedee.*" She asked Deedee to arrange for a meeting of the Alphabet Soup at ten o'clock the next morning. Her mentor and sometime lover protested at first, reminding Courtney that the next day was a Saturday; but when Courtney explained the agenda for the meeting, she immediately agreed to take action. Courtney's agenda was *Courtney.*

Chapter 83

Courtney remained working in her office with the door open until she saw that all members of the editorial board had passed by and entered the conference room. She got up from her desk and joined them, taking her usual place at the far end of the conference table.

"Thank you for coming," she said uncharacteristically humble and with sincere appreciation in her voice. "I need your help."

The three board members looked at her expectantly, clearly eager to offer whatever help and advice they could to this, their soul sister, whom they dearly loved.

"Let me start at the beginning," Courtney began. "I've been very secretive about my relationship with George Cleary, but you need to know a few things."

"George and I go way back. I've known him since I was a junior at college. I was a cheerleader and he was a student manager for the Lions basketball team. He was kind of a nerd then, and I didn't notice him really. He kept coming around as if he wanted something but he didn't say anything so it was easy to ignore him.

"You have all heard about what happened next. In my senior year. It was...you know, horrible. I went to this party for the basketball players and... I don't want to even say it. I've tried to put it out of my mind but I couldn't. At least until now. What made it worse was that George appeared at the door and...watched. He didn't say or do anything. He could have saved me but he just stood there.

"What I know now is why he did that. He told me. He froze and I can understand that. People react differently in emergencies. With some it spurs them into action. Others are paralyzed. George just couldn't... move.

"Not only did that experience almost ruin my life, it has haunted George ever since. I went my way and started this magazine. He went his and focused on making money. He was driven and it worked for him. He's made a *lot* of money.

"When we needed money to pay Billy, I turned to him and he came through for us. He invested. I think it was out of guilt. It partly made up for what he had done, or not done, when I was…raped. But I think it was more than that. I think he wanted to impress me so I would pay attention to him. You heard when he said he had a crush on me back then. I didn't know it because he was too shy to say something to me. I don't know how I would have reacted if he told me. I probably would have rejected him because he was so nerdy, and that could have left its scars too.

"Anyway, you asked me if anything happened when we went to Vermont together a month ago. He invited me, and against my better judgment I agreed to go. I didn't know him that well and I wanted to keep a tight rein on our relationship. He took me up there in his private plane. I couldn't help but be impressed. We then stayed overnight at a beautiful inn: the Woodstock Inn. We had separate rooms. We had dinner together and he kissed me goodnight on the cheek. He was the perfect gentleman. I was beginning to like him.

"The next day we went hiking together on the Appalachian Trail. It was lovely. We talked while we walked through the woods just at the time the leaves were turning. I can't tell you how divine that was. I was entranced. And George was so pleasant to be with.

"I didn't want it to end but there came a storm. A thunderstorm. It started to rain, just lightly at first so we headed back to the car as fast as we could. We didn't make it in time though. We got drenched. George said he knew of a place we might go: a B&B he had heard of. He called ahead and it turned out they had room.

"The storm was raging and it didn't look like it would end any time soon, so we stayed overnight at the B&B instead of going back to the Woodstock Inn. In one room this time.

"To make a long story short, we had a lovely dinner at a restaurant nearby and a lot of wine, and when we got back to the room he kissed me. Really kissed me. I kind of…gave in, and we made love. Sort of kinky love I should say. I didn't let him…penetrate me. We didn't have sex the old fashioned way. Like Bill Clinton with Monica Lewinsky, I suppose. It was defintely sex, yet it wasn't really." The three women at the table stared at her open-mouthed at this point. "I could honestly say that I didn't have sex with George. Nor did I want to have sex with…a *man*.

"Well since then you know how helpful George has been in getting back at the three rapists. Ronnie told me they finally found their way home but they haven't gone to the police so far as we know. The whole plan would not have worked without George's airplane. Fact is, they paid dearly for what they did and I feel much better now. We got evidence that could convict them too, but I'm not going to go to the authorities unless they try to get back at me. I'm done with them.

"On the way back from that trip, George asked me to go to Vermont with him again. I didn't think it was such a good idea because I didn't want to lead him on, but he told me something that changed my mind. Ronnie was after him. I…I didn't want to lose my chance. I didn't know if I loved him or not. I liked him, but like is not enough for me. I've never been in love before so I don't really know when 'like' becomes 'love.' This was all new for me. I was feeling my way along, so I said 'yes' to going with him.

"We went up there again…to the same B&B. It is nice there and the people who own it are very nice. I had a good feeling about it and about George. We had a lovely dinner again, at the same place as before. I was a bit tipsy when we left, but George had a lot more wine than I did. I knew he wanted to have sex. Real sex this time. And I might have been okay with that. I don't know. Like I said, I'd had some wine.

"George went up to his room but I got to talking to one of the owners of the B&B. I found out that George lied to me the last time we went up there. He had planned the whole trip to try and get me into bed with him. He knew the storm was coming and he'd made a reservation at the B&B ahead of time. Going there to get out of the storm was just a ruse to stay overnight with him in the same room. I freaked out. George was not the gentleman I thought he was. He was almost as bad as those rapists. I was so mad that I took the car he rented and drove all the way back here to the City. I left him there.

"I'm a helpless wreck. Right now I'm boiling over. I won't be able to stand the sight of George for a long time to come for what he's done. I feel betrayed. He almost succeeded in having sex with me. Thank God that didn't happen. But he's still an investor in this magazine. We owe him for that. But sex, *never*.

"What should we do? What should *I* do?"

After this long monologue Courtney looked expectantly at the three intelligent, savvy women who sat around the table. She was flying in the dark, way beyond her ability and expertise, and she desperately needed their advice.

Chapter 84

Brash Ashley spoke up first. "I agree with you, Courtney," she said angrily. "That stinks. That's just like a man to try to get you into bed. That's exactly what *Women Rising* is all about. We've got to fight back."

Bailey was not so supportive. "Have you never heard the expression, 'All's fair in love and war?' There have been court cases on this: whether it's rape to entice a woman into bed by deception and deceit. Short answer: It's *not*.

"I'm afraid there's nothing you can do, Courtney. It's in men's DNA to get into your pants. You've got to suck it up, then get back out there again to fight another day.

"It's a good thing you found out what that son-of-a-bitch is made of before you plunged into bed with him," she added, more sympathetically now. "Once a cad, always a cad, I say."

Courtney turned at last to Deedee for guidance and comfort. Her eyes pleaded for some scrap of wisdom she could hold onto in the weeks, months and years ahead. Deedee was the person she trusted most to keep a level head and to make sense out of the confusing events that were overtaking her as she stumbled forward on the rough and rocky road that was her life.

"We've known each other a very long time," Deedee began with deep empathy in her voice. "Over these many years I've wondered when and if you'd ever fall in love with a man. On the one hand I hoped you would, for your sake. Deep in my heart I knew it would be good for you. It would erase some of what you've had to endure and allow you to become that wonderfully wanton woman that I know you are. On the other hand, I selfishly wanted you to remain a *pioneer*: that person who's had it up to *here* with the problems and the heartache caused by the unrestrained aggressiveness of men. I felt you'd lose that fire in your belly: that drive you've had to make us aware of what is wrong with men. Once you've found a soul mate, I feared, you'd become accepting of the way things are and stop leading all of us on to the way things ought to be."

Deedee paused and looked at the other women in the room as if to telegraph what was to come. "I know, first hand, that you're a sexual being," she said. "You and I have had our moments."

Ashley and Bailey stared back at Deedee, their faces blank. Deedee had just confirmed what they had suspected for quite some time: that she, Deedee, had been more than a mentor to Courtney. She was a lesbian who had awakened Courtney sexually. They had also come to learn that Courtney had been sexually attracted to George, which meant it was high time she seek and find a life partner of the opposite sex.

Deedee continued, "Before I give you my advice, Courtney, I'd like your assurance that you'll continue with *Women Rising* magazine. I'm worried you'll become complacent. Please tell me that if you have a relationship with a man, you won't let him seduce you into accepting the status quo. Even if you should marry, have children and create a new life for yourself with a home in the suburbs, a dog and a cat, you won't be distracted and lose your focus on what is important to the world."

"I'm not even sure I can find a man I can love," Courtney replied somewhat woefully. "I don't know if I can love a man at all. I've been resentful of men for so long, I don't know if I have it in me. One thing I'm certain of, though: the facts are the facts. Men are the problem. But if men were more like us women, would we live in a better world?"

Ashley, who had been listening intently to Deedee's sidebar with Courtney, finally broke in. "Well, I'm glad *that's* settled," she said. "Men are men and men are a problem, but itsn't that what we love about them? It's in our DNA. Now let's get on with the business of finding Courtney her Mr. Right."

"Whoa," Courtney held up her hands. "Not so fast. I didn't say…"

"She's right, Courtney," Bailey added. "You want our advice, so let's have at it. You think you're the first woman in the world to have a problem with a man? We've all had our ups and downs but, as Deedee said, you have to pick yourself up and keep on trying."

"Let's start from scratch. What characteristics do you want in a man?" Deedee asked. "The more we know about your likes and dislikes, the better the advice we can offer you."

"We should make a list," Deedee suggested. "Let's put the qualities you want on the board." She stood up and walked to the whiteboard on the conference room wall. She picked up a blue felt-tipped marker and, centered at the top of the board, she printed the heading "COURTNEY'S MAN." She then divided the panel into three columns by drawing two vertical lines from top to bottom, spaced apart beneath the heading. At the top of the left column she wrote and underlined, "*Likes*," at the top center she wrote, "*Don't Care*," and at the top of the right-hand column she wrote, "*Dislikes*."

"Now," she said, turning to Courtney. "We just need to fill in the blanks."

Courtney blushed rose red. "Isn't this overkill?" she protested. "I don't know what kind of man I like, and in any case I don't know that many men."

"There's always the Internet," Ashley reminded her. "There are a million men out there just dying to meet a wonderful woman like you. You have to know what you want. You have to be selective."

"Let's list the 'likes' first. How about the guy's looks?" Bailey asked. "Where do you stand on, say, 'tall, dark and handsome'?"

"I really don't care about looks," Courtney said honestly. "As long as I love him and he has a good heart, that won't make any difference."

"Okay, Put that down also under '*Don't Care*,'" Bailey said. Deedee did so.

"What are your '*likes*' then?" Deedee asked, getting somewhat impatient. "Come on. Let's list them."

Courtney took a moment to reflect. She then said, "I want my man to have a good heart. That's the most important thing. A kind person. Kind to people and also kind to animals. And gentle too. A 'gentleman.' That's second. A good sense of humor would be a close third. Intelligent would be fourth. Yes, I think if my man had those four qualities, that's all I'd need."

Deedee wrote '*kind*,' '*gentle*, '*sense of humor*' and '*intelligent*' on the whiteboard in the left-hand column. "Heck, what you've described so far is a *woman*, not a man."

"How about 'sexy'?" Deedee asked. "You'll want to have sex with him."

"Yeah," Ashley seconded the thought. "*Lots* of sex."

"How about dislikes?" Bailey asked. "That should be telling."

"That's easy," Courtney said. "I don't like a man to be arrogant. Self-centered. Vain." Deedee wrote as fast as she could as Courtney tossed out the adjectives. "No one likes those qualities anyway, but I particularly dislike dishonesty. I want my man to tell the truth at all times, even if it hurts him to do so. And to never cheat others. My man should be guided by a good moral compass. I want him to be fair to his fellow man and to foster goodwill. I want…"

"Stop, stop." Deedee interrupted. "I can't write that fast, but I think we get the idea. We have your wish list. Now let's start looking for a man who fits the list."

"I see George is out," Ashley said.

"Oh? Why?" Bailey asked rhetorically. He seems to have the qualities Courtney wants. As far as I've heard, he's kind, he's a gentleman and he has a sense of humor. He's not arrogant, self-centered or vain. And he's not exactly *dishonest*. He didn't tell Courtney about the thunderstorm but heck; like they say, 'All's fair in love and war.'"

"You're forgetting one thing. Or maybe you don't know," Ashley replied. "It's his business."

"What business?"

"He explained it when he spoke at the Wednesday Assembly at Horace Greeley High School in Chappaqua," Ashley said. "I was there. He's kind of a Robin Hood in reverse."

"What does that mean?"

"He takes money from other peoples' pension funds – legally to be sure, but is it 'fair'? – to give to *himself*. The worst part of it is, he has no idea that what he is doing is *wrong*."

Chapter 85

"All right, ladies. Who else do we know with all those good qualities?" Deedee looked around the room expectantly. "Let's rack our brains and come through for Courtney."

At first there was stone silence. They could think of no one.

"Men are flawed," Deedee commented flatly. "But there has to be someone."

"Or they're married," Ashley added. "Even at my age the good ones are getting picked off. And, sorry to say, I don't know many guys over thirty."

"How about you, Bailey?" Deedee asked. "You should know some eligible bachelors in their thirties or forties who are coming off their first marriages."

"That's the trouble," Bailey answered. "The ones I know that have never been married are too self-centered, and the ones who are divorced are the walking wounded."

Deedee shook her head. "I've never been in the market you know. So I can't be very helpful. But Courtney? I should have asked you first. How about you? Do you have eyes on anyone who fits the profile?"

Courtney looked more dejected than when this whole exercise started. "I guess there just isn't anyone out there for me," she said hopelessly. "Or maybe my expectations are too high."

"For every woman there's someone she can love," Bailey offered. "Look at me. I'm your age and still looking, but I know that he's out there. I'm a romantic."

"Don't look at *me*." Deedee said. "You know I'm not into men. Never have been."

"Is there anyone we can call?" Ashley asked, rolling her eyes. "This is bad. I never realized the pickings were so slim."

The women looked at each other and then at Courtney.

"What?" Courtney uttered, confused as to why the women were staring at her.

"How about your friend Emily?" Deedee asked. "She knows a lot of people."

"We could call her. But I don't think she knows that many eligible men. She's the Queen Bee of gorgeous women, but they suck all the young bachelors out of the room. She doesn't have much time to go looking for herself."

"Let's find out," Deedee pressed.

Courtney took out her cellphone and dialed a number. While it was ringing she pressed "Speaker" and laid the phone on the table. Emily answered on the second ring.

"Hello, Bitch. What are you doing, calling on a Saturday? Shouldn't you be up in Vermont some place, bedding down your new honey… what's his name, George?"

That raised a chuckle from Ashley and Bailey. Deedee remained stone faced.

"I'm in my conference room in New York with my editorial board. You're on speaker," Courtney added the last comment so Emily would watch what she said. "George and I had a falling out. That's why we're calling, actually. I've had a pretty bad experience with George and I'm here licking my wounds. We wonder if you can help."

"Help *you*, Bitch? I always thought you had it together. But you know I'll do anything. What's up?"

Deedee broke in and said, "It's me, Emily. I'm Deedee. We're here as a board to advise Courtney as best we can. You won't believe this, but we've narrowed it down. There's only one thing that Courtney needs right now."

"What's that? A defibrillator to resuscitate her failing magazine?"

"As a matter of fact, the magazine's doing really well at the moment. No, Courtney needs something else."

"Okay, I'll bite. What is it?" Emily asked.

"A man."

"A what?"

"A man. A perfect man she can call her own." Deedee said this without hesitation, as if it were the commonest thing in the world for a woman to want a perfect man.

"*She* needs a…*man*? I thought men were the *enemy* for her?"

"Not just men or *any* man. She wants and needs one 'ideal man'. We've worked it out. We know the kind of guy she's looking for; we just don't know anyone who fits her specs."

"Really? What are these 'specs'?"

"The man needs to be kind and gentle, have a sense of humor, be intelligent and of good moral character. That last is very important. And by the way, he can't be arrogant, self-centered or vain."

"Gee, the Bitch doesn't want much, does she?"

"That's why we called you. We're stumped."

"I'll bet she wants him 'tall, dark and handsome' too. And rich. Don't they all…"

"As a matter of fact, that's not true. She doesn't care what he looks like or how much he makes."

"Is that so? I should have guessed. It's just like Courtney, going for what's inside the package rather than on the outside."

"There's always the Internet, but men lie about themselves. Especially the arrogant, self-centered and vain ones."

"Tell me about it. Courtney, are you still there listening?"

"Yes, I'm here, Emily."

"You already know the perfect man. He's right there, under your nose."

"I do? Who?"

"*Roger Thornwood.*"

Ashley, Bailey and Deedee stared at Courtney. It was as if a flashbulb just went off in the room.

Deedee spoke loudly so Emily could hear clearly via the phone, "You think?"

"He's a dear," Emily said. "Trust me, I've spent some quality time with him. He's a diamond in the rough. I'd go for him myself if I were twenty years younger."

"Thank you, Emily," Deedee glanced at her colleagues as she spoke for the group, and then added, "You may have just changed Courtney's life. Forever."

"You're welcome. S'long, Bitch. You have some catching up to do. *Go get your guy.* 'Bye everyone."

The phone on the table went silent.

No one said anything for the longest moment. They all sat there, each thinking her own thoughts.

Deedee finally broke the silence. "A penny for your thoughts, Courtney."

The other women looked at Courtney, expectantly.

"I…I like Roger…very much. I do. He's just a friend. I enjoy his company. But I don't think of him…that way."

"There's only one way to find out," Deedee said, her voice serious now.

"Oh? How do I do that?"

"Get him into bed. You'll know in an instant."

"How do I do that?"

"It all starts with a *kiss.*"

Chapter 86

"Get *going*." Deedee said to Courtney. "There's not a minute to lose. For all you know some other woman has her designs on him already."

"I think you're right. I...I guess this meeting is over. Thank you everyone." Courtney got up from her chair, as did the others. "I need to call him."

The three women hugged her in turn and wished her good luck before leaving.

Ashley waited until the others had gone and, before leaving herself, she said, "One more thing, Courtney."

"Sure. Anything."

"What's George's cell number?"

"You want to call him? You can have him. He's yours."

"It's not for me—."

"Oh? Who then?"

"Ronnie. She's got the hots for him, real bad. I'll give her his number. She can take it from there."

Courtney smiled. "I *though*t something like that was going on. Yes, do that."

"You think they'll make a good match?"

"I do. I know about one thing they have in common, at least."

"What's that?"

"They both like a lot of *sex*."

* * * *

After everyone left, Courtney called Roger's cell number. The call went to voicemail and she left a message. She next dialed four-one-one and got the number for the main switchboard at Aberdeen Proving Grounds. She called it and asked the receptionist to put her through to Roger at his lab.

"You know it's a Saturday?" the female voice said. "No one is in."

"Any idea how I can reach him. It's *very* urgent. A family matter." Courtney remembered that the last time she tried to call him at APG, they pretended not to know him.

"I can try to connect you with Eve. She's the administrative assistant to the Post Commander. Maybe she can help."

"Okay. Please do."

Courtney waited and eventually a sleepy voice came on the line.

"Hello?"

"Are you Eve?"

"Yes?"

"My name's Courtney Stillwell. I'm a magazine publisher in New York City. It's very urgent that I get in touch with Roger Thornwood. Can you help me please?"

Courtney heard a male voice in the background. "Who's that, baby? Who the fuck's calling on a Saturday?" She then heard "Sssh, quiet," and Eve came back on and said, "Roger's on a field trip. He can't be reached."

"Do you know where he went?"

"I'm not at liberty to say. May I ask what this is about?"

"I…can't say either. It's…personal."

"Oh?" From the tone of the voice that said "oh," Courtney could tell she had pricked Eve's interest.

"Yes, I met him in New York and—."

"*Right.* I know you. You're the one who was going to publish an article about his secret program."

"Yes, that's me."

"Did you…publish?"

"No, I agreed not to."

"Well, Girl, let me say: You did the right thing. You could have ruined…everything."

"I know. He told me."

"So what do you want?"

"I want to…uh, see him."

"Really?"

"Yes, really."

"Why? Whatever it is you have to say, can't you just tell it to him on the phone?"

"No, I need to…see him again."

"Duh. Now I get it. I'm a little slow on the uptake sometimes. Sorry. You want to…um, turn up the heat?"

"Something like that."

"Hello. Earth to Venus Girl: *Go for it*. He's a catch."

"I know," was all Courtney could think to say.

"I'd put you in touch with him if I could, but they don't keep me in the loop on all the super secret stuff they do. I know someone who can, though."

"You do? Who?"

"Nobody you'll want to ask over for dinner, trust me."

"Who?"

"He'll refuse to take your call, but I'm going to help you."

"Who is he, for gosh sakes?"

"The Chairman of the Joint Chiefs of Staff."

Chapter 87

General Mason, Roger, Jim and the three other Navy SEALs sat around the table in a conference room of their hotel and discussed their plan to "Nemodate" the water supply in the City of Damascus. Mason had been in contact with "Agent Joe" at the CIA, and Joe had explained the lay of the land. The CIA had undercover agents on the ground in Syria to monitor the activities of all three combatants: the Syrian Government led by Bashar al-Assad, the rebel insurgents and the "Islamic State of Iraq and Syria" known as "ISIS."

The CIA spies posed as double agents with these various groups, exchanging information to earn the trust of whatever locals they were able to infiltrate, and passed a steady stream of intel up to Joe through radio messages, midnight Syrian time which was midday Eastern Standard Time.

To the extent they could do so, they also monitored the activities of the Russian fighters who stockpiled material and made bombing runs from their base in Latakia.

Joe issued instructions to his secret agents every day to direct their intelligence gathering and to warn them of any person who might pose a danger, or who otherwise threatened to expose them. On more than one occasion Joe had ordered the termination of such a suspicious person, whereupon his agents discreetly "took him out" without leaving a trace.

The plan for "Project Nemo" required the secret agents to rent a box truck and drive to a remote, secluded area in the dead of night. There they would meet up with Mason's team, which would be flown in, together with the supply of Nemo, by a pair of Black Hawk helicopters.

The truck would travel to Damascus by a circuitous route and park near the water pumping facility that was at the base of the water tower. The team would pose as a water inspection and maintenance crew. If anyone on the ground appeared suspicious of their activities, they were authorized to take him or her out and seclude this person's body on the truck for extraction by helicopter when they returned to the "safe zone" for their escape to Israel.

The drop was scheduled for zero-two hundred hours, the early morning of the very next day. After discussing and mapping the plan, Mason asked everyone to retire to their rooms and knock themselves out for six hours with Ambien, to log some sleep they would surely need later on.

Just as they were about to disband, Mason received a call from the Chairman. He got up from his chair, phone to his ear, and walked out of the room at the same time raising a hand as a signal for the others to stay put. "Sir? This is General Mason," he said when he was out of earshot. "Today's code is...." Mason rattled off a set of alphanumeric characters from a slip of paper he took from his shirt pocket to verify his identity. Immediately following, he compared a set of characters the Chairman gave him with those on the slip to confirm that the Chairman was the person whom he said he was.

"Okay, go ahead," Mason said. "We're clear and were encrypted."

"Good. Mason, to be frank we're getting nervous here. This mission is absolutely critical and it's got to go on under the radar. Do you have it buttoned up?"

"Yes, Sir. We do. The team from the CIA is already working inside the theater. We're meeting at zero-two hundred Zulu to drop the powder and take it to the water supply."

"I've got to tell you, the President is extremely nervous. More than I've ever seen him. He's not going to sleep until we let him know we've completed the mission without a breach in the circle of secrecy."

"Then he's going to have one long night, Sir. Even if all goes as planned, we won't be back here on friendly soil until zero-eight hundred. That's one o'clock your time."

"We can't have any slip-ups. You understand me, Mason?"

"No slip-ups. Understood, Sir."

"It's going to be hard to keep the President in check. He's micromanaging this."

"Yes, Sir. We'll do our part."

"Oh, and Mason: one more thing. Tell Thornwood there's something nice waiting for him here when he gets back."

"Something?"

"Well, someone. Tell him it's 'someone'."

"You won't say who?"

"Nope. It's a huge surprise.

* * * *

Tommy-gun Mason and Roger rode in one of the two Black Hawk helicopters, together with Jim and the SEALs, touching down in a sugar beet field at precisely two in the morning. They were thirty-five miles from Damascus as the crow flies, but about fifty miles away by circuitous back roads and highways. One of the SEALs operated each of the choppers.

The undercover agents of the CIA had parked the truck at the edge of the open field. When the choppers landed they drove the truck toward them over the rough ground, leaving heavy tire tracks on the pristine rows of the beet crop.

All of the men, except the two chopper pilots who remained in their seats keeping the rotors slowly turning, jumped out and set about unloading their tools and the cases of Nemo from one of the choppers and reloading them into the truck. This took them exactly twenty-two minutes, and when they were done, Roger, Jim and the remaining SEAL jumped into the back of the truck with three CIA agents while Mason climbed into the passenger seat. Another one of the CIA operatives climbed in behind the wheel and started the engine. As the truck pulled away, the two helicopters rose and disappeared into the black sky.

Roger sat on the floor of the truck, his back leaning against one of the cases of Nemo. The truck's cargo bay was pitch black inside so he couldn't see any of the comrades, even those who sat next to him. Using his hands for balance, he kept himself sitting upright as the truck jostled its way over the rows of crops, but the ride smoothed out somewhat when they reached the road. Someone in the back used his phone to contact the driver and asked him to turn on the light.

"Mason said it's okay, as long as the rear door is closed," came the reply. "When we stop I'll have to kill the light again."

The ceiling light came on and Roger instantly recognized the man sitting next to him. It was *Jamal.* Roger stared at him and his jaw dropped. He had difficulty believing what he saw.

"Ja…Jamal." Roger stuttered. "What the—.?"

"*Surprise,*" Jamal exclaimed, grinning broadly. "I wasn't at liberty to tell you anything before. I'm really sorry. I'm a U.S. agent. Been working in Syria for almost three years now. I was recruited because I can speak Arabic. Learned it at home. My dad is Syrian. He caught the attention of the CIA because he works for a military contractor and one thing led to another—."

"The other guys you were with? Were they—?"

"One of them was. The rest were locals. We were a small team, working in Aleppo to gather intel. We found out there might be a plot to poison the water so we went out there to check the facility. We found a guy there who was about to add some really toxic stuff to the system. We killed him, but then you guys showed up. We figured you as terrorists too so we went after you."

"You mean you never intended to…uh, kill me? When you found me there?"

"I didn't want to, but I couldn't tell you that. It would have killed our cover. I had to make a choice, though. I was compromised so I decided the best thing for me to do was to surrender. Pretend I was a misguided terrorist sympathizer. That way the rest of the team could continue working in Syria. I almost didn't make it when Jim here decided it was time for me to die. You truly saved my life, you know."

Jim, who was sitting in the back by the rear hatch, looked over and acknowledged that was true. "But all's well that ends well," he added. "You never know who you might meet out there in a war zone."

Roger shuddered, as if trying to clear his head. "It's a good thing I'm sitting down," he said. "You could knock me over with a feather." He nodded toward the two other CIA agents who sat in the back with them. "These guys?" Roger asked. "And the guy driving this truck?"

"Yup. They were the ones who were with me out there in the woods when you showed up."

Chapter 88

The truck stopped in front of the water tower an hour later. The driver switched off the light in the back, then got out and walked around to the rear where he raised the hatch, which rolled up like a window shade into a recess in the roof. All except one of the men in the back climbed out, leaving a SEAL inside to hand out the cases of Nemo when the others were ready to unload it. From earlier recons of the area they knew the tower was unguarded and no resistance was expected.

General Mason also climbed down from the front passenger seat and stood watch for possible interference by the local populace. As did all the other men on the mission, Mason had on civilian clothes of the type worn by a tradesmen and handworkers in Syria. Like the others too, he carried a concealed handgun and a few extra magazines of ammunition.

The water tower was a tall, square, stone structure of such height that it dominated the cityscape. It was nearly a hundred years old and its façade was in great need of repair. Pock-marked in places, one might say it had accumulated the graffiti of time. Although the original design had been inspired by the spires of Moslem mosques, the top of the tower had lost its handsome turret and was only a drab reminder of its once distinctive, and some say historic, past. Originally the tower had housed a steam-powered reciprocating piston mechanism to pump the water upward into a large tank at the top, but this contrivance had long since been replaced by electric rotary pumps that depended on an electrical grid that intermittently lost power. Over the years the tower had served the city well to provide water at a constant, steady pressure, especially during outbreaks of rebellion against the then current regime with the resulting bomb-created fires that required massive amounts of water to extinguish.

Roger stood by as Jim and the secret agents made quick work of opening the locked wooden door at the base of the tower. Once inside, the agents switched on their mini MagLites and peered around. Roger followed them in, carrying his equipment, and turned on his own flashlight. Inside he saw a jumble of plumbing, some new, and some old and rusty, within a cavernous space above a dirt floor. The system of pipes, pumps and valves looked complicated at first but Roger quickly traced the various paths the water took as it entered the facility, was initially filtered and then pumped upward into the tank at the top. Coming down from the tank, the water exited through a manifold of pipes to different districts in the city.

Looking for a way to climb up to the tank, Roger saw a set of stone steps along one wall, leading to an opening in the high ceiling. "I'm going up," he whispered to Jim. He went over and began to climb, counting the number of steps as he did so.

Feeling the pull of vertigo whenever he looked down, he continued upward, using his flashlight to illuminate the steps. Making his way through the opening in the ceiling he kept going, counting the steps as he climbed higher and higher until he reached the level of the huge tank enclosed in the top of the tower. By this time he had counted one hundred and forty-two steps and had passed several oval openings in the outer wall that served as windows, allowing light in during the day. At this time of night it was pitch black outside, and the only illumination was the light from Roger's flashlight that reflected off the drab earth-tone masonry.

Roger looked over the upper lip of the tank, which, being under the roof of the tower, was open at the top. He aimed his flashlight inside and saw black murky water. He could imagine there being snakes and various other kinds of creatures in the water, but he knew they'd have no way of getting in there.

He looked up again and saw a trap door above him in the roof. The stairs led up further so he continued climbing until he reached it and pushed against it. The door was stuck closed so he banged it hard with his fist. It broke free after the second try and flipped upward, hinged on one side, revealing the stars overhead.

Roger squeezed through the opening and climbed out onto the flat roof. Looking around, he saw a round manhole cover a few feet away. He walked over, knelt down next to it and grabbed two handles that protruded from the top. He lifted the cover away and, taking care not to accidentally slip and fall into the hole, he peered downward and saw the dark water. "Yes. We can do this," he thought to himself.

Standing up again, he looked outward and took in the view of the entire city, lights twinkling beneath the clear night sky. He then walked to the rim at the edge of the roof and stared down at the truck far below. He pointed his flashlight downward at the men standing nearby and wobbled the light to attract their attention. When they looked up, he aimed the flashlight at his own face so they would recognize him. They all waved silently and he waved back. In the near darkness he couldn't recognize faces or tell who was who.

Roger pulled out his com device and called Jim. "How's the view from up there?" Jim asked.

"You've gotta come up here. It's a great-looking city at night."

"Well let's hope we won't see it in the daylight…and they won't see *us*."

"Roger to that," Roger replied, realizing the double entendre after he'd said it. "Bring up the winch and cable. We can drop the Nemo into the tank from up here."

"You got it. Sit tight. We're coming right up."

"Roger that," Roger said again, his tension briefly eased by the use of his own name.

Within ten minutes Jim arrived, assisted by the other SEAL, hauling up the equipment they needed to lift the cases of Nemo up to the roof. In the meantime the ground crew had spread out a rope net behind the truck and had placed on it the containers of Nemo.

Jim and his partner secured the winch to the side of the roof and unwound the cable, throwing the end hook over the rim and lowering it quickly down to the ground. The ground crew attached the four corners of the net to the hook and waved, signaling Jim to lift the pile of containers. Jim and his partner took turns winding the crank on the winch and the net, with its load, slowly rose higher and higher until it reached the edge of the roof. Roger then helped them lift off the containers, carry them over to the open manhole and pour their contents into the dark interior.

Daylight was just beginning to appear on the eastern horizon when all the Nemo from the containers had been finally dispensed and dispersed into the dark water in the tank. Roger assembled the empty containers at the edge of the roof and was about to reload them into the net, when he heard a commotion below.

It began with some shouting. Roger peered over the edge of the roof and saw men running away from the truck. Other men appeared around corners and from behind buildings and opened fire. Several men near the truck fell, either wounded or killed, shouting out in agony as they slumped to the ground. Roger stared down, aghast, as pure pandemonium erupted on the street below.

Chapter 89

Jim immediately grabbed for his satellite com and called to his SEALs in the two choppers. "Mayday. Mayday. Need air support *now*. Being attacked. Men down."

Roger heard some return chatter, but all he could make out was the word "Roger." He wondered how the attackers, with their assault rifles and rocket launchers, knew that they were there.

As Jim directed his helicopter pilots via com, Roger ran over and replaced the cover on the manhole. He and the other SEAL then worked together furiously, carrying the empty containers that lay strewn around the manhole back to the roof edge, and stacking them in a pile on top of the open net. When that task was finished they worked to unbolt the cable winch from the railing in readiness for their evacuation.

Jim directed his men on the street to take cover inside the tower, taking with them the wounded and the dead. From his vantage point on the roof Jim fired on the attackers, wounding one and causing the others to scatter and take cover around the corners of the tower and behind adjacent buildings. There were ten or fifteen of them now and their number seemed to be increasing by the minute.In the distance Roger heard the familiar and welcome sound of the helicopters. He looked out and saw two black dots emerge on the horizon, becoming gnat-like with fluttering blades as they grew larger.

Within seconds the choppers were upon them, one descending onto the roof as Roger and the two SEALs stood aside, and the other descending onto the plaza below.

As soon as the first chopper touched down on the roof, Roger worked with Jim and the other SEAL to load their equipment into its open side door. They dragged the net with the pile of containers over and hooked its corners onto a cable that dangled from an extended arm. The slack in the cable disappeared as the onboard winch drew it in and hoisted the net with the containers off the roof surface. Roger climbed in first, expecting the others to follow, and the chopper immediately lifted off. He turned around and saw the two SEALs rush to the side of the roof and begin firing on the attackers below. "Wait!" he screamed at the pilot. "You're leaving the others." But the chopper kept rising.

The helicopter pilot looked back at Roger as he flew and shouted, "That's the plan."

Roger slumped into his seat and watched through the open door as the scene slipped away. Within a minute all he could see was the tower, standing tall in the city but rapidly receding from view, as the helicopter headed for Israel.

Rather than relieved, Roger felt dejected and also inwardly guilty at leaving his comrades under attack while he rode to safety. He needed to return just as soon as the helicopter landed and discharged its load of containers and equipment: the telltale evidence of their mission to add Nemo to the water of Damascus.

The ride back took only an hour but it seemed like two to Roger. When they finally landed in the far corner of Tel Aviv airport, he noticed an unusual military jet on the tarmac that had not been there when they left. It was black and its shape reminded him of a Stealth bomber he had seen in pictures. That aircraft, he'd heard, was the fastest in the U.S. arsenal.

Roger un-strapped himself and stood in the open side door, ready to jump down as the landing skids of the chopper touched the ground. A ground crew ran up to unhook the net filled with the empty containers and grab the winch equipment that lay next to him on the floor of the craft. A fuel truck pulled up alongside and two men jumped out to rapidly refuel. "Stay on board!" shouted the pilot, who kept the rotors spinning above their heads.

Roger stepped back and chanced to look out toward the nearby open hanger. He saw two figures walking toward him. Thinking it strange, he looked more closely and realized they were a man and a woman. It took a second before he recognized the *Chairman* and *Courtney*.

Chapter 90

When Courtney saw Roger standing in the open side door of the helicopter she broke into a run, leaving the Chairman behind her on the tarmac. "*Roger*," she shouted as she approached the aircraft. "Are you all right? We heard there's been an *attack*."

Roger stared at her in disbelief and jumped down to the ground. "Why are you here?" he asked. "And how did you get here?"

"We rode in *that* thing," she said, pointing in the direction of the sleek, all-black aircraft. "It went pretty fast."

"Huh…fast? How fast?"

"I don't know. They didn't tell me. All I know is we left Washington two and a half hours ago and *here we are*."

"Yeah, but…how come you got a ride? What are you doing here?"

"She wanted desperately to see *you*," the Chairman said with a grin as he walked up.

"*Me*?"

"Yes. But she's here as my staff assistant and a reporter. We saw there was trouble so we had to come. General Mason's been shot and…"

"General Mason?" Roger's jaw dropped. "I didn't know… How did you—?"

"We monitored your mission every step of the way."

"I saw some people shot, but—."

"That's right. General Mason and a couple of our agents too. Mason took a direct hit and was killed."

"Oh, no!" Roger buried his face in his hands.

The Chairman and Courtney stood there sympathetically, waiting a moment for Roger to compose himself.

"There are only four people on U.S. soil who know about your operation," the Chairman said after a beat. "The President, the CIA handler 'Joe,' Courtney here, and me. We could see what happening from a camera on the General's helmet. It wasn't pretty, believe me."

"I…I didn't know—." Roger stammered.

"The General's gone. So I came."

"But Courtney—?" Roger looked at her.

"She came to me just as you were starting your mission. She insisted on coming too so I let her. It's against all regulations. I made a judgment call."

Courtney embraced Roger and buried her face in his shoulder. "I was so worried—," she sobbed in full realization of what it meant to her that Roger was safe, at the same time surprising him with her display of emotion.

"I'm all right," Roger assured her. He took her head gently in his hands and looked squarely at her face, suddenly feeling an almost irresitable pull of attraction. She gazed back at him as if in a trance, moving her lips slowly towards his for a kiss but reached nothing but empty air. Roger, getting a grip on himself, realized the urgency of returning to Damascus to rescue the others and backed away.

"I've got to go, *now*," he exclaimed.

In the meantime, the ground crew had finished emptying the containers and equipment from the open bay, and the refueling crew had finished their job and were climbing back into the tank truck. In addition to refueling the main tanks they had topped off the level in the four external tank pods. Another crew, in charge of ordnance, took the opportunity to re-check the Hellfire missiles and Hydra 70 rockets that bristled from both sides of the aircraft.

"You're both staying *here*," the Chairman commanded. "I've got to go there to take charge and see this through." He took hold of a handle on the side of the helicopter and swung himself up into the open bay doorway.

Roger looked up at him and shouted above the noise as the aircraft's rotors increased in speed and started biting the air. "I have to go back there too. I've got to test the water. We couldn't tell how much water was in the tank so we didn't know how much to put in. We dumped in all we had, but that might have been too much or, worse yet, too little."

"You have to test it?" the Chairman shouted back, trying to understand what Roger needed to do.

"I left my test kit in the tower, right near the water pumps."

The Chairman made a blitz decision. "Okay then. Climb aboard." He held out his hand and pulled Roger in.

Roger looked back at Courtney as the Black Hawk helicopter lifted off and started to turn toward the northeast, the direction of Syria.

Courtney frantically grabbed her cellphone and held it high in the air. "*Skype me.*" she shouted, her reddish blonde hair blowing in the backwash of the helicopter as it rose. Roger barely made out the words over the engine roar and the beat of the blades as he looked back and watched her figure recede. He couldn't help thinking how beautiful she was.

* * * *

As they flew toward Damascus, Roger briefed the Chairman on what had transpired. He told him they had finished pouring Nemo into the tank and had closed the opening on the roof. They had been able to remove all evidence of having done so while General Mason, Jamal and all the other CIA agents were undergoing the attack. As far as he understood, the men who were still alive were still battling the fierce attackers: hostiles who were dead set on killing them all.

"They blew up the truck and did major damage to our other helicopter," the Chairman said. "Our job now is to evacuate the bodies and everyone who's left."

"The roof should be safe," Roger replied. "The assailants are going to be careful not to damage the tower. It's their only water source."

"Good thinking, Roger. We need an angle like that. Right now our chances of getting everyone out don't look very good."

On the way the Chairman and Roger worked out their strategy. The Chairman made a call to Jim, and by the time the tower was in sight their plan was set. They would use the structure as a fortress and try to bring everyone on board the helicopter. This would exceed maximum weight limit, but to leave someone out there would mean almost certain death.

Chapter 91

The stealth helicopter came in fast and banged loudly when it hit the flat surface of the roof. Roger unstrapped himself, jumped down and headed immediately for the trap door. He climbed in and started his descent to the base of the tower. As he hurried down the steps he passed members of the American team near each window, taking aim and firing at the attackers that surrounded the tower under cover of the adjacent buildings. As he passed by he told them to make their way to the roof as soon as possible to be evacuated by helicopter.

When he reached the ground floor he looked around and found his water test kit just where he'd left it, next to the complex system of plumbing. No one else was there. The assailants had been busy in the fight outside and had not yet stormed the tower through the ancient wood door. Roger knew that would happen soon when they finally figured out that his men had moved up to the higher vantage points at the windows, leaving the ground floor unguarded.

Expecting them to storm through the door at any minute, Roger grabbed a plastic beaker from his test kit and opened a spigot to tap into the water supply. He let the water flow for a few seconds before inserting the beaker into the stream, filling the container and then dumping its contents on the ground. He did this a second time and, after closing the tap, added a precise number of drops of three different chemicals to the water sample he'd collected. Holding the beaker up to the faint light in the room, he smiled faintly. "A little heavy on the Nemo," he said to himself. "But that should change things around here."

Gathering up the parts to his test kit, he returned them to the leather case and snapped the flap closed on the top. Grabbing the case he quickly headed for the steps. Except for the small amount of water that he'd released from the tap, there was nothing in the cavernous space that would in any way reveal that he'd doctored the water supply.

As he ran for the steps he heard men finally crashing through the door behind him. He reached the steps just as the men charged in and spotted him. "*Up there.*" Roger thought he heard a familiar voice shout in English as he climbed the steps as fast as his two legs would take him. "*Jamal?*"

Roger knew it was a long way to the top, and under normal circumstances he would need to stop to take a breath every twenty steps or so. But these were not normal circumstances. He charged up the steps and kept going. By the time he was nearly halfway up, the first hundred or so out of the two hundred and fifty steps, he was totally out of breath and his legs were sore. But he heard the clattering of men down below who were following, and this drove him on. He passed window after window, but he didn't even dare to look out as he went. All his men had moved up to the roof by this time. His climb upwards became slower and he was panting heavily. The men behind him seemed to be getting closer. He sensed they were shouting something in Arabic but wasn't sure. He had to keep going, He thought one of the voices seemed familiar but that was crazy. He was losing his grip. He continued to climb. He knew now he couldn't make it to the top. Just too weak. Maybe he could stop for a second.

"*Roger.*" He heard his name being called from up ahead. That voice was familiar too. What little strength he had left was fast ebbing away. He felt he was losing consciousness. He stumbled. He felt a firm hand grab his arm and catch his fall. He looked up and saw Jim, his chiseled face firm, his body strong. He felt Jim lift him and carry him up the remaining few stairs to the top. To the trap door. To safety. Jim pushed him upward through the small opening and Roger felt himself crawl out onto the roof and let go of the leather case. Jim was right behind. And so was the sound of their pursuers. One of them shouted, "Grab his legs." Roger recognized that voice now. It *was…Jamal*.

Chapter 92

Roger turned to look down at Jim, who had saved him from the clutches of the assailants. What he saw made him freeze with fright. Jamal was right behind Jim holding a gun to his head. Roger was about to shout, "Please help." when the remaining SEAL materialized at his side. He too looked down as Jim was dragged backward down the steps by two other assailants while Jamal held the gun. Like Jamal, the other men remained behind Jim, using him as a shield.

"*No!*" Roger screamed frantically, moving out of the way so the SEAL could jump down into the opening in an attempt to rescue his colleague. Shouting came from below, just as the Chairman joined Roger and peered down into the opening.

A bullet came whizzing up past his head followed by the sound of the gunshot.

"*Shit.*" the Chairman cried and jumped back, looking at Roger helplessly.

"We have to save our guys," Roger said urgently. "We can't leave without them."

"There's no other way," the Chairman replied. He pulled out his com and spoke to the SEAL who was piloting the helicopter, ready to fly it away. "We're heading back to the base," he commanded. "Roger, get back on the chopper, *now*. That's an *order*."

"No, no!" Roger protested, shouting now. "That will take too long. Once they get our guys out of the tower, we won't know where they take them. We have to save them *now*."

"We need a force to deal with that," the Chairman shouted back. "A force we don't have." As he spoke the chopper behind him started spooling up, its engine sound increasing to a roar, its rotors gaining momentum in anticipation of lifting off with its heavy load of men.

"Stop him." Roger screamed. "I have a plan."

The Chairman stared angrily at Roger. "We have to go. There's no way we can save them without going down there."

"Yes there *is*." Roger shouted at the Chairman emphatically. "We *can*."

The Chairman was livid from Roger's refusal to obey orders, but he hesitated for a fraction of a second, then lifted his com and spoke again to the pilot. "Hold it." he barked.

The engine roar subsided.

"Okay, then. What's the plan?"

"All SEALs are sharpshooters, right?"

"The best of the best, or they don't make the grade."

"They're using Jim as a shield."

"So?"

"That means they'll come out of the tower door *first*."

"And?"

"Our SEAL can pick them off from up here." Roger pointed to the edge of the roof.

"*That's* the plan? There are hostiles all around down there. As soon as he gets near that edge, he's a sitting duck. We'll lose our *pilot*."

Roger didn't have an answer. In his eagerness to save his friends he had come up with the first steps of a rescue plan, but he had not worked it through. He knew there were attackers all around the tower with guns trained on the edges of the roof. Maybe saving his friends was impossible. Maybe there was nothing they could do except cut and run. They'd have to leave Jim and the other SEAL in the hands of the enemy to be tortured and killed. But that was unthinkable. He had to find a way. Find a way to bring them back to safety. Back to the base in Israel. His mind flashed on the image of Courtney, standing on the tarmac, looking up at him, her long hair blowing in the backwash of the helicopter, holding her phone high in the air.

"I'll use my *cellphone*." Roger stared wide-eyed at the Chairman as his mind worked out the rest of the plan.

"Your cellphone?" the Chairman replied, almost derisively. "We use *satellite coms*."

Roger grabbed his smartphone from his pocket and pressed Skype to call Courtney.

"What the…" The Chairman looked at Roger as if he had gone insane.

"Courtney. It's me. Can you see me?" Roger pressed the speaker button and the instrument became, miraculously, the representation of Courtney. Her face could be seen on its screen and her voice could be heard from its loudspeaker. It almost seemed that the tiny box had *become* Courtney.

"Listen carefully," Roger said. "I'm going to hold the phone over the edge of this tower, looking down. You tell me if you can see the door, down at the bottom."

"Is everything all right, Roger? You worry me."

"I have to admit, it's not alright. But you can help us." As he spoke Roger got down on his hands and knees and crawled toward the edge of the roof holding the phone in his right hand. "Just a minute while I get to the edge," he said to Courtney. The Chairman, in the meantime, had understood the plan and he ordered the SEAL pilot to shut down the helicopter and come out with a sniper rifle "on the double."

As Roger came close to the edge he dropped from his knees to a belly crawl. Finally, he held out the phone and laid it flat, face up on the ledge that bordered the edge of the roof. Before he did so, he pressed a button to switch to the camera facing down.

"The screen went blank." Courtney's voice came from the speaker.

"I know." Roger replied. "I'm going to push the phone out. Tell me when you see something."

Roger carefully pressed the phone forward until its top edge came even with the far edge of the ledge on the side of the roof. Lying as flat as he could to keep out of sight, he felt the ledge with his hand and pushed the phone a bit further, so that it extended out slightly beyond the far edge until its camera eye, near the top of the instrument, could look straight down.

"I see light again." Courtney's voice said. "It's focusing. Yes. I can see the ground down below."

"Do you see a door? The door to the tower?"

"I'm not sure. No, I can't see a door. But I can see where the door must be. There's a kind of path in the dirt where people go in and out."

"That's *it*. Now watch and tell me when you see someone come out."

Out of the corner of his eye, Roger could see the SEAL with his rifle coming up along side him, crouching down and ready to spring.

"There's someone coming out." shouted Courtney. "He's backing out of the tower. There's another one too. he's….holding on… to a third person. Pulling him backwards. The two people…they have guns."

The SEAL jumped up, took aim through the rifle-scope, and fired. He then fired again and jumped back from the ledge. A second later a barrage of bullets whistled up past his head, and a few ricocheted off the side of the tower with a "pocketa-pocketa" sound.

"Got 'em both," he said matter-of-factly, after stepping back from the brink to the relative safety of the roof. Roger pressed the button on the iPhone and snapped a photo.

Chapter 93

"Get back in the chopper." shouted the Chairman. "When our boys arrive they'll be followed by a shitload of hostiles."

The SEAL with the sniper rifle ran for the helicopter followed by Roger, and the two of them climbed up into the open side door. The SEAL stepped carefully over the men sitting on the floor and, moving to the front, took his place in the cockpit. He quickly spooled up the engines and began turning the rotors.

The Chairman stood by the helicopter door and waited for Jim and his colleague to join them after running up the two hundred and fifty steps from down below. Within minutes Jim's head appeared in the trap door opening and he climbed out onto the roof. His fellow SEAL immediately followed and the two men sprinted toward the helicopter. They jumped aboard and both reached out to pull in the Chairman. As the side door slid shut, the engines roared and the rotor blades spun faster and faster until they were a gray blur.

Roger sat on the floor of the chopper, together with the other men squeezed together in the cramped space. The rated cargo capacity for the Black Hawk was eleven troops without armaments, a weight limit that was far exceeded by the men, guns, missiles and rockets that now weighted it down. He held his breath as he heard and *felt* the rotors straining to lift the craft. The seat beneath him vibrated uncomfortably but it did not rise.

The pilot tried all the tricks in the manual to raise the craft, trying different angles at which the rotor blades bit the air when they reached their rated speed, but the craft would not budge. He increased the RPM before changing the blade angle, and the craft vibrated violently but still did not rise. After several tries he throttled back and spoke into the intercom, "No can do. We've got to lighten the load."

"Can we drop the external fuel tanks?" Roger heard Jim say.

"It takes two men fifteen minutes with a portable lift to do that. Besides, we'll need the extra fuel to get back home with this load," came the response from the pilot.

"How about shedding the missiles and rockets?"

"I can fire them off but they'll kill civilians on the ground for sure."

"Can we disarm them?"

The Chairman interrupted the exchange. "That's doable. We had a tactical talk about that at the Pentagon. Didn't want our missiles to be used by the enemy. There's a way to render them harmless."

"How do we do that?" asked Jim.

"I don't know," The Chairman replied haplessly. "All I know is they're designed to stand down if they fall into enemy hands."

"I can try," Roger spoke up. "I work at Aberdeen Proving Ground, remember? I've watched them test these things."

"Let's do it then. Go." Jim slid open the side door and jumped out together with the Chairman and the other SEAL. Roger followed them as the rotor blades spun at high speed above their heads. The roar of the engines had subsided but it was still deafening.

As the Chairman and two SEALs removed each missile from the missile launchers on both sides of the Black Hawk, Roger entered a code on a flat keypad on the missile surface near the ogive to disable both its propulsion and its warhead.

"How about the rockets?" Jim asked. He was shouting because of the noise and due to the urgency.

"Leave them," the Chairman shouted back. "They're not heavy. Besides, we can't disarm those."

"Let's get in then." All four men climbed back into the helicopter and Jim shut the door. The engines spun up and the rotors beat faster. The pilot tried to raise the craft but again it vibrated violently without levitating. First one skid and then the other lifted off slightly but, try as he might, he could not get them to both lift together from the roof of the tower.

"I have an idea." Roger shouted. "Fire the rockets."

"They're armed," the Chairman shouted back.

"We can take off the nose cones. We'll aim the rockets upward and they'll give us a boost."

Jim again slid open the door and jumped out.

"I need a hex key." Roger shouted above the engine noise, standing up inside the cramped space of the chopper.

"There's an Allen wrench set in the toolkit," the pilot screamed. "Right *here*." He pointed with his thumb to a flap on the back of his seat.

Roger opened the flap and grabbed the set of wrenches. Next he jumped over the sitting men and leaped out the door to the ground.

There were four rockets on the Black Hawk, two on each side. Roger found the correct wrench and loosened a locking screw on one of them. He rotated the warhead to unscrew it from the rocket shaft and handed it to Jim. Jim, in turn, carried the explosive device to the open doorway and handed it up to the Chairman, who placed it carefully in the leather pilot's pouch in the cockpit. They repeated this process for the other three rockets as fast as they could and then jumped back on board.

The pilot revved the engines and the blades spun faster. He aimed the rockets straight up and, when the blades reached takeoff speed, he pulled up on the collective to change their pitch and at the same time fired the rockets. The sound was deafening.

Through the window, Roger could see men popping up from the trap door on the roof, like bubbles erupting from the surface of boiling oil. A few of them had guns and they prepared to take aim at the aircraft.

Suddenly startled by the rockets, these men stepped back as the helicopter lifted itself slowly into the air. The fiery blast of the four rockets sizzled the roof, causing sparks to fly in every direction. Finally able to clear the ledge, the chopper pilot pushed forward on the cyclic control and the craft moved ahead, slowly at first, over the edge of the tower and flew out in a southerly direction. The rockets that had kept the hostiles at bay exhausted their fuel and ceased firing, each with a "pop" and a puff of smoke. The craft dropped down slightly below the level of the roof, out of sight from the rooftop assailants, and then steadied itself and maintained a level altitude.

As the Black Hawk helicopter burned through its fuel it grew lighter and became more and more airworthy.

Meanwhile the hostiles ran to the edge of the roof and fired their guns, both handguns and rifles, at the tail of the receding aircraft. Inside the hold, Roger and all the other men sat squeezed together next to the dead body of General Mason, praying and holding their collective breath until they were well out of range. Perhaps because of this, none of the enemy gun shots hit home or did damage.

A grateful sigh of relief could be heard throughout the cabin as they sped away south to the Golan Heights and the safety of Israel.

Chapter 94

Courtney was sick with worry about what happened to the men, particularly Roger, and she couldn't understand why. Normally, she would think men deserved what they got for fighting each other, like mobsters shooting it out in the name of revenge. But this was different, wasn't it? They were fighting for truth and justice, weren't they? They were the good guys fighting the bad guys, and wasn't it okay to want the good men to win?

She wondered if perhaps there might be something more at stake. She genuinely *liked* the men, particularly Roger, and wanted them to be safe. Wanted the men to come home, wanted *him* to be home, safe with *her*. It was a new feeling she wasn't at all used to.

When Roger called, her heart had leaped. She felt giddy as a schoolgirl. It was *him*. But she knew instantly something was amiss. From the tone of his voice and the look on his face, she *knew*. She did just as she was told, but then her phone went dead. She tried to call back but he didn't pick up. Oh my God, what could have happened to those men? To *him*?

She was almost beside herself now. She didn't know whom to turn to: whom to ask if they were all right. No one was supposed to know about this operation except the President of the United States and "Joe," the CIA agent in charge. He was monitoring the mission with the POTUS in the Situation Room. She had no idea how to contact him. If the mission failed, would he contact *her*?

But if the Chairman of the Joint Chiefs of Staff, the highest-ranking officer in the entire United States military, did not come back from this mission in the field, the *whole world* would know. All Courtney could do was to wait and stand watch.

An hour passed as she watched the skies. Dots in the air appeared silently out of the blue and grew larger as they approached. Almost all of them turned out to be winged aircraft that landed on a nearby runway. One helicopter did appear but it was flying east to west and must have landed elsewhere too. She kept vigil, watching the northerly skies just above the horizon for a tiny gnat, wings fluttering, flying her way, bringing her man home. She wished; she hoped, but her hope was fading with each passing moment she watched and waited. The skies were empty. Except... There was another dot. It was growing slowly larger. It was possibly... a helicopter... heading toward her... Yes, definitely a helicopter. Dared she hope? Feelings of relief came sneaking up. She waited. Then a rush of *joy* surged through her. Please, let it be. Let it be *Roger*.

Within seconds she was sure. She recognized the Black Hawk helicopter that had taken him away only a few hours before. It was coming home now. Bringing Roger back to *her*.

Courtney stood on the tarmac as the helicopter approached noisily and settled down with a clatter and a blast of air. She could see the pilot through his windshield, concentrating on bringing the craft safely down and, when it made contact with the pad, throttling back the engines and allowing the rotors to spin gradually to a stop. The side door slid open and the Chairman jumped out, followed by Jim and a number of other men, one after the other. But Roger was not one of them. She scanned all the arrivals, all of whom remained standing there, but didn't see him. She felt a painful stab of angst. Her emotions welled up suddenly. She felt herself about to cry. Why did she *care* so much?

She saw soldiers in military dress walk rapidly past her, pushing what looked like stretchers on wheels, two men on each side. They came from somewhere in a building, a hanger, behind her. They were solemn, marching nearly in lock step. *Oh my God. Roger.*

She sprinted forward toward the helicopter. As she ran she saw the men who had assembled next to it part to make room for the soldiers with the stretchers. She got to the Black Hawk well before the soldiers and looked up into the open doorway. The SEAL who piloted the craft, and also *Roger*, were standing inside next to two wounded agents and the prone dead body of General Thomas Mason.

"Roger!" she shouted breathlessly looking up at him. "Is everything all right?" She quickly checked herself when she realized how inappropriate the question was.

"I...I'm sorry. I shouldn't have—." Courtney stepped back, embarrassed. Roger looked back at her, his face signalling his inner joy at seeing her there, but said nothing, obviously otherwise occupied and apparently embarrassed: embarrassed for *her*. She felt mortified.

The soldiers with the gurneys came up and the mood became suddenly somber again. Roger and some of the other men assisted in transferring the wounded and the General's body from the helicopter to the gurneys. The Chairman, Jim and the other SEALs, as well as the uniformed soldiers, saluted solemnly.

Courtney stood nearby as the men respectfully draped a white sheet, and then an American flag, over the General's body that lay on the gurney. She tried to calm herself as they did so, but her heart was full of conflicting emotions: in turmoil because of the fear of losing Roger, the joy of seeing him alive and her embarrassment at disrespecting General Mason. All she could think of was that caring about a man wasn't easy for a woman. In fact, it really *hurt* inside. But at the same time she knew she was more than ready, willing and able to take on that burden as most women do. Maybe it was in a woman's DNA, she thought. More than anything right now she wanted Roger to want *her*.

Roger jumped down from inside the helicopter and walked over. She held out her arms and embraced him, holding her face up to kiss him but he didn't reciprocate. Instead he hugged her perfunctorily and gave her a gentle push away.

"Thank you, Courtney," he said earnestly. "Without your help we could not have made our escape."

She wanted to give him another bear hug and mash her lips against his, but she knew it would embarrass him so she merely nodded and quietly accepted his thoughtful expression of appreciation.

What in heaven was happening to her? She was regressing to being that schoolgirl in "BC" -- before Columbia -- she thought. She desperately wanted to share her feelings with Roger.

Instead, she walked solemnly with the group of men who respectfully followed behind the gurney carrying General Mason's body and the gurneys carrying the wounded, as they were rolled carefully toward the nearby hanger. She made an effort to appear appropriate, although Roger was the only thing on her mind at that moment.

Chapter 95

Having been up all night, everyone who came back on the helicopter crashed at the hotel and slept for the rest of the day. They met that evening at the hotel cocktail lounge to celebrate the success of the mission. Only the Chairman was absent. Once General Mason's body had been placed in a coffin and loaded onto a transport plane, the Chairman had flown back to Washington on the supersonic jet.

Having succeeded in secretly salting the water in Damascus, the group gathered to both recap what had happened the previous night and project what effect the Nemo might have on the residents of the city. After ordering drinks from the bartender, they all assembled in a darkened corner of the lounge to avoid being overheard. Courtney stood next to Roger and listened quietly before eventually joining in the conversation.

Roger took out his cellphone, pressed the camera app and quickly pulled up the last picture he took. It was of Jamal, who lay dead in front of the tower door. One of his ISIS colleagues lay next to him. Both had bullet holes in the head.

"I think Jamal was a true double agent," Roger said. "He was serving both sides of the fight, but in the end his loyalties were clearly with ISIS."

"You can't serve two masters," Jim commented.

"He did for a while, at least. He provided the CIA with some good intelligence. Otherwise they would have found him out."

"You could have knocked me over with a feather when you started shooting," Jim said to the SEAL who fired the shots. "I sure didn't see that coming."

"That was our one and only chance," Roger explained. "If they took you away from that water tower, only God would know where to find you."

"Things were looking pretty grim at that point," Jim admitted. "But what I want to know is, how'd you get a shot off at Jamal without getting shot at yourself? You guys were sitting ducks up there on that roof."

"He kept out of sight until Jamal opened the door of the tower, with you right behind him," Roger replied. "We figured everyone on the ground would be distracted by that, so we had a couple of seconds to take the shots."

"We figured that?" commented the SEAL who fired the shots, pretending to be surprised. He added, "That's the first I heard that I wasn't committing *suicide*."

"That's why we SEALs make the *big bucks*," Jim joked. "But seriously, how did you know when Jamal would come out that door?"

"We knew there were about two hundred and fifty steps to the bottom of the tower," explained Roger. "We calculated it would take exactly a half a second to take each step, so we ran the numbers."

"Cut the crap, " Jim protested. "If that's how you did it, you were really stupid. Seriously, how'd you do it?"

"He used his cell phone," the SEAL explained with a grin. "Imagine *that*."

"Really?" Jim was astounded. "Who'd he call?"

"He called Courtney here."

"Courtney?" Jim gave her a surprised but appreciative look. "You told them when Jamal came out of the tower?"

"Well, kind of," responded Courtney hesitantly.

"Kind of?"

"Okay, then. Yes, I did." Courtney said, catching the drift and following along.

"But how'd you know?"

"We women know things."

"But how?"

Courtney rolled her eyes. "We just *know*, stupid."

Jim shot her a knowing look. "Believe it or not, I'm tempted to believe you. We should recruit more women to help us fight the enemy. We could make use of your feminine intuition."

"We're lovers not fighters. If you men want to kill each other, I say go right ahead, but leave us out of it."

Roger put his arm around Courtney's shoulder and came to her defense. "Men should be providing women protection, not the other way around," he said.

Courtney looked up at him and her mouth moved toward his. Once more she tried to entice a kiss from Roger but he didn't even notice.

"By the way, how'd you get yourself over here?" Jim asked.

"I came with the Chairman of the Joint Chiefs. He was nice enough to bring me along in his super-jet."

"*What*? You came in *that*?" Jim appeared incredulous. "No one gets to ride in that thing. Not even the *President.*"

"The President has his own private jet," Courtney said smartly.

"I'm serious. No SEAL has ever flown in one of those."

"Well, I guess I'm special then."

"I know the Chairman. No one's *that* special in his book."

Courtney looked at Roger for help.

"As a matter of fact, I was wondering the same thing," he said, holding his hands out questioningly. "Tell us the secret."

"Okay, okay. I used some leverage."

"*Leverage*? What leverage?" Jim's eyes bore down on her. All the other men, including Roger, leaned in to hear the answer.

"I told him I knew about Nemo, which I do. I hinted I'd write an article about it." Courtney gritted her teeth and looked sheepishly back at the men.

"Oh, *no*." said Roger and raised a palm to his forehead. "The Chairman didn't know about our deal to keep Nemo a secret?"

"Okay, you know all about it and you're a woman," Jim said. "So tell us then: What's going to happen to al-Assad and his men in Damascus when they drink the KoolAid?"

"The same as I told the Chairman," Courtney replied. "They'll finally act like gentlemen and sue for peace."

"You told the Chairman *that*?"

"Yes I did, and you know what he said?"

"Tell us."

"He said he wanted those guys to act like women and suck your dicks."

"Damn!" Jim shook his head in disgust. "That sexist son-of-a-bitch."

He nevertheless raised his glass. "Let's drink to the Chairman," he shouted.

"To the Chairman." everyone repeated. They all raised their glasses and downed their drinks, paying their due respects to the highest-ranking officer in the U.S. military.

* * * *

Courtney sat with Roger at a candle-lit table for two in the hotel dining room. Courtney thought at first she might finally be getting somewhere with the "perfect gentleman" she imagined he was, but she was becoming more and more frustrated as the dinner unfolded. She was sending out female sexual signals right and left, which weren't backed up by a whole lot of experience to be sure, but Roger wasn't picking up on any of them. As far as she could tell, he had no idea why she was there or what she wanted.

Over dinner the talk turned to what might happen to Bashar al-Assad after a couple of days of drinking the tap water. "This is the ultimate test for me," Roger confided. "This is my life's work so far. If al-Assad doesn't turn, I've wasted a whole lot of years."

"This may be a good time to move on to other things," Courtney said sympathetically. "Let other men take over, now that you've shown the way."

"You may be right. Maybe it's time for me to start a new project, but what?"

"Ever thought about getting married?"

"To be honest, I haven't had time. I don't even have a girlfriend."

"Well I'm kind of in the same boat. I'm not married and don't have a boyfriend."

"I guess we're even then."

"Yup. Even Steven."

"Then maybe we both should start a new project."

"We could work on same project."

"The same pro—?" Roger stopped short and Courtney felt his eyes fixed on her. He stood up and came around to Courtney's side of the table, reached out his hand and she took it. As Courtney rose she felt herself being swept into his arms. She let herself go and he embraced her with a kiss. She saw sparks flying everywhere.

"He's the *one*," she thought excitedly. At that moment, "*The Rape of Courtney*" was erased forever from her mind.

Chapter 96

Five minutes later they were in Roger's hotel room, kissing passionately and literally ripping each other's clothes off. Courtney reached down and felt the bulge in Roger's pants. She massaged it gently and he responded with a soft moan. His passion fueled hers, and she felt a warm glow between her legs.

Courtney pushed Roger backward onto the bed and pulled off his pants and his under-shorts. His prong stood straight up, hard and *huge*. She grasped it with her right hand and knelt on the floor in front of him. Rubbing it gently up and down, she put its tip in her mouth and sucked. She could feel it throbbing between her lips and suddenly, with a final convulsive throb, it filled her mouth with a white creamy liquid.

Roger uttered a guttural "Ooh." and fell still as he lay on his back. His member shrank in size and fell over, like a soft rag doll.

Courtney climbed up onto the bed and lay on her right side, next to him. She gazed in his face. "Was that good for you?" She surprised herself by how much she really cared to give him pleasure. She realized it was just as satisfying to give sexual pleasure to a man as it was to receive it.

Roger took a moment to compose himself, then said simply, "I'm sorry."

"Sorry? About what?"

"Not having you come first."

"It was my pleasure to do you."

"No, really. I'm serious."

Courtney shot him a sly smile and, with her left hand began to explore the hair on his chest. "We're not finished, you idiot," she teased.

Roger reached up and lightly squeezed her breasts.

"I know a position," she offered, "where we can both get off at the same time."

"Oh, yeah?"

"Sit up."

Roger did so and sat on the edge of the bed.

Courtney stood and slowly finished undressing in front of him. She did a strip tease, undoing and slowly lowering her slacks over her hips, revealing her white panties while gyrating as if to music. She saw Roger's eyes become larger.

She slid her slacks all the way down and then started playing with her panties.

Inch by inch she lowered them until some pubic hair could be seen, appearing shyly above the top edge. She put her hand inside the front and slipped it slowly down between her legs, undulating as she did so. She could feel the warmth and wetness.

She watched Roger's reaction as she went through her routine, and she could see his member waking. It no longer drooped but was rising slowly. It grew in size and stature until it again stood ramrod straight.

Courtney pressed her panties down below her hips and revealed her prize. She bent down to kiss Roger, allowing him as she did a brief view of the wet lips behind her bush. They held each other's faces in their hands and they kissed, tenderly at first and then more passionately as she pressed her tongue deeply into his mouth, providing him a faint taste of his own semen.

She let go of his face and climbed up upon his lap, kneeling, her legs on either side. She carefully lowered herself down and allowed his prong to slide slowly into the wet hollow between her thighs. It felt wonderful.

Facing Roger and watching his expression she began to work her pelvis, forward and back, up and down. He assisted her with his hands holding her butt, and they worked together, forming a rhythm, doing whatever felt good, slowly and easily at first and then with ever-increasing urgency.

Courtney felt Roger deep within her body and with each stroke she tried to drive him deeper inside. It was a more satisfying feeling than she had ever known. She tightened her vagina around him to increase the pleasure and increased the rhythm, gyrating faster. She pounded against him, up and down, up and down, until she felt her vagina convulse and explode with a searing orgasm.

At that moment she realized Roger was experiencing the same sensations and was coming inside of her, filling her with his essence, the thought increasing her delight even more.

They came together, locked tightly in their passionate embrace, before they fell sideways on the bed, still hugging each other, exhausted and spent.

Chapter 97

On their way to Chappaqua for their final trip to Horace Greeley High School, Ashley and Ronnie talked about the upcoming Wednesday Assembly. A local husband and wife team, Bill and Hillary Clinton, were going to address the student body. The subject was the war in Syria.

"That Nemo really works," Ashley was saying. "My cheerleaders are getting sooo frustrated. The boys are ignoring them and it's driving them *crazy*."

"You know what I heard on the grapevine?" Ronnie commented. "The girls' grades are sinking like a stone. The boys are getting better grades than the girls now."

Ashley shook her head. "That won't last. It's been a month now and the Nemo is going to wear off. The guys will start getting horny again and go back to obsessing about getting laid."

"So maybe the Nemo's a good thing. No wait; what am I *saying*." Ronnie laughed. "It practically ruined my love life with Billy. It turned everything upside down. I had to chase *him*."

"Yeah, you sure had a rough patch. You have to admit, though, that it kick-started your writing career. The article you wrote for *Cosmo*? Even *I* bought that sex magazine because of it. You did good, Ronnie. Keep it going."

"I'm doing even better now with my new boyfriend."

"You mean George? You're doing George now?"

"Yup, and he's loving it. Says it's the best sex he ever had."

"I hope he's doing you too."

"Not so much. He gets off too quick mostly, and I'm left holding the you know what. I have to get myself off sometimes when he's not looking."

"Maybe he could use some Nemo," Ashley said brightly. "It would slow him down some."

"Yeah, why didn't *I* think of that? A new cure for PE. Could be the answer women are looking for."

"PE? What's PE?"

"Premature ejaculation," Ronnie reminded Ashley. "The bane of all women. Maybe we should talk to Roger about it. Come out with a new drug for men. We could patent it and make a bloody *fortune*." Ronnie looked over at Ashley who was focusing on a traffic slowdown on the road ahead. "What do you think?"

"We'd never get men to take it. They won't buy it."

"So? We women will buy it and slip it into their water or, better yet, their beer. We rule the kitchen, remember. They'll never know what hit them between the legs."

"Shut *up*. Women won't do such a thing. That's fighting *dirty*."

"Women have been using our feminine wiles to manipulate men since time began."

"Maybe so, but this is just the *opposite*. Turning our men *off* to get what we want."

"It would help any woman who can't get the big "O" because of PE. Believe me, women will do *anything* for better sex."

The two women drove on up the Saw Mill River Parkway toward Chappaqua, brainstorming excitedly about their new idea for curing PE, exchanging ideas and laughing at the possibilities.

"What should we call this new blockbuster drug?" Ashley asked eventually.

"That's a no-brainer," Ronnie responded. "We'll call it 'Nemo'."

"Yeah, Nemo. That's pretty obvious, I guess. And after our drug is a terrific success, people will ask how we thought this up. We'll think back on this, our last trip up to Horace Greeley, and reminisce on how we made our great invention. You know what we should tell them?"

"How we made this mad medicine?" Ronnie joked.

"No."

"How we crafted this cool creation?"

"No."

"Searched for such a slick solution?"

"Not even close."

"Okay, okay. I give up. What were we doing?" Ronnie laughed, exasperated at having exhausted the possibilities.

"We were *finding Nemo*."

* * * *

Bill and Hillary Clinton walked onto the stage and sat down on two comfortable chairs facing the packed auditorium. Ashley and Ronnie stood in the back with most of the school faculty because the seats were filled to overflowing by the excited student body.

Principal Barbara Westerhoff stood at the podium and introduced the honored guest speakers. Although residents of Chappaqua, the Clintons had not addressed the high school before because, it was assumed, to do so would raise questions of "politicking" with a "Democratic bias" on the sons and daughters of the largely wealthy, and therefore largely Republican, Chappaqua parents.

"You are in for a treat today," Principal Westerhoff was saying. "It has been a long time in coming, but they are finally here. Our neighbors, Bill and Hillary Clinton, live only a mile away from Horace Greeley High as the crow flies, but from what we've heard of their activities, they're not home very often." Principal Westerhoff turned briefly and shot the guests behind her a quick smile. "As you know they travel the world," she continued, facing the audience again. "They need no introduction so I won't waste any time. Let's give a warm HGHS welcome to President Bill Clinton and his wife Hillary." She raised her voice as she said this and the audience came to its feet, most of them clapping enthusiastically, some only respectfully but applauding nevertheless, as Bill Clinton came forward to the podium. Principal Westerhoff shook his hand warmly and then receded to a third chair that was on stage. Bill stood before the microphone and waited with a wry smile for the audience to sit, and for the applause to die down.

The auditorium fell suddenly silent. Only a random cough now and then interrupted the quiet as the audience waited with great anticipation.

"It's good to be here," Bill began. "It's good to be anywhere at my age, I guess, but here mostly. Of all the places in the country to settle down, Hillary and I chose Chappaqua."

The audience stood up again, applauding wildly and shouting out excitedly, showing their appreciation that the ex-President and his wife, now famous in her own right, chose to live in their town.

Bill waited until they had finally calmed down and sat again in their seats. Ashley and Ronnie both clapped, but not unreservedly so.

"Hillary and I are here to give you our perspectives on some very grave events that are right now going on and are affecting us and our nation. We are calling this talk 'Problems in the Middle East' but we'll focus mostly on the Islamic State of Iraq and Syria: what we call ISIS, and how that organization affects the Middle East region, and has affected the world. I understand we have about an hour to be together here, so the way we'll work this is as follows: I'll speak for about fifteen minutes and then Hillary will do the same. After that we'll take questions. Is that okay?"

The question was asked rhetorically but Bill took a moment to look out at the rapt faces and make eye contact with many. He had just begun his talk and he already had them spellbound.

Bill spoke for the promised fifteen minutes, then turned and sat down amid thunderous applause. As he did so, Hillary came forward and stood at the podium wearing her trademark smile. The applause continued unabated until she held her hands in the air to plead for silence. The audience complied, whereupon she spoke for her allotted fifteen minutes, providing additional background on reasons for disaffection and unrest in the Middle East and outlining how she thought the United States should deal with what she called this "challenge to democratic principles." When she concluded her talk Principal Westerhoff came forward, clapping as she came, and spoke into the microphone. "Aren't these two terrific? Aren't we lucky to have them as neighbors?" The crowd continued to cheer and clap enthusiastically as Bill left his chair and joined his wife and Principal Westerhoff at the front of the stage.

"Now, it is time for questions," Principal Westerhoff announced. "Raise your hand and I'll call on you. One of our volunteers will come over and pass you a roving mike. State your name and your question, and tell us whom you would like to answer the question: Bill or Hillary."

A small scattering of students immediately raised their hands. Principal Westerhoff scanned the crowd. All of them were boys, except for an attractive-looking girl. "I see only one brave girl out there," she said, pointing. "Murial, you get to go first. What is your question?"

The girl stood and waited for the roving microphone to arrive. When it did she held it with both hands in front of her mouth, but then hesitated. After a beat she composed herself and spoke clearly but slowly. "I'm a senior here at Horace Greeley. My question is directed to you, Hillary. What all the girls want to know is, when you found out your husband was cheating on you, not just once but many times, why didn't you divorce him?"

Chapter 98

On the trip back to Manhattan, Ashley and Ronnie couldn't stop laughing.

"That look on Hillary's face: it was *priceless*." Ronnie howled, looking over at Ashley who was doing her best to stifle her laughter so she could keep her focus on driving.

"And did you see Bill?" Ronnie added. "If he could, he would have sunk through the floor and *disappeared*."

She and Ashley laughed until tears flowed down their faces.

Finally settling down, the two enjoyed the ride by exchanging details of their private lives. It was all girl talk from then on.

"How's your writing coming?" Ashley asked. "You working on another article for *Cosmo*?"

"Funny you should ask. Emily has given me a big advance to write about me and George."

"Oh, yeah?" Ashley's ears perked up. "What about you and George?"

"The article's gonna be called, '*How to Marry a Billionaire*'. You know, the next level up from 'How to Marry a Millionaire'."

"Hmmm," replied Ashley, grinning. "You lost the alliteration of 'Marry a Millionaire'. Maybe you should call it 'How to *Bed* a Billionaire'."

"That works for *me*. I'll suggest it to Emily. It's really how I got to him in the first place. Bedding him was first base. Making him laugh was second base. Getting him to commit was third base. And now I'm heading for home."

"What? You're engaged to be *married*? Why didn't you tell me, girl?"

"He didn't give me the ring yet, but I feel it coming. It's just a matter of time."

"But you should have said something. That's *fantastic*."

"I didn't want to jinx it."

"Yeah, you're probably right to play close to your chest. Guys are really weird sometimes. They're easily spooked."

"I'll play it close to my *boobs*. He loves my boobs."

Ashley shot Ronnie a warm smile. "You're a lucky girl, you know. Just a few months ago you were having trouble getting it on with that biker, Billy. Now you're about to marry a *billionaire*. Maybe you should call that article 'From Biker to Billionaire'."

Ronnie frowned in disapproval.

"Just *joking*." Ashley added hurriedly.

"That's not funny," Ronnie said. "I'm serious about this guy. He's really nice and I think he loves me."

"Do you love him? That's what's most important." Ashley asked.

"Yes, I think I do. It's kind of a new feeling for me. Up to now it's been all fun and games, but it's...it's *different* now. You know what? I'd like to have his baby."

Ashley fell silent and concentrated on her driving for a bit. She eventually looked over at Ronnie and said, "I'm jealous. You may have found true love. That's *huge*."

* * * *

The Alphabet Soup met in the boardroom of the *Women Rising* office the very next day. The four board members sat in their usual places around the conference table with Courtney at the head. Courtney called the meeting to order at precisely two o'clock.

"Okay, Courtney. Spill the beans," Deedee demanded. From the inquisitive looks on the faces of the other board members, it was clear she was speaking for them too. "It's been a week now. Did you ever find Roger?"

"Yes, I did." Courtney couldn't help radiating how she felt, and at that moment she felt really good. "And he's a wonderful guy. Not bad looking for a geeky scientist, and he's kind, he's a gentleman and really smart. He's also humble to a fault."

"Does he turn you on? Is he good for you in bed?" Deedee asked. "That's what's most important."

"He's sexy to *me*," Courtney replied, smiling. She was practically glowing with happiness.

After a beat, Deedee cleared her throat and said, "Well... where does that leave us?"

"What do you mean?" Courtney asked.

"The magazine. That's our first priority. All of ours," Deedee reminded Courtney, rather sternly.

"The magazine? What about it."

"We have to carry on. We have to be motivated. We can't be sidetracked and lose our momentum just because—."

"Oh, I see. Because of a *man*, you were going to say."

"You said it. I didn't."

"Well, now that you bring the subject up, we might as well deal with that. I wasn't going to drop the bomb so early, but I guess now's as good a time as any."

"The *bomb*?" Bailey stared sharply at Courtney. "What bomb?"

"I think we should close down the magazine. I've been thinking, men are not all that bad. And they have some good qualities too. If you're lucky enough to find the right one, he can change your life for the better. All in a heartbeat. I mean *really*. Just think of it."

"Have you gone *crazy*?" Deedee almost shouted. "All that we've worked for these past three years? You want to give men a pass, like women have done for thousands of years? We're finally calling them on their abusive, terrible behavior. We're getting women to fight *back*. I can't let you do this."

Courtney remained calm. The other women were clearly shocked and looking upset.

"I was just *messing* with you." Courtney said, laughing. "Of *course* I want to continue with our *Women Rising*."

Chapter 99

HOW TO MARRY A BILLIONAIRE
by Veronica Miller

On my first date with Joe (not his real name) I could feel the heat. He and his driver Isaac (his real name) picked me up from my apartment with his stretch limousine. While my roommates watched from the window, green with envy, Isaac assisted as I climbed in and sank into in the soft leather seat next to my new billionaire boyfriend. My boyfriend couldn't take his eyes off me all evening and treated me like a beautiful princess.

If you're reading Cosmo *and paying attention to the advice you're getting, you are drop dead gorgeous and can attract any man like a fly to a light bulb. And if you chose wisely, like I have, you may end up marrying a billionaire. Yes, that's billionaire with a "B." Don't be intimidated by such a man. A billionaire is no different than other men; he just has more money.*

And right off the bat you have a problem. What do you do about that Pre-Nup he's going to ask you to sign before you tie the knot?

If you're like me, you'll sign anything to marry the guy. Easy come, easy go, right? And anyway, a diamond is forever and you can always sell that huge sparkling rock he gives you when he's so hot to trot he can't think straight. But hear me out.

At first this man is going to change your life for the better in ways you can't even dream of. In a way, it's not fair to all you other gorgeous, sexy women that I got chosen to be his wife, but who do I complain to? He can't marry every beautiful bachelorette although he'd probably like to. You hit the jackpot and you're going to love it, believe me.

You'll be the queen of a lovely home, which you can decorate to suit your every whim. You'll choose a second, vacation home and maybe a third. You'll entertain his quests, with maids and servants of course, and with a caterer if need be.

You'll go to high-end parties and meet celebrities like Kim Kardashian (if you like that sort of thing – I don't). Watch out, though. There will be other drop-dead gorgeous women there who would give anything to trade places with you.

You'll travel the globe, first class, visiting places on your bucket list (if you don't yet have such a list, it'll come to you soon when you realize the great things you can see and do in this wide, wonderful world).

You'll dine at fabulous restaurants and be entertained by the best concerts and shows in New York City.

You'll enjoy flying in his airplane and sailing on his yacht.

And here's the best part: As his wife, you'll receive a credit card with unlimited spending power.

All of this because… well, just because you're you.

Now take a breath and think about how you'll feel when all of this comes to an end - when someone prettier, someone younger and sexier, catches his eye. You'll have a terrific ride while it lasts, but let's be realistic. Just between us girls, your ride won't last forever. Then what?

That's where the prenuptial agreement comes in. Before he marries you, he'll want you to sign away your right to his money. If he divorces you or even if he passes to the great beyond, you'll get nothing. Bupcus. You'll be right back where you started, financially flat, before you gave him the keys to your heart and soul and threw caution to the wind.

It will be great while it lasts but it won't last, believe me. So protect yourself. Get a good lawyer and negotiate like crazy. If he wants you bad enough he'll give a little – just a little – of his vast wealth. He'll agree to leave you with a million or two, or maybe even five or ten. In any case, make sure its enough to live on comfortably for the rest of your life.

Why? Why would a man pay you more money than you could ever dream of earning on your own? There is one little word for that. It's all about the SEX.

After Ronnie finished writing this, proofed it, and was about to press "send" to transmit it to Emily, her cell phone rang. She saw it was George and immediately picked up.

"Hi," she said brightly. She was as ready as she'd ever be to meet his challenge.

"About that Pre-Nuptial Agreement I gave you yesterday?"

"Yes, I've read it. I was about to—."

"Well, tear it up. I've got plenty of money. I realized that if you took half of it, I'd still have more than enough to live on. I'd even have some left over to fly my airplane.

"Anyway, we're going to stay together, right? We're going to share and witness each other's lives, and I'm in it for the long journey with you."

Chapter 100

It was an all-female party and the cosmopolitans were flowing like water. They were in the reception area of *Cosmopolitan,* after hours with the main office door shut and locked to outsiders. The Alphabet Soup was there, joining the distaff staff members and all the supermodels who worked for the magazine.

No men had been invited to join in the celebration. Not a single male staff member, deliveryman or repairman was on the premises.

On the wall behind the reception desk a flat television, tuned to CNN, showed images of world events, but no one was paying attention. Emily, the Editor-in-Chief, outdid herself this time in celebrating the lives of her dear friends Courtney and Ronnie, both of whom were engaged to be married.

The women crowded around admiring the proof positive: Courtney's ring had a modest diamond, but it sparkled brightly in the beams from the overhead lighting. Ronnie's was absolutely amazing. It was *huge* – out of modesty Ronnie wouldn't say how huge – and looked almost out of place on Ronnie's slender finger.

"Eat your hearts out, ladies," Ronnie boasted as she held it up so it flashed in their faces.

"Let's *hear* it for the brides-to-be." Emily held up her funnel-shaped stemmed glass filled with the pink elixir, and everyone followed her lead. "I want to say that I had a part in this mating ritual but that would be unfair to our honored guests. Courtney and Ronnie managed to get it done all by themselves." Emily downed her drink with one gulp and looked around, encouraging everyone else to do the same. She grabbed a pitcher from the reception desk that served as a temporary bar and made the rounds pouring the elixer into all of their funnel-shaped glasses.

"Speech! Speech!" The chant arose spontaneously from the assembled women as Emily refilled everyone's glass. Courtney, smiling with genuine appreciation for the emotional support she was feeling, raised her hand. "I do want to say something—." The crowd fell suddenly silent.

"While it's true that men are the cause of most of our frustrations and our problems, I'm not convinced any more that the world would be a better place without them. Although they can be horrible sometimes, we still need them.

"If we want to get something done, and we don't just want to talk about it or write about it, we need to get ourselves a man. And if we want to have fun – the kind of fun that *rocks our world* -- we need to get a man."

"So let's hear it for the *men* in our lives." she shouted, her voice reflecting her celebratory mood. She held her glass high and then downed its contents.

"To *men!*" someone shouted and all the women cheered and drank their cosmopolitans.

"But if a man speaks his mind in a forest, and no woman hears him, is he still wrong?" one of the fashion models asked rhetorically.

"*Yes,*" all the women shouted back.

Emily kept the drinks flowing and that kept the women laughing and enjoying the party. As the event continued on the jokes started coming more frequently and becoming more and more risqué.

"You should have let Chester stay," one of the young models said. "He's always the life of the party."

"Who's Chester?" Ronnie asked, squinting, trying to recall where she'd heard that name before.

"He's our fashion maven," Emily told her. "He's at the center of everything we do around here."

"Not *everything* we do," the model noted with a wink and making a pretend pouty face. "And believe me, I tried my best."

"Although I must admit he thinks like one of *us,*" Emily replied, "he's still a guy."

"Why does a woman always have the last word in an argument?" one of the partiers asked everyone.

"I don't know." another partier said. "Why?".

"Because when the guy says anything, that's the beginning of another argument."

"Why are boyfriends like parking spaces?" someone else asked.

"Why are they?" someone replied.

"The good ones are always taken."

"To Courtney and Ronnie!" Emily raised her glass again, newly filled with elixer. "May they live happily ever after." Everyone followed her example and took a long drink.

"To *marriage*," Emily then shouted, and after everyone took another drink, she added, "I have a marriage joke. This woman got married, but her husband was abusive and he hit her, so she divorced him. She got remarried and that husband ran out on her. She married a third time and that husband failed to deliver the goods in bed. She finally put an ad in the paper: 'Looking for a man who won't abuse me, won't leave me, and is good in bed.' The next day, the doorbell rings. She opens the door and there's a man in a wheelchair with no arms and no legs. 'Hello, I saw your ad in the paper,' he tells her. 'You're here about the ad?' she asks him. 'Yeah, I am,' he says. 'I have no arms, so I can't hit you. I have no legs, so I can't run out on you.' 'But how do I know you're good in bed?' she asks, and he replies, 'How do you think I rang the doorbell?'"

From this point on the jokes came from all quarters of the room, one after another.

"When a woman marries a man she expects him to change, but he never does. When a man marries a woman he expects she won't change, but she always does."

"A woman tells her boyfriend, 'After we get married I'll let you kiss me where no one else has kissed me.' 'Oh yeah? And where's that?' the guy asks her. 'In Paris.'"

"This man comes up to the beautiful woman in the supermarket and says, 'I've lost my wife. Mind if I talk with you for a few minutes?' 'Why?' she asks. 'Because every time I talk to a beautiful woman my wife appears out of nowhere.'"

During this jokefest someone noticed the breaking news on television.

"Just a minute everybody. Look at the TV!" One of the models pointed to the screen.

Over the banner "BREAKING NEWS," CNN was telecasting a press conference in Syria. Bashar al-Assad stood before a bevy of microphones, speaking in Arabic with a simultaneous English translation.

"...because I can't allow the turmoil and bloodshed to continue," he was saying. "As of noon tomorrow I will step down from the presidency. My family and I have been offered safe haven in Russia where we will stay indefinitely, guarded day and night by Russian security.

"Before I leave I want to apologize to the Syrian people for the death and destruction that has been caused by our military forces. It has been unconscionable and without precedent. I want you to know, however, that they have acted under my orders, even to the extent of using chemical weapons against you, our citizens. With a heavy heart I take full responsibility for all of this and ask that, over time, you will not judge me too harshly. I can only hope that you will forgive and eventually forget this terrible past.

"For the future belongs to *you* now. I have asked the United Nations to establish a committee to draft a new constitution as the basis for a democracy—."

The women were stunned by the news at first. They looked at each other in astonishment and then, all together, they broke out into a joyous, New York *Cosmopolitan* cheer.

Epilogue

The New York Times had one of its rare banner headlines, the width of the entire front page:

AL-ASSAD ABDICATES PRESIDENCY OF SYRIA AND SEEKS REFUGE IN RUSSIA. UNITED NATIONS ASKED TO DRAFT CONSTITUTION AND ESTABLISH DEMOCRATIC GOVERNMENT. U.S. AND ALLIED COUNTRIES DISCLAIM ADVANCE KNOWLEDGE; PRAISE AL-ASSAD'S BOLD ACTION
Al-Assad Accepts Responsibility for All Actions of the Syrian Military Including Use of Chemical Weapons against Syrian Citizens; Huge Liability for Damage Claims Possible

The announcement created one of the greatest media firestorms that anyone could remember. Journalists from around the globe descended on Damascus and spread out throughout the country to gather news stories about the war-torn nation.

The United Nations coordinated world support to provide food and medical services for the Syrian people still left in the country and for those who wished to return.

Thousands of refugees from Jordan, Europe and Africa streamed back into Syria, returning to their devastated homes, and started the process of rebuilding.

Advisors from the U.S. and Russian governments worked together for the first time to maintain order and to rebuild the infrastructure: the roads, the railroads, the airports, the power plants and electrical grid, the communications networks, and the fresh water and waste water systems.

ISIS initially remained aloof from this reconstruction but then, fearing the loss of their constituency by appearing to favor the impairment of vital human services, some jihadists joined in assisting those in need. As one journalist reported, an admitted affiliate of ISIS "sounded more like a volunteer from Rotary than a terrorist."

A major portion of *The New York Times* was given over to detailing the sequence of events leading up to al-Assad's abdication in an attempt to document his sudden turnabout. Those high placed in the Syrian government had no explanation but feared the consequences. Their main concern was about losing their jobs under the provisional government set up by the U.N. Commission.

CBS's Scott Pelley interviewed the President of the United States for the next *60 Minutes* broadcast and lobbed questions at him for over an hour. During this interview the President appeared to reveal he knew more than he was able to disclose to the public.

PELLEY: Mr. President, is there nothing at all you can say to the American public about the role the United States played in the events that unfolded. We must have done something to make this happen.

POTUS: I'm not at liberty to say—.

PELLEY: Did our government play a role? Any role at all?

POTUS: Now if I told you that, you would immediately ask, 'What role?'"

PELLEY: Of course. That's my job, Mr. President.

POTUS: And it's my job to secure and protect the American people.

* * * *

Courtney switched off the television and turned to Roger, who was sitting at his desk in his home office making notes. "You really started something," she said. "Now that President al-Assad is leaving, maybe the Syrians will finally stop fighting each other."

"I don't know. The Nemo wears off remember, and I don't think we're going back there any time soon to put more of it in the water."

"But you can always use it again, can't you? Whenever there's a problem somewhere in the world?"

"As long as no one finds out about it. If they do, that will be the end of Nemo. People will figure out how test the water for it, the way they can do for lead or for anything else."

"Well then maybe you'll get credit for what you did in Syria. I'm so proud of you, Roger."

"Thanks, Courtney. But we can't tell anyone. It has to remain our little secret."

"Won't there come a time when we can at least tell our grandchildren?"

"We've got to be careful not to let anything slip. Even though we had good intentions and we achieved a good result this time, it's a Pandora's Box that had best be kept closed. There's no telling what might happen if Nemo falls into the wrong hands."

Courtney thought about this a moment. "Oh…I understand," she said. "At least I think I do. So what are you going to do now?"

Roger looked at Courtney with a curious smile. "The first thing I'm going to do is to marry you."

"*Definitely.* I'm not letting you off the hook on that plan." Courtney waved the ring on her left hand in his face. "I mean, after that."

"Then we're going to go far away on our honeymoon."

"Not to the Middle East, I hope."

"No. We've been there. Done that."

"Okay, at least that's settled. Then what will you do?"

"Invent the next big thing."

"Oh, *really*? What will it be?"

"I have no idea. I was hoping you'd help me with that."

THE END

Printed in the United States
By Bookmasters